D1054592

Siren's Call

A Dark Tides Novel

DEVYN QUINN

A SIGNET ECLIPSE BOOK

SIGNET ECLIPSE
Published by New American Library, a division of
Penguin Group (USA) Inc., 375 Hudson Street,
New York, New York 10014, USA
Penguin Group (Canada), 90 Eglinton Avenue East, Suite 700, Toronto,
Ontario M4P 2Y3, Canada (a division of Pearson Penguin Canada Inc.)
Penguin Books Ltd., 80 Strand, London WC2R 0RL, England
Penguin Ireland, 25 St. Stephen's Green, Dublin 2,
Ireland (a division of Penguin Books Ltd.)
Penguin Group (Australia), 250 Camberwell Road, Camberwell, Victoria 3124,
Australia (a division of Pearson Australia Group Pty. Ltd.)
Penguin Books India Pvt. Ltd., 11 Community Centre, Panchsheel Park,
New Delhi - 110 017, India
Penguin Group (NZ), 67 Apollo Drive, Rosedale, North Shore 0632,
New Zealand (a division of Pearson New Zealand Ltd.)
Penguin Books (South Africa) (Pty.) Ltd., 24 Sturdee Avenue,
Rosebank, Johannesburg 2196, South Africa

Penguin Books Ltd., Registered Offices:
80 Strand, London WC2R 0RL, England

First published by Signet Eclipse, an imprint of New American Library,
a division of Penguin Group (USA) Inc.

First Printing, August 2010
10   9   8   7   6   5   4   3   2   1

For Termunkle,
who sat on my shoulder and purred as I wrote this book

ACKNOWLEDGMENTS

This book could not have been written without the input of the following people. It is with much gratitude that I must mention the following:

Roberta Brown is my absolutely brilliant agent. Not only does she always encourage me to aim higher and do better with my writing, but she's always there to hold my hand when I'm melting down with doubt. I could not function without her sane and sensible advice helping me navigate through the pitfalls of a writer's career.

Jhanteigh Kupihea is my amazing editor, whose insight and experience helped to shape the manuscript from a bare-bones synopsis of a few pages to a completed book. She was kind enough to call and speak to me in person whenever I hit the panic button. Her insight and clearheaded thinking keeps me on track.

Bestselling author Kate Douglas generously took time out of her own crazy schedule of deadlines to cheer me along and read the opening drafts of this book. She also delivered a few well-deserved kicks to the rear whenever I began whining about my lack of talent to write a decent sentence. I also need to mention my beta readers, Lea Franczak and Tracey Anderson. Both ladies suffered through those first early drafts and encouraged me with words of praise and support. And I can't forget my circle of girlfriends on whom I rely for advice, support, and friendship: Jodi Lynn Copeland, Anya Howard, Sara Reinke, Sarah Parr, Marianne LaCroix, and Del "Buddy" Garrett.

Greg Eschenbauch, a talented artist in his own right, kindly loaned me the vision of a mermaid when I had none. Thanks for letting me borrow her. . . . You can't have her back.

Last, I would like to thank the musicians of Nox Arcana for creating the music that gave me back my inspiration. No, I don't know these fellows personally, but their CDs played constantly as I wrote. Listening to their compositions reminded me why I wanted to create something others might enjoy.

Prologue

Kenneth Randall walked along the craggy beach. Hands shoved into the pockets of his jacket, he watched ever-rising waves lap against the shoreline. Gray, brooding clouds hung low in the sky. Lightning scratched like an angry animal at their fat bellies. Thunder rumbled in the distance, ominously warning of the deluge soon to arrive. A foghorn blast from the lighthouse standing about a mile off the bay warned stragglers off the water. When the storm finally made shore, it would hit with vicious force.

The bitter sea wind kicked up, driving the water harder against the land. An icy blast of air threaded through his hair, as intimate as the caress of a lover. It seemed the water spoke, although Kenneth knew—just knew—the voice couldn't be anything but the echo of the wind. Its mournful whisper traveled through the air, brushing against his ears.

Join me, came the ocean's song. *I can take your pain away.*

Brooding, he studied the restless sea. A vision of sinking beneath the waves immediately unfurled across his mind's eye, sending a forbidding chill through his veins. It would be easy to do. Wiser inhabitants of Point Rock Harbor had already made their way to shelter. No boats lingered on the water, nor people on the beach.

He was all alone.

Heart thudding dully against his ribs, Kenneth headed closer to the water's edge. He took one step, and then another, moving with the determination of a man who'd made up his mind. Stopping at the edge of the beach, he felt the water seep into his heavy boots. The unexpected sensation of wet and ooze sent a shiver down his spine.

Bending, he fumbled with the laces, working the heavy, wet things off his feet with clumsy fingers. The Arctic airstream driving the storm had given the water a brisk, eye-opening nip. It was chilly, but not yet unbearable. Self-preservation tugged at the back of his mind where logic still lingered. He really should turn around and head back, go to the hotel room he'd rented for the duration of his monthlong vacation.

His mouth drew into a downward arch. He'd kept the reservations only because there was no refund on the anniversary package he'd booked months ago. He'd been looking forward to the idea of being holed up in a quaint little seaside hotel, making passionate love to his wife. Now he dreaded it.

Traveling alone was the hardest part.

Blinking to clear his blurry vision, Kenneth pulled off his soggy boots and set them aside. His socks followed. It didn't feel like half a year had passed since he'd laid Jennifer to rest. The trip to Maine had been his idea, an attempt to get Jennifer away from the stress of work and family. It would be just the two of them, reconnecting, rediscovering the old spark of passion.

Instead of celebrating their life together, he was left alone. Mourning Jennifer's loss.

And looking for a way out, he thought.

Today, the opportunity presented itself.

Thrusting logic back in its box and locking the mental lid, Kenneth gazed out over the open space. Past Little Mer Island there was nothing but water and more water. The lighthouse located there stood alone, wrapped in its own cloak of isolation. Privately owned, the grounds, dwelling, and tower were off-limits to tourists.

"Might as well take advantage," he murmured. He doubted the owners would mind his swimming past. After all, he wasn't planning to stop by for a visit.

Swallowing down the lump forming in his throat, Kenneth took off his jacket and lifted it into the air. The wind quickly whipped it out of his hand, carrying it out of sight. His shirt followed. Goose pimples spread across exposed skin lashed by the blustering wind. The brackish scent of the incoming sea filled his nostrils, clearing away the apathy dulling his senses for so long.

For the first time in months he actually felt energetic, as though a great and terrible weight had lifted off his shoulders.

Clarity gave him a vision. The renewed burst of energy gave him the strength to carry it out.

Jaw tightening, he undid the buttons of his jeans. With a gasp of mingled agony and relief, he slid them down his hips and legs. Stepping neatly out of the pile, his gaze lingered over the last of his clothing. As naked as the day he was born, it was also the way he wanted to leave this life behind. It seemed only fitting the gloomy, unwelcoming waters of the bay would be his grave—the exact opposite of the warm, nurturing womb that had given birth to him.

The storm rolled closer, bearing down on the land like a locomotive without brakes. Lightning flashed, illuminating the shoreline with an eerie glow. Flung down with a vengeance, rain stung his bare skin.

Naked and exposed, Kenneth knew death by drowning wouldn't be easy. But it would be merciful. That was all that counted. It would probably be a few days before the hotel staff figured out he was missing. Didn't matter. It probably wasn't the first time some tourist had gotten himself drowned. His wallet with his driver's license was still in the pocket of his pants and his SUV was parked nearby. It wouldn't be hard to identify his remains.

The voices from the water were stronger now, louder. To ignore their call was impossible. Even if he'd wanted to, Kenneth doubted he could've found the strength to turn away. He was too weak, his psyche battered by grief, loss, and an agony no amount of time could ever dull.

. Losing Jennifer and the child she carried hurt more than he had ever dreamed. As a human being living on planet Earth, one expected life to inflict its tragedies. But expecting and experiencing them were two different things. The subtle rips living inflicted on the heart became a jagged chasm when death reached out to claim someone a man cherished.

Somewhere, somehow, she's out there. Waiting for me.

Exhausted by the long reach of memory, his shoulders slumped. Suicide wasn't the answer and he knew it, but somehow he couldn't break the spell of the water. And, truth be told, he didn't really want to.

Steeling himself against the incoming wash of waves, Kenneth walked into the water. Each determined step took him farther out into the all-consuming sea . . .

*   *   *

The fool. The *damn* fool.

Binoculars pressed to her eyes, Tessa Lonike frowned as she watched the man standing onshore strip off his clothing. What was it about these extreme athletes that made them think a swim in the bay during a severe thunderstorm would be a good idea? Given the temperature of the water, it would take only minutes for hypothermia to set in.

She sighed. Humans should know they weren't made for the water.

Leaning into the rail circling the deck of the thirty-foot-high lighthouse, Tessa adjusted the focus on her high-powered binoculars, zooming in for a closer view.

Even from a distance she could tell he was tall, at least six feet, thin, definitely a swimmer's physique. Though his features were indefinable, the long dark hair whipping around his face and shoulders gave him a sexy, bad-boy appeal. If he thought he could take on the water and win, more power to him.

Her breath caught in her throat when he unbuttoned his jeans and pushed them off his hips. She was expecting to see a pair of those lycra-jammer swim trunks so popular with the local male swimmers.

A gasp rolled past her lips when he revealed himself to be one hundred percent bare-ass naked. Stepping out of his jeans, he stood proud and unashamed at the water's edge. He didn't flinch when a roll of thunder released a torrent of rain, the heavy drops slashing at his pale skin with brutal intent. The man was obviously an exhibitionist.

As the keeper of the Little Mer Island lighthouse and one of the area's search-and-rescue volunteers, it was her job to keep an eye on the bay. With a storm about to make landfall, most people knew to get the hell off—or out of—the water. Summer had passed without a single incident. Soon fall would settle in, and then the freezing snows of winter. She'd be locked on this frickin' island with little more to do than twiddle her thumbs until spring's thaw.

Wiping the water off her lenses, Tessa lifted her binoculars for another look. Surely now that the rain had arrived, he'd give up his insane idea and go home. Thunderstorms blowing in off the North Atlantic had a tendency to get dangerous. High winds and crashing waves were sure to drive boats and bodies alike against the rocky shoreline. Not to mention the powerful undertows that could drag you under in the blink of an eye.

As if to second her concerns, thunder clapped around her, shaking the lighthouse. Lightning streaked to earth, striking the tower's aluminum rod that was designed to take its charge safely into the ground.

"Get out of the water, idiot," she murmured.

Instead of abandoning shore, the naked man entered the sea. Making slow progress against the waves, he began to swim, traveling through the water with strong, determined strokes. Within seconds it became clear he wasn't heading toward the lighthouse, the usual destination of endurance swimmers. Though the isle was privately owned by her family, it didn't stop stragglers from coming ashore.

The man unexpectedly stopped, treading water. Then he dove. Disappeared.

A long minute stretched into two.

Nothing.

The water grew choppier. Waves crashed harder against the shores. Rain fell in sheets, obscuring her view. The wind howled, a banshee singing the doom of another soul taken under by the unforgiving bay.

"Aw, shit," she cursed lightly under her breath. The damn fool was a suicidal fool.

And my idiot lack of focus could cost the man his life.

Tearing off the deck, Tessa took the stairs two at a time heading to the first floor. There, the lighthouse was outfitted with the emergency radio system allowing her to communicate with the Harbor Department on the mainland. Moored at the docks, a twenty-seven-foot Boston Whaler waited for action. Her sister Addison would be one of the women piloting the rescue boat. She wouldn't be happy either. Addison hated being called to pull a dead body out of the water.

By the time she'd hit the last step, Tessa had already figured out it was too late to summon help. She'd have to handle this one herself. Cold shock could severely limit a swimmer's ability to rescue themselves. It could also cause them to ingest water into the lungs, especially if they gasped while under the surface or while submerged by a wave. Drowning was death from suffocation. Anyone who wanted to commit suicide in the water need only take a few gulping breaths. Asphyxia would soon occur.

Leaving the lighthouse behind, she ran the short distance toward the edge of the island. On the north side was a stony ledge that was good for diving.

Barely stopping to strip out of her clothing, Tessa launched her body over the rocks and into the water with a single smooth motion. Her aim was that of the expert swimmer, her slender figure slicing through the churning waves like a knife.

Disappearing beneath the surface, Tessa felt the telltale prickle of iridescent scales rippling across her skin.

She caught her breath, anticipating her shift from an inhabitant of the land into a being of the sea.

From the waist down an instantaneous metamorphosis took place. Bone and muscle twined, fusing her two human legs into one before reshaping them into a long, slender, fishlike tail. Painless and swift, the sorcery of her modification from human to Mer occurred within the span of a second.

Born and raised in these waters, Tessa had always known she was different from the humans living onshore. Though human beings and mermaids were anatomically similar on land, all those similarities vanished once she hit the water. Far beneath the waves, where no human eyes could see her, Tessa became her true self—a strong, vital, confident woman of the seas.

Churned by the storm wailing above, the water was muddy and as dark as a tomb. The murk boiled around her, thick and almost impenetrable even to her super-sharp eyes.

Propelling herself at top speed, Tessa headed in the direction where she'd last seen the suicidal swimmer.

Precious seconds ticked away as she searched for the man she'd seen onshore. Beneath the surface, the water was bone-chillingly cold. As a Mer, Tessa was comfortable hot or cold. For a human, surviving would be difficult. In this temperature he'd have perhaps ten minutes before muscle impairment set in.

Struggling past the impulse to panic, Tessa forced herself to slow down. The water filtered in and out of her lungs as easily and naturally as she breathed air.

If he's dead . . .

She clamped her teeth against the acidic nausea of dread. No! She would find him. She would save him. It was her fault he'd gotten this far out into the water in the first place. If she'd been paying attention instead of worrying about her starved libido, she would have recognized the warning signs sooner.

Making several more passes through the area, she sensed rather than visually recognized his presence. A shadow. A wisp. Hair loose and tangled.

Head whipping around, she zeroed in on the body gently bobbing beneath the water's surface. His arms were floating outward, as if he were reaching for her in appeal. But his unseeing gaze stared right through her. There was no light, no life, in his eyes.

Fear lanced through her. Was she too late to help him?

Gasping painfully, Tessa quickly swam over to the fading man.

If he still has any life, I can save him. The thought offered a glimmer of hope.

Reaching out, Tessa cupped the man's face between her palms. Beneath the water, a mermaid's kiss could save a man's life, granting him the ability to breathe. She took a deep breath, filling her lungs with the precious air he needed to survive.

Tilting her head, she pressed her mouth to his. Summoning the magic known only to the Mer, she exhaled, passing the vital spark of life from her body to his . . .

Chapter 1

Port Rock, Maine
Ten months later

The boat skimmed across water as clear and shiny as a newly polished mirror. Though the bay was calm and untroubled, Kenneth Randall felt his stomach make a slow backflip. Swallowing hard against the rise of nausea, he quietly fought the urge to vomit. *Good grief.* He'd had no idea a quick trip across the Penobscot would make him sick as a dog.

Tightening his grip on the edge of the flat-bottomed skiff, he glanced down into a depth unfathomable to the naked eye. A prickling sensation ran up his spine. The bay looked unwelcoming, ominously unpredictable. Because the weather changed from day to day, its tides often presented intimidating challenges to navigation and piloting.

Kenneth shivered. His muscles bunched with tension. Though the water was tranquil, he couldn't help thinking back to the day he'd almost sacrificed his life to that all-consuming abyss in a moment of despair.

He frowned as images of walking into the choppy water flashed across his mind's eye. Through the hazy labyrinth of time and distance he still couldn't remember what had happened after he'd gone under. Every time he tried to put the pieces together, the indistinct pictures melted away, slipping back into the murky void lingering around the edges of his skull.

Despite the fact that it felt strange to admit it, he had a feeling he hadn't been under the water alone. Someone—some*thing*, some benevolent presence—had hovered nearby, keeping him alive when he should have perished. Whether it was the design of a higher power or the provenance of pure luck, somehow he'd survived. And while he wouldn't go so far as to label the underwater presence an angel, he couldn't shake the deeply rooted notion he'd been visited by a being of purity and beauty.

Digging deeper into the murk surrounding that day, Kenneth's stomach tightened at the fleeting, half-conscious impressions crowding into his brain. *Female*. Yes, he was absolutely sure the presence was a feminine one.

A flush prickled his skin as his heart sped up, filling his veins with hot adrenaline. Since that time the same faceless siren had visited his dreams, ushering in a sensually erotic delight. He was absolutely convinced he'd experienced the feel of her hands caressing his skin with a sensitive, compassionate touch. The breath seeping from his lungs had been restored by her kiss . . .

Kenneth choked down a lump of frustration before taking a few quick breaths to calm his fluttering stomach. "I definitely need to get my head on straight," he muttered under his breath.

The idea his sea nymph was nothing more than the

apparition of a mind gone awry had occurred to him on more than one occasion. The siren had to be the figment of a desperate imagination. He'd spent months in therapy working through that day. His therapist had even identified the notion to be part of post-traumatic stress disorder.

Survivor's guilt in the wake of two painful events had obviously put a lot of pressure on his subconscious mind. His body was relieving the stress in the only way it knew how, through sleep. Coming from the mouth of a professional, it all made perfect sense.

Forcing his gaze away from the water, Kenneth settled his attention on the island ahead. As the transport motored closer, he could see a traditional Cape Cod–style home—right down to the whitewashed exterior and gray-shingled roof—that stood several hundred feet behind a high concrete wall designed to break the worst of the waves.

The lighthouse was perched staunchly nearby, a guardian warning ships away from the dangers of land ahead. According to what he'd been told, he'd washed up, battered by the rocks and unconscious, on the island's rocky shore during the storm. The island's owner had reportedly pulled him to safety, alerting shore patrol to the emergency.

Kenneth hoped by returning to the island he could talk to the woman who'd rescued him. Surely she could help him put the final pieces of that day together.

"You guys never last." A raspy voice shattered Kenneth's internal monologue, reminding him he wasn't alone on this voyage into the unknown.

Kenneth glanced over his shoulder. Outfitted in clothing that had seen better days, the owner of the boat manned the rudder. Loaded with supplies destined for the island, the motor-powered vessel wasn't the prettiest or fastest on the bay. Rather, she was seaworthy and worked hard, a necessity for people who made their living in the coastal waters off Maine's shores. Dubbed *Lucky's Lady*, the small craft was as sun-weathered as the grizzled old man piloting her.

Feeling a twinge of tension in his shoulders, Kenneth loosened his grip on the edge of the boat. "I didn't catch what you said," he admitted, shouting his words over the whine of the motor.

Pushing back a cap that barely covered a fall of shoulder-length silvery hair, the old man spat a wad of phlegm over the edge of the boat. His expression was one of amusement. "Tessa," he yelled back, nodding toward the island. "She eats up the help and spits them out. Can't keep a handyman to save her life."

Ah, right. Now he understood why the old man had been so willing to ferry him across the bay. Clad in a pair of jeans coupled with a short-sleeved knit shirt and heavy boots, he most likely looked like he needed a job. Failing to correct the notion, he signaled his understanding. "Is she hard to work for?"

The skipper sucked his lower lip against his bottom teeth, then spat again. "That's saying a mouthful." He flashed a grin, showing more of his gums than teeth. "I reckon you're about the fifth or maybe sixth man I've taken across in the last few months."

Kenneth grimaced at the idea of nursing on a wad of tobacco. Disgusting habit, worse than his own addiction to nicotine. At least he tried to be polite about his smokes. "That's a lot of men," he yelled back. The mental picture of a sour old fishwife was beginning to take shape. The woman sounded like a shrew from hell, impossible to please.

The old sea dog guided the skiff up beside a small dock reigning over a rocky shoal; more than a little creaky and none too well cared for. Battered by the elements, it clearly wouldn't survive many more storms. "Tessa's a real ballbuster," he spat, throttling the Evinrude into blissful silence. "No man can satisfy her, no matter how hard he works." He briefly scrubbed a hand across his silvery whiskers. "Nobody lasts more than a week— maybe two—before they head back to the mainland. No man has managed to stand up to her yet."

"You're still around."

"Gwen—that's her sister—pays me to bring over the supplies and do a little tinkering with the lighthouse radio system. Past that . . ." He shook his head. "I'm too damn old to put up with any woman's lashing tongue."

Kenneth nodded his understanding. That made sense. "So Tessa never leaves the island?"

The skipper stood up and expertly looped a rope around one pillar to keep the skiff from drifting. Unloading a few items onto the dock, the old man climbed out of the boat. "The Lonikes have always kept to themselves, minded their own business. Tessa's sisters are nice enough, I suppose, seeing as they work in town. I like 'em both. As for Tessa, she's best left to herself."

Kenneth began to rethink the day's journey. Perhaps hitching a ride to the island wasn't such a wise notion after all. "Maybe I'd better stay here," he ventured.

The old salt snorted. "Tucking your tail between your legs?"

Those were fighting words. And one thing Kenneth had already decided in this life was that he wasn't backing away from anything ever again. He'd folded like a wet paper sack once. A second time wouldn't be acceptable. Besides, it wasn't like he actually wanted the damn job. He'd simply find the woman, and thank her.

Simple enough.

Fighting to keep his balance, which wasn't half as assured as the skipper's, Kenneth scrambled onto the dock. Though the ride hadn't taken more than ten minutes, he felt better having his feet closer to solid land.

He eyed the sign prominently nailed to a post. NO TRESPASSING. The locals clearly respected the privacy of people living off the mainland and their desire for peace and solitude. As an uninvited guest, he had to wonder how soon it would be before the island's reclusive owner sent him packing. *Too late to second-guess my decision now.*

"What's she like?" he asked, wanting to keep the conversation going just a moment longer.

The skipper shrugged. "She's as stubborn and ornery as a jackass. She won't listen to anyone and does what she damn well wants when she wants to. As for answering to a man . . . not anytime soon. You can take her, or leave her." A chuckle slipped between his chaw-stained lips. "Most of 'em leave."

"Got a feeling I'll be leaving soon," Kenneth muttered under his breath. Pushing his sunglasses up onto his head, he surveyed the island stretched out in front of him. A strange sense of familiarity crept in, seeping up from the darker corners of his mind.

The fine hairs on the back of his neck rose. His lungs seemed to freeze, holding on to the oxygen. Bit by bit, a sense of recognition began to return. Even though the sky held nary a cloud, he fancied he heard the rumble of thunder preceding a rain redoubling its angry assault on the earth. He vaguely recalled the wind kicking up, slashing at his bare skin. The chill was painful, penetrating all the way to the bone . . .

With more than a little relief, Kenneth released the breath he'd been holding. For once the cells in his short-circuited brain were beginning to spark, the soggy mass of gray matter finally assuming coherent shape.

The presence is here. He definitely felt it. *Her.*

Relief mingled with a tinge of anxiety. Most of the memories were still a blur, the details yet to be clarified. Despite the signs warning strangers away, he hoped Tessa Lonike would give him a few minutes of her time. All he wanted was information, enough to fill in the blanks. Once his need was satisfied, it would be time to close the door on the past and move on.

The skipper gave him a hard poke. "You going to stand there all day?" he demanded irritably. "I ain't got all day to be foolin' around here."

Jarred out of his thoughts, Kenneth refocused on the matter at hand. The skipper thought he was here to work. Best to get a move on and get going. "Just tell me what to do." Being agreeable was the best way to get along with people, especially strangers. The small community was a tight-knit one, where everybody knew everyone else's business. The best way for an outsider to gain acceptance was simply to go with the flow.

The old man made a sound just this side of a deep hack before spitting a wad of phlegm into the water. "You'll have a better chance of getting on Tessa's good side if you make yourself useful." He pointed to one of the parcels he'd unloaded onto the dock. "She's waitin' on a new motor for the swamp cooler. The sooner you get it in, the happier she will be."

Kenneth picked up the part, tucking it under one arm. "Can do."

"Just go on around back," the old man continued, pointing out a path leading toward the house. "I'll finish unloading the supplies. Once you're done there, we'll carry it all up to the house. I'd like to be home for supper before sundown, so get a move on."

Kenneth blew out his cheeks in a sigh. "Whatever you say, boss."

The trail leading from the dock to the house was made up of half-buried stepping-stones zigzagging over soil eroded from continual assault of water driven by furious winds. One wrong step would twist an ankle, or worse, break a bone. The walkway could clearly use improvements.

Leaving the rocky path behind, Kenneth stepped onto an overgrown lawn. Up close the place wasn't as picturesque as it appeared from a distance. Grass curled around his ankles, thick and squishy underfoot from recent rains. The thick, loamy scent of pine nettles and decaying leaves from trees clustered around the house filled his nostrils. They needed to be clipped and thinned, as did the low hedges edging both sides of the house. The house also needed a lot of work. The roof had lost more than its share of shingles to high winds. The white paint covering its walls had faded, cracking and slowly peeling away. Plywood nailed over a broken corner window lent the house a sad, neglected air.

It looked picture-perfect when viewed from a distance. However, the fairy-tale allure faded as perspective changed. The enchantment had long ago faded away.

"Needs a lot of work," Kenneth muttered under his breath. Despite the neglect, he recognized a lot of potential in the property. The house clearly had a solid foundation. Why the owner had let the place go when repairs would be so easy to make was beyond him.

He eyed the house, making a mental note here and there. "It could be fixed up." A new roof and a fresh coat of paint would go a long way toward restoring it to its former glory.

Closer now, the sound of angry voices drifted around the corner of the house.

Kenneth cocked his head, straining to hear the words. Though he couldn't make out the gist of the conversation, he clearly recognized the anger filling two female voices. An argument was under way and getting louder by the moment. Neither one of the participants was happy.

Feeling a little bit like an intruder, Kenneth tightened his hold on the motor. By the sounds of things, the girls were going at it tooth and nail. They probably wouldn't welcome any interruptions, especially from a stranger who'd invited himself onto the property.

Maybe I should go while the going's good. . . .

Despite the thought, his feet had other ideas. He'd come here for a reason, to settle his mind. Leave now and he'd just be back to that first frustrating square.

Walking with more confidence than he felt, Kenneth skirted the side of the house, skimming between the hedge and wall. He emerged into an overgrown backyard.

His gaze settled on two women standing beside the remains of a derelict swamp cooler. Someone had taken off the panels and gutted it, scattering the parts without much thought toward reassembly. Perched on a base constructed of cinder blocks and plywood, the old air conditioner looked ready to topple at any given moment.

His gaze shifted, refocusing his attention. Two women, two fiery redheads, were squared off against each other. The fur was flying, fast and energetically furious. By the look of things, neither was backing down.

Kenneth dragged in a breath. Talk about timing. He'd blundered straight into a hornet's nest.

He grimaced. *It's my own fault if I get stung.*

Tessa Lonike's eyes narrowed as she caught sight of the stranger. If she hadn't been so damn spitting mad at Gwen, she might even have welcomed his arrival. He carried the much-needed motor for the swamp cooler, back-ordered for more than a month. She'd been waiting all day for Lucky to show up with supplies. What she hadn't counted on seeing was a total stranger.

A twinge of suspicion rose. "You know him?" she demanded peevishly.

Gwen followed Tessa's gaze and shook her head. "No, but I hope to." Pasting on a grin, she lifted a hand in the air. "Over here," she called, motioning for the stranger to join them.

Screwdriver in hand, Tessa waved the tool toward her sister. "Don't lie."

Realizing the jig was up, Gwen pled out. "I put another ad in the paper," she admitted sheepishly. "I was beginning to think no one was going to show."

Shooting a glare toward the man, Tessa frowned. Gwen was determined to step all over her authority as the eldest. "I've told you before I don't want strangers here. I can handle this place myself."

"No, you can't." Gwen's hand shot out, delivering a sharp jab to Tessa's chest. "Now, be nice and hope he wants to work."

Grumbling under her breath, Tessa rubbed her aching boob. This was the last thing she wanted to deal with today. Her to-do list was already too long. "I have no intention of being nice." Hot and sweaty from wrangling with the swamp cooler, she didn't feel like kissing ass.

Gwen ignored her. Quirking a brow, she gave the approaching man an appreciative twice-over. "He's got potential."

Eyes rolling skyward, Tessa huffed. That was Gwen. Hot for anything in a pair of tight jeans.

Folding her arms across her chest, she narrowed her gaze toward the oncoming man. He stood well over six feet, most of it long, endless legs. Lean and buff to the max, he appeared to have a strong physique. Broad shoulders ruled over a rippling abdomen and narrow hips. His short-sleeved work shirt revealed biceps well defined from heavy lifting. Though faded, his jeans were clean, fitting him like a second skin. His confident stride ate up the ground.

As the distance separating them narrowed, Tessa got a clearer look at his face. His features reminded her of the rough-hewn statues of ancient athletes: subtly, oddly imperfect yet nevertheless appealing. He wore his brown hair short and spiky, a style complementing the shape of his face. A pair of stylish sunglasses obscured his eyes, adding to his bad-boy vibe. A Harley was probably waiting for him back on the mainland.

There was something familiar about the man, something that made her inner antennae perk up and hum. When she'd first glanced at him, heat had risen in her core, as if she'd been plunged straight into a pot of boiling water. Without intending for it to happen, her interest in the stranger had definitely been piqued.

Tightening her grip on her screwdriver, she immediately tamped down her attraction. Oh, this was so not the kind of man to be paying attention to. He had a rough appearance, one suggesting he was most comfortable hanging out with the guys, drinking tons of beer, and slapping chicks on the ass.

Tessa mentally gritted her teeth and stiffened her spine. *You ain't staying on, dude.*

The approaching stranger offered a smile. "Afternoon, ladies." He lifted the motor. "I believe you've been waiting on this."

Gwen beamed. "Yes, we are." She offered her hand. "Thanks for coming out with Lucky, Mr.—"

"Randall," he said, accepting her gesture. "Kenneth Randall."

His name flew over Tessa's head. She really didn't care who he was. Her attention was focused on the precious motor.

"Nice to meet you. I'm Gwen Lonike." Her sister made a vague gesture. "And the shrew standing beside me is Tessa."

Tessa pulled a face. *Bitch.*

He offered his hand. "Nice to meet you."

Ignoring him, Tessa reached for her motor. "I'll take that."

"All yours." He handed it over.

She nodded. "Thanks for bringing in the parts."

He shrugged. "No problem."

Gwen pounced. "This is the third one you've ordered. You shorted out the other two, brand-new."

Tessa rounded on her sister, then caught herself. Yes, it was true she'd burnt two motors to cinders with a bit of faulty wiring. She was sure she'd figured out the problem. The third time should be the charm. She just needed to do a little more tinkering. "I can handle it."

Gwen ignored her. "You ever do any electrical work?" she asked the newcomer.

Kenneth Randall smiled enough to show his teeth, slightly crooked on the bottom. His eyes crinkled at the corners, revealing the beginning of crow's feet. "I've done a little bit of everything."

Tessa silently simmered. Oh, no! Gwen wasn't the boss here.

"A little bit of everything isn't a whole lot of experience for anything." Her words came out, sharp and withering.

The tone of her voice immediately registered on Kenneth Randall's face. "I didn't come here looking for a job, ma'am." Skimming a hand through his thick hair, he took a step back.

Giving herself a swift mental kick, Tessa silently cursed her rudeness. There wasn't anything wrong with a man looking for honest work. And it wasn't his fault he was human. She just didn't like having them around. "What I meant to say is I don't need any help," she added quickly, trying to make amends. She softened her voice a little, proving she could carry on a conversation without being a complete ass.

"That's okay. No harm, no foul." Jerking a thumb over one shoulder, he offered an easy smile. "I just caught a ride with the old man because I wanted to come by and say thanks."

Casting her sister a suspicious glance, Gwen's fine brow puckered. "What for?"

He slid off his sunglasses, propping them on top of his head. His irises were deep brown, like puppy eyes. The hard-ass edge hovering around him evaporated. "Last year a lady living here fished me out of the water." An ironic smile curved his lips. "Maybe you remember the naked idiot who tried to take a swim in the bay."

Tessa barely kept her jaw from dropping off. Recognition crashed in like a ton of bricks. *Oh shit.*

There was no way in hell she'd have compared this tan, fit specimen of a male with the drenched man she'd pulled out of the water last year. Now she understood why her first impression had been one of familiarity. When she'd last seen him his hair was shoulder length, his body whipcord thin from the neglect that came from missing regular meals. When she'd reached him he'd been half-drowned. He almost hadn't survived.

A chilling thought flashed through her mind. Her stomach clenched painfully. *He wasn't supposed to come back.*

Tessa tightened her grip on the motor, thankful for its anchoring weight in her hands. Her heart sped up, thudding heavily against her ribs. She'd deliberately tucked the day away, forcing herself to forget it and move on.

That was a damn near impossible thing to manage.

Throat squeezing tight, she vividly recalled the feel of his naked, chilled skin pressed against her own warm flesh. Her stomach squeezed, blood heating from the fleeting memory of holding him in her arms. She'd sensed his need to touch and to be touched, and she'd answered in the only way she knew how. With her body.

Tessa drew a long breath.

What if he remembers?

Fighting to collect her wits, Tessa licked her papery lips. It was taking a supreme effort to think, to keep her thoughts on track.

She needed to get rid of him, and double quick.

Vaguely aware some response was expected, Tessa cleared her throat. She set the motor down, trying to hide her trembling hands. "I was just doing my job." She tried to keep from looking him directly in the eyes. She was too afraid of what she might find if she looked into their depths a second time. "You don't owe me anything."

"I owe you my life." Unwilling to let her off the hook, he cocked a brow toward the swamp cooler. "So why don't you let me repay you by lending a hand? I've done my share of work on those old puppies. Not hard to fix at all."

Tessa frowned and shook her head. "Really, you're not obligated in any way. What I did for you, I'd do for anyone."

Lines of disappointment furrowed his brow. "Is this where I pick up your hint to leave?"

Tessa stubbornly held her place. Getting him to go away was priority number one. "Yeah, pretty much."

Gwen broke in. "If he's offering a hand, you should take it." Disapproval colored her tone. "You've already been rude enough."

She was about to get a little ruder.

Grabbing her sister's arm, Tessa shoved Gwen to one side. "I have my reasons," she gritted. "I just want him gone." Later, when they were alone, she'd explain things. She'd never shared the details of the day, not even with her sisters.

Kenneth Randall couldn't fail to overhear. "I think that's my cue to catch a ride out with Lucky." He turned and simply walked away. A moment later he disappeared around the corner.

Watching him go, Tessa felt her tension drain away. Thanks be to the goddess. He wasn't going to be an ass and force himself into a place he wasn't wanted.

Tessa ran her palms across her face. Her skin felt clammy, cold. That was a bullet she didn't care to dodge again. The fact he'd come looking for her was a bad sign. What if he remembered that part of that day, including the fact she'd been in the water, wearing a tail? Being busted was simply not an option. Mers already had a hard enough time surviving in this unfriendly world.

She shot a surreptitious glance toward her sister. Gwen would have a stroke if she knew Tessa had been swimming around any humans in full Mer form. It wouldn't matter that the man was more than half-drowned and close to death.

Best not think about that now. She'd deal with the fallout, when and if it arrived.

Tessa switched back to the problem at hand. With temperatures climbing past the nineties, the relief of a cool house would be welcome. "Now I can get back to fixing this old piece of junk."

She didn't quite get the relief she was counting on.

Gwen stepped in to continue the fight. "This time I'm putting my foot down," she insisted, taking up where they'd left off. "You don't know your ass from a hole in the ground." She threw up her hands. "Look at this place. All you've done since Mom and Dad died is let it go to hell in a handbasket."

Startled by the intensity behind Gwen's attack, Tessa's hackles rose. "I'm doing my best. But you know as well as I do money's tight and finding someone who'll work for a reasonable wage is damn near impossible. Not to mention the cost of materials to do the repairs. I can handle things, but only one at a time."

Gwen pressed her lips into a line, and she crossed her arms over her chest. "That's the trouble. Nothing's getting done. This place is too much for one person and the money's running out. It's true I can funnel more cash over from the hotel, but I'm not inclined to do that anymore. As much as you don't like it, you've got to face facts. It's time to let the island go."

Tessa felt a stab of anger-driven pain so sharp it went straight through her core. "I'm not selling the island. This is my—our—home. It's the only place we belong."

Gwen slowly shook her head. "It's time to give it up, Tess. Move onto the mainland and live a normal life."

Normal? What was normal about their fucking lives? As much as she tried to act human and play the part, Gwen knew damn good and well that mermaids and humans didn't mix well.

Planting her feet as though the act would anchor her to the ground, Tessa glared daggers. If looks could kill, Gwen would be pushing up daisies about now. "I'm the oldest. I decide what happens here. You tell Addie I'm not selling it. Not today, tomorrow, or ever."

Gwen countered with her own fierce glower. "We each have an equal share, and Addison agrees with me. Two votes add up to the majority, and we've decided to sell." Her sister's ultimatum hit like a blast of arctic air on naked flesh.

Tessa gasped. She'd hoped Gwen wouldn't feel compelled to make that threat.

A chill snatched the air from her throat. She'd been outplayed. Her sisters could sell everything out from under her and she was powerless to stop them. "Fuck you both," she mumbled, feeling like she'd been pummeled to tiny pieces.

Gwen sighed heavily. "This didn't go as well as I'd hoped."

Irritation flickered. "I think I've heard enough."

Gwen raised her hands, palms out. "Just listen. Please."

"Why should I?" Tessa replied, forcing her eyes open wide so she could stall the threat of tears. There was no way she'd let her younger sibling see her cry. Hell would freeze over first.

Gwen paused, pursing her lips. "Because we won't sell if you'll just hire someone to help out." She spread her arms. "It's that simple."

It was the same old dilemma, except Gwen had some serious leverage behind her threat. And while Tessa didn't want to share the island with a human, she also didn't want to be packing her bags to move to the mainland.

Tessa considered her options. *None.* It felt like Gwen had cut her legs off at the knee. She was down and had no way to get up. "Fine. You find a guy who wants to work for nothing and he's hired." She didn't need to look at her checkbook to know the balance was perilously low. The island was considered a prime piece of real estate and even though it belonged to her family, the taxes on the land weren't cheap. Uncle Sam was eating her sack lunch, leaving only crumbs behind.

To Tessa's surprise, Gwen wasn't the one who answered.

Kenneth Randall reappeared, easing around the corner of the house. "I couldn't help overhearing," he said, offering a sheepish grin and a shrug. "Maybe I can help out."

Tessa launched a glare his way. He was supposed to be gone. For good. "Eavesdropping isn't polite."

Dark eyes met hers. He was too confident—and too damn sexy to easily ignore. "Neither is walking away when someone needs help."

His heavy gaze burned right through Tessa, causing her body temperature to inch dangerously higher. She clenched her jaw against the tremor of awareness flooding her veins. He affected her on such a physical level.

Tessa swallowed over the lump in her throat. "I'm not a charity case. I can do for myself."

"I didn't say you were." An easy laugh escaped him. "I'm in between jobs, so I've got time on my hands."

Nostrils flaring, Tessa looked at him doubtfully. "There's a lot to do. The house needs a new roof, a fresh coat of paint, and it's got a few plumbing issues. Not to mention the lighthouse."

"And the cracked front window," he reminded.

Tessa winced. The list was endless. No wonder she'd gotten so far behind. "I could use an extra pair of hands."

Kenneth caught her gaze, holding it for a long moment. "If it helps, I'm a certified mechanic. And I did a lot of construction to pay my way through college. Hell, I could even drag up a reference or two if necessary." His reply was natural and sincere. He clearly meant every word he said.

Tessa wavered. "I can't pay much," she admitted. "In fact, it's almost nothing."

He ignored the fact. "If you've a place I can stow my stuff and can throw me a sandwich now and again, I'm good."

"We do!" Gwen clapped her hands. "And I can hit the deli and stock up today."

Tessa drew in a long, shaking breath. Everything was slipping out of her control with alarming speed. It all sounded too good to be true. Kenneth Randall *seemed* too good to be true. "You'd do that?" she asked, still a little dazed by the sudden turn of events. "Work for free?"

"Not for free," he corrected. "I'll work for room and board." A slow, wry smile parted his lips. "If nothing else, maybe it'll keep me out of the water."

"You've got a job, then," Gwen said, sealing the deal by offering her hand.

Tessa opened her mouth, trying to think of a reasonable protest but nothing came out. Just like that, a decision had been made. On some secret, selfish level she was relieved to be spared further argument. But that didn't stop her stomach from rolling over. Whether or not she agreed with the notion, she had no choice.

She'd have to share her island. With a man she'd seen at his most vulnerable, stripped bare and struggling to find the will to live.

A man she couldn't help but admit she desired a little.

A flush pricked Tessa's skin even as her heart sped up, filling her mouth with a vaguely coppery taste. Sweat plastered her thin T-shirt to her back. Thinking about her new handyman undressed and aroused was like grabbing on to a hot-wire fence. Hang on tight and she'd get one hell of a buzz.

Foreboding sent a chill down her spine. She had a feeling the island wasn't going to be big enough for both of them.

Chapter 2

A smile tugged at the corner of Kenneth's mouth as he followed Tessa Lonike up the narrow circular staircase leading to the second floor of the lighthouse.

As befitting the warm afternoon, Tessa was casually dressed in a pair of shorts and a tank top. A sports bra hugged her breasts, a no-frills undergarment that nevertheless managed to look sexy beneath her stained work shirt. The shorts accentuated her slender waist and peach-firm rear, their high cut displaying endless, tightly muscled legs. She'd twirled up her long hair, securing it with something that looked like a set of chopsticks. Her locks shimmered with a thousand flames, fiery to pale reds and effervescent coppers. A few stubborn strands refused to be tamed, straggling around her face and neck. Aside from a delicate gold chain holding a simple crystal pendant, she wore no jewelry. Her body undulated with a particular feline grace each time she lifted a foot.

Kenneth had already imagined brushing those curls off her slender nape before planting a soft kiss on the enticing curve. But her tight shoulders and distant at-

titude indicated making time with the boss wouldn't be
one of the perks of the job.

At this point she was being civil. Nothing more. Nothing less. Considering he'd made himself welcome on her
turf, he didn't blame her. But if taking the job meant he
could remain on the island, then he'd gladly roll up his
sleeves and go to work.

He still wanted to know what the hell was in the
water.

As for the perks, he had to admit following Tessa
around wasn't a bad way to spend an afternoon. Truth
be told, he was having the time of his life. If nothing else,
the view was terrific. Even more interesting was the fact
her bare arms were heavily tattooed with some sort of
a tribal pattern. The design appeared to continue down
her back and over her abdomen, reappearing again on
her legs. The pattern ended at her ankles, just above the
unlaced combat boots she wore. On any other woman
the design would be vulgar. On her the tattoos were
strangely alluring.

Kenneth winced. That much needlework had to be
extremely painful. "The tats are awesome," he said,
eager to break the silence hanging between them. She
didn't seem to be the chatty kind, speaking only when
spoken to.

Tessa didn't stop walking, nor did she turn her head.
"Thanks," was all she said.

He tried again. "Must have taken years to get done."

She kept on climbing. "Seems like a lifetime." Her
tone was noncommittal. She simply answered, giving no
invitation to continue the conversation.

Kenneth pressed on anyway. He'd had enough of silence in his life lately. Surely it wouldn't hurt her to talk

a little. "How'd you come up with the design? Tribal, isn't it?"

Tessa shot a glance over one shoulder.

"It just kind of happened," she said. "In fact, you might say it grew on me."

Kenneth cocked his head. For a moment it seemed her voice had changed a bit, taking on a tinge of bitterness.

Conversation stalled as they reached the second level.

Tessa stepped into a small vaulted vestibule, flicking on an overhead light. The single bulb cast a soft, luminescent glow throughout the loft. Though the ceiling was ridiculously high, the space was more than a little cramped due to the circular construction of the lighthouse.

Easing in behind her, Kenneth set his duffel bag on the floor. It was the sole piece of luggage he had. It didn't take long to look the place over because there wasn't much to look at. The simple design had enough room for the bare basics: a small kitchenette, adjoining bathroom, and, shoved under the staircase that continued up toward the control tower, a bed. A small dinette set and a lounge completed the furnishings. A couple of portholes broke up the solidity of the walls. The natural wood of the walls was austere, the floor bare except for a few necessary throw rugs.

Though not the newest or the most expensive, every item in the small apartment was clean and well kept. The bed was a single, neatly made up with a patchwork quilt. A yellow tomcat had made himself welcome, stomping down the pillows and stretching out on top.

For the first time that day, Tessa showed a bit of animation. "There you are, Jasper." Crossing the small space, she scooped the cat up, giving him a quick scratch

behind the ears. "Sorry, big fella. You're being evicted."
Cat in hand, she turned around. "This is as good as it
gets."

Ken coughed in the damp atmosphere. The loft was
stuffy and humid, the air smelling of the sea. The humidity in the attic created a fine sheen of perspiration on
his skin. Catching sight of the fan propped on the coun-
tertop, it vaguely occurred to him the lighthouse didn't
have any sort of cooling system.

He couldn't complain. After all, it was his decision to
stick his nose into Tessa's business. It was his own fault if
he sweltered and suffered the heat. Fortunately Maine
summers were short; the winters were long and fierce. It
wouldn't be long before the island would be blanketed
in snow, its inhabitants digging in against the cold.

Realizing she expected an answer, he nodded. "It's
good."

She knew he'd spotted the inadequacies right away.
"This is the old keeper's dwelling. It's not really up to
date, but it's private."

He nodded his approval. "It's nicer than I thought it
would be." Since deciding to pack up and leave Jersey, he
presently owned nothing more than the clothes he carried and his vehicle. He'd disposed of everything else.

A snort of disbelief escaped her. "Yeah, right."

"What's that supposed to mean?"

Tessa eyed him a long moment. "I'm wondering how
long you will last," she finally answered, frowning. "A lot
of the guys Gwen's hired treat the island like their own
private getaway. I can't tell you how many I've caught
smoking dope, getting high. One guy was even smug-
gling, for heaven's sake." She shook her head. "Can't
trust anyone nowadays."

Kenneth couldn't imagine being a woman alone, a

mile from the mainland. That in itself was a recipe for disaster. Tessa had no business living alone. She clearly needed someone trustworthy and reliable.

Like me, came his niggling, intrusive inner voice.

Kenneth immediately backed away from the thought. It was one thing to offer a hand. He might even amuse himself with a few harmless fantasies. But barreling into this woman's life like a steamroller wasn't the way to impress her. That smacked of desperation. And desperate people—*lonely people*—were scary.

"I agree," Kenneth said, choosing each word carefully. "The world isn't a safe place." It was definitely a fact he knew too well.

Tessa laughed shortly. "I don't mind if a man wants to kick back and have a beer after a hard day's work, but I definitely don't need the party-hearty types." She paused, her face taking on a serious look. "You might think Gwen pretty much strong-armed me into hiring you, but that's not true. I'm not blind and I'm not dense. I know this place is falling down around my ears. If you're offering honest help, I could use it."

Her unexpected admission was a breakthrough. It was the first allowance she'd made that she wouldn't mind having him hang around. Not a great gesture of welcome, but it was a step in the right direction. It offered a chance they might get along, maybe even like each other.

Past that, he wouldn't push. Right now just having a place to live and something to do was a godsend. In fact, it was exactly what he needed, a project to take his mind off the fact he was still drifting.

"That's exactly what I'm doing."

Tessa studied him, her gaze simmering with suspicion and wariness. "My mother always told me that if it seemed too good to be true, it must be some kind of a con."

"And my mother used to say *seeing is believing*," he countered. "So why not just give me a chance and judge for yourself?"

She crossed her arms, nodding with resolution. "You've got a two-week trial. If things don't work out, you leave. No questions asked."

He nodded. "That's fair enough."

She lifted a hand, pointing a finger his way in a scolding manner. "I've got some rules, though."

Kenneth smiled politely. "And those are?"

Tessa jabbed her finger his way. "On the mainland, what you do is your business. Here, what you do is my business. I don't like strangers, so bringing girls here is off-limits. So are drugs. If you use them, you might as well leave now."

Uh-oh. Better get this one out of the way. "I do have one drug."

Her gaze clouded. "What?" Jaw tightening, her tone was icy.

He grinned. "Nicotine. Okay if I smoke?"

Tessa relaxed, voice returning to normal. "Outside, if you must."

Kenneth laughed. "I must."

Tessa's nose wrinkled. "Stinky habit."

"I'm working on quitting." The habit was new, a stress thing he hoped to give up in time. For now it was the best therapy for jumpy nerves. He'd rejected medication for his depression, preferring to work through the problem himself. "Got to admit I've got a carton packed, though."

Tessa eyed the single duffel bag he'd returned to the mainland to retrieve. "That all you got?"

He shrugged. "Pretty much, but it's crammed full. I think I've got about a week's worth of clothes."

She paused a beat. "You travel light."

Kenneth nodded, but didn't explain. At this point in his life, he wasn't into being weighed down with useless possessions. "I hope you have a washing machine. Otherwise I'll have to work naked." His tone came out a little huskier than he intended. The statement he'd jokingly offered sounded like a blatant come-on.

He mentally gave himself a swift kick and prayed his brand-new boss would take no offense. He wouldn't blame her if she tossed his duffel in the water and told him to start swimming.

A tinge of pink immediately crept into Tessa Lonike's cheeks. Her grip on the cat tightened, causing poor old Jasper to meow heartily and wiggle in disapproval. "You can have laundry privileges once a week," she allowed.

Kenneth psychically released the breath he'd been holding. A relief. She could be a good sport. Perhaps there was even a sense of humor lurking under her queen-bee attitude. No time like the present to find out. He couldn't resist taking another poke at her. "Don't think you could handle me naked again?"

Catching on, Tessa resumed her normal, cool demeanor. She arched a brow, pursing her sensual mouth. Vivid jade green eyes ruled over the sexy arch of her full, sensual lips. "I've seen you nude," she sniffed. "And it's nothing to get excited about."

Ken winced. *Ouch*. He'd thrust and she'd parried with perfect precision, unsheathing her claws and digging them deeply into his skin.

Too bad. All work and no play made things dull.

He tried again. "Any chance you might change your mind if you see me again with my shirt off?" He was pretty proud of his body, and he worked out regularly to regain the weight and muscle he'd lost after Jen died. For a while, the only nutrition he'd been consuming consisted of whiskey straight from the bottle. It was no way to live and yet another terrible way to commit suicide. Working out daily had helped ease his many frustrations. While pumping iron, he didn't have to think. Just do.

Pressing her mouth into a flat line, Tessa vehemently shook her head. "Not going to happen. I'm single, free, and I like it that way."

He couldn't help smiling. She looked like a little girl resisting a bite of food she found displeasing. "So what do you do for a thrill?"

"I get a book and a glass of wine," she shot back drily. "Unlike a man, that entertainment never disappoints me."

He studied her, intrigued. She didn't even crack a smile when she said it. "I'm always willing to try something new. Maybe you can recommend a few good books."

It dimly occurred to him he was doing something he hadn't thought would be possible ever again. He was flirting. With a woman he found absolutely and utterly adorable.

The realization hit like lightning streaking from the sky. For the longest time he hadn't been living. He'd been existing, a prisoner trapped in the gray, numbing fog of grief. Living with Jen's ghost had been an exhausting endeavor. He could second-guess and reshape the facts in his head, but nothing would change the actual event of her murder. If he wanted to stay sane, stay alive, then the past had to be put to rest.

Survival meant moving on. To a place he wanted to be.

He was thirty-six years old and starting life over, from scratch. For the first time in a long time he felt good. Maybe even happy.

Tessa pulled a face. "Don't be expecting any hearts-and-flowers romances. I like horror, a lot of good, bloody gore."

By the look of her extreme tats, that one should have been a no-brainer.

He nodded. "I'll keep that in mind."

Realizing he relied on her good graces to allow him to live on the island, Ken backed off. She'd made it pretty clear she wasn't particularly interested in him. In fact, she didn't even really seem to like men. Anytime a woman ragged on men it usually meant some heart-smashing bastard lurked in her past. And if that were indeed true, then the son of a bitch deserved a good ass kicking.

Unzipping his duffel bag, he dug out a fresh pack of cigarettes.

Tessa frowned her disapproval and immediately pointed to the tower. "Up there, please." She plopped the cat back on the bed, and Jasper yawned, content to return to his nap. The big cat stretched out. The bed was his and he wasn't sharing.

Continuing their walk, they followed the stairs to the lighthouse tower. Bypassing the service room, where radio and other communication equipment was kept, they stepped onto a catwalk surrounding the massive enclosed lantern. A circular iron awning overhead offered protection from the elements.

Tearing the cellophane wrapper off his cigarettes, Ken tapped one out. "So that still work?" he asked, digging in his pocket for his lighter.

Tessa nodded. "In olden times the lamp was powered

by oil. It's electric now, drawing its charge off a small generator. And it still works." She patted the clear glass surrounding and protecting the lantern. "It's one of the oldest working lighthouses in Maine, built in 1870. Right now we stand one hundred and sixty-five feet above sea level." She smiled, truly animated for the first time since he'd arrived.

Flicking his lighter, Kenneth lit up and inhaled. A rush of calming nicotine filled his lungs. Now that the sun was beginning to set, the day was cooling off. The salty breeze riffling in from the sea carried a hint of the coming change in seasons. Winter would be fierce. "I would call that job security."

"It's been in the family so long, it's like an actual member."

"So this is where your people come from?"

Smile dimming a little, Tessa turned and leaned against the waist-high rail. "Considering my family has owned this island for more than a hundred and forty years, I guess you could say that." Despite her answer, she cast her gaze over the wide expanse of the all-consuming sea. "Before that, who knows . . . ?"

"A lot of history in this place."

"More than you'll ever know," Tessa muttered under her breath. "What about you, Mr. Randall? Why did you come back to Little Mer Island?"

Taking one final drag off his cigarette, Kenneth smashed out the remnant. Realizing he had no place to discard the leftover butt, he tucked it back in the pack. "Looks like I'm going to need a few ashtrays."

Tessa nodded. At least he hadn't just tossed it over the railing. The idea of a pile of butts littering the base of the lighthouse wasn't appealing in the least. She didn't like the habit, but she could tolerate it as long as he kept his smoking outside.

"You been smoking long?"

Shaking his head, Kenneth turned and leaned into the rail. "Off and on," he said. "Mostly on lately."

"So is that part of the story you're going to tell me?"

He didn't get it. "Story?"

"The one about who you are, where you came from, and how you ended up here." Tessa's reason for asking wasn't entirely because she was interested in his life. She wanted a few details. Details she knew Gwen was already checking on the Internet.

As owner of By the Sea, a hotel on the mainland, her sister often ran background checks on applicants. No doubt Gwen was already doing a search as they spoke. Gwen was more trusting of the human race—but only so far. It helped that Kenneth had been staying at Gwen's place. Her sister would already have his driver's license and vehicle plate on file.

If there was anything lurking in the man's past, Gwen would find it. But Tessa also wanted to run her own litmus test. Just how honest would he be, face-to-face?

She already knew looks were deceiving. She'd been misled before by a handsome face and charismatic personality. And one time was enough. She wasn't anybody's fool anymore.

Hr shrugged. "Not much to tell. I was born. I grew up. I moved to Maine. End of story."

"Not much of a story."

"It's pretty boring."

The man played his cards close to his vest. Tessa wanted a peek. "If I were to ask you if your life was a drama, a comedy, or a tragedy, what would you choose?"

A long silence ensued. By the look on his face, her question struck a definite nerve. She already knew what the answer wouldn't be. Like a lightbulb shorting out, his expression instantly darkened. Whatever was going through his mind wasn't pleasant.

The sun was beginning to disappear on the far horizon, bathing the lighthouse in cool shadows. His face, too, was shadowed, closed. The easy rapport of the last few minutes had vanished like a ghost in fog. "You really want an answer to that?"

"Yeah."

He scrubbed his face with his hands. "Tragedy."

Tessa's stomach curled into tight knots. She'd seen him at his weakest. Whatever his past held, it was enough to bring this strapping man down to his knees. "Would it have anything to do with what happened last year?"

Fidgeting a little, his mouth pulled down. "You could say that." The turn in conversation appeared to be making him uncomfortable. She wondered when he would snap, tell her to back off and mind her own business.

Tessa considered, wondering just how much she should reveal from her point of view. Lying, pretending she hadn't seen him go into the water, simply wasn't an option. She didn't want to downplay the seriousness of the day. If the man required help—real help—she needed to know. The island was remote, not readily accessible. If any emergency arose, she was on her own.

"I was in the tower and I saw you go into the water that day," she admitted at last. "I've got a pretty good view up here, as you now know." Not wanting to spook him, she tried to keep her tone noncommittal. All she could do was show a willingness to listen and hope he wanted to talk.

Kenneth barely suppressed a groan. "I didn't think anyone actually lived on the island. All the signs say 'private property' and 'no trespassing.'"

A vague sense of uneasiness rippled through her. "Well, now you know differently. That's the way life is on an island with a working lighthouse . . . that and the shore patrol I handle. All part of the job of being a Lonike."

Amazed, he shook his head. "I can't believe you rescued me all by yourself." He was trying to take a detour, turning conversation away from himself.

Tessa motored straight ahead. "Training. I knew when you went under you didn't intend to come up again." There. She'd said it. He wasn't the first suicidal person she'd pulled out of the murky depths of the bay.

A deep, body-shuddering sigh suddenly moved him. "At the time, I didn't intend to." His muscles perceptibly bunched with tension. He clutched the railing with such a tight grip his knuckles began to turn white.

Holding him at arm's length was going to be difficult. He understood the pain of being alone, feeling lost in this world.

"I think we've all had those moments."

Kenneth's right hand moved to his left, fingering the plain gold band he wore. "I've had more than my share, that's for sure."

Tessa's eyes followed the movement. It was the first time she'd noticed. He wore a wedding ring. "You're married," she murmured, unaware she spoke aloud.

Gaze dropping to his hand, he hesitated an interminable moment. "Widowed. My wife died about a year and a half ago." He swallowed thickly. "You must have thought I was a cheat for hitting on you."

Tessa felt like a twit. She'd judged him on looks alone,

and had been totally wrong. "I honestly didn't notice. I was too busy being pissed off at you."

He nodded in agreement. "I did kind of invite myself." A pause. "You want me to leave?"

Tessa considered the idea, then shook her head. "I'll cut you some slack. At least two weeks' worth."

Relief brightened Kenneth's eyes. He nodded. "Thanks. I'll take every bit I can get."

"If you just want to kick back—"

With a shake of his head, he cut her off. "Thank you for the offer, but I actually want to work. It'll help take my mind off the pity party I've been throwing for myself since Jen died. I know I've got to get my shit together and bag it. I've just been dragging my ass."

Tessa studied him, taking in the beginnings of gray sprouting at his temples, the fine lines beginning to etch themselves at the corners of his eyes. She judged him to be in his late thirties, which meant his wife must have been young when she passed away. "You mentioned your wife is no longer living," she ventured. "Was she ill?"

His jaw tightened seconds before he shook his head. "Murdered," he grated. "Some punk robbing a convenience store needed a getaway car. Jen had just pulled in to grab a cup of coffee, just like she did every day before work. He shot her and took her car. She didn't survive."

His answer was one Tessa hadn't expected. "That's horrible. I hope they caught the man who did it."

Shifting away from her, Kenneth dragged a hand down his face in agitation. His fingers rasped against the stubble he'd neglected to shave off. "They did, and the bastard got the death penalty. But it wasn't enough in my opinion. He didn't just kill Jen; he killed our baby." His words tumbled out unchecked, a burden he seemed incapable of bearing any longer than necessary.

His words delivered a jolt. Shock ran through her, a dismay so sharp she had to gulp down the sudden rise of bitter acid.

Tessa reached for the crystal hanging from her neck. "By the goddess." Events such as he'd narrated would bring even the strongest man to his knees. Losing a wife and a child to a random act of senseless violence had rightly torn his soul asunder.

Human beings can be such savage, horrible beasts.

A breathless moment passed before Kenneth's dark gaze met hers. He tried to smile, but failed. "Sorry. I didn't mean to lay all that on you."

"I did ask," she reminded him. "I'm the one who should apologize."

"Don't. It happened and I can't keep sticking my head into the sand." A deep line formed between his brows. "That day I went into the bay . . . I'd looked at my life and didn't see anything beyond the water. All of a sudden the answer was there. I wasn't thinking when I did what I did."

Tessa glanced at his face. His brown eyes were shadowed, sad. He'd lost his place in the world, belonging nowhere. She realized his search had brought him back to the island. "I'm sorry to remind you."

Giving no reply, Kenneth shifted his attention back toward the water. "Thanks for saving my life. I appreciate it."

Tessa quickly shook her head. "Don't even mention it," she mumbled. Of course, there was no way to tell him the real truth: that she hadn't immediately dragged him ashore. Because of the storm's severity, she'd ended up pulling him far beneath the waves, taking him to an underwater shoal. She'd held him in her arms, sharing her breath with him, keeping him alive until the waters calmed enough to return him to the mainland beach. Chances were he had no memory of the event whatsoever.

He shook his head. "From my side, the chance to say thank you is absolutely necessary. I was really wearing my dunce hat that day."

Wondering how thin the ice beneath her feet might possibly be, Tessa ventured, "Do you remember much?"

Frowning, he shook his head. "Nothing's really clear until the hospital in Port Rock. I got admitted on a 5150, an involuntary psychiatric hold."

Working with mainland search and rescue, Tessa knew the emergency codes all too well. "That must have sucked."

He laughed shortly. "Yeah, it definitely did. I had a lot of explaining to do to the resident shrink. Somehow I managed to turn my vacation into a one-way trip to the nuthouse."

"Sorry. I had to tell them what I saw."

Kenneth started to say something, stopped, then shrugged. "Don't be. The rest of the story's pretty simple. I went home to Jersey, but I couldn't get back on track, couldn't get a grasp on normal. It took a lot of sessions in therapy for me to figure out my life would never be normal again."

The breeze off the sea shifted, bringing his personal odor to her nostrils. He was standing so close she could smell the clean scent of his body spray, the alluring combination of musk and sandalwood.

Close enough to breathe in his masculine scent, Tessa licked her suddenly dry lips. Her inhumanly acute senses zeroed in on the pheromones emanating from his scent.

He smelled like sex—a rich, dark, ravenous scent that emanated from every pore.

Breath catching in a hitch, need immediately surged through her. Knees weakening, her head began to spin.

Fighting to regain control, Tessa pressed her fingers against her temple.

She forced herself to take in air, tamping down her body's response to the silent but urgent call. Acutely aware of his longing, her body's response was natural, one she couldn't control. As a Mer, Tessa was extrasensitive to a male's unspoken reaction to her presence. It helped her gauge the suitability of a prospective mate.

And there was no denying Kenneth Randall's unconscious craving. All the verbal and physical signals pointed in one direction.

He wanted her.

The only question that remained was whether or not she intended to respond. The temptation was certainly there.

Kenneth caught her move. "Headache?" Concern laced his words.

Hearing his voice, Tessa's hand immediately dropped. "A little." She cast around for a quick excuse. There was no way she'd ever admit she was suffering the effects of intense arousal. "I've been fighting with the damn swamp cooler all day." The sensible thing to do right now was keep her distance.

Toying with his cigarettes, Kenneth sifted out a fresh one. Lit it. "Sorry. I guess I kind of barreled in on you." He took a deep drag. Smoke rushed through his nostrils, reminding her of the steam of a boiling volcano. His movements were suddenly awkward, uncomfortable. "Guess I was wondering what the hell I thought I'd do when I got here. Sold the house, quit my job, and hit the road. Sounds like a plan, right?"

Tessa cleared her throat before allowing a brief smile. "Just stay out of the water, okay? I'm not saving your raggedy ass twice."

He drew another lungful of smoke. The tip glowed red before dying in gray ashes. "What I'm looking for isn't there anymore," he said quietly.

Tessa recognized the strain in his eyes, the uncertainty hovering beneath his calm facade. He'd obviously picked up the vibes her body was giving off, but hadn't yet recognized the tension humming between them to be erotic in nature.

Heart doing a war dance in her chest, a little laugh slipped past her lips. Every nerve in her body was stretched taut. A thousand emotions were all tangled up inside her psyche, but she froze at the thought of acting on a single impulse. If he touched her now, she'd shatter.

She took a step back, putting a little distance between them. It wasn't easy to resist the electricity flickering between them. It was taking a supreme effort to pull her thoughts together, keep them coherent. This was something she wasn't ready to deal with. The day was already crazy enough without having to have sexual pressure added to the mix.

Back off, she warned herself. *And take things slow.*

Tessa's heart sped up. She swallowed hard, panicky yet intrigued by the expression on his face. "What are you looking for?" she asked, almost afraid of what the answer might be.

Kenneth shook his head. "I'm not sure," he admitted. "But I hoped by coming back I'd be able to find it again."

Chapter 3

Careful not to make a sound, Tessa crept toward the western edge of the island. There, craggy boulders gave way to a small cul-de-sac, the eroded remnants of a sandy reef. At low tide smaller rocks dotted the white sand, nature's perfect seat for sitting and just gazing at the ocean. Before the lighthouse had been constructed, this side of the island had caused a lot of damage to ships attempting to make landfall.

Because of the abundance of water in the Port Rock area, fishing and swimming were among the most popular activities. Sea kayaking and boat tours were also popular, which often meant the island saw more than its share of trespassers. Drawn by the lighthouse, many tourists chose to ignore the warning signs. If someone was in need, Tessa was glad to offer help. Otherwise she'd been known to get snappish, especially when people pulled out their cameras and started tramping around to get shots of the popular landmark.

Casting a furtive glance toward the lighthouse, Tessa breathed a little sigh of relief. It was dark, nary a sign of light or life about it. Its new occupant appeared to have

settled in for the night. She'd waited until well after mid-
night to venture out, needing some time alone to contemplate the abrupt change in her solitary life.

A human had invaded her sacred space. And this visitor wasn't just any human, but one who had a direct tie
to her. Worse than that, pieces of the past were beginning to surface in his mind. It didn't take a rocket scientist to figure out what would be revealed if the picture
were completed.

Not that she intended to help him figure things out.
Anything Kenneth Randall thought might be bona fide
could easily be explained away by emotional trauma.

Tessa grinned to herself, enjoying her role as keeper
of the secrets. Despite the fact she genuinely liked the
man, her inner Mer still wanted to crack the whip. Control was all important in her world. A wicked thought
slithered out of the darkest corner of her mind. *And the
proof is in the tail.*

In other words, she'd swear it was all a lie.

As one of the mermaids actually dwelling on Little
Mer Island, Tessa knew the indigenous Native Americans regarded stories of the sea creatures inhabiting
these waters as absolutely true. Those who lived in Port
Rock also did their share to keep the lore alive, many
doing a thriving business in mermaid-themed parapher-
nalia when tourists visited the isolated port. Fishermen
working in the harbor were glad to encourage belief
with stories of their own.

Some of those stories might even have a grain or two
of truth.

Most of them didn't. Most of the tales were nothing
more than fiction spun by locals who needed tourist dollars to keep their businesses in the black. According to
them, the bay was teeming with mermaids.

Not true.

Aside from her own close-knit family, Tessa knew of no others. And unless she and her sisters found mates and had daughters of their own, their bloodline would soon be extinct in these parts.

Tessa glanced around, making double sure she was alone. The moon hung in the velvety sky, full and silvery, casting its luminous glow on the surface of the water. On calm nights the bay was a wonderful place to swim. She'd have about an hour to swim before the tide rolled back in and reclaimed the reef.

She slipped off her terry-cloth robe, tossing it over a nearby boulder. The cool night air lovingly caressed her bare skin. She wore not a single stitch, not even the skimpy pieces of a bikini. The only thing she wore around her neck was her soul-stone, which she was never without. Upon birth a Mer was given her own crystal, which contained the vital part of the magic she'd learn to wield, including the ability to shift. At this point in her life, Tessa still hadn't grasped the full scope of a Mer's abilities. Neither had her sisters. Their mother had passed away just as she'd begun to pass on her knowledge to her three daughters. Tessa was barely fifteen years old when the automobile accident claimed both her parents.

Tessa followed the narrow beach to the water's edge. She didn't stop to test the temperature of the water, stepping straightaway into the chilly depth. Wet sand oozed up between her toes and she sank a little. She walked until the sandy bottom fell away beneath her feet, suddenly plunging into an endless depth.

Sighing with contentment, she treaded water for a few minutes. Her legs were bothering her, a restless sensation that wouldn't settle down. Her body felt crawly, like thousands of tiny insects skittered beneath the surface of her skin. The only remedy was a swim, where she could shift into her true form. Once in the water, she could swim herself into exhaustion. After that, she'd be able to rest.

Taking a deep breath, Tessa dived. As the water rippled around her naked flesh, she shifted. Beneath the surface, her lungs filtered water like air. Her vision adjusted perfectly to the shadowy depths. Her movements driven by incredible flexibility and strength, she swam with strong, sure stokes.

Spotting a school of blue-tinted bass, Tessa darted through the pack. Offended by the disturbance, the fish scattered in a dozen different directions.

Drifting lazily in their wake, Tessa laughed. She could almost imagine them shaking their fins in anger. She wondered what they might be thinking, seeing a half-human, half–sea creature swimming among them. Contrary to popular belief, mermaids could not communicate with sea life, not even the more intelligent species. Just as people couldn't understand a cat's meow or a dog's bark, she had no earthly clue what the chirps and whistles of a dolphin might mean.

It was a silly part of the legend that annoyed her. Mermaids might be able to live on land *and* sea, but their main components were designed to mesh with those of oxygen breathing Homo sapiens. After all, there were no mer*men*. Mer females still needed human males to impregnate them.

A tremor unexpectedly shook her that had nothing to do with the fish she'd disturbed, but had everything to do with Kenneth Randall. His presence had sparked something inside her, a hunger she'd almost forgotten existed. Though she tried to deny it—had fought against it—the Mer were a highly sensual species. The desire to mate came as naturally as breathing. Having gone without physical relations for several years, a man's touch, however causal, was guaranteed to set her on fire.

It was my choice to live alone, she reluctantly reminded herself. *My choice to stay here and not move to Port Rock*. But in choosing the solitary island over the populated mainland, she'd mostly cut herself off from the outside world.

From all human contact.

Coming to a dead halt, Tessa closed her eyes and allowed herself to sink. She refused to breathe, doing her best to ignore the arousal Kenneth Randall had inadvertently piqued. She was attracted to him. No doubt there. His appeal had definitely set her body to simmering.

Three years had passed since she'd been dumped by Jake Massey. Surely that was long enough to get her emotional equilibrium back. Just because she'd gotten kicked to the curb didn't mean all men were pigs. It just meant she hadn't chosen the right man.

Tessa winced, drawing an involuntary breath. Good grief, she'd really dodged a bullet there. Thank the goddess they hadn't gone through with the mating ceremony. Once a mermaid linked with her human *Breema*, her breed-mate, the ties binding them could never be undone. It would have destroyed her to be married to a man who couldn't keep his dick in his pants.

Jake had broken off their engagement the night before the ceremony. Tessa had spent the evening drinking too much wine and crying. Jake had spent it wrapped in the arms of some stripper he'd met at his bachelor party. As great a guy as Jake had appeared to be, she'd had to learn the hard way he was a self-centered, selfish individual. He thought only about his wants, his needs, and his satisfaction. Jake didn't care who he hurt as long as he got his way.

Having drifted beneath the surface long enough, Tessa reluctantly opened her eyes. Shifting her position, she broke through the surface of the water a few moments later. Lights from the mainland sparkled in the distance.

Ignoring their lure, Tessa flipped over onto her back and just let herself float. She relaxed and drifted with the currents, allowing the water to take her where it wanted. Her mind drifted, too, inevitably turning toward the man who'd invaded her island. Much to her surprise, she wasn't as angry as she'd thought she'd be by his intrusion.

In fact, she welcomed it.

She needed a change, something to shake up the boring rut she'd fallen into. The idea of taking a lover hovered at the far recesses of her mind.

Tessa's internal temperature hitched up a notch. So did the heat in certain parts of her body. Oh, it had been such a long time since she'd allowed herself to revel in a man's touch, enjoy sex for the sake of pure physical gratification. There were some needs that just couldn't be slaked with a battery-operated boyfriend.

Shuddering with need, Tessa ran her hands over her skin, palms lightly tracing the curve of her breasts, then the soft slope of her belly. It was perfectly acceptable for a Mer to have many partners before settling on her breed-mate, the male she would eventually choose to father her children.

She mulled the idea of finding a boyfriend on the mainland. Both Addison and Gwen had tried to set her up on blind dates.

Heart hammering against her rib cage, Tessa caught

her breath. Did she really have the nerve to take a lover?

She definitely ached for physical contact, for a man's hard caresses on her hungry skin. The sexual hunger driving her species was inborn, necessary.

Giving the plan more consideration, Tessa had to admit the idea held a lot of appeal. She could definitely use a no-strings-attached affair. And no law said she had to invest her emotions. She was almost thirty years old, for heaven's sake. No reason to let life entirely pass her by. Laying eyes on a hunk of man like Kenneth Randall reminded her exactly what she'd been missing out on. Had he not been so psychically damaged, she would have put him at the top of her list.

She made a quick decision. *Time to loosen up and have some fun.*

Reanimating her limp body, Tessa reluctantly forced herself to swim back toward the island. She'd drifted at least two miles, maybe more. Putting her tail in motion, she quickly closed the distance. An Olympic swimmer would have been envious of her speed and agility.

She reached the reef a few minutes later. She'd stayed in the water too long. The rising tide lapped at the hem of her abandoned robe. In a few more minutes it would carry the garment out to sea.

Tessa rescued the skimpy piece of clothing. Lose it now and she'd be walking home naked as a jaybird.

Still not tired of wearing her tail, she swam toward a boulder jutting out from a rocky outcropping. She tossed the robe, watching it hit its mark.

With a grace belying her clumsy proportions, she hefted herself up onto the weathered surface. Worn smooth and flat by the erosions of wind and water, the boulder provided the perfect place to stretch out and enjoy the view.

Flipping the tip of her tail in the water, she stared at the lights flickering on the distant mainland. A few years ago both her sisters had abandoned the island for human ways.

Gwen and Addison each maintained opposing views regarding their inborn talents. To Gwen being a Mer was a curse, something that kept her from fully integrating into the human community.

Addison was on the other side of the fence. Working in search and rescue, she'd learned to put her unique talent to good use. She was often called to all parts of the country to help in underwater recovery efforts. Where other divers would fail to bring up the goods, Addison succeeded nine times out of ten.

Turning her face up to feel the night breeze, Tessa heaved a sigh. She'd never felt more alone. Abandoned.

While her sisters had both forged successful ties to the mainland, Tessa was the sole holdout. The island was the last link to the Mer, who'd settled in these waters back when the land was still untamed wilderness. And while she knew her kind came from waters far away, she had no idea where that place might have once been on this earth. Like the legendary Atlantis, the fabled Mer homeland of Ishaldi appeared to have vanished far beneath the ocean's surface, all traces forever obliterated.

Sometimes Ishaldi was a place Tessa didn't think ever really existed. She'd listened with rapt attention to the stories her grandmother recounted, shivering as she imagined the devastating events that had sent the great seaport to a watery grave.

But she'd taken those stories with a grain of salt. Several grains, actually.

If Ishaldi had ever truly existed, its whereabouts remained a mystery. The seven seas, all consuming but ever silent, weren't going to give up their secrets. Not even to the daughters the salty waters had spawned.

A hot burn unexpectedly stung her lids, blurring her vision. Her throat closed, clogging with emotion. Thin tendrils of fog had begun to drift in from the sea. Taking on a shimmering ghostly form, the luminous mist undulated across the water. The mainland vanished, lights winking out of existence as the cloak thickened.

Tessa was all alone.

She shivered. "We're a part of this world," she whispered to the silent water. "But I don't think we've ever belonged."

Kenneth couldn't sleep.

Though he had the fan turned on high and had both windows open to let in the night breeze, the room was sticky and hot. Stripped down to the buff, he lay naked on top of the patchwork quilt. Beads of perspiration dotted his skin. The heat clung like a giant's smothering hand.

He sat up, rubbing his hands across his freshly shaved face. He'd already tried an ice-cold shower, and then another, to cool himself down. He'd even made an ice pack, wrapping cubes from the dorm-sized fridge into a washrag and icing himself down. And he'd already guzzled several of the beers Gwen had generously supplied. Having been off the booze for six months solid, the dark foreign brew she'd picked out had given him quite a buzz.

But the ability to close his eyes and simply drowse off eluded him. It was too hot and muggy.

Lowering his hands, he looked at the digital on the nightstand. The red numbers read 1:20. It didn't help that the fat yellow moon cast its shine through the thin sheaf of curtains covering the window, lighting the narrow room up like a Christmas tree. A pair of blinds would be welcome.

He glanced around. Just as soon as he could manage it, he'd be installing a few things, including an air conditioner. He suspected part of the reason Tessa went through handymen so fast was because the quarters were uncomfortable.

Past providing the basics, there was nothing in the way of entertainment. No television or DVD player. Hell, not even a shelf of books. A man could work only so long. And once the day's chores were accomplished, a little entertainment was usually on a guy's mind. And while Tessa had made it clear he would be free to party on the mainland, no funny business would be allowed on her island.

He'd already decided that would suit him just fine. Right now he wasn't quite ready to get back into the social swing. The main thing he wanted to do was establish himself as a resident, get to know the locals, and familiarize himself with the lay of the land. Once he'd settled in, he figured he might be ready to venture on to the next step on the social ladder.

Finding some female companionship.

As it stood, he had a place to live and a job. Sure, the pay sucked. In fact, there wasn't any. Aside from agreeing to put a roof over his head and feed him, there would be no other compensation. Gwen had offered a small cash stipend, but he'd turned her down.

Truth be told, he didn't need the money.

Stare grimly fixed on the ceiling, Kenneth shivered,

suddenly feeling the chill of Jennifer's murder all the
way to his bones. His muscles bunched with tension.
Right now there was no way he'd ever consider spending the money he'd inherited from her passing. It was
tainted with her blood. He'd even added more to the
balance by selling the house and his half interest of the
garage and salvage yard he owned with a buddy from
high school.

The money was presently sitting, drawing interest.
He kept half in liquid cash. The other half was invested,
a tidy stock portfolio. He lived off the interest, never
touching the principal. The monthly stipend added up to
a very nice chunk of change. If he never wanted to work
another day in his life, he didn't have to.

As far as he was concerned, his present job would
suit him just fine. By the looks of the house and grounds,
the list of repairs was a long one. He had at least six
months of work ahead. Perhaps more. By that time he'd
probably have his head on a little straighter. Maybe he'd
even have a better idea about what he wanted to do with
his life.

He looked around the room again. Despite its auster-
ity, the place had potential. A big-screen television and
a satellite dish would definitely add to its charm. Maybe
he'd even look for an island of his own to buy. He liked
the idea of living in the middle of the ocean, surrounded
on all sides by water. The mainland was close enough to
be accessible without having to suffer the annoyances of
living in a tourist town. No wonder Tessa wouldn't give
the island up.

Tessa . . .

He flopped back onto the bed, spreading out his arms
and legs. Oh, boy. That redheaded spitfire was enough to
raise his temperature all by herself. Remembering the

skimpy attire she'd been wearing when he arrived was enough to send his internal mercury straight into the danger zone.

He licked dry lips. Just thinking about Tessa sent a fluttering sensation straight through his gut, sparking off an even deeper throb below. Certain parts of his lower anatomy were beginning to stir. It had been a long time since he'd considered getting physical with any woman.

Shuddering with need, a soft moan slipped between his lips. Although he knew his body was trying to tell him something, he'd steadfastly ignored the blatant signals. As much as he didn't want to admit it, he needed to get laid. No ifs, ands, or buts about it.

Groaning with frustration, Kenneth rolled off the bed, heading toward the bathroom. Turning on the cold tap, he stepped into the shower. Icy needles dug at his skin. There. That should help cool him down a little.

Drying off, he dug in his duffel for a clean pair of shorts. He'd slept in the buff since college and didn't own any pajamas, not even a pair of sweatpants. Next time he made a trip into town, he'd remedy the deficiencies in his personal wardrobe.

Feeling a twinge at the back of his throat, he reached for his cigarettes on the night table. *No can do*, he thought, recalling Tessa's strict admonition. He'd have to go outside.

Ken briefly considered skipping the smoke and going back to bed. Rethinking the oppressive heat and adding in the fact he was wound up tighter than a dime store yo-yo, he pulled on his clothes. Snagging another beer, he carried his drink and smokes down the winding stairs. The trip down was actually shorter than the trip up to the catwalk.

Plopping himself onto the ground at the base of the

lighthouse, he twisted the cap off the bottle. The malted liquor went down smooth. He enjoyed the alcohol's burn on the back of his throat. Setting the bottle down, he lit up. The day had certainly taken a turn he hadn't expected. All in all, he felt strangely content.

Leaning back, he stared out over the bay. Soft waves rippled gently, illuminated by the light of a full moon.

Taking another drag off his cigarette, he tipped his head back. Lazy tendrils of smoke curled through the air, disappearing into the tangy salt-scented breeze. While the loft might be a sweat box, the night air was cool, refreshing. He had a feeling he would be camping out as long as the weather was good. According to Tessa, Lucky came to the island only once a month. He'd burn to a crisp before he managed to order and install a cooler in his place.

Turning his head, he glanced toward the house. The back of it was dark, the windows staring out over the ocean with dead, blank eyes. Tessa had snapped the lights out promptly at ten o'clock. The swamp cooler hummed like a charm, working perfectly.

Ken had to grin. It had taken about ten minutes to replace the motor. But it had taken another two hours to replace the wiring she'd somehow messed up. She would sleep in comfort while he sweated and simmered.

He briefly wondered what kind of pajamas she slept in. Would she have some sort of lacy baby doll gown? Maybe pink or a really sexy red. Nah. Not her style. Tessa had more tattoos than a Hells Angel biker and wore cutoffs and combat boots. He guessed she'd eschew the frills for something sensible.

Something sensible being nothing at all.

That idea definitely made him smile. It probably wasn't true, but he sure did like thinking about Tessa

naked. He couldn't help it. There was something about
her he found very appealing; something beyond her face
and killer body. Perhaps it was her stubbornness, her in-
sistence on relying on herself even when she knew she
was fighting a losing battle.

After he'd gone back around the corner earlier that
day, he'd paused, something he normally didn't do. Listening in uninvited wasn't a thing he intended to do. It
just happened. If he'd heard correctly, Tessa was down
to counting dimes instead of dollars.

He mused. *I have the money and she has the island.*
If things worked out, maybe he'd approach her about
buying a share. As far as he could guess, the island was
about 640 acres, or roughly a mile in size. A lot of it was
uncultivated, occupied by trees and other wildlife. He
wouldn't mind having a house of his own. Buying a couple of acres might help her out, without invading her
space too much.

Yeah, right. Tessa would probably have a stroke if he
ever actually got up the nerve to ask.

Building castles in the air was easy. It couldn't be a
bad thing. The future had once felt so bleak, empty.

Not anymore.

The black clouds over his head were finally moving
on, letting the sun shine down. He'd survive. Oh, the
guilt would still linger, the sadness over what might have
been. But that chapter of his life was now closed. Time
to write a new one, fill a blank page with new adven-
tures. Somehow he felt Jen would smile, and approve.

The tenseness in his shoulders eased. Cigarette done,
he poked the remnant through the mouth of his empty
beer bottle. Feeling a slight burning sensation behind his
lids, he rubbed his eyes. The need for sleep, real sleep,
was beginning to set in. Eyeing the soft patch of grass,

he yawned. A lazy sense of comfort had settled into his bones. He didn't want to get up.

Kenneth was close to drifting off when the sound of something paddling at the water's edge jarred him back awake. Eyes snapping open, he stared toward the direction he believed the sound had come from. Moonlight glistened, reflecting off the silvery waters of the bay.

Something flapped again, louder and more insistent. He thought he heard a woman's voice, cursing.

Curious as to the cause of the disturbance, he hurried in the direction of the sounds. The western edge of the island faced the mainland, which became less and less clear as a thick fog began to roll in off the sea. Little more than a jagged shoal, the craggy ground was unstable and dangerous. One wrong step could twist an ankle.

He arrived at the edge just in time to see a woman's head and shoulders break through the surface of the water. Her hand lifted. She tossed some dripping piece of clothing up onto a flat rock overhanging the water.

Reaching up to catch the edge, she hefted her body up. Moving with the grace of one accustomed to the life beside the bay, she plopped herself onto the rock. A mass of wet curls streamed down her back. She wore not a single stitch.

Kenneth started to back away. *I'm intruding.* Feet defying his mental command, he didn't move.

Except for Tessa's silent form, the water was deserted. Unaware of his presence, she sat brooding, staring off into the distance.

Kenneth eased a little closer, admiring the view. His gaze dipped, briefly taking in the delicate curves of her body. Eyes reaching the level of her waist, the fine hairs at the nape of his neck rose. It only took seconds to real-

ize something about her appearance wasn't normal. Her
slender limbs had changed shape.

Kenneth stood for a moment in dumb surprise. His
heart skipped a beat even as his breath stalled in his
lungs. Rubbing his bleary eyes in disbelief, he stared,
dumbfounded. Guts twisting, the bottom dropped out
of his stomach.

Impossible!

His gaze darted back and forth over Tessa's elon-
gated form, taking in every inch. From the top of her
head to . . .

He gulped. *The tip of her . . . tail?*

Kenneth felt his knees wobble as reality began to
slip from his grasp. His stomach lurched. Without even
knowing it, he'd stepped through some kind of strange
prism, entering a world where beautiful women had the
torso of an aquatic creature instead of legs.

Looking down at the woman, he felt himself begin
to shake.

"Oh my God. Tessa . . . ?"

Chapter 4

Startled by the voice behind her, Tessa swiveled around. She caught sight of her newly hired handyman standing just above her rocky perch. She was fully exposed, and out in the open.

And she hadn't shifted back to human form.

Her heartbeat doubled, pulse pounding in her ears. Every instinct demanded she scuttle away, dive back into the water and disappear.

She felt sick, but angrily shook off the unbidden emotion. Instead she frowned, resisting the urge to flee, hide herself from human eyes. *I have nothing to be ashamed of*, came her irate thought. He's the one who intruded, interrupted her private moment. She should have known better than to allow a stranger onto her island.

Snatching her soggy robe, Tessa flipped it over her lap before crossing her arms over her naked breasts. At least she had a little cover. She'd never felt so vulnerable. So exposed.

"What are you staring at?" she snapped, lacing her tone with an edge of displeasure.

Kenneth blinked at the question. His face was chalky

white. "I'm sorry," he said, holding his hands out and backing away. "I didn't mean to bother you."

She studied him suspiciously. Had he seen *it*? She couldn't be sure. And this was a conversation she definitely didn't want to have. Damn it all! Why did he have to come snooping around and invade her privacy?

"Well, you are," she grated, wishing he would turn around and make fast tracks. The sooner he got the hell out of there, she sooner she could shift and go home.

Much to her displeasure, Kenneth came to a sudden halt. "I thought I was crazy," he confessed in a rush. "But I wasn't hallucinating. You're her, the thing in the water. It was you all along."

Her brows rose. Had he really just called her a *thing*?

There was a moment of awkward silence.

Tessa's anger unexpectedly faded. Realizing how tired she was of perpetuating the lie, she sighed. No reason to let the poor man think he'd lost his grasp on his sanity. That would be cruel. Besides, what would he do with the knowledge?

Flicking the soggy robe aside, she revealed her long tail in all its glory. "You're right." She wiggled her appendage, splashing the tip in the water. Her scales were bright, glimmering with soft iridescence. A mix of pinks and blues, her tail was also elaborately patterned with symbols etched in black. The pattern extended up her back and arms. Most people mistook the markings for tattoos. She rarely corrected the misperception.

Disbelief slowly drained from Kenneth's face. Another look replaced it. Relief. "Thank God," he breathed on a note of revelation. "I haven't lost my ever-loving mind."

Tessa shrugged. "Guess not." She studied him, wondering if she hadn't unconsciously wanted to be un-masked. He'd told her his secrets. Now he knew hers.

In uneasy awe, he asked, "Can I come a little closer?"

Tessa involuntary stiffened. She wasn't used to having people nearby when she was in Mer form. Still, she had to wonder what he must be feeling. For him, everything about the world had suddenly turned upside down. "If you have to," she grudgingly agreed.

Easing his way onto the flat boulder, Kenneth knelt beside her. He blinked hard. "Man alive, I was sure that beer had gone to my head. I thought I drank too much and passed out." Pulling a hand through his already di-sheveled hair, he briefly glanced up. "I'm half expecting to see a winged horse fly by."

Allowing herself to relax a little, Tessa laughed. The constriction in her chest eased. "No Pegasus here, I'm afraid, though it would be pretty cool to have one." All in all, he seemed to be taking the truth fairly well.

His gaze fixed on her lower half. "Have you been like this all your life?"

She swished her tail. "If you mean was I born a mer-maid, the answer is yes. Of course."

He arched an inquiring brow. His compelling gaze explored every inch of her lower half. "What does it feel like to have a tail?"

Tessa glanced down, eyeing her bottom half. She'd never given it a second thought. It wasn't half as uncom-fortable to wear as it looked. "It's like having your legs strapped together with duct tape."

He laughed. "Really?"

"Really."

Kenneth studied her, intrigued. "Amazing." He started to reach out toward her, but his hand froze in midair. A nervous laugh escaped him. "Sorry. I just wanted to see what it felt like."

Tessa nibbled her lower lip. She usually didn't let anyone close enough to cop a feel. "I guess it would be okay."

Keeping one hand across her bare breasts, she used her other to take his, guiding his fingers toward where her left thigh would usually be. "I'm not a fish. I'm warm-blooded."

Eyeing her with pure admiration, he let his hand linger. "Beautiful," he murmured. "Feels like hot velvet." His fingers brushed across her scales, sending a tremor down her spine.

Tessa shivered. His touch, strangely welcome, felt wonderful. Her breasts felt particularly sensitive behind the shield of her arm. Unbidden heat bubbled up from her core. Her body was slowly awakening from the long slumber of self-imposed celibacy.

She closed her eyes, secretly enjoying the contact. A vision of their bodies coming together flashed through her mind. Her senses went off-kilter, as if she'd downed ten shots of hundred-proof whiskey after days of drinking nothing but water.

"Have a little care there." Her voice sounded strangely husky, more than a little bit needy. "Certain parts of my anatomy are anatomically correct."

Kenneth's brows shot up. "You mean—" He immediately lifted his hand.

Suppressing a groan, Tessa nodded. Arousal rolled through her, sweeping away the last of her self-protective instincts. "Brush those scales aside and everything's still there, right where it's supposed to be."

He nodded thoughtfully. "I suppose that makes sense."

Hesitating, Tessa licked papery lips. Many people would consider the idea of mermaids an abomination, a freak of nature. That wasn't true. Mermaids had the same feelings, the same emotions as any human being. The fact she carried genes that allowed her to adapt to living on land or immersion in water made little difference. Deep inside she was still a woman, and had a woman's feelings. Love. Hate. Desire. She'd experienced them all at one time or another in her life.

Especially desire . . .

"I'm still a female, in every way." Oh goddess above, she wished he'd touch her again. Just one more time.

I want him, her ravenous body clamored. *So very much*.

She could almost taste those full, sensuous lips of his. And his hands. They had the power and the strength of a man used to handling heavy equipment. She wondered what those hands would feel like spread across her waist as he guided her down onto . . .

Oh!

Tessa's skin suddenly felt way too small to fit over her bones. She drew a quick breath, mentally willing her out-of-control libido to stand down. His simple, curious touch shouldn't have hit her so hard. Right now she'd probably mistake a simple handshake for foreplay.

Rocking back on his heels, a rich, deep laugh escaped him. "I would definitely agree." He gave her a glance that swept every inch of her body. "You're a beautiful woman." His tone was humble, awed.

Attempting to cool herself off, Tessa dipped the tip of her tail in the bay. She tossed it into the air, splattering them both with salty water. "Flattery will get you everywhere."

Kenneth swiped his hands across his face, wiping the

droplets away. "I mean every word. With or without the tail, I think you're one hot chick."

Damn, she liked him. Instead of treating her like a freak and running off to call the media, he was talking to her like a real person. One who had a brain, a soul, and could understand plain English. "You're not just saying that?"

He shook his head. "Not at all." Tense with nerves, he dragged his fingers through his hair, spiking it wildly. The sexy, punk style suited him. "Now I know how the guy felt in *Splash.*"

Tessa snorted with amusement. "Good grief. You're comparing what happened to you to something you saw in a movie?"

Grin a mile wide, he nodded. "All I know about mermaids comes from movies, actually. It isn't like you stumble on one every day."

She shook her head. "I think you were sneaking." Pointing to her temple, she pretended to think a moment. "Yes, I'm pretty sure you were creeping up with the intention to spy on me."

Kenneth eyed her. "Honestly, I had no idea you were here. I just heard something in the water."

She rolled her eyes. "I still say you were sneaking."

He held up his hands in mock defeat. "I'll cop a plea and just admit to being curious." A hand moved to his heart. "And I swear to God I haven't tried to sneak up on a woman and get a peek since college."

"Oh?" She looked him up and down. "You don't look like the kind who'd have any trouble getting a private show from a co-ed."

Kenneth chuckled, a rich, warm sound. "Eighteen years ago, I was bone thin, had more acne than skin, and couldn't make time with a freshman to save my life.

Making panty raids on the girl's dorm was as close as I usually got to a living, breathing female."

"Old habits die hard, eh?"

"Yeah, well, those were the days."

"And time marched on."

He rolled his eyes. "In a big way. Never thought middle age would ever come my way."

Tessa swallowed a laugh. "Oh, please. You aren't *that* old."

He had the audacity to grin. "That's probably what I should be saying to you. What are you? Twenty-four, twenty-five . . . ?"

She raised a scolding finger. "Oh, no! A woman never tells her age."

Kenneth's gaze settled on her face, intense and focused.

Stomach clenching with desire, Tessa sucked in a startled breath. Just the idea of him touching her in other, more intimate places made her senses hum with a sexual awareness she couldn't possibly ignore.

She self-consciously ran her fingers through her hair, trying to neaten the damp strands, arrange them into something remotely presentable. Her shoulder-length hair was usually a wild tangle, out of control. Taming the mass of loose curls was almost impossible.

"I'm about to turn thirty," she said to cut through the tension.

A lot of people often mistook her to be much younger than her actual years. A mermaid was capable of surviving for more than a few centuries if she kept her soulstone intact. Humans lived very short lives, a pittance in terms of time. Given their extraordinary genetic structure, a Mer could also deliver a child at an age most humans couldn't even begin to imagine.

Clearly surprised, Kenneth rocked back on his heels. "I'd have never guessed."

Tessa sighed. "There are a lot of things people would never guess about me." She reached for her robe. Her butt was getting more than a little bit numb from sitting on the hard surface. "You've got a lot to learn about Mers."

He cocked his head. "I hope you'll fill me in."

She handed him the robe. "I'll consider it if you promise not to sneak up on me again. You've got a bad habit of putting your nose where it doesn't belong." Since it was too late to drown him and hide the evidence, she supposed she'd have to put up with him. He'd already proved himself valuable by fixing the swamp cooler, and good help that worked cheap was hard to find.

Kenneth accepted the dripping thing, shaking it out and holding it open. "No more sneaking and peeking," he promised.

Tessa fought to keep her expression stern. He spoke as if he visited with Merfolk every day of the week. "Well, no peeking now. I like to shift in private."

"I won't look." A grin split his face. "Unless you ask me to."

Tessa pondered a moment. She found the idea appealing, but decided to pass for the moment. Maybe she'd think about it. *Later.*

"We'll see about that."

He grinned. "Promise?"

"Keep it up and you'll go back into the water," she muttered. "I can guarantee you won't come out a second time."

"Oh. Feisty. I like that."

Tessa shot him a scowl, even though he couldn't see it. "Put a lid on it or you'll be sleeping with the fishes." She smacked her tail on the water to emphasize her point. "Mermaids are known for their bad tempers."

"Sounds like you have issues." His smile widened. "I'll show you mine if you show me yours."

"Shove yours, please. And close your eyes."

He gallantly closed his eyes. "Closed."

"About time."

Tessa reached for the crystal hanging around her neck and concentrated. Her tail began to reshape itself. Within seconds two normal legs replaced it.

She climbed to her feet, slipping into the robe and belting the tie around her waist. "All done."

Kenneth opened his eyes. Looking her up and down, he smiled his approval. "I'm sorry I didn't get to see more."

She gave him a level stare. "It's all anatomy. If you've seen one Mer, you've seen them all." She steadied her footing on the slippery rock. The wind was beginning to kick up, the mist thickening. "I think it's time to go in."

One corner of his mouth kicked up. "I suppose that's my cue to buzz off." He clearly didn't want to go.

Half distrust, half pleasure filled her. He was doing a damn good job of worming his way into the rest of her night.

Unwilling to make things too easy for him, she snorted. "Buzz away."

He cocked his head at her. "Oh, great. Send me off while I'm way too wound up to sleep." He threw her a flashing grin.

Tessa's heart tripped at the sexy arch of his full, sensual mouth. He really knew how to put that pirate's smile to good use. Something in his lost-boy appeal sent a rush of adrenaline through her veins.

Whether or not she wanted to admit it, Tessa genuinely liked the man. He had a good sense of humor and seemed to be a hard worker. Having him around might not be as bad as she'd imagined. He appeared able to handle the fact she wasn't entirely human.

Sick of holding everyone at arm's length, Tessa gave in. She was tired of hating herself for being different, of yearning uselessly to be human. Most of all she was tired of being alone.

She drew a deep breath. "Then you might as well come inside. I think I could use a drink." A shaky laugh escaped. "It's not every day I get to show off my tail."

Kenneth grinned. "It's a nice tail." And he'd like to see more of her.

With or without it on.

As for that drink, he could use one, too. He was wide-awake and too damn wired to even consider sleeping now. Sleep wouldn't be coming anytime soon. He'd probably regret staying up so late, but dragging himself away from Tessa's company was impossible. He could snooze anytime.

Heart thudding in his chest, Kenneth followed her lead. Obscured by the thick mist settling across the land, the moonlight no longer cast its light on the earth below. The night had deepened, darkened. The island felt deserted, wrapped in a cottony soft cocoon.

Tessa moved like a gazelle, sure-footed and graceful as they negotiated the craggy shore. He stumbled like a clod with two left feet, silently cursing the effects of too many beers.

A moment later a door opened and the night disappeared, shut outside.

Tessa flashed an apologetic smile. "Hang on a minute.

I want to put on something dry." Disappearing down a short hallway, she left him standing in a warm, cozy living room.

Kenneth looked around, taking in the simple decor. The house offered a reflection of its inhabitants, right down to the heavy wooden furniture one expected to see in an old New England oceanfront, complete with faded wallpaper and a multitude of family photographs stretching back through a couple of generations. Though immaculately clean, it was an old house. The place was obviously lived in, and comfortable to its inhabitants.

Tessa reappeared. "That's better." She'd thrown on a sweat suit, obscuring the curves that had been so obvious earlier. Her long hair was twirled up, secured with a clip. A few damp strands refused to be tamed, straggling around her face and neck in a most alluring way. Untouched by makeup, her skin was flawless, and deeply tanned.

After seeing her mostly naked, Kenneth hadn't thought she could get any better. He was wrong. Even bundled in baggy sweatpants and a baggier sweatshirt, with her hair soaking wet, she looked sexy as hell.

He cleared his throat, turning away before a certain part of his anatomy revealed his thoughts. "You look great." It had been a long time since he'd considered getting physical with any woman.

Kenneth mentally put the brakes on. They'd known each other barely a single day. True, he'd thought about her, dreamed about her, for months. But at that point in time she was little more than a vague impression in his mind, a faceless phantom siren. Now that he knew her to be real and not a figment of his imagination, the fantasy was no longer acceptable.

He wanted the real woman.

But does she want me? His internal question nagged.

There was only one answer: Wait and find out.

Kenneth darted a glance around. "So you live here all by yourself?" He wanted to know everything about her. At least a hundred questions rolled through his mind, but he revisited the urge to pelt her with one right after the other.

Even though she had accepted his intrusion with good grace, he could tell by the aloofness in her manner that she wasn't entirely comfortable. It would take time for her to trust him. And until she did, he'd have to be patient. Answers would come. Later.

First he wanted her to be comfortable. He wanted her to trust him. It came without saying that he would have to earn it.

The barest hint of sadness touched Tessa's lips. A trace of shadows lingered behind her vibrant gaze. Loneliness . . . or something else? Whatever it was, it vanished as soon as it had arrived. "Just me and the lighthouse, and Jasper," she said honestly. "And now you."

"Your sister doesn't live here?"

"Sisters," she corrected. "Gwen and Addison moved over to Port Rock a few years ago. They prefer the human way of life."

Though she appeared calm, a vibe of uneasiness hovered around her. Given the circumstances behind his discovery, it was entirely understandable she would feel ill at ease.

"Must get lonely, being left behind."

A frown crossed her face. "Sometimes." A visible shiver coursed through her. "I think I need that drink to take the chill off. Join me?"

He nodded. "Sure." He didn't really need any more booze, but a gentleman didn't let a lady drink all by herself.

Tessa indicated the sofa with a nod of her head. "Sit. I'll pour."

Kenneth took a seat. A hand-crocheted throw was tossed over the back of a well-worn sofa. Though it sagged a little in the middle, its thick cushions were comfortable. A twenty-gallon tank sat behind it, teeming with a multitude of colorful fish. He settled back, watching the fish swim in their tranquil environment.

He jerked a thumb toward the tank. "So these would be your cousins, right?"

Tessa put her hands on her hips. She had the grace to grin, flashing perfectly white teeth. "Cute." Her green eyes shimmered with good humor. "You're a real funny guy."

Kenneth held her gaze and winked. "Humor's a good defense. If you don't laugh, you'll cry. And you look like a lady who needs a little laughter in her life."

Lips the shade of fresh strawberries settled into a sexy smirk. "You think so?"

He spread his hands. "Definitely." Right then and there he vowed to taste her lips before morning arrived. At the moment, the notion didn't seem far-fetched at all.

Tessa raised a mock fist. "Sit down before I knock you on your ass, please."

Kenneth did a mental comparison. Tall and willowy, Tessa wasn't a shrinking violet. She stood at least five-ten, fairly tall for a woman. That pretty package probably carried a lot of dynamite.

Still, he couldn't resist challenging her. He arched an eyebrow and shot back, "You really think you could?"

Tessa's brows arched higher. She stepped right up to the plate and swung hard. "I'm a lot stronger than I look." She pointedly eyed him from head to foot.

"And don't forget who dragged your sorry ass out of the bay."

She'd hit a home run. The proverbial ball sailed right over his head. He flinched. "You've got a point."

She stuck out her tongue and pulled a face. "And they stick out all over my body, I know. Nobody's ever accused me of being a nice bitch."

Well, at least she knew herself. Most people didn't.

Kenneth held his hands up, signaling a time-out. "Maybe we could skip the bitch part and try for pleasant."

She shook her head. "Pleasant is the polite way of saying I'll tolerate you for now. If you want me to be civil, I need a drink."

"If it will help your mood, by all means, proceed."

Tessa rolled her eyes. "About time." She walked over to a small wet bar tucked in one corner.

Kenneth watched her walk, enjoying the sight. Tessa cracked open a bottle. Splashing a generous amount into two glasses, she delivered one to him. "Best service on the island."

He accepted the drink. "And delivered by the prettiest girl."

Tessa settled down across from him. The distinct aroma of sea water and warm female skin tickled his nostrils. He inhaled, enjoying her unique scent. "You may imbibe liberally and be merry."

He eyed the amber liquid. It smelled vaguely like apricot brandy. Not his favorite, but he'd grin and drink it and pretend to enjoy it. Now that he'd gotten inside the house, he wanted to stay. The fact that she had a working swamp cooler had nothing to do with it, either. "Can't say I really need this."

She raised her glass in a brief toast. "Be merry tonight, hungover tomorrow. We'll both probably be dragging ass for staying up so late." She downed hers. "Good thing I'm sleeping in."

A woman who took her booze straight and neat. Impressive. "Am I going to have that luxury?"

She considered. "Entertain me well and you might."

Tipping the glass, he swallowed his shot in a single gulp. It added to the warm glow in his belly. "I'll sing and dance, and offer a little romance." The words sounded insipid coming out of his mouth, but he didn't care. Right now he was having a good time. It seemed like forever and a day had passed since he'd enjoyed a woman's company and just laughed.

Tessa eyed him over the rim of her glass. "Don't make promises you can't keep."

Kenneth willingly swallowed the bait. He felt positively giddy. "So if I'm good, maybe you'll show me your tail again?"

Tessa released a tremulous breath. Uncertainty hovered beneath her calm facade. The subject loomed between them like an invisible wall. "It's been a long time since I showed my tail to a strange man."

Remembering how uniquely beautiful she'd looked sitting on the rock, tension knotted his stomach. Moonlight had lit the incoming mist, lending a magical touch to the scene of the mermaid staring out over the water.

Kenneth wished he'd had a camera to capture the fleeting moment. As it stood, he doubted he'd ever be able to forget his first glimpse of Tessa in her true form. "If it helps, yours is the first tail I've ever laid eyes on," he said, trying to keep the conversation light, nonthreatening. "And now that you know me, why are you calling me strange?"

She visibly relaxed. "What would you like me to call you?" she quipped back. "A cab?"

Ken laid a hand over his heart and put on a Groucho Marx leer. "How about calling me your boyfriend?"

Eyes widening with surprise, Tessa delicately coughed into her hand. She looked at him as if deciding whether or not to take the bait. All she had to say was no, and it was game over.

Her tongue darted out, moistening her tempting lips. "Is that something you'd want?"

He leaned closer. Oh, yeah. He definitely did. "Is it something you'd consider?" Though he fully expected to be turned down, it was fun to ask. It was part of what made chasing the fairer sex interesting.

Tessa hesitated. She looked both startled and pleased. "Maybe." Her answer intrigued.

Kenneth went one step further. The ground could crumble beneath his feet at any moment, but he didn't care. Even if she shot him down, he had to ask. "So how do I turn maybe into yes?"

She gave a bemused smile. "You could try asking."

The desire to be funny vanished. He leaned forward, reaching out to trace her cheek with the tips of his fingers. "So if I asked for a kiss, do you think I'd get one?" He wasn't sure if he was teasing or not. If she allowed it, he'd definitely follow through.

Tessa tipped her head to one side. "You've already had a kiss."

Kenneth gulped back a moan. Keeping his thoughts on track wasn't easy. Right now he'd love to nuzzle the gentle curve between her neck and shoulder. "Oh, I think I'd remember kissing you."

One corner of her fine mouth edged up. "Guess you don't remember all that mouth-to-mouth."

Ken's pulse spiked. He'd always had the notion they'd already had some kind of physical connection. "Is that all it was? Simple mouth-to-mouth?"

Tessa's gaze never wavered. Eyes he could drown in glittered mysteriously. "There was a teeny bit of Mer magic involved." She lifted her hand, measuring off about a half inch between her thumb and forefinger.

Given the fact she could shift her shape, he wasn't surprised. Banter evaporated, replaced with something a little more serious. Things were beginning to get a little bit more complicated and tangled than he'd initially imagined.

"Magic?" A burning sensation settled in the pit of his stomach. "As in some kind of enchantment?"

The light faded from her gaze. "Of a sort," she answered vaguely, her expression shuttered.

Her answer was a blow against his breastbone. It vaguely occurred to him that his perception of Tessa might be—manipulated. What if his intense attraction wasn't real, but something she'd conjured? Could he even trust his mind, his own feelings, anymore?

He wasn't sure.

Frowning deeply, Kenneth cleared his throat. "Are you saying that you put some kind of a spell on me?"

Chapter 5

Pulse missing a beat, Tessa's breath caught. She was in trouble. The shit was definitely hip deep and rising by the second.

By the look on his face, Kenneth Randall wasn't a happy man. The last thing humans wanted to hear was their emotions had been manipulated by an inhuman force.

Her brain raced as she attempted to put the pieces together in a way a human would understand. She'd known when Kenneth brought up that day he was opening a door best left closed.

Closed, and locked tight.

Lying would do no good. She might as well tell the truth. After that, she'd deal with the consequences. She silently chastised herself. *Messing around with Mercraft always comes back and bites you on the ass.*

Tessa hastened to explain, make an attempt to soothe his ruffled feathers. "I didn't mean to do it. The magic of a Mer's kiss is supposed to break once you come out of the water."

He looked at her strangely, as if measuring her every

word for truth. "A mermaid's kiss?" he asked. "I don't understand. Why would you kiss me?"

Tessa shook her head. "When you were under the water, you were almost dead. I gave you back your breath, helped you to breathe under the water. Most people never remember a Mer's kiss. I'm not sure, but I think the connection between us wasn't broken." She winced the moment the words came out of her mouth. That sounded lame. Really lame.

Setting his glass down, Kenneth scrubbed his face with his hands. Confusion sped across his visage, darkening his features. "Excuse me for making a total ass out of myself." He let his hands drop limply in his lap. "Man, I feel like a fool."

It was Tessa's turn to frown. "Why?"

A weak laugh escaped him. "This is going to sound really strange, but I've dreamed about the woman in the water. The feel of her lips pressed against mine, her body . . ." Catching himself, he clenched his fists in frustration. "You say I'm not supposed to remember that, but I do. Not clearly, but it's there. It's been there for months, haunting me every damn day. Now that I know the truth, I don't know if what I'm feeling for you is real or something conjured up."

Tessa's stomach squeezed. Frustration coiled and burned in her gut like barbed wire. "I'm sorry. I didn't mean to leave you feeling invaded by my presence."

I shouldn't have tried to mess with things I don't understand, she thought, laying a mental whip across her back. There was no telling what kind of damage she might have inflicted on the human's mind. What if more memories surfaced, images he might find even more confusing or frightening?

He shook his head. "It's not your fault I twisted survival with desire." Giving a quick, rueful smile, he made a helpless gesture in the air. "I've been lusting after you like a hormonal teenager, and you were only trying to save my life." Laced with intense disappointment, his words sounded forlorn.

Nodding tightly, Tessa swallowed over the lump forming in her throat. An uncomfortable feeling rose in the pit of her stomach. She knew he'd believed his attraction for her to be genuine.

Now he wasn't so sure.

She hastened to take the blame. "It was entirely my blunder. I've never spent that long in the water with anyone."

He looked at her hard. "How long was I under?"

Tessa searched her memory. The details weren't hard to locate. As much as she'd tried to put them away, they'd lingered. She couldn't stop her thoughts from sneaking back to the disastrous event.

"At least a couple of hours, maybe more. The storm was out of control by the time I reached you. I couldn't get you to shore so I took you down, deeper."

His brows rose in surprise. "Deeper?"

Tessa squeezed her eyes shut a moment. Maritime lore painted mermaids as malevolent creatures. After luring sailors to destroy their ships on the rocks, they were known to take survivors and drown them. Such stories didn't exactly inspire confidence in her species. Mers were said to be destructive and mean, their dislike of humans legendary.

"Not far," she said, hoping to reassure him. "The island is riddled with underwater caves. I pulled you into one. You were perfectly safe."

Kenneth studied her closely as she spoke. His gaze

never wavered, recording every twitch she made. "Am I still under this hex?"

Tessa nibbled her bottom lip. "It wasn't a hex, and I don't know. I've only had a crash course in Mercraft." The words came out in a rush, almost apologetic.

Kenneth applied his hand to his forehead. "Oh terrific. A mermaid with a learner's permit."

At least he hadn't lost his sense of humor.

Tessa picked up her glass, belatedly realizing it was empty. Damn. She could use another drink right now. A double. And a lot of them. "I haven't had a lot of practice." She'd only recently learned to add simple verbal commands to the energies she generated, and was still a little unsure of the shape and form they might manifest into.

Hand dropping, a worried expression crossed his face. "You're not going to experiment on me again, are you?"

She cleared her throat. "It wasn't an experiment," she insisted. "If I had done it right, you wouldn't have remembered a thing."

Kenneth unexpectedly laid a hand on her arm. A prickling sensation ran up her spine, as if his touch carried an electric charge. His compelling gaze settled on her face, intense and focused, a visual caress he clearly hesitated to make physical.

"I'm glad I did," he said softly. "I wouldn't ever want to forget you, Tessa."

Whoa!

Tessa immediately hit reverse, backing up. "You're kidding, right??"

Kenneth leaned toward her, his face intent. "I probably shouldn't say this, but one of the reasons I wanted to live was because of what happened in the water."

Blinking hard, Tessa swallowed over the lump forming in her throat. She knew she was staring at him, but she couldn't seem to tear her gaze off his face. The air between them was shifting, thickening.

She gave him a half-nervous smile. "Seriously?" Keenly aware of the heat suffusing her body, she sounded too breathless for her own comfort.

He reached out, caressing her face with the tips of his fingers. "All this time I believed I'd been touched by something extraordinary, some out-of-this-world being that chose to let me live when I rightly should have died. You restored my life, and for that I'm grateful."

Tessa squeezed her eyes shut a moment, enjoying the feel of his fingers against her needy skin. Clenched muscles trembled. Oh, she wanted him. To pull her close, touch her all over. To fill the emptiness inside.

"I didn't make that choice," she murmured. "You did."

Kenneth cupped his palm around her cheek. His skin barely made contact with hers, as though he held something so fragile he was afraid the merest touch would shatter it. "I kept telling myself the woman in the water couldn't be real . . ."

Tessa's internal temperature hitched up another notch. So did the heat in certain parts of her body. Inside, her emotions were threatening to unravel. The emotions of loneliness churning through her were suddenly quelled. This man had sought her out. She didn't know how or why he had come back into her life at this particular moment. She didn't care.

"Yet here I am."

Closing the narrow distance separating them, Kenneth's mouth brushed hers, deliberately light and excruciatingly slow. "Right in front of me, a dream come true," he whispered against her lips. His voice was sweetly humble.

Before she could think of a reply, he deepened the kiss. His lips were firm, his mouth eager with passion and a longing she'd never felt from a man before.

Heart pounding fast and furious, a ribbon of pure need knotted inside Tessa's core. The shock of his mouth on hers rocked her hard. "Oh, my." The rest of her sentence became little more than a garbled moan.

The voice of reason called out for her to pull away, put some distance between them before something happened. But the hunger for his touch was much more powerful. Every nerve in her body zinged with tension even as a thousand emotions and words tangled inside her mind.

His gaze locked with hers. "I can't tell you how many times I've made love to you in my mind."

Tessa gasped. She would have swallowed but her mouth was dry. "It's all happening so fast . . ." A shudder ripped through her as she realized the implications. And the complications.

Sensing her hesitation, Kenneth pulled away. The warmth building between them immediately vanished. "I'm sorry."

Tessa blinked. The air in her chest locked painfully. Head still spinning, she tried to corral her hormones. Though her body was willing, it was probably best to slow down and think before things went too far. Kenneth Randall wasn't exactly the poster boy for emotional stability. For once, someone else's baggage was heavier than her own.

"It's okay," she murmured, drawing a breath to still the unfulfilled energy pounding through her veins.

He ran nervous fingers through his hair, further mussing the short style into an even spikier mess. "I didn't mean to put the make on you like that."

She laid a hand on his arm. "Things happen. It's easy to get carried away."

Kenneth's entire body trembled in reaction. "I'm just being a fool."

"You didn't do anything wrong," she countered softly. "We're both adults and at the moment it felt right, that's all."

The slightest hint of a smile tugged at his lips. "I haven't been with a woman since my wife died." He hesitated and then blurted, "I haven't wanted anyone else. Until I met you."

Silence followed. Silence in which no sound came but the soft hum of the swamp cooler.

Tessa considered her options. Even though she'd been displeased at his arrival on her island, the intervening hours had delivered a revelation. She liked the man. After learning the reasons why he'd gone into the water, he had begun to matter. She no longer viewed him as an intrusive human. He was simply a lonely man, trying to rebuild his life. And if she were to delve a little deeper, she'd have to admit she was attracted to him.

The conclusion, of course, was inevitable. But if they were going to do this, she wanted to be completely honest. "I understand the need to be with someone," she said slowly, measuring every word carefully. "And I'm open to having company of the adult kind."

Kenneth nodded. "I see."

She took another mental step, testing the ground beneath her feet. "But I'm not looking for complications."

His dark eyes met hers. "Meaning?"

She cleared her throat. "If we were to consider getting together, I'd like to keep things casual."

A spark glinted in the depths of his eyes. He was beginning to catch on. "How casual?"

Heat scorched her cheeks. "Let's say we just satisfy each other, relieve a little tension. You know, we could share a bed for fun."

He cocked a knowing eyebrow. "And when it's over we each go our own way?"

She nodded. "Right. No complications."

His gaze cooled. "That's not what I'm looking for."

"You'd miss the chance to sleep with your fantasy?" she asked defensively.

Kenneth pinned her under a get-real look. "I don't want to fuck the fantasy." His hand slipped under her chin, tipping back her head. "I want to make love to the living, breathing woman I'm looking at now. And when I'm done I want to hold her in my arms until she falls asleep."

She swallowed thickly. By the look on his face, the man was absolutely serious. Wow. She'd simply assumed he wouldn't be ready to tie himself down with another woman.

"No shit?"

His hand dropped. "No shit," he repeated. "Just having sex with you wouldn't begin to satisfy me. I'm looking for something solid, something real. So if you just want a fuck buddy, I'm not the guy."

Tessa studied his face. "You're really serious."

Kenneth nodded. "Dead serious. Life is too short to play games. I've been given a second chance and I'm not willing to blow it this time around. It's all or nothing."

A tremor of yearning shimmied down her spine. "And if I said I don't want to get involved with a human?"

His face was tight. "Then I would say good night."

The thought made her heart squeeze. "And if I take a chance?"

Conflict warring on his face, he cleared his throat. "I don't know what tomorrow will bring, but I'm willing to find out."

Tessa considered. It would be easy to bare her body to this man. But her soul? She couldn't give him that kind of power over her. When she'd considered taking a new lover, she'd imagined an affair with no strings attached.

Kenneth Randall was making it clear: He wanted strings.

A slew of thoughts crept up from the shadowy corners of her mind. She was tempted to take him on, but she didn't want to get tangled up in another knotty relationship. Problems invariably arose whenever she dared to let a man into her world. Somehow a Mer woman was too much for a human male to handle.

Just three years ago, she'd come close to marrying the man she'd chosen to be her breed-mate. She'd been ready to be in a committed relationship, even though it meant giving up the longevity of the Mer. She couldn't make the shift toward fertility until she synchronized her body's internal clock with that of her mate. After that, she would begin to age normally, like a human.

Jake Massey had backed out at the last minute, leaving her high and dry.

And while she wasn't ready to say yes to a new engagement and set the date, she had to admit she wanted a partner. Unless she took the first step and let a new man into her life, she was doomed to spend a lot more nights alone.

She had to make a decision. Either she wanted Kenneth, or she didn't. One way or another he deserved an answer.

Tessa gestured toward her body. "Do you honestly think you could handle all this enchantment?"

"You, I can handle." He drew a deep breath. "Just take it easy with the Mer-magic, okay?"

She nodded solemnly. "I promise not to lay any more whammies on you."

He raised an eyebrow. "Whammies?" He shook his head. "I'm still trying to wrap my head around the whole sea-witch thing."

"I can't stop being a Mer," she admitted honestly. "What you see is what you get."

Reaching out, Kenneth twirled a strand of copper-shaded hair around his finger, tugging lightly. "What I see is what I want. Nothing less will satisfy me, tonight or any other night. Just tell me what you want me to do. Stay or walk out." His gaze darkened subtly. "But I'm warning you now. Throw me out and I'll be right back on your doorstep tomorrow. I'm serious."

Tessa lifted her eyes, staring into his handsome face. Her heart beat rapidly inside her chest. "You think it's that easy? That I should trust and believe a complete stranger?"

A grin tugged at his lips, making her want to lay claim to his sexy mouth. "Give me tonight and I won't be a stranger anymore."

Before she could answer, Kenneth brushed a kiss over her lips. He meant to take it slow, but the fire between them flared fast.

Fantastic, he thought. *Absolute heaven.*

Tongue plumbing her mouth, he worked a hand under her sweatshirt. She wasn't wearing a bra and her nipple pushed taut against his palm. Finding the sensitive tip, he rolled it between thumb and forefinger.

Her response was instant. And encouraging. "That feels so good," she murmured against his lips.

"It's about to feel better." Reaching for the bottom of her shirt, he eased it up to bare her breasts. Lowering his head, he captured one pink tip between his teeth. At the same time, he slipped a hand into the waistband of her sweatpants. Her knees separated, allowing him full access. His fingers continued their exploration.

Tessa released a sound somewhere between a moan and a whimper. The contentment behind that tiny noise hinted he was definitely headed in the right direction. Stroking her softness, he slid a finger into her moist depth. Her heat simmered under his touch.

Driven by pure impulse, she automatically lifted her hips, pressing against his hand. A purr rumbled deep in her throat. "Oh, goddess," she breathed. "Don't stop . . ."

He took her breasts more deeply into his mouth, tonguing her sensitive nipples as his fingers delved below.

Tangling her fingers in his thick hair, Tessa held him close. Breath coming fast and hard, her entire body began to tremble, slowly engulfing her in heated convulsions. She climaxed with a loud moan. After a few minutes she went limp, seemingly stunned in the aftermath.

Kenneth slowly pulled away. Gaze locked on her face, he brushed away a few curls clinging to her damp forehead. A fine sheen of perspiration slicked her tanned skin. "Good?"

Opening her eyes, Tessa slowly dragged her tongue

over her lips. "Fantastic." Heat crept into her face, red-dening her cheeks. "But I didn't mean to come that fast."

He grinned at her. "It's not like it's the only one you'll have tonight."

She looked at him through sparkling green eyes. "Don't go making promises you can't keep." Her voice had changed, sounding deeper, huskier than before.

Tugging her sweatshirt over her head, Kenneth tossed it aside. "Oh, it's a promise I intend to keep." Her sweat-pants followed.

His gaze swept her naked body, appreciating every inch. He wanted to savor the moment, commit every inch of her to memory. "You're so beautiful."

Tessa was definitely all woman: peach-firm breasts, long torso, and even longer legs. Her eyes were electric, sparking with the mysterious, primitive power only fe-males possessed.

A faint blush heated her cheeks. "This isn't fair."

He lifted an eyebrow. "Why?"

A bandit's grin lit up her face. Her rose-shaded nip-ples jutted. "I'm naked."

Kenneth grinned back, savoring the sight. He cupped a breast, thumb brushing the erect nipple. The hard little peak puckered, then blossomed. Her skin was warm, bronzed perfection. "I noticed."

She laughed and tugged at his clothes. "And you have way too much on."

He lifted a wicked brow. "What should I do about that?"

"Take it off," she said coyly. "Take it all off."

Kenneth groaned in frustration. "I think I can handle that request just fine." Beyond refusing her anything she wanted, he stood and slipped his shirt over his head. If she would have asked for the keys to his vehicle and every credit card he had in his wallet, he would have handed them over without question.

He'd give anything to make her happy. And keep her in his bed.

Tessa's hungry gaze eagerly roamed his hard physique. She followed the line of his abdomen down to the top of the jeans hugging his slender waist.

She reached out, eager to take him.

Kenneth shook his head. "Not just yet." He wanted to make love to her slowly, give her the gift of delicious pleasure without the pressure to reciprocate.

Moving the coffee table aside, he dropped to his knees. Light from the nearby lamp reflected the fine sheen of perspiration on her tanned skin.

Kenneth's hand brushed her face. "I've wanted to do this all damn day." He leaned forward and nibbled at the soft flesh under her jaw, just below her ear.

Tessa let her head fall back. Lashes a mile long fanned across her cheeks. "Then do." She moaned softly, encouraging him to continue his enticing torment. "I feel that all the way inside." Her arms circled his neck. Their mouths came together again with ravenous intensity. She tasted like sweet, tangy apricots—a delicious, mind-drugging nectar.

He drank deep and long, savoring every drop.

After a long time he broke away, separating their bodies.

"Lay back," he murmured. "And enjoy."

Kenneth licked his way down her abdomen, his tongue tracing one of the thick black lines marking her skin. They wound round her body from shoulders to ankle, forming an elaborate pattern. "These are so damn sexy."

He kissed his way down her abdomen. Unlike some women who were all skin and bone, Tessa had a sexy, full belly. Then he moved lower. His hand parted her thighs.

But before he went farther, he stood up, leaving Tessa with a pleading look on her face. Claiming one of their empty glasses, he walked to the bar and filled the glass with two fingers' worth of apricot brandy. Coming back to his place, he tipped the glass over, letting a bit of the fragrant alcohol trickle into her belly button.

Tessa squealed, then dissolved into a fit of giggles. "Oh, I don't believe you're doing this."

Kenneth dipped his tongue into her navel. "Tastes like the nectar of the gods." He dripped more of the sweet brandy onto her skin, then lapped it up. "I could get used to a diet like this."

Eyes smoldering with heat, Tessa rolled her hips. "Feast away."

Feast, he did.

She gave a primitive cry when he parted her legs again. Adding a splash of brandy, his tongue immediately followed.

Tessa released a strangled cry. "Oh, heavens!" she gasped. "That's so wonderful." Her moans and deep sighs mingled with the soft hum emanating from the swamp cooler.

Kenneth's hand replaced his mouth. In moments, Tessa voiced a lusty moan of pleasure. Limp in the aftermath of rapture, it took her a few moments to catch her breath. But it wasn't long before Tessa's fingers plucked at the top button of his jeans. "I want more."

He pulled back, trying to ignore the bulge in his pants straining for freedom beneath the tight denim. "Damn." Stomach twisting with disappointment, he swallowed hard. "I haven't got a condom." As much as he wanted her, there was no reason to take risky chances.

A soft voice cut through his frustration. "It's okay. Mers don't carry disease, and we can't catch anything from humans."

Kenneth's jaw tightened. Holding himself back was a misery within itself. "What about . . . ?"

He held his breath, waiting for her answer. Backing off now wasn't going to be easy, but he'd find some other way to relieve his fierce need if he had to. Neither one of them needed an unexpected complication.

Tessa's fingers worked into the top of his jeans, tugging his hips toward hers. She tilted her chin up. Her touch was intimate, her gaze even more so. "A Mer can't get pregnant unless she's breed-mated."

He caressed her cheek. The bulge in his pants swelled, pulsing even harder. The pressure had gone from uncomfortable to out-and-out unbearable. "I don't know what that is, but it sounds serious."

Tessa deftly undid the single button. "It means we choose only a single male to sire our offspring." His zipper crunched down, delivering welcome freedom. "But until that time comes, I can't conceive."

Kenneth drew a sharp breath as she pushed his jeans down. The sheer intensity of waiting was beginning to shred him to pieces. His hands slid into her long hair, sending a mass of curls tumbling down around her neck and shoulders. Tilting back her head, he sought her mouth. Their lips came together in a hungry crush.

Somehow their bodies came together, all the separate parts meshing with perfect synchronicity. Tessa curled her legs around his waist. "I want you inside me." It was all he needed to hear.

Kenneth's self-control snapped. He plunged deep, savoring the silken glide into her depth. Bracing his hands against the cushions, he began to thrust. Blood pounded in his temples, spurring him on. Pleasure built with every excruciating second. Waves of liquid heat shimmered through his veins. A long groan of surrender broke from his throat. His hips moved with a rhythm all their own.

All gentleness was lost between them as Tessa welcomed thrust after thrust. Gripping his shoulders, she dug her nails deep into his skin. Their bodies weren't just joined.

They were one.

Chapter 6

Sunlight was flooding the room when Kenneth forced himself to wake up. His muscles ached, and the temptation to succumb to two or three additional hours of sleep was difficult to resist. Punching his pillow, he rolled over on his side and snuggled deeper under the blanket. He immediately felt a naked female body pressing against the length of his.

As visions of the previous night unspooled across his mind's eye, Kenneth opened his eyes. The first thing he saw was a luxurious length of red hair covering the pillow next to his. Tessa lay beside him, sleeping peacefully.

He shook his head in disbelief. *I can't believe I'm really with her.*

Kenneth eased himself up on an elbow. Aftershocks still rippled through his system. Muscles he hadn't used in a long time ached, reminding him just how long it had been since he'd spent the night with a woman. He doubted he'd ever walk normally again.

A grin split his lips. He had to admit he liked those feelings. A lot. It felt good waking up next to another warm body. He'd like to do it more often. Every day, if he could arrange it.

At first he'd been afraid of making a move on her, afraid he'd make a fool of himself with a woman he'd known barely a day. But when she'd accepted his kiss and gave him the chance to keep going, he'd grabbed on with both hands.

Everything since last night had felt like a dream.

After making love to her in the living room, he'd been so damn wasted he barely remembered making the move to her bedroom. His head had barely touched the pillow before he'd fallen asleep, vaguely aware of Tessa curling into him for warmth. Good sex had put him out like a candle in a hurricane-force wind.

Last night there hadn't been time for regrets or second thoughts. He had plenty of opportunity now. Much to his surprise, he couldn't find a single reason why they shouldn't have made love last night. They'd both needed someone, and they'd both satisfied each other. Completely.

On every level, lying beside Tessa felt right.

He didn't know why. It just did.

Kenneth glanced around Tessa's bedroom. You could tell a lot about a woman by the way she kept her private space. Seaside blues and sandy creams dominated the color scheme. The furniture was basic with a slight French flair and many of the pieces had a worn yet comfortable look. Though a little battered by years of use, everything was neatly arranged, clean, the seascapes hanging on the walls painted with a lively hand. Beneath the combat boots and cutoffs beat the heart of a woman grounded in the traditional style of the place she grew up.

As for lace and other frills, there wasn't a single one to be found. What you saw was what you got.

Kenneth had to admit there was something sexy about a naked woman wrapped in a patchwork quilt and plain cotton sheets scented with a barest hint of sandalwood and spicy cinnamon.

He reached out, caressing her cheek. A pair of vibrant green eyes blinked, and then looked into his.

Kenneth smiled. "Morning." He leaned over and tried to brush a warm kiss over her cheek.

Neatly avoiding contact, Tessa rolled over onto her back. Throwing her arms wide, she stretched and sat up. The bedding slipped down, revealing her nudity.

Making a quick attempt to cover herself, she regarded him through half-lidded eyes. "Hi." The expression flitting across her face said everything.

She hadn't expected to wake up to company.

Ah, damn. The morning after was always awkward. As comfortable as he felt, he had to consider that Tessa might be having postsex regrets. He had to wonder how she felt, having a naked man sprawled in her bed. "You okay?"

Tessa bit down on her lower lip. "Yeah, I think so." Her voice was husky, like gravel rolling over silk. She hesitated a moment. "You?"

Kenneth pressed his fingers to his temple. A slight thud be-bopped behind his eyes, accompanied by the achy feeling one usually felt the morning after imbibing too much booze on an empty stomach. He hadn't eaten a bite since yesterday's breakfast, and that meal was long gone. Too keyed up and nervous about coming to the island, he'd missed lunch. Dinner, too, had gotten a pass in favor of those tempting beers.

"I'm a little beat, but I'll survive." He mentally pictured a nice, hearty breakfast, one that included heaps of bacon and lots of buttered toast.

Dragging her fingers through her tangled hair, Tessa yawned again. "Oh, me, too." She plopped back onto the mattress. Rolling onto her side, she pulled the covers up to her chin before drawing her knees up to her chest. "I'm definitely sleeping in." She scrunched her eyes shut. Her body language was stiff, and the message was clear: Do not touch.

She might as well have put up a brick wall between them.

Kenneth glanced at the clock on her bed table: 8:40. Early enough to sleep a little longer and still get up before noon.

Except that Tessa didn't seem to want any company.

"I guess this is the part where I have to make the walk of shame?" At least he'd managed to make it upstairs with half his clothes on. His jeans were tossed across a nearby chair, his boots and socks nearby. Getting up was the problem. He didn't want to go.

Tessa cracked an eye. "If I had any energy I'd put my foot on your ass and boot you out of my bed so I could get my beauty rest."

His stomach tightened. "I get the hint." He started to slide out of bed. Right about now he could use a shower and a hot cup of extrastrong coffee. Several cups. And some aspirin, to chase away that headachy feeling. "I'll think about trying to make nice with you later. You sure are grouchy in the morning."

The creases in her forehead deepened. "Grouch smouch," she grumbled. "All I want to do is snatch a little more snooze."

He grinned and leaned over her. "And all I want to do is snatch a little more snuggle." His lips brushed hers.

She didn't uncurl. "You're a pain in the ass," she whispered against his mouth.

He didn't pull back. "Then let me kiss it and make it all better."

Tessa's throat worked. "Right now I'm not sure about letting you anywhere near me."

Kenneth froze. His stomach balled into tight, hard knots. "Did I do something wrong?"

He heard her suck in a ragged breath. "This is usually the time when we part company."

Caught short by her statement, Kenneth sifted through his brain cells, attempting to pull all the various elements together. Through the haze of his hangover and just plain excitement, he was aware he'd said some mighty sweet-sounding words.

Kenneth reached out, tracing the tense line of her jaw. "And this is my cue to tell you I meant it when I said I wasn't a one-night-stand kind of man. Anything I do, I'm in for the long haul."

Her gaze met his, honing in. "So you're telling me you've never slept with a woman you've just met? Never did it just for the sex?"

He shook his head. "Honestly? No. I never have. You're my first."

Tessa appeared to believe him. She uncurled, stretching out and propping herself up on an elbow. "So I popped your *one-nighter* cherry?"

At least she was thawing out a bit. How did the old saying go? Women traded sex for intimacy and men swapped intimacy for sex.

. Not that he minded. If it bought him a few more minutes in her company, he'd gladly welcome the bedroom confidences.

"I'm not saying I haven't wanted to. It's just something I haven't made a practice of."

Tessa's mouth drew down. "I've done it before."

His brows rose. That was something he never would have guessed. "Oh?"

She blew out a frustrated huff of breath. "Mers are very sexual. We need a lot."

Kenneth considered her confession. Though he wouldn't have asked, he thought it generous of her to volunteer the information. When it came to tallying numbers, he'd always believed discretion to be the better part of valor. Unlike some men he'd worked with, he never kissed and then shared the dirty details.

"I appreciate your honesty."

She flashed him a skeptical look. "In case you're wondering, I've had a lot of men."

He shook his head. "I wasn't wondering. But thanks for telling me I was just another notch in your bedpost."

"A warm male body with a hard-on always does it for me." She shrugged. "Sorry. I couldn't control my hormones."

His jaw tightened. "So you're telling me last night meant nothing."

Her gaze skittered. She wouldn't look him in the eyes. "I just used you," she confirmed. "It's what Mers do. You humans mean nothing to us."

Kenneth's stomach did a cartwheel. What the hell was her game? This definitely wasn't the woman he'd made love to last night. Something had changed. "Glad I could accommodate your need for an orgasm."

She snorted. "Oh, come on. Get real and grow up. You didn't go to bed with me. You went to bed with the fantasy mermaid who kissed you crazy under the water." Her eyes narrowed. "Hard waking up with the real bitch, isn't it?"

Hearing her words, a light immediately came on in his head. It occurred to him Tessa was afraid he'd wanted her because she was exotic.

A curiosity.

Now that the passion of the night was over, things probably appeared a lot different to her in the bright light of day. She most likely suspected he'd said a lot of persuasive words so he could work his way into her panties.

Something in his gut told him she wasn't being truthful. It was easier for her to push him away first. She believed she was being a big girl, too smart to put her heart on the line for a single night of sex.

"I don't believe you're a bitch, Tessa," he replied calmly. "I just think you don't trust men. Is that it? Men don't play straight, or fair, so why should you?"

By the look on her face, he'd struck a nerve. A very raw and exposed one.

The wall she'd tried to hide behind suddenly collapsed. Her expression grew somber. "When I'm with a human, I always wonder how long it's going to be before the guy figures out I'm not really so special after all."

"You are special." No thinking required there. He truly believed it.

Tessa's throat worked as she swallowed. By the look on her face, she believed he was feeding her a line of pure bullshit.

"No, not really. I mean, once the exotic Mer thing wears off, I'm just like a human woman. Hormones make me bitchy, my skin breaks out, and I cry when I get depressed."

A chuckle escaped him. "Is that all?"

She shot him a look. "It's not funny. I'm trying to be serious, warts and all. Mers aren't easy to be around."

His hand curled under her chin. "This may come as a surprise to you, but that's 99.9 percent of the women alive on the earth today. And as far as I know, it has everything to do with being female and nothing to do with being a mermaid."

Tessa refused to be mollified by his words. "So you think you could find me tolerable?" She huffed. "Wait till you find out I can't even fry an egg. If it doesn't go in a microwave or come out of a tin can, I can't cook it."

Her words came out in a rush, as if she were making a confession too dreadful to be spoken aloud.

It didn't take a genius to figure out what she was doing. She was tossing excuses. Stalling. Doing her best to discourage him.

Too bad it wasn't going to work.

"Believe it or not, most men aren't worried about that," he informed her. "I can cook for myself. I'm pretty damn good at doing my own laundry. Hell, I can even handle a needle when pressed."

The determination to be stubborn continued to shadow her expression. "If you can do all that, why would you possibly want any woman?"

Kenneth answered by tugging the covers off her body. "Nothing can compare to being with and making love to a woman you desire."

Eyelids fluttering, a soft moan escaped Tessa's lips. "You almost make me believe you're serious."

"If I wasn't serious, I wouldn't be here now," he said. Everything about Tessa appealed to him; from her prickly personality to the sight of her luscious body. He loved the feel of her soft skin and full curves beneath his hands.

A soft laugh escaped her. "I wonder if I should tell you I don't believe in love at first sight." Although her eyes glinted with pleasure, he picked up a hint of melancholy behind her words.

Kenneth swept his palm over her rib cage, letting his hand rest on the soft curve of her belly. "If the attraction's there, I believe anything's possible."

Tessa's sparkling gaze warmed his face. "Damn, you're good." Her breath caught. "You've definitely got the touch. I bet you could sweet-talk the birds out of the trees."

Kenneth's hand inched lower beneath the sheets. A white-hot dart of fire shot through his body, his own need rising by the second. "All the talk in the world won't be any good if no one's listening."

Tessa shivered as his fingers touched her. A rush of air escaped her. "Maybe I could listen a little more."

Just as things were about to go into round two, the jarring sound of a newcomer's voice cut through the bedroom. "Oh my God," came the exclamation filled with delight. "Tessa got laid!"

Losing the intensity behind the moment, Tessa groaned in frustration. Rolling off Kenneth, she scrambled to pull the bedding over their naked bodies. The last thing she wanted to do was give her little sister a nice view of the man she'd just slept with.

Frustration simmering in her chest, she fixed a laser beam stare on Addison. Of course the little twit stood in the doorway, grinning like a monkey. "What the hell do you want?"

Addison put more wattage behind her smile. "Lucky said you hired a new guy, so I came by to see how he was working out." She eyed the rumpled bed. "Looks to me like he's got everything under control."

Tessa glanced at Kenneth, who was doing his best not

to look like a man who'd just been caught in bed with his new boss. Mortification scaled his face. The poor guy had literally been caught with his pants not only down, but completely off and lying across the room.

And knowing Addison, she wouldn't let him get dressed without giving him a good razzing.

"I'm sorry," Tessa said, trying to come up with a decent apology. "The person who hasn't learned to respect other people's privacy is Addison, best known around here as *Addled Brain*."

Kenneth cleared his throat. "Nice to meet you, Addison."

Addison grinned and gave a little toodle-loo wave back. "You deserve hazard pay for taming the witch." She rolled her eyes. "We were beginning to fear Tessa wouldn't ever have sex again. Every time a guy comes near her, she bites his head off."

Feeling her blood pressure rise, Tessa glared harder. Exasperation bubbled like hot oil. "We'd like some privacy, please."

Enjoying their discomfort, Addison leaned against the doorframe. "Oh, don't mind little old me. I'll just hang around while you get dressed."

Oh, no. That definitely wasn't going to happen.

Tessa snatched up an old stuffed tiger propped on the headboard. Though one ear was missing and most of its fur had fallen out, it still made a hefty missile. "Get out!" The motley feline whizzed through the air.

Addison easily caught the flying animal. "That's no way to treat Tiggs."

Tessa gritted her teeth. Her little sister's cute act was beginning to wear thin. One more second and she'd jump out of bed stark naked and pummel Addison into the floor. "Just get out."

Tossing the tiger back on the bed, Addison raised her hands in mock defeat. "Okay, okay, I'm going." She disappeared. A cheery song floated back into the bedroom. "Ding-dong, the witch is dead . . ."

Kenneth raised a brow. "Um, she's different."

Tessa shook her head. "She's an idiot. It's hard to believe she's my sister sometimes."

Slipping out of bed, Kenneth reached for his jeans. Tessa got a nice glimpse of his muscular body as he pulled them up around his slender waist. "Both your sisters look a lot like you. Can't mistake that red hair."

Tessa climbed out of bed, reaching for her robe. Just looking at Kenneth caused her pulse to ratchet up another notch. "She's still an idiot." She slipped it on. Her fingers shook more than a little, making it difficult to tie a knot around her waist. Her body still hummed with unfulfilled sexual energy.

Kenneth sat down to put on his boots. "Sounds like she's pretty happy, though." A laugh rumbled deep in his chest. He sounded more than pleased himself.

Her face heated. She might as well come clean. So far nothing she'd done to deter him seemed to be working. "I was lying when I said I've had a lot of one-night stands. The truth is I haven't had sex in more than three years."

He shrugged. "No reason to lie about it. There's nothing to be ashamed of if you've been celibate a while. I've been there and done that."

His statement made her uncomfortable. She tried to dodge around it. "You had a pretty good excuse."

Kenneth's eyes momentarily darkened. "Trust me. It wasn't my choice."

Tessa pressed her lips into a flat line. "Sorry. I didn't mean to throw it in your face."

His gaze cleared. "I can take it," he said softly. "Now tell me what you're dealing with. I've been straight with you. The least you can do is return the courtesy."

Tessa stood there, feeling awkward. *Say it*, she ordered herself. *It's time to spit it out.*

Tilting her head back, she blew out a long sigh. Her already erratic pulse skipped another beat. "If you want to know, it's because my fiancé ran off with a stripper."

Kenneth winced. "Ouch."

The thorn went a little deeper. "On the night before our joining ceremony."

Pulling on a sock, Kenneth pushed his foot into his black leather boot. "And now you think all men are bastards?"

An awkward silence hung between them.

Tessa clutched her robe and swallowed back a wave of queasiness. Even though several years had passed, her heart still had cracks. No, they weren't quite as deep nowadays, but they were still there. She thought she'd done a good job of putting the pieces back together.

Before Addison had interrupted, she'd been willing to fall for Kenneth's seduction. He said all the right words. He definitely made all the right moves. But was she going to accept him because she wanted to scratch a physical itch or because she really wanted to start working on a solid relationship?

She didn't know. And confusion meant indecision. Indecision meant uncertainty. And uncertainty was beginning to lead her down the path of just plain thumbs down.

Tessa swallowed, unnerved by the quiet. Trepidation washed over her. Attempting to explain everything would be pointless. There was so much more to the story than she was willing to divulge.

"It's not just that. Not only do I have the whole fucking human-versus-Mer thing going on, there are other things I'm dealing with that aren't going away anytime soon." She raised her hands, palms out. "You have to understand where I'm coming from. Right now it's just easier to keep my distance."

Shifting his lean frame, Kenneth slipped on his other boot. "You weren't feeling very distant ten minutes ago."

Arms dropping, her hands curled into fists. "It's obvious we both have desires. But we also have too many issues that go along with those needs. I think I—we—made a mistake rushing into sex."

Pushing out of the chair, Kenneth closed the brief distance between them. He was still bare-chested. The rest of his clothing was downstairs.

One hand settled on her hip. His fingers worked into the belt loop of her robe, tugging her body toward his. His touch jolted like the current through a hot-wire fence. "What happened last night didn't feel like a mistake."

Tessa gasped in surprise as warmth flooded her veins. The solid length of his body pressed against hers, feeling oh so right.

A twinge twisted her gut. The hours since his arrival had felt like a dream. He was a generous and attentive lover, taking care of her needs in every way.

"The sex was good," she admitted, trying to keep her mind on track. Hard to do when an awesomely hot man stood not an inch away. "It's what comes after we get out of bed that I'm not ready for."

Kenneth's face was only a few short inches from hers. He was so close she could feel the brush of his breath against her lips. "Then let's just stay in bed."

Tessa pressed her hands against his chest. His skin was warm, the beat of his heart steady under her palm.

A tremor shook her that had nothing to do with desire, and everything to do with fear. It would be easy to fall fast and hard for this man. Really easy. But she wasn't ready to put her heart back on the market just yet.

"Would that actually be satisfying?"

Kenneth cocked his head to one side. His gaze probed hers, seeking. "I'm willing to take the time to find out."

Taking a deep breath, Tessa pulled back, breaking contact. The last thing she wanted to come off as was a needy, clinging woman who'd settle on a man she'd known less than twenty-four hours.

She squared her shoulders. "I might be lonely, but I'm not desperate. I haven't exactly been sitting around waiting for a guy to rush in and give me an orgasm so I'll feel like a woman again."

Kenneth immediately made a time-out sign. Muscles rippled in his shoulders and abdomen. "Put the claws away, babe. I don't need a new asshole."

Tessa pressed a palm to her forehead and closed her eyes. "I'm sorry," she heard herself say. "Everything's just happening so fast. I've slept alone for three years and now there's a man in my damn bed." Her jaw clenched, cutting off the rest of what she was going to say. *A man I desire.*

The feel of his hand claiming her free one jolted. His was a light touch, but the heat from his fingers seeped straight through her skin, hitting her bloodstream with a potent shot of pure electricity.

His voice penetrated her self-imposed darkness. "Then all you have to say is slow down."

Tessa shivered and opened her eyes. "Is it really that easy?"

Mouth curving in a rueful smile, his head bobbed once. "I didn't mean to come in like a bulldozer and roll over you. If you need some space, tell me to back off. I can find somewhere else to be."

The thought made her stomach curl unpleasantly. Her throat tightened painfully. "I'm not saying go away," she tried to explain. "I'm just not ready to get involved."

Taut muscle rippled when he shrugged his shoulders. "We were involved the moment we took off our clothes." His stare held hers. "And I didn't hear you say *no*."

The way his gaze caressed her sent a rush of heat straight to her inner core. Last night she would have sworn his irises were dark brown. With the morning sun lighting the room the shade had lightened out to a breathtaking golden hue.

She pulled her hand away, feeling strangely awkward. He was so damn appealing. And seemed so sincere. Saying no when looking into his eyes was impossible . . .

Shaking her head, Tessa stood her ground. "Maybe I should have."

"I don't think you wanted to."

His statement caught her off guard.

Tilting her head back, Tessa covered her face with both hands and released a long sigh. "I don't know what I wanted last night. I'm just one neurotic, messed-up Mer." Hands falling, she made a helpless gesture. "So much for the fantasy, eh?"

Giving her a smile that would melt chocolate, Kenneth swiped a hand over his stubble-covered jaw. "I get that you have trust issues, on several levels. It must be hard to let someone into your world."

Emptiness boiled in her chest. She felt hollow, gutted

by isolation and doubt. "It's like standing on the outside always looking in. I don't seem to belong anywhere."

"Maybe you're standing on the inside, looking out. There's a door there, I know. You might consider opening it, letting someone in."

She shook her head. Tears welled up in her eyes, as years of pent-up emotion boiled over in her chest. She blinked hard, refusing to cry. "Right now's it's got to stay closed. Maybe not locked, but closed. Until I'm sure."

Kenneth nodded. "I can handle that." He shrugged. "Can't say that I haven't got a few hang-ups that need to be examined a little closer."

Lowering her hands, Tessa inhaled a few shallow breaths to ease the ache building in her chest. "Exactly." The timing just wasn't right.

Kenneth looked at her in all seriousness. "Just don't keep letting the bad times hold you back. Believe it or not, things do get better." His voice was low and soft.

She swallowed and took another deep breath. "The voice of experience?" Her words came out in a raw, husky whisper.

Standing so close to him made it hard to breathe. The musky scent of their lovemaking still clung to his warm skin, reminding her of everything they'd done. The intoxicating scent filled her with indescribable longing.

He nodded. "Absolutely. Been there, done that. There comes a point when you have to decide to move forward and rebuild your life with the pieces you've got left. It isn't easy, but it's possible."

Despite the glimmer of hope, her shoulders drooped. There was so much more to the story he just didn't know. Her love life, or lack thereof, was just the tip of the iceberg. "Sometimes I wonder if I have the strength to do it again."

Kenneth cocked his head. "I can be patient." His eyes crinkled slightly when he smiled. "And if you need some help working things through, you know where I'm at, sweetie." Flicking a quick wink her way, he turned and strode out of her bedroom without saying another word.

Tessa's jaw dropped. She stared in his wake, speechless.

Sweetie? Nobody had called her sweetie since her parents were alive, and they'd been in the grave since she was a teenager.

"Absolutely incredible," she muttered.

Somehow his response reassured. He didn't get mad and stomp off. Instead, he'd stepped back and given her the space she'd asked for. That's the way a responsible adult male acted. A man said his piece and stood his ground. He didn't run off, jump in bed with the first woman who came his way.

She shook her head. Kenneth Randall was too damn good to be true.

Chapter 7

Addison immediately sailed into the bedroom with a frown on her face and fire in her eyes. "Are you a nut?"

Still digesting the last few minutes of her conversation with Kenneth, Tessa's gaze narrowed. "What are you talking about?"

Addison waved her hands. "Hello! I heard everything, and by the sound of it you're cutting him loose."

Tessa frowned. "Lot of eavesdropping going on here lately."

"Uh, yeah. When there's something as important as this. Getting it on with the hot handyman is as cliché as it comes, but whatever gets you out of your rut is good."

Tessa felt her face heat. *Unsettling, out of character, and disturbing is more like it.* "We weren't getting it on."

Shaking a finger, Addison's grin widened. "That's not what it looked like to me, missy, so don't try to lie. The living room looks like a hurricane hit with full force. If the couch wasn't sagging before, it damn sure is now. Can't say I blame you, either. I passed Mr. Hunk in the hall and he's—" Addison fanned herself with a hand. "Hot! Wow, you could bite a hole through that chest."

Tessa shook her head, refusing to be baited. "I'm not discussing my sex life with you."

Addison ignored her. "I want all the details, blow by blow." She giggled. "I saw the hands on him. Bet he knows how to use them, too."

Tessa's already erratic pulse skipped a beat. Tightening her hold on her robe, she stiffened and put on a fierce frown.

The last thing she wanted to do was discuss the incident with her little sister. Sex was a private thing, to be shared between two lovers. Though she cherished her sisters, revealing the intimacies of her sex life was something she'd never consider. She'd always been the oldest, had taken care of the girls after their parents were killed. She had to be the responsible one, the levelheaded one.

And that meant acting like an adult. Though she'd made a mistake, she'd done her best to nip it in the bud. Nothing ever had to happen between her and Kenneth again. At first it would be awkward, but if he couldn't accept her decision, then he knew how to get off the island.

Addison stuck out her tongue. "Killjoy. This is the best thing that's happened to you in a long time, and you're already turning your nose up."

Her little sister certainly had sharp ears. She hadn't missed a thing. "I'm not being stuck-up. I simply told him the truth. I'm not ready for anything serious."

Addison shifted her stance. "I didn't hear him asking you to marry him, Tess. Right now it looks like all the guy wants is a chance to be with you."

"He's been here one day."

"So? Mom and Dad met on a Friday and married on a Monday. In three days they knew they had something real."

Tessa cringed. "Well, I guess I don't spot them as good as Mom did. I thought what I had with Jake was real, and look how that turned out."

Addison blew out a breath. "Jake was . . . a jerk. He might have been a bad apple, but that doesn't mean all the fruit has worms."

"So I'm being a little more careful before I bite this time."

Addison laughed. "Oh, what a line of bullshit."

Tessa smacked her sister on the arm. "I've heard enough out of you, Addled Brain."

Addison rubbed her wounded limb. "At least tell me you're going to give the guy a chance."

"I don't know," she said curtly. "It depends."

Addison folded her arms over her chest. "On what?"

"On—" Tessa gestured helplessly, then let her arms drop. "Oh, hell. I don't know." She sat down on the bed, lowering her head into her hands. "Right now I'm just confused."

Addison walked over and sat down beside her. "Are you okay?"

Tessa pulled in a deep, slow breath. "He saw me, with my tail on."

Addison gasped. "He knows you're a Mer?"

She sat up. "Yes, he knows. I took a swim late last night and he caught me in full shift."

"Did he freak?"

Tessa shook her head. "He took it pretty well, actually."

"That's fabulous!"

Her sister's response shocked her. Tessa wasn't sure

she heard her correctly. "Fabulous?" she repeated. "He knows about me. About us."

Addison shrugged. "So what? Is it going to bring him any fame or money?"

It took a moment for Tessa to wrap her head around the implications . . . and realize there were none. She was making a mountain out of a molehill. "Well, probably not."

"It's not like other people don't know about us. Lucky, Jake . . . the guys at the station. Once they get over the idea we have tails, they're usually pretty cool with it. Plus, they couldn't supply evidence, even if they wanted to."

Tessa shot a look at her sister. "The guys you work with know?" Though her sister worked a human's job, underwater search and rescue, she'd had no idea Addison was close enough to anyone to tell them the truth about their origins.

Addison's brows hunkered together. "I haven't told everyone, but I have told a few of the guys. I mean, they know I can get into places a diver with normal gear can't possibly reach. Someone's got to watch my back when we're down that deep."

Her sister's confession was an eye-opener.

Tessa had always believed both her sisters to be tight-lipped about their Mer side. Apparently she was wrong. The veil of secrecy was slowly beginning to fall away and she hadn't even realized it.

"I didn't think you'd ever tell anyone. I don't even think Gwen has."

Addison frowned. "Gwen's still trying to live and be like a human. But that doesn't mean she doesn't play on the folklore about Mer in these waters. Her hotel relies on tourists wanting to come here. Stories of mermaids living in the bay are famous and she does her part by making sure they have plenty of merchandise to buy in the gift shop."

Tessa twisted her fingers tightly together. "So you think it's fine Kenneth knows about us?"

"Of course it's fine. You don't want to start a new relationship with a secret like that hanging between you."

Tessa nibbled her bottom lip. "No, I don't suppose secrets are good for any relationship."

She could certainly relate. All the while Jake was romancing her, he'd also had a slew of quickies on the side. Yes, he knew all about her. But she'd had no clue about his extracurricular activities until after he'd said goodbye. It vaguely occurred to her he might have done her a favor when he'd dumped her and left town.

Addison skewered her with a pointed look. "Kenneth obviously finds you desirable even though you sometimes look like half a fillet. If a guy can overlook that, he can overlook a lot about your bitchy personality."

Tessa sniffed. "I'm not a bitch. I just know what I want."

"Then start going after it. If the attraction is there, take advantage of it. Have fun, and enjoy life for a change."

She allowed a weak smile. "I've been pathetic, haven't I?"

Addison grinned, showing off the cute split between her front teeth. With her short, spiky red hair and tons of freckles, she looked like a teenager, no older than sixteen, maybe seventeen at the most. Most people found it difficult to believe she was an accomplished EMT and could handle a fire truck just as well as she piloted the rescue boat.

"Beyond pathetic. Snivel-worthy, as a matter of fact.

You've moped around so much I've wanted to put a pillow over your face just to put you out of our misery."

Tessa regarded her younger sister. At twenty-six years of age, Addison had made a place for herself in a world that didn't exactly welcome those who were different or special. Gwen, too, had made a place for herself as a local business owner on the mainland.

Only Tessa, the oldest, who should have been the wisest, was floundering. *I haven't found my place yet.* She wondered if she ever would.

"I guess I really deserved that one."

Addison made a wringing motion with her hands. "Only ninety percent of the time."

Tessa sighed. "I've been so busy trying to keep things together here," she said. "Yet everything's still falling apart around me."

"The money Mom and Dad left stretched only so far," Addison reminded her. "Hanging on to the island, putting me and Gwen through college, then having Jake dump all over you. You've had a rough time."

Rubbing her face with her hands, Tessa glanced up at the ceiling. The plaster had begun to flake and crack, rotting away because of a leak in the roof. "This place is falling apart around my ears." The house needed a lot of repairs. Too many for one person on a limited budget to handle.

"We've had a good offer," Addison ventured. "It would take a lot of pressure off your hands."

Tessa frowned. She wasn't really sure Addison understood the implications behind selling. "I know you and Gwen could outvote me and sell if you wanted to, but I think it would be a huge mistake. This place is more than our home; it's been the home of the Mer since our kind first swam into these waters."

Addison nodded. "That's true. But we haven't prospered here. Most Mer have left these waters behind, moved onto land to integrate with the humans. We're a dying breed now."

Tessa glowered at her sister. "Just because we're facing extinction doesn't mean we have to roll over and die. Someday we will all have daughters of our own. Are you truly going to deny your child the gift of the sea?"

Her sister's lips quirked down. "I guess I hadn't thought of the daughters I might have someday. I'm enjoying my life too much to even think about children now."

"All I'm saying is that whatever may come, I want my girls to have a place they can feel safe. A bit of land that belongs to them, where they can live in peace if they so choose."

Addison looked at her. "It's really important to you, isn't it?"

Tessa allowed a thin smile. "Important enough that I promise not to fire the handyman."

"Well, now I have to take it seriously. You think he'll last more than two weeks?"

Tessa considered. "He's had a rough time," she allowed.

"The name seems familiar . . . I'd swear I knew him."

Tessa pressed her lips together, wondering how much she should tell. Might as well spill. It wasn't like Addison couldn't Google him. "That's the guy I pulled out of the water last year."

Addison's brows shot up. "The nut who tried to drown himself?"

Tessa swallowed back her frustration. The question squeezed her heart. "He's not a nut. His wife had passed away and he needed to work through some problems."

Hearing her own words, she almost had to stop and shake her head in wonder. How was it she found it so easy to rush to his defense? Kenneth Randall was, for all intents and purposes, a stranger.

Shadows of unease flitted through Addison's eyes. "You've got big problems if you try to fucking off yourself," she said quietly. Now that she had a few facts, her earlier enthusiasm quickly faded. She'd gone on the defensive. Though they might not always agree, when push came to shove, the Lonike girls always stuck together. "Are you sure he's stable?"

For a moment air wouldn't flow through Tessa's windpipe. She cleared her throat. "We actually talked about it. He's had some therapy, grief counseling. Right now he's kind of kicking around, looking for a new place to settle."

Addison's brows knitted. "Kind of funny he'd come back here, isn't it?"

"That kind of comes back around to the whole Mer thing."

"Oh?"

"He came back because he remembered being in the water. With me." She struggled to sound unruffled.

"But you only gave him the kiss of breath, right?"

She hesitated. "Yes."

Addison's brow puckered in confusion. "The spell's supposed to break once they come out of the water. They're not supposed to remember us."

"And we're not exactly experts in Mercraft," Tessa reminded her. "I'd just begun learning when Mom died. The bits and pieces I know don't even begin to reveal our talents."

Addison nodded her agreement. "This is definitely

where we could use that handbook on how to be a Mer."

"Well, we didn't get one. Anyway, he didn't remember me clearly, or even know that I was a mermaid. But he did remember enough to want to come back and find me."

Addison eyed the robe Tessa had on. At the moment it was the only thing covering her body. "Looks like he found you, and then some."

Tessa's back stiffened. "I didn't mean for that to happen. It just . . ." She gestured helplessly. "Did."

Addison ruffled a hand through her short hair. "I still think you should give me all the details."

Tessa wouldn't budge. "My lips are sealed." Taking off her robe, she stepped into the shower and closed the glass door. Angling the faucet away from her body, she turned on the taps and adjusted the water to a bearable temperature. It took a few minutes for the wheezy old water heater in the basement to kick in, but somehow it did the job. Steam soon billowed around her.

Her sister tapped on the glass. "Come on, please. I haven't gotten laid in months. The least you could do is let me live vicariously through you."

"Get a vibrator," Tessa called back. "It'll do wonders for you." Flipping open the lid on the shampoo bottle, she poured the pearlescent liquid into her hand. It smelled of coconut, her favorite scent. A moment later fragrant suds covered her from head to toe.

"You're going back to bitchy."

Giving herself a quick rinse, Tessa shut off the water ten minutes later. "The bitch would like a towel, please."

Addison tossed one over the top of the shower. "I

should make you stand there until I get some of the juicier details."

Tessa dried off, then wrapped the towel around her damp body. It felt good to be squeaky clean. "You're getting to be a pain in my rear, Addie," she said, breezing past her sister and back into her bedroom. She dug a pair of faded jeans and a T-shirt out of the bureau.

Addison nipped at her heels like a bloodhound. "I still say—" Her words broke off abruptly. She sniffed the air. Her sister's elfin face curved in a wry grin "Hey, is that bacon I smell?"

Slipping into her clothes, Tessa gave the air a sniff. The potent aroma of frying bacon mingled with the distinct scent of freshly brewed coffee.

She exchanged an incredulous look with her sister. "I think so." Her stomach backed up the scintillating olfactory evidence, rumbling in response. She usually drank instant coffee and it had been years since she'd eaten more than a bowl of cold cereal for breakfast.

Addison clapped with delight. "Oh my God! A man who cooks!"

Cup in hand, Kenneth measured out a level amount of dry mix, then dumped it in a mixing bowl. While he wasn't fond of instant batter mixes, he supposed it would do in a pinch. Adding in a few extras to improve the taste, he stirred the batter until all the lumps disappeared.

As he whisked, he cocked an eye toward the coffeepot. The old machine grunted alarmingly, but the coffeepot was steadily beginning to fill. God, yes. He couldn't wait for a cup of fresh-brewed coffee. That instant crap he'd found in Tessa's cupboard didn't cut it with him.

Bacon sizzled in a heavy cast-iron skillet on the

stovetop. Another sat nearby, warming on the opposite burner. He could start the pancakes now. And just as soon as the bacon was done, he'd crack some eggs and fry them in the leftover grease.

The breakfast he prepared was decadent, an artery-clogging meal with at least a bazillion calories. He didn't care. Last night he'd worked up an appetite and he intended to eat.

Even though it might be the only meal I get to eat on this island.

After he'd left Tessa's bedroom, he'd hit the living room to claim his shirt and beat a hasty retreat back to the lighthouse. Even though her sister had given him two thumbs up as they'd passed in the hallway, he wasn't so sure he should be hanging around. Tessa had already decided they'd made a mistake. The best thing to do was get out of her sight.

Twenty minutes later he'd showered, then changed into a fresh pair of jeans and a T-shirt. The list of repairs staring him in the face was a long one. The rumbling in his gut reminded him he'd need to get something in his stomach before going to work.

But the idea of eating breakfast alone bothered him. A lot.

He'd just slept with Tessa, and now he wasn't man enough to sit down at a table and eat with her. No matter that she was the one begging for distance. It still didn't feel right. Neither one of them had done anything to be ashamed of. They were both consenting adults. If Tessa had doubts or guilt or whatever, well, she'd just have to deal with it.

Part of the agreement he'd made with the sisters included meals. He wasn't going to slink off like a servant and find some corner to eat in.

Marching back to the main house, Kenneth had been surprised to find the kitchen empty. Voices drifted down from upstairs, along with the distant sound of running water. He figured the girls were doing what women did when they got together: gossiping like hens. In the back of his mind he hoped Addison was pleading his case.

Two thumbs up had to count for something.

Since the bargain had covered only food, but not service, Kenneth set to making breakfast himself. Hunting though the cabinets, he had familiarized himself with the whereabouts of the necessary staples. Gwen had made sure they'd eat well, loading up the kitchen with enough food to feed a small army.

The appliances were older models, but still functional. Since natural gas wasn't available on the island, everything was powered by electricity. As no power lines stretched from the mainland, he suspected everything was run off a generator, probably located in the shed abutting the house. If nothing else, the island seemed self-sufficient.

He was just about to pour the pancake batter on the hot skillet when two curious redheads peeked around the doorframe.

Addison took a deep breath and squealed, "Oh my God. I haven't smelled anything so heavenly since Mom was alive."

Tessa nodded her agreement. "It's been years since anyone cooked on that stove."

Addison's eyes settled on the wheezing coffeemaker. "And is that real brewed coffee I smell?"

Setting down the mixing bowl, Kenneth reached for the coffee cups he'd set out. "One hundred percent Colombian." He poured three cups. "I hope you're both hungry."

Addison's face split into a grin. "Oh, you are so frickin' right I am!"

He delivered the cups to the kitchen table. Instant creamer and sugar occupied a lazy Susan, along with a set of salt and pepper shakers and a napkin holder. "Sit down. I've almost got everything ready." Anticipating that he wouldn't be eating alone, he'd set out enough silverware for three. It was purely a move of optimism. The women he knew freaked out at the thought of eating more than a piece of whole wheat toast and a half slice of grapefruit.

Addison zoomed to the table. "Bless you."

Tessa followed at a slower pace. Pulling out a chair, she plopped down on the farthest side. "If I'd have known you cooked," she said, wrapping her hands around a thick mug, "I'd have hired you faster."

Kenneth returned to the stove, poking the bacon with a fork. It was sizzling nicely. "Thought I'd treat you both to breakfast," he said casually, making sure to include Addison.

"It does smell good," Tessa allowed.

He reached for the bread, popping a few slices into the toaster. "I think I remember you saying you didn't cook much." He was going all out, missing no detail. Besides, nothing went better with fried eggs and bacon than slices of buttery toast loaded with sweet jam. The kitchen was redolent with the aroma of cooking.

Loading her coffee with cream and tons of sugar, a hint of a smile touched Tessa's lips. He couldn't tell if she was genuinely amused or just tolerating him to be polite. Once Addison left, those claws of hers might come.

Be nice if she'd rake them down my back. The sexually charged notion buzzed through his mind like a hornet heading in for the sting. It could be a problem if all he thought about was sex every time he looked at Tessa.

But he'd promised her he'd keep his distance. If nothing else, he was a man of his word. No matter how damn hard it might be to keep his hands off her luscious body, he'd be nothing but a perfect gentleman.

Unless she changed her mind ...

Tessa sipped her drink, now a pale milky white liquid barely recognizable as good Colombian coffee. "I don't. And I'm not going to start now."

Kenneth cleared his throat. "Guess I'll just have to handle that for you." He winked. "I hope you don't mind a masculine touch."

A blush immediately rose to Tessa's cheeks. "I think we've had enough touching around here for one day," she mumbled into her mug. "I could have made do with a bowl of cereal."

Addison pretended not to be listening. "I'll take the freshly cooked hot food, thank you very much." She jabbed a finger his way. "Just let him handle things and you'll eat a lot better. All that junk food you eat is scary." She rolled her eyes. "Who seriously eats a box of Triscuits and calls it a meal?"

Tessa pounced on her sister. "Those crackers are made out of shredded wheat. Lots of fiber."

"Which makes you full of shit," Addison retorted. "I hate to disillusion you, but potato chips and salsa isn't a meal either."

"I've got better things to do than cook," Tessa huffed. "So sue me."

The two set to bickering, going back and forth on the benefits of a healthful diet versus the convenience of junk food.

For the moment, Kenneth was content to let them argue.

He sipped his coffee, trying not to look at Tessa over the rim of his cup. Casually dressed in jeans and a faded goth-metal tee, she looked great. She'd braided her long hair into a rope stretching down her back. As an extra touch, she'd put on a bit of makeup: mascara, eye shadow, and gloss. Not enough to be showy, but subtle. Yesterday her face hadn't had a lick of cosmetics.

A little smile tweaked up one corner of his mouth. *Maybe she's making that effort for me.*

Maybe there was hope she'd give him a chance.

From what he'd seen of Gwen, and now the youngest, all three of the girls were real lookers. He couldn't imagine being attracted to either one of the other sisters, though. Tessa had a spark, a certain bristly manner that reminded him of a semi-wild cat. Half-eager to be stroked, but wary of human hands. She'd run if spooked, fast and hard.

So he wasn't going to chase. He'd just let things happen.

Addison rubbed her hands together. "So when's that food coming, bud?"

"Coming right up."

Setting down his cup, Kenneth flipped the pancakes over. Mooning over Tessa, he'd almost forgotten them. To his relief, they were a nice golden brown. Good. He'd hate to serve burnt food. He forked the bacon, laying it across paper towels he'd spread on a plate to soak up the excess grease.

Finishing the pancakes, he carried them to the table with a bottle of maple syrup. "Might as well get started while I get the rest done." He eyed the girls. "How do you like your eggs?"

Addison forked up a couple of pancakes, then slathered them with butter and at least half a cup of maple syrup. "Over easy, please." Taking a huge bite, she rolled her eyes. "Delicious. Did you make these from scratch?"

"It's just a mix," he admitted. "But I used milk instead of water, and added in some blueberries."

Addison paused long enough to swallow. "They're perfect." She wiped her syrupy chin with a napkin. "The best I've eaten."

"You flatter me, I'm sure." Kenneth looked to Tessa. "Want to try one?"

Tessa's brows puckered, and then she shrugged. "Sure." Adding a pancake to her plate, she was a little more cautious with the extras. "I usually don't eat much this early in the day." She took a bite, chewing slowly.

"It's almost eleven, so call it brunch." Kenneth watched her swallow. "Okay?"

"Good." She forked up another bite, tucking it in her mouth with a little more gusto. "In fact, they're better than I thought they'd be. I never could make that mix taste decent."

"It's all in the extras." He smiled. "You want eggs?"

Tessa visually took his measure, as if she didn't quite trust whatever he might be up to. He could tell by the look on her face that it had been a long time since anyone had waited on her. "Two, please. Over easy. And I like my bacon crisp."

"Hungrier than you thought you were?"

Relaxing a little, Tessa allowed a little smile. Her face immediately changed from merely pretty to beautiful. "Guess I am."

Kenneth headed back to the stove. "Then I'd better get those eggs going." Cracking a half dozen into the still-sizzling bacon grease, he set them to frying before popping more toast in.

Addison watched him with stars in her eyes. "Gwen said you're a mechanic, have worked in construction, and now we find out you can cook. If you want to move in with me, I think I could find a place for you."

Tessa cut another bite out of her pancake. "You have a one-room apartment so small you can't even turn around in it," she reminded after she'd swallowed her food. "Where would you possibly put him?"

Addison smiled and winked. "I bet I could find a place to tuck you in."

Kenneth retrieved the hot toast, stacking it on a plate. Addison was flirting outrageously and it was beginning to piss Tessa off. Good. "I'll keep the thought in mind. If things don't work out here, it might be worth considering."

Tessa immediately put the kibosh on the idea. "Back off! I've got a to-do list at least three miles long. The man's got plenty to handle around here."

Kenneth liked the sound of that. It seemed like Tessa wasn't going to give him a boot to the ass and send him packing. In the back of his mind he hoped he'd be handling more than tools and spatulas.

Eggs done, he added the bacon and toast. He delivered three heaping plates of food to the table. "With a list like that, I'd better eat up." Pouring everyone a second cup of fresh coffee, he took his own place at the table. "Dig in, ladies."

The sound of silverware going into serious action filled the kitchen.

Addison pointed toward the last pancake. "Anyone going to eat that?"

"Not me," Tessa said between bites. "I've got enough."

"Feel free," Kenneth added.

Addison stretched out an arm, snagging the pancake with her fork. "Thanks."

Kenneth eyed her bare arm. Addison was dressed much like her sister, except her T-shirt had an EMT's emblem on it, and was emblazoned with SEARCH AND RESCUE in big red letters across the back.

"Nice tats."

"Thanks," Addison said between bites. "I like 'em."

"Yours match Tessa's."

Addison shrugged and forked in a mouthful of eggs. "We each chose the same designs."

"Tribal, right?"

The two women exchanged a quick glance. Blank stares and silence followed, as if he'd lifted his leg and stuck a foot in his mouth.

"So let's drop the bullshit," Addison finally said. "I know you saw Tess wearing her tail, so you know the tats are part of our scale pattern." She gave him the stink eye as if daring him to make a big deal of the issue. "What do you think of that?"

Keeping his face neutral, Kenneth sipped his coffee. "Well, truth be told, I think it's pretty awesome."

Addison speared her butter knife his way. "I know you're the dude Tess hauled out of the water last year."

He nodded. "I guess I'm not going to live that one down."

"You're lucky you did live. Tessa told me about your wife, so I won't ask you to explain the reason why you did that."

Tessa glanced at her little sister sharply. "That's enough," she warned. "Shut the hell up."

Kenneth shrugged. "It's okay. I was just having a moment."

"Just don't have another one." Addison made a face. "I hate hauling dead bodies out of the water."

He nodded again. The girl was certainly blunt. "I'm good and done with my nervous breakdown."

Tessa gave her sister another verbal poke. "Change the subject or shut up, Addie."

Kenneth smiled to himself. Ah, Tessa. Prickly as a cactus. Reach out and touch and you'd get a nasty jab.

Sitting at the table with two pretty women, he realized how much he'd missed the simplicity of sharing a meal with other people. Because of her busy schedule, Jen had never done more than grab a cup of coffee and a piece of fruit before heading out to work at the hospital. They rarely met for lunch and dinner was catch as can.

He'd known when he married her that Jen's career was important. She was an up-and-coming young neurosurgeon. Her parents had freaked when she'd agreed to marry him, a mechanic and junkman. After Jen's murder, they'd cut him cold. He knew why, too. In their eyes he wasn't good enough. Not highly educated, just a plain workingman. He didn't fit in with their country-club lifestyle.

Glancing around the kitchen with its faded wallpaper and peeling linoleum, it vaguely occurred to him why he felt so comfortable sitting down to the table with its scratched surface and creaky chairs. It reminded him of the place he'd grown up, one of the tract houses across the railroad tracks that separated the good side of town from the poorer side. When he was a kid, his mother had encouraged him to work hard and do better. He'd married up, to the manor born.

But he'd never been comfortable.

Scraping her plate with the last of her toast, Addison popped the final bite in her mouth. "My God, I'm stuffed." She patted her stomach. "This is the best breakfast I've ever eaten."

Having wiped out his own food with the speed of light, Kenneth sipped his coffee. "Glad you enjoyed it." He glanced at Tessa. Though she hadn't cleaned her plate, she'd eaten a good portion. "Edible?"

She gave one of her slight, fleeting smiles. "I think I just gained ten pounds," she allowed. "All that greasy food is going to go straight to my hips."

He smiled. "I can do healthy."

"I thought you were a mechanic. Where'd you learn to cook?"

Her probe for information wasn't graceful or subtle.

As a general rule, Kenneth didn't care to share his childhood. Along with the memories came the fear he'd end up as bitter and alone as his mother had. She'd tolerated people, but never allowed them to get close. In the end, she'd pushed everyone away, including her own children.

But since Tessa was a woman who also eyed all men with suspicion, he supposed it would be best to open up and be honest. He really had nothing to hide. But what he had to share wasn't pleasant, or encouraging.

"My mother was a single parent. I guess you could say I kind of grew up having to look out for myself. Mom worked two jobs to keep a roof over our heads, so she didn't have a lot of time to cook or clean. Since I was the oldest, I tried to help out."

Pushing her empty plate away, Addison propped her elbows on the table. "You have brothers and sisters?"

"A brother. Jason. Three years younger than me."

Addison waggled her brows. "Maybe you could introduce us sometime?"

Tessa smacked her younger sister's shoulder. "Stop it, Addie. He gets that you're on the make."

Addison eyed her sister. "Keep your hands to yourself, or I may be hitting back." She raised a mock fist. "I got one that'll send you to the moon, babe."

Kenneth couldn't help but laugh. It was clear when these two got going, they'd entertain for hours. He wished he'd had that kind of connection with his own sibling.

Regret prickled along his nerves. "As much as I would like to see him with a girl like you," he said, "that's not possible. Jason got into drugs really deep when he was a teenager. Even though he was in and out of jail, he never could shake the habit. Rehab didn't work either. Last I heard, he was a carnie traveling with some fly-by-night circus. You know, the kind that blows into town, sets up for a week or so, then blows back out." He shook his head regretfully. "No keeping up with those kinds of people. I lost track of him a few years ago. I don't know if he's dead or alive."

Tessa's grip visibly tightened on her cup. Her expression grew somber. "I'm sorry to hear that. What about your dad?"

Kenneth fiddled with his own empty cup. This was a part of his story he'd like to skip. "Dad walked out when Jason was three and I was six. I spent most of my life after that listening to Mom rant about what a bastard our father was. She blamed him for everything that went wrong, for everything we didn't have. Poverty wasn't just a word, it was a way of life."

Tessa's hand slipped over his arm. "I'm sorry. That must have been tough."

Heart tripping in his chest, Kenneth glanced down

in surprise. Tessa reaching out to him was something he definitely hadn't expected. By sharing a bit about his life he'd unwittingly set up a thaw, cracking through her icy wall of self-protection.

Swallowing hard, he shrugged. "The rest is pretty simple. I grew up and moved on."

As if she recognized the implications behind her touch, Tessa got up and began to clear the table. She obviously needed to put some distance between them. She piled the dishes in the sink.

Kenneth watched her work. As he'd gotten older, he'd tried to help his mother out. But nothing he did to please her was ever good enough. In her eyes, all men were pigs. Swine. Out for nothing but a good time and a quick lay.

It was exactly how Tessa seemed to view men. She'd lumped him into the category occupied by cheats, losers, and liars.

That wasn't true, though. He wasn't a man who used women.

Kenneth had decided at an early age that he wasn't going to grow up and be like his father. He'd work hard, be responsible, and take care of the woman he married.

He inwardly flinched. Jen, however, didn't need much taking care of.

Maybe that's why they'd begun to flounder . . .

Unwilling to let Tessa look like the heroine for taking over kitchen duty, Addison immediately butted in. "I can handle those dishes."

Soppy washrag in hand, Tessa raised a brow. "Don't you have someplace to be? Like work?"

"I've done my four twelves; now I have three beautiful days off." Addison reached for a dry towel. "You wash, I'll put away."

Pushing away from the table, Kenneth headed toward the coffeepot. There was just enough for one more cup; then he supposed he'd have to quit lollygagging and find something useful to do. Tessa had pointed out a work shed where the tools were kept yesterday. He supposed he'd better sort through them and see what he had to work with. If he needed anything, he could send the list back to the mainland with Addison.

Not that it looked like Addison was going to leave anytime soon. She seemed determined to park herself at the house and rag away on Tessa. It was worth it, though, if it helped keep her older sister in a good mood.

"I'll be glad to cook more often, as long as I get to watch two pretty ladies clean up the mess," he offered.

Putting away the last of the dishes, Addison flipped the damp dish towel over her shoulder. By the look on her face, she was about to say something totally inappropriate when a newcomer arrived. Without warning, the back door flew open.

Gwen sailed in. Sunglasses perched on top of her head, she was dressed in one of the fashionable business suits he'd come to recognize as her human uniform. The long sleeves of her blazer and her slacks hid the markings she seemed determined to keep from the world. For all intents and purposes, Gwen Lonike lived as a human being. Like Tessa, Addison made no attempt to hide hers. The younger woman's punk persona and cocky attitude suited the idea that she was a tattooed badass.

Sniffing the still fragrant air, Gwen looked around. The kitchen had been thoroughly cleaned, everything put back in its place. She groaned. "Why do I miss the good stuff?"

"Maybe 'cause you don't live here anymore," Addison ventured sensibly. "But, man, do I have some juicy gossip for you."

Tessa shot Addison a glare hot enough to scald. "Don't say a frickin' word if you want to live." A double-hot look landed on Kenneth. "Same goes for you."

Kenneth raised his hands. "I know nothing," he mumbled, taking on a comic accent. "I'm just the handyman." He really didn't want Tessa to follow through with her earlier threat to toss him back in the bay. He doubted he'd come up a second time.

Lightening her glare to a look of annoyance, Tessa looked to Gwen. "What are you even doing here anyway? I don't see you two for months, and now the place is Grand Central Station at noon."

Gwen waved a distracted hand. "I wanted to be the first to tell you."

Tessa stiffened. "Tell me what? If it's about the taxes, I've already written the check."

"No, it's not about that. It's something bigger."

Tessa snorted inelegantly and shook her head. "We're not selling our home, either."

Gwen frowned, tipping her chin to a pugnacious angle. "Shut up for a minute, would you? You're not listening to a thing I'm saying."

Gaze growing wary, Tessa crossed her arms. "You haven't said anything worth listening to."

"I'm about to." Gwen took a breath. "It's Jake. He's back in town and he wants to see us. All of us."

Chapter 8

Two hours later, all four of them were standing on the dock like bystanders waiting for the parade to start. Lucky's skiff was puttering toward the island, and on board was the last man Tessa wanted to see in the world.

"Why did you tell him he could come here?" she grumbled to Gwen. She really didn't want to lay eyes on the man again. She hadn't seen him since the day he'd dumped her, which had probably been for the best. It had made the break cleaner, though no easier to deal with. "Considering how he tried to exploit us, you should have told him to take a flying leap."

Eyes shielded behind an impenetrable pair of sunglasses, Gwen kept her eyes fixed straight ahead. "I did consider that. But it's actually because of you that I told him to come over."

Tessa felt her stomach drop to the ground. "Me? If you think having him say I'm sorry now is going to make things all better, you're wrong."

"It's not Jake I'm thinking about, Tess," Gwen told

her. "It's what he says he has I'm interested in. I think you will be, too."

Tessa sniffed. "He's got nothing I want."

Addison leaned over, bumping Gwen's shoulder with her own. "What's he got?"

"A few days ago he sent an e-mail telling me he was about to break his theory wide-open. He says he's found indisputable proof in some artifacts brought up from a recent recovery."

"Artifacts, my ass." Tessa rolled her eyes. "We've heard that one before. And hell would freeze over before I'd help him prove them true."

As an archaeologist, Jake Massey had centered his studies on lost civilizations and their rediscovery. In academia that was perfectly acceptable, as many of his colleagues also searched for the same elusive destinations throughout the world.

After he'd ended their relationship, Jake had begun to present a series of lectures about lost sea-based civilizations like Atlantis and Ishaldi, claiming in his course program that such places had actually existed.

On paper his thesis sounded plausible, and was actually published in *Archaeology Today*, a bimonthly magazine for professionals in the field. He'd based his research on the accounts of several excerpts reputedly penned by the Greek philosopher and mathematician Hypatia of Alexandria.

The rediscovery of Hypatia's work—which had been previously considered forever lost—occurred in the earlier part of the eighteenth century. At first archaeologists of the time had been immensely excited by her account of a sea-born people. Unfortunately, her work was later judged to be pale imitations of others such as Plato, and her account of the vanished isle of Ishaldi was believed to be no more than a romanticized version of Plato's account of the sinking of Atlantis.

Judging her version to be utterly authentic, Jake had taken his theory a step further, adding that lost civilization had actually been founded by an intelligent nonhuman species.

A species he claimed survived to this very day.

Addison leaned in close. "You know he ended up getting bounced out of U Maine a few years ago because of his support of the"—she raised her hands and made quote marks with her fingers—"'intelligent nonhuman species' he says exists. I heard he lost his sea grants shortly after for lack of hard evidence. The scientific community blasted his theories as no more than junk science."

Folding her arms over her chest, Tessa nodded smugly. "Serves him right to try to take advantage of us like that."

Listening quietly to their conversation, Kenneth raised a brow. "He told people about you?"

Though there'd been no real reason to include him in their meeting with Jake, there hadn't been a reason to exclude him, either. After all, he did know they were mermaids.

"He did it purely to advance his career," Gwen said, answering his question. "Fortunately, it seems to have backfired on him."

"Man, did it ever." Addison rolled her eyes. "According to the last gossip I heard around town, he'd gotten a job working as chief archaeologist with a group called Recoveries, Inc., which is supposedly working toward the recovery and conservation of underwater artifacts."

Tessa frowned. "In other words, he's a fucking treasure hunter."

Addison patted her arm. "Don't worry. Whatever he's got up his sleeve, we're here to cut him off at the pass," she said, unintentionally mixing her metaphors.

"Jake's e-mail said he has proof beyond a doubt about our origins," Gwen warned. "He promised we'd be the first to see what he's found." She pressed a hand to her forehead. "If something's about to break, we need to know."

Tessa shrugged. "I see no reason to panic, Gwen. I really doubt whatever his so-called discovery is even concerns us. If it were really anything groundbreaking, he'd be front and center on the six o'clock news."

"Oh, an exposé on the secret lives of mermaids." Addison giggled and grinned. "We'd be stars."

"I don't think it's funny," Gwen huffed through a deep frown. "I have a business to run and a reputation to uphold. That's the reason we keep things on the QT. In this world, different is not acceptable to most people." She shot a glance at Tessa. "And it's why we should keep our tails tucked away out of sight."

Tessa shrugged helplessly. "I was going to marry the man," she started to say in her own defense. "How was I supposed to know he'd be a total mercenary bastard?"

"Uh, excuse me." Gwen pointed at Kenneth. "So this is your next husband?"

Tessa elbowed Addison. "Big mouth."

Grinning, Addison elbowed back. "She wanted to know how you two were getting along." She tried to affect an angelic expression, but it came out as all mischief. "I simply told the truth."

Kenneth lifted his hands as if to ward off blows. "And I'm not saying one freaking word about anything. I'd like to keep my job, thanks very much."

Tessa covered her face with her hands. "Great," she

muttered. "Just great." This was already shaping up to be a hell of a day.

Everyone watched as Lucky guided the skiff up to the dock. This time the old boat wasn't carrying supplies, but a single passenger.

A tall man clad in slacks, a crisp white shirt, and a trendy blazer stepped onto the dock. His face was all hollows and angles, male-model perfect. He had shoulder-length blond hair tied at the nape of his neck in that trendy metrosexual style, and a day's worth of stubble covered his face. He looked like a preppy academic slumming among the regular folk.

Tessa's stomach did a dozen fast cartwheels. Oh, man. Jake Massey was so hot—and so not her type. When they first started dating, she'd been impressed by his intelligence and well-spoken manner. But darkness lurked behind his hundred-watt smile and charming facade. She'd learned the hard way that the only person Jake was interested in taking care of was himself.

Jake slipped off a pair of expensive designer sunglasses, tucking them in the pocket of his blazer. His piercing gaze regarded her with intimate familiarity. His smile beamed out of his deeply tanned face. The power behind it was meant to send a woman straight to her knees. "Tessa, darling, it's been so long since I've seen you."

Tessa's back stiffened. There was something distinctly phony in his greeting, as if they'd parted on the best of terms and were the dearest of friends. It was all she could do not to rip that pretty smile off his face and toss it in the bay.

Acrimonious feelings welled up from all sides, swamping her. *How dare he*, she seethed.

The liar. The hypocrite. The bastard.

Her fists clenched, fingernails digging into her palms. "As I recall, that was entirely your choice." An undertone of rebellion sounded clearly in her voice.

Jake stepped forward and pulled her toward him. His touch seared into her skin. "Let's just forgive and forget, shall we?" His lips brushed her cheek. "I've been dying to see you."

Tessa twisted out of his grasp. "There's only one thing I've been dying to do to you!" Before she could think the action through, her hand flew straight for his face. Her open palm connected with his cheek. A sound like a shot echoed across the bay.

Man, that felt good.

Rubbing his stinging cheek, Jake eyed her from head to foot. A slow grin parted his sensual mouth. "I suppose I deserved that."

"You're fucking right you did, you conniving bastard!" Jaw thrust out, Tessa's voice chilled with offense. Suddenly, she felt filled with a torrent of indefinable strength and anger.

Her words seemed to amuse Jake. His sardonic grin lit up his electric blue eyes. "Did it make you feel any better?"

Tessa refused to back down or let him see her waver. *What the hell is he grinning about?* She gritted her teeth. "Yes." She lifted her hand again. "Just as soon as I get a few more licks in."

Gwen caught her hand. "Let it go, Tess. The damage can't be undone. It's time to move on."

Jake grinned at her. "Once you see what I've got, I think all will be forgiven."

Tessa's pulse picked up speed. "That's not likely."

His smile faded. "Putting you and me aside—"

Tessa resisted the urge to roll her eyes, then decided

the action perfectly suited the moment. "Considering you walked out on me the night before our wedding, that's kind of hard for me to do."

Jake bent, closing the distance between them. "I'll admit up-front that I made a mistake, Tess. At least give me the benefit of the doubt. I've come back to try to make things right." He spoke with tense directness. A bit of his former bravado seemed to have faded.

Frowning, Tessa stepped back and skewered him with her most scathing look. On the surface Jake was so damn appealing, with those blue eyes and cleft in his chin. But looks were only skin deep. On the inside, he was a manipulator. A user.

The last thing she needed was for Jake to try to walk back into her life. She'd been fooled once. She didn't intend to be fooled a second time.

Tessa hit her forehead with the heel of her hand. "You'll never be able to fix that one, Jake. As it is, it'll take a hell of a lot of work for you to earn back everyone's trust."

"That's not as far-fetched as you may think, Tess," he said. "Just give me a second chance."

"Like you deserve one," she sniffed.

Addison stepped up. "I heard you got bounced out of the university on your ass." She waggled mocking brows. "Everyone thinks you're a nut now."

Jake regarded Addison through a cool gaze. "It's not going to be that way much longer, Addie. The one thing archaeology absolutely demands is hard evidence. It took a while to get it, but this time I've got solid proof."

Gwen interrupted. "I've told the girls about your discovery. As you can imagine, we're all eager to see it."

"Of course." Jake gestured toward the skiff. A large wooden packing crate had been lashed in the center of the boat. "I've actually been very anxious to get the artifacts here for you to examine."

Gwen nodded. "Let's get them unloaded."

Jake shifted his stance. "Well, then, let's not have any further delays." His gaze fell on Kenneth, taking in the plainclothes of a workingman. "You, there." He snapped his fingers like the lord of the manor. "Get that crate, will you?"

Kenneth shrugged. "Sure."

Jake watched him go by, stepping down into the skiff. Lucky helped him heft the crate onto the dock. "Careful now, you—" He snapped his fingers again. "What is your name?"

Kenneth clamored back onto the dock. "Kenneth Randall," he said affably, offering his hand. "I'm the handyman."

Jake ignored his offering, rubbing his hands together. "By the looks of these rotten boards on the deck, you're not very handy."

Tessa's jaw tightened. Jake had always flaunted his superior attitude, treating people who worked blue-collar jobs as though they were a lesser species. Their only function was to serve him. In other words, he was just plain rude. She wondered what she'd ever found attractive about the man. The old saying of *love is blind* must be absolutely true. Amazing how a little time and distance could open a person's eyes.

Her mouth quirked down. *Hindsight is always twenty-twenty.* There was no way she was going to let Jake treat Kenneth like a doormat to be walked all over. Tessa cleared her throat. "Actually Kenneth's my boyfriend."

The lie popped out easily and naturally. Walking up to join him, she put her arm around his waist. "He's just moved in."

Jake's brows rose. His expression darkened subtly, taking on strain and tension. Her statement had clearly taken him by surprise. "Well, this is quite something I hadn't expected."

Kenneth's mouth curved in a slight smile of befuddlement. "You could have knocked me over with a feather." Patting her on the rear, he eyed her closely. "In fact, I'm always wondering what she'll do next."

The feel of Kenneth's hand on her ass jolted Tessa. Earlier she'd told him she needed her distance. Now she was pawing all over him. Thankfully, he seemed willing to go along with it.

Jake had done her wrong, no doubt about it. She wanted him to see she'd gotten over the heartbreak, had moved on. Kenneth's arrival had helped jolt her out of lethargy. It was time to drain the black pool of her depression and get back to walking among the living.

"We've got a ton of plans for the house," Tessa added, verbally pushing the thorn a little deeper into Jake's side. "It's just come to the point where it was easier to move in together."

Jake's knee-weakening smile brightened, albeit reluctantly. "Lucky man," he said, detouring around her news by refusing to address it. "But let's get back to the subject at hand." He gestured toward the crate. "If Ken will just give me a hand with this, we'll get it inside."

Sliding a crowbar in between the seams of the crate, Kenneth gave the tool a sharp upward jerk. Nails holding the lid in place gave way to the pressure, separating from the wood.

Jake, of course, was supervising. "Try not to crack the wood when you lift the lid." Staring down his nose, he delivered his instructions in a crisp voice untainted by any local inflection.

Shooting Jake a quick glance, Kenneth narrowed his eyes. *I don't see a damn thing in him.* Of all the men he'd imagined Tessa might be attracted to, this prissy girlie man with his fashionable blazer and perfectly creased slacks didn't seem to be her type at all.

Kenneth moved to the second corner. "Whatever you say, boss." He repeated the action, easily prying the nails out of the wood.

"Careful, please," Jake chimed in again. "It's vital you don't damage the items inside."

Biting down on his tongue to keep from laughing at the pompous ass, Kenneth repeated the action on the other two sides. He lifted the lid off the crate and set it aside. "I think I managed to not break anything."

The girls had cleared the center of the living room, giving him ample space to work. Standing at the perimeter, the three sisters peered anxiously at the crate. By the looks on their faces, some strange and terrible creature had entered the house. One they clearly did not welcome.

Jake glanced at Kenneth, then cut a look to the three sisters. "Since you're a couple, I'm going to assume he's in the know."

Tessa looked at Kenneth. Frowning a little, she nevertheless nodded. "He's aware we're mermaids."

Kenneth set the crowbar aside. "Of course I know. She told me on our first night together." He didn't bother to mention the small detail that their first night was last night.

He'd already figured out he was just playing a part, filling a role. When Tessa had claimed him as her boyfriend, he'd recognized the act to be one of pure self-defense on her side. She needed a wall between herself and any lingering feelings she felt for Jake, so she'd thrown him up as protection.

Jake gave him a thumbs-up. "The tail is magnificent, isn't it?"

Kenneth refused to be baited. He had a feeling such talk made all the sisters self-conscious and embarrassed them. From what he'd seen, they were doing their best to fit into human society, live as normally as possible. "It's nothing I'm interested in. I like her just as well when she's standing on two legs."

Jake smirked knowingly. "She's much better when she's in the water. Some of the moves she can do with that appendage will make your co—"

Tessa silenced him with a single finger cutting through the air. "Don't you dare go there!" Her frigid eyes glittered with offense. "Say one more word about us and I'll kill you and hide the body, Jake. No one will find you at the bottom of the bay."

"I'll help her," Addison chimed in.

"Me, too," Gwen warned. "You're here on a trial basis only. Blow it and you're gone." She snapped her fingers. "Like that."

Chastised by three fierce expressions, Jake backed down. "Okay, okay. I was just joking," he grumbled. "There was a time when you had a sense of humor, Tess."

Tessa huffed out a long breath of disgust. "I'm not the blind fool I used to be."

The atmosphere in the room was beginning to turn hostile, toxic.

Feeling his muscles knot, Kenneth stepped up. He hadn't liked Jake on sight and the idea of punching him in the face wasn't exactly unappealing. "One more crack out of you and the girls won't be the ones showing you the door." He'd always felt contempt for men who made unflattering sexual remarks about the women they'd slept with. It wasn't only immature; it was disrespectful.

Jake held up his hands in appeal. This time his smile wasn't so self-assured, cocky. "I'm a jerk, I get that," he said through a cold stretch of his lips.

Tessa nodded her agreement. "That's saying the least of it."

Kenneth placed a hand on Tessa's shoulder. She tensed momentarily, then relaxed and accepted his touch. "Instead of going at it tooth and nail, just stay to the business at hand."

Gaze cooling, Tessa nodded her agreement. "The sooner you show us, the sooner you can leave."

Jake stepped up to the crate, reaching inside to retrieve an object protected by layers of heavy bubble wrap. "You won't kick me out once you've seen this." Going down on his knees as though weighed down by an object of great and holy reverence, he unwrapped the package. "Keep in mind this has been underwater for a long time. It took months to restore, though I think my team did a pretty good job."

A statue about three feet in length was revealed. The top half of the figure was instantly recognizable as a woman: long hair, full breasts, slender waist. Her bottom half didn't show two legs, as would be expected. From the waist down, her figure was that of a sea creature. The mermaid appeared to be poised as though to rise from the water, her left arm extended toward the sky. What the figure might have held in her hand had gone missing centuries ago.

Jake slowly lifted the statue, showing all angles. Painstakingly cleaned and polished, it was a striking piece. "Isn't she beautiful? The detailing is perfect."

"Heavenly goddess," Gwen murmured, reaching for the crystal hanging around her neck. "It's a Mer."

"I don't believe it," Addison added. "It looks just like . . ."

"Us," Tessa finished grimly.

Awed by the craftsmanship that had gone into the piece, Kenneth whistled under his breath. "It's a stunning piece of work." What had been merely curious had truly become fascinating. The twists and turns of the last twenty-four hours were something he could never have dreamed up. He was definitely hooked.

Pleased to be the center of attention, Jake nodded. "What you are looking at is one of the few preserved original bronze statues of the Severe Style, notable for the exquisite rendering of motion and anatomy. It's most assuredly the hand of a great sculptor, one probably hailing from the time of the early Grecian Classical period."

Tessa shrugged. "So it's a Greek statue. That doesn't prove anything. It's probably meant to represent one of Poseidon's sea nymphs."

Jake shook his head. "Many would jump to that conclusion. Except in this case there is more than one relic pointing to the origins of this particular piece."

Tessa snorted. By the look on her face, she was doing her very best to disbelieve everything Jake presented as false and misleading. "What relics?"

Jake Massey graced everyone with a Cheshire's grin. "Though we've only been able to work with underwater subs, we've found enough remnants to convince us that a small island once inhabited the area."

Gwen's brows shot clear off her forehead. "You are fucking kidding."

"I am absolutely serious, Gwen," Jake countered dryly. "Though I have to admit the ruins are far beyond the location I'd initially guessed."

"What kind of remains are there?" Addison asked.

Jake reached back into his crate, drawing out more pieces. "Literally, everything you could imagine. Though we didn't have long to explore the area because of some tricky laws about who the waters belong to, we did manage to bring up a few significant items. Our biggest challenge has been the sheer depth. There are a lot of deep crevasses we just can't penetrate, even with a rover." He unwrapped about half a dozen packages, including a stash of gold coins, a few oddly shaped vases made out of pottery, a marble bust that looked like the head of a woman. The last piece was most puzzling, a long and spiraling loop fashioned out of gold.

"If you look closely, the image cut into the coins also resembles the face of this woman," Jake said, pointing to the marble bust. He handed a couple of the coins to Gwen. "Do you know that woman?"

Looking at the coins, Gwen paled. "Atargatis," she murmured. "The mother-creator of all Mer."

Tessa snatched one of the coins. "It can't be."

Addison looked at the small marble head. "I think it is."

Kenneth glanced over Tessa's shoulder. The coin, about the size of a silver dollar, wasn't perfectly shaped, but it was brilliantly engraved with the face of a woman in profile. A series of strange symbols was stamped in front of her face. The edges of the coin were decorated with a sort of ornamental pattern.

Looking at the piece, he remembered the sudden

cold prickle of disbelief that had crept over him when he'd seen Tessa in her mermaid form. It began to dawn on him that the Mer were an actual people with a viable history, a race that had existed alongside mankind for millennia uncounted. Yet few knew of their existence. He couldn't imagine belonging to a race that had lost its identity, its place in the world. He suddenly understood Tessa's earlier remark, when she'd said she felt like an outsider, always looking in.

"Turn it over," he suggested.

Tessa hesitated, then turned over the coin. A small gasp of surprise escaped her. "It's the Mer," she murmured, casting a glance at the bronze statue Jake had unwrapped. The figure on the coin left no doubt as to what might have been in the statue's upraised hand: a thunderbolt. "I don't believe my eyes."

Jake's grin widened. "I didn't believe it, either. But it's there. It's all there, and so much more."

Tessa's fingers closed around the coin. Kenneth couldn't fail to notice her hand shook. "Where did you find it?"

Jake swept his long bangs away from his angular forehead. One could almost imagine him primping for his close-up. "I wasn't the actual discoverer," he admitted. "The bronze statue there was snagged by accident by Libyan fishermen. My crew and I just happened to be doing some research in Benghazi when they brought some pieces they'd salvaged in to sell."

Addison grimaced. "Lucky break for you."

Jake scrubbed his fashionably stubble-covered jaw. "Not so lucky, actually. It took more than two years to pinpoint the location where the artifacts came from. There's been a lot of volcanic upheaval through the centuries, and the remains are literally scattered for miles across the bottom of the sea. It would take years to map out every square inch of the site, tag, and preserve every artifact."

Addison studied the coins she held, comparing them with the small marble bust about the size of a fist. "It's amazing to think I could be holding something a kinswoman of mine might have held more than a millennium ago."

"Not 'might have held,'" Jake broke in. "Did. Based on the dives I've made, I am convinced the ruins belong to Ishaldi."

"But it's not one hundred percent positive?" Tessa asked.

Jake considered a few of the coins. "Not one hundred percent," he allowed. "But I'd stake my reputation on ninety-eight percent."

Addison snorted a scornful laugh. "Your reputation sucks, Jake. People think you're a nut."

"And a gold digger," Gwen added, no more tactful than her younger sister. "They say you've sold out for working with commercial treasure hunters."

There was a long silence.

Jake Massey's confidence wavered in the wake of their criticism. "It's true I went about presenting my theories in a ham-fisted manner," he said, clasping his hands behind his back and rocking on his heels. "But I've always felt the evidence would be found."

Kenneth listened closely as Jake explained his find. He had to admit the subject fascinated him. As a person who had just learned of the existence of mermaids, he was still in the early stages of discovery. Sure, his initial disbelief had passed. He'd seen Tessa in her Mer form with his own eyes. And now that he knew her, he wanted to know more about her kind.

And even though he didn't like the presenter behind the information, he couldn't resist the niggle of curiosity. "Now that you've found what you believe to be the location, how exactly will you go about presenting proof of their existence?" he asked. "Short of having a mermaid show up, it's all still pretty much speculation, right?"

Jake scowled at the interruption. His cool gaze raked over Kenneth, though not as dismissively as before. "Although there is a lot of lore surrounding the Mer, I believe I can absolutely present their existence as fact."

Spreading his hands, Kenneth gave him his best *show me* expression. "How?" he asked.

"I'd like to know that one myself," Gwen broke in.

Tessa and Addison nodded, too.

Jake looked at the girls. "You've already given me a good foundation to build on by identifying your mother-goddess. It's true, isn't it, that you were taught to acknowledge Atargatis as the creator of the Mer?"

Addison nodded and began to recite from memory, "As God created mankind in his image to live on land, Atargatis created Mer women in hers to occupy the seas. So that the two species could live in harmony, the Mer were granted the ability to shift on land and interact— and mate—with human males."

Jake nodded. "The first known Mer lore dates back to Assyria, which gives us a region to begin the search for artifacts."

Tessa wrinkled her brow. "But wasn't Assyria a primarily desert region?"

Jake beamed, enjoying his glory as the in-resident expert. "At one time the Neo-Assyrian Empire actually extended all the way to the Mediterranean Sea," he corrected. "And while most legends of sea gods and goddesses come out of Greece and Rome in the form of Poseidon and the like, the Assyrian empire actually predates those myths, perhaps even inspired them."

Tessa blinked and fingered the coin she held. Half elation, half disbelief colored her features. "I've always wondered about where we came from, where we might have belonged."

Jake nodded. "To this day we're still uncovering artifacts that prove what many take for myth is based on actual fact."

Gwen shook her head. "I've always thought Ishaldi was a myth, and I'm a Mer." A short laugh escaped her.

Addison eyed her sisters with a searching look. "I think that's why the Mer have become endangered." She looked at her sisters. "We've spent most of our lives trying not to be Mer."

Tessa nodded. "That's true. Part of the reason Mom and Aunt Gail fought so much was because Gail wanted to raise her girls as human. Gail even sold her share in the island to our parents, because she wanted to leave everything behind. I'm afraid that's what broke our grandmother's heart so much. Grandma wanted us to hang on to our Mer heritage, however little of it we had to hang on to."

"So you have relatives living on the mainland?" Kenneth asked.

Tessa frowned. "Oh, yeah. But Aunt Gail cut contact years ago, when Gwen was still in diapers and Addison was just a twinkle in Daddy's eyes. I barely remember my cousins."

"It would be logical the Mer moved inland and integrated with humans," Jake added. "As I mentioned before, there were a lot of volcanic upheavals on land and at sea during those times, which might explain the destruction. One that stands out in my mind is the Crete earthquake of AD 365. The quake was followed by a tsunami that devastated several coasts on the Mediterranean."

"Something like that could have taken a small island under," Addison said. "I mean, look at the recent earthquakes in Haiti and China. The devastation is almost endless."

"Based on the account I found in Hypatia's writings and the fact she lived during the time the events took place, it would seem as close to an eyewitness account as can be found." Jake shook his head. "More of the Mer might have been known if only the library of Alexandria had survived."

Gwen thought a moment. "That's underwater now, isn't it? Alexandria, I mean."

Jake nodded. "Very little of the ancient city has survived into the present day. Much of the royal and civic quarters sank beneath the harbor due to the earthquake I mentioned earlier. What remained has been built over in modern times."

Kenneth listened closely, putting the pieces together for himself. Even without Massey's explanations, the facts were beginning to stack up. "You can't argue with what he's shown you so far."

Addison knelt down on the rug Jake used to showcase the artifacts. "Holding these pieces in your hands does make it all seem real." Previously overlooked, the spiraling circle caught her attention. She pointed. "That's gold, isn't it?"

Jake picked up the artifact, turning it every which way. "Pure gold." He indicated some of the finer details. "Damned if I know what it was used for. Something ornamental, I'm sure. Maybe it would be easier to identify if all the pieces were intact."

Tessa suddenly made an involuntary sound. Something about the piece sparked recognition in her eyes. "Hot damn," she muttered. "I think I've seen one of those before."

Gwen frowned. "Where would you have seen something like that?" her sister demanded, asking the question everyone was thinking.

Raking her hands through her long hair, Tessa's face took on a shadowed, guilty look. "When I was about to turn fifteen, Mom showed me some . . . things she had stored away in the basement."

Kenneth felt his heart skip a beat. His gaze tracked hers, focusing on the mysterious artifact Jake held. It didn't look like anything special. Her admission intrigued, spreading the infection of curiosity. He couldn't remember the last time he'd been so fascinated by a woman. "What kind of things?"

Breath hitching, Tessa laced her fingers together, pressing her hands under her chin. For a moment she looked like a kid who'd gotten caught stealing forbidden cookies out of the jar. "Magical stuff," she mumbled. "Mom told me I had to take care when using them. They're the keys to a Mer's power."

Chapter 9

Tessa shivered as she led the way down into the basement. As a young girl, her mother had shown her a secret, then warned her she must never let her curiosity overcome common sense.

As a young girl, she'd heeded the warning. As a grown woman, she'd become more and more drawn to the Pandora's box of secrets her mother had entrusted to her care.

Gwen followed closely at her heels. "Does anyone get the feeling we're walking into the mouth of doom?"

"Yeah, isn't this the part where the monster reaches out and drags one of us off into the darkness?" Addison added.

"Actually, I think this is the part where Scooby asks Shaggy for a snack," Kenneth put in. "And then the monster pops up."

Jake brought up the rear. "And this is the part where the archaeologist pukes from all the pop culture references before he proceeds to dazzle you all with his brilliance."

Tessa shined her flashlight toward the ceiling, looking for the cord dangling from the overhead lightbulb. Spying it, she reached out and pulled it down. A wash of bright light flooded the basement, instantly chasing away the shadows.

She huffed. "And this is where the leader of the pack says you're all nuts and to stop acting like morons."

Everyone blinked, looking around the basement. Gwen snapped off her flashlight. "We really need to get that light at the top of the staircase fixed," she grumbled.

Tessa frowned. "It's on my to-do list," she said tartly. She never did understand why Gwen offered to pay for repairs on the house, but never quite came through with the money. She suspected the hotel wasn't doing as well as Gwen wanted her to believe. In a tight economy, people just didn't spend a lot of money on vacation and travel.

Addison looked around. "Man, I don't think I've been down here in at least a decade."

It was true. At one time the basement had been out-fitted as a family room, filled with old comfortable furniture, an entertainment center, and a Ping-Pong table. It even branched off to a small bedroom with an attached bathroom.

Gwen yanked away the sheet covering the Ping-Pong table. "Nobody plays anymore," she said, looking at the silent paddles and balls.

"Not since Mom and Dad died, that's for sure," Addison said.

Jake glanced up. "Car accident, if I remember correctly."

Gwen tossed the crumpled sheet on the table. "Yeah," she filled in. "Some teenager with a learner's permit and a lead foot ran a red light at an intersection. They both died instantly. Hard to believe the little fucker walked away without a scratch."

Scrubbing a hand across his face, Kenneth shook his head. "Man," he muttered. "That isn't right or fair."

At the mention of their parents Tessa felt her heart squeeze as if the organ was caught in the grip of an iron fist. "There just wasn't any more time for games."

At fifteen she'd had the weight and responsibility of two younger sisters thrust upon her. Gwen was only thirteen, Addison two years younger. Not only did she have to finish raising the girls, she'd had to deal with teaching them how to navigate the angst-ridden world of being Mer teenagers. Though they'd had a relative on their father's side to help handle the finances until Tessa turned eighteen, their befuddled, never-married uncle Jay knew nothing about raising children.

Hands on her hips, Gwen scanned the basement. "So where is this hidden alcove containing all the secrets of Merdom?" She frowned. "And how come you never told me or Addie about it?"

Tessa stiffened. Of course the shit would hit the fan right after she'd opened her mouth about recognizing one of the artifacts Jake had recovered. "I've wanted to tell you both," she admitted. "But the time never seemed right. I mean, both you and Gwen never really seemed interested in the Mer side."

Addison frowned. "That really sucks that you kept this all to yourself," she said. "I mean, we're both Mer, too. We have a right to know about what we are. *Who* we are."

Tessa passed her hands across her face. "It's not that you didn't have the right to know," she said, almost wishing she'd made no mention of the hidden items. "It's because of the power these things have. You know. The craft Mom warned us not to use."

Addison and Gwen exchanged a look.

"Ah, right," Addison said. "Don't want to be messing with that."

"That can be some bad mojo," Gwen added.

The men just looked confused.

"What the hell is bad mojo?" Jake demanded.

Drawing a deep breath, Tessa indicated the Ping-Pong table. "It's easier to explain if I show you," she said. "Put some muscle into moving that thing, won't you?"

Kenneth headed toward the table. "You going to help?" he asked Jake, cocking his head toward the other side.

"Guess I'd better." Jake took his end. The two men moved the table aside. "This okay?"

"Fine." She pointed to the rug the table had sat on. "Roll that up," she told Gwen and Addison.

The girls rolled. As the rug disappeared, a segment of the floor was revealed. Though the basement floor was bare concrete, the large rug had covered a secret: a section of the floor was hollowed out and covered with a thick piece of plywood.

Addison whistled under her breath. "I never knew that was there."

Tessa knelt, working her fingers into the crack between the plywood and the concrete. "You weren't supposed to know." The plywood wasn't easy to lift. She'd last opened the secret recess almost a year ago, eager to try her hand at a little more Mer-magic.

The experiment hadn't been a success.

Kenneth knelt beside her. "Let me help." Fishing out

a pocketknife, he slid the blade in between the cracks and lifted one corner.

"Thanks." Tessa slid her fingers into the narrow crack and lifted. Jake claimed the section of plywood, setting it aside.

Gwen and Addison shined their flashlights into the narrow recess.

"What's there?" Gwen asked.

Tessa bent, lifting out a small box. "Everything we are as Mer is here." Opening the box, she turned it so everyone could look inside. An elaborate choker fashioned out of gold and diamonds glinted against the black felt lining the box.

Gwen's eyes almost popped out of her head. "Holy shit, is that what I think it is?"

Tessa nodded. "They're not the kind of diamonds you think they are, Gwen," she said. "They're Herkimer diamond crystals, not very valuable at all."

Gwen frowned. "Then why hide them away?"

Jake pointed to the crystal hanging around Gwen's neck. "Crystal magic. Herkimer diamonds have the unique ability to convert one form of energy into another."

Addison raised her brows. "Is that so?"

Jake nodded. "As an example, when pressure is applied to a crystal, energy is released in the form of heat, light, and electrical voltage. This is what is known as 'piezoelectricity.'"

Tessa slowly closed the box. "This crystal is very powerful. Herkimer can be used to enhance telepathy and out-of-body travel, as well as generate manifestation energy." She took out another box, opened it. A small clear crystal orb about the size of an orange nestled on black felt.

"This is what the necklaces we wear are made out of. Crystal quartz, which is the basic stone of all magic. It can be used as the amplifier of other stone energies. It also enhances psychic ability."

Addison reached for the stone around her neck. "Hot damn! That's why we can do what we can do, right?"

Tessa nodded and picked up yet a third box. Opening it, she revealed a variety of gemstones and other crystals. "These stones each have a magical property. Using them can help enhance our own inherited abilities, which we use as shifters to adapt from land to water. It's the power we were all born with as Mer."

Thrusting her hands out in front of her body, Gwen staunchly shook her head. "Oh, no, no! I refuse to mess with that shit."

Tessa looked at her middle sister. "I happen to know you have a very strong talent with this so-called shit, Gwen."

Kenneth picked up one of the random stones, balancing it between thumb and forefinger. "How can a stone be magic?"

Jake scratched his chin. "I suspect it would be in the psi-kinetics, an ability all of us seem to have been born with but few can use."

Kenneth put the stone down. "You just flew over my head with that one."

Having an insider's edge, Jake chuckled wryly. "Try the ability to move things with just a thought. Energy is all around us, and using crystals is one of the ways to tap into that power. What we call magic, the Mers would actually call science."

Kenneth's brows shot up. He looked at Tessa, all wonder and surprise. "You can do that?"

Tessa sighed. "I can, in a limited fashion. So can Addison. Gwen's the best at it, though. She can really get things to jumping when she sets her mind to it."

Gwen stepped away from the hidden recess. "No, don't get me started. I don't do that shit, you hear me."

Tessa looked at her younger sister, so obviously frightened and upset by the day's revelations. "It's a part of what we are, Gwen, a part of our power as Mer."

"And it's something Mom warned us to be careful with," Gwen shot back. "The first thing we learned was not to embrace our inner selves, the darker side of our minds."

Jake looked into the recess. "You said you recognized the artifact upstairs."

Tessa retrieved a larger piece. "This is it," she said, tugging at the silky material cushioning the object. "Except its whole. There were so many pieces missing on the other that I almost didn't make the connection." The wrapping fell away to reveal the complete relic, a glorious piece fashioned of gold and studded with several semiprecious stones.

Jake's blue eyes glittered with greed. "Jesus, it's in pristine condition."

Tessa lifted her brows. "And it's deadly as hell."

It was Jake's turn to look surprised. "Deadly?"

Tessa slipped her arm through the spirals. A bar halted her hand's progress. Her fingers curled around the grip. A large clear-cut stone rested across the top of her knuckles. Other, smaller stones were woven into the gold braid.

Jake's face immediately paled. His eyes narrowed, and the fine lines around his mouth tightened. "Holy Christ, that's not a—" he started to say, ratcheting to his feet. Fear made his voice an octave higher than normal.

Catching Jake's worry, Kenneth also looked more than a little alarmed. "What is that thing?"

Tessa couldn't help grinning. She liked seeing Jake scared shitless. Kenneth Randall had only just walked into the world of the Mer, so he had no idea of what she could do. Jake had a little more experience. Which was probably the reason he'd cut and left town as soon as possible. Simply put, he wasn't taking any chances.

"Mom said it's called a *Ri'kah*," she explained, identifying the deceptively designed, jewel-encrusted gauntlet. "In the old days it's how we defended ourselves."

Stretching her arm straight out in front of her, she closed her eyes and centered her energy. All she needed was one tiny little spark to activate the thing. Catching a glimmer in her mind's eye, she concentrated, pushing the force outward. For a moment sound and light fused, filling and engulfing her with a pulsing, bright static energy.

Feeling heat rise up from inside her, Tessa growled a soft spell, channeling the force she'd whipped up in her mind into the stones. The crystals around her arm began to glow. Almost simultaneously a shot of pure red-hot light beamed from the crystal across her knuckle. It struck the far wall, blasting a small hole into the plaster. Like a Fourth of July firework, sparks showered in a thousand different directions.

Everyone could only stare, thunderstruck.

Addison was the first to break the silence. "Holy shit, I love that!" she said, close to dancing with delight. "How fucking awesome was that?" She headed toward Tessa. "I've got to try that thing."

Frowning severely, Gwen cut her off. "Nobody's going to be playing with it anymore. We don't know

what we've got there and it's too damn dangerous."
She turned toward Tessa, pointing a threatening finger.
"You've got no right to be playing around with things
you don't understand. Take it off. Right now."

Though her initial instinct was to buck Gwen's demands, Tessa decided caution was best. She'd only just
begun to grasp the fundamentals of Mercraft. Right now
a lot of it was pure guesswork. She could do some serious damage without intending to.

"You're right," she said, sliding the weapon off her
arm. "I haven't really gotten the hang of it yet."

Face pale, Jake looked at her through eyes as wide as
saucers. "You could have blown my fucking head off,"
he spat, wiping beads of sweat off his forehead.

Tessa tossed her head. "I wasn't even aiming at you,
idiot." She slipped the weapon off her arm, rewrapping
it, and tucked it back into its hiding place.

Jake's lips twisted with anger. "Bullshit! I saw the
look on your face . . ." For once words seemed to fail
him.

Addison groaned. "Hey, I wanted to try it out."

Gwen frowned and shook her head. "No way am I
letting you play with that, Addie. Knowing you, you'd
find a way to blow the moon out of space."

Addison's face lit up. "Oh, man, that would be fucking fantastic, wouldn't it?"

Tessa snuck a glance toward Kenneth, wondering
what he'd thought of this little display of Mer-magic. He
seemed to be the only one not caught up in the drama.
He was a watcher, an observer, taking everything in its
stride.

Hanging on the periphery of the group, he walked
over to the wall, examining the damage. Scorched pieces

of plaster crumbled into dust when he brushed curious fingers against the deep hole. "Going to take a lot of filler to repair this" was his only comment.

Tessa struggled to tamp down her smirk. Jake was definitely freaked-out, no doubt about it. Good. Let him wonder just what else she had up her sleeve. There was no way she'd ever admit her use of the Ri'kah was more luck than skill. She'd only just figured out what the thing was, and had yet to make it do more than sputter and spark.

Alarm spiked across Gwen's face. "How long have you been messing with this stuff?"

A shiver crawled down Tessa's spine. Inside she felt as if someone had turned up her body's temperature to blazing hot. On the outside, though, her skin felt strangely chilled. Her heart beat hollowly in her chest. Black spots still danced in front of her eyes, part of the aftereffect of focusing her psi-energies.

"I've been dabbling with it off and on for years," she finally admitted. "Mom always promised she'd teach us to use it, control it."

Addison's face lit up. "There's so much we could do if we knew how."

Dismay flashed across Gwen's face. "It's something best left alone."

Shivering harder, Tessa pressed her fingers against the pulse beating in her temple. Though the pressure was beginning to lessen behind her eyes, she could feel a new, sharper ache building. Her stomach clenched, bowels going liquid. She'd drawn out the energy too quickly and was going to pay the price.

She clenched her jaw and swallowed hard to keep the nausea at bay. "It's time we stop denying what we are, Gwen. Our magic is part of our heritage. If we deny it, we deny ourselves. And as long as we keep denying ourselves, we'll never be whole."

Listening to the conversation taking place behind him, Kenneth leaned closer to the damage. The hole Tessa had blasted into the wall was about the size of a fifty-cent piece. The edges were blackened, scorched.

When she'd slid on the arm piece, he'd physically felt her gathering energy, as if sucking it out of the bodies around her and pulling it into her own. The fine hairs on the back of his neck had risen and his skin had gone chilly with goose bumps. Tessa was definitely a phenomenon and he'd experienced the power behind her will.

Curious, he poked his index finger into the blackened cavity. His hand didn't stop until he'd reached the knuckle. Even then he couldn't feel anything under the tip. Though the moment had passed, energy still swirled around the affected area, snapping and crackling. Narrowing his eyes, he could almost catch a glimpse of the tiny charged particles.

Holy cow. If that thing had hit flesh, it would have burned right through it. At first he'd been worried about the idea of a woman living alone in a deserted place. No need for that. It looked like Tessa Lonike was more than capable of taking care of herself. With her fiery red hair and weapon at the ready, she had the appearance of a warrior goddess: fierce, determined, and ready to go to battle again her foes.

In short, she was awesome. Fucking awesome.

And the men better look out.

Leaving the damage behind, he looked toward Tessa. He felt his heart skip a beat. She was still kneeling beside the alcove she'd uncovered. Arms wrapped across her chest, she rubbed her hands vigorously up and down over her skin.

Sensing her distress, Kenneth walked over to her. Bending down beside her, he settled a hand on her back. A strange vibration emanated from her, driven with so much pressure that he felt the force of untapped energy surging through her veins. She was literally trembling to keep it all contained inside.

Resisting the urge to pull his hand away, Kenneth held his palm in place. "Are you okay?"

Mouth tightening, Tessa cast an uneasy stare his way. Her eyes were huge as saucers, her face pale as wax. She looked a little dazed. "I just need to back it down." She blinked hard and drew a deep breath. "Put the leash back on the black dog."

He kept his hand in place. "The black dog?"

"It's what we call the darker side of our power," Gwen said quietly. "When you have a force, a presence living inside you, you have to be careful to keep it under control."

Kenneth looked at Gwen. Arms locked across her chest, her stance was tense, tight. She clearly didn't like talking about the Mer or their capabilities. "What do you mean, a presence living inside you?"

Jake glanced at the girls sharply. By the look on his face, his mind was working furiously. "You're not talking about some sort of symbiote, are you?"

Gwen nodded. "It happens in the womb, I think. Something in our genetic structure destroys the traits of our human fathers and reshapes us into Mer." One of her hands lifted to the crystal around her neck. "It may seem ghoulish, but Mer are born inanimate. It's at birth we receive the *breofe*, or the breath of life and our crystals."

A cold chill washed over Kenneth. "You mean Mer are born dead?" He didn't like the idea of dead babies. It creeped him out.

Reining in her inner energies, Tessa's skin began to return to a normal temperature. She lifted her chin. "Not dead," she corrected. "Just inert." She thrust out her arms, showing the pattern on her bare skin. "That's how you know something's inside you. It grows, from the inside out."

The other two girls showed their markings.

"When we're born, our skin is clear. But by the time a Mer turns eleven or twelve, her symbiote begins to emerge," Addison explained. "When human girls are getting their menstrual cycles, we're beginning to see our symbiote mature. It's about that time we begin to learn to control the energies necessary for the shift."

"And it's about that time you learn you'd better be careful with what you think," Gwen added through a deep frown. "It isn't funny when a stray thought manifests into something physical."

Jake nodded. "That's entirely feasible. Such paranormal activity has been noted in some adolescent girls. I can't help but wonder if those girls have a bit of diluted Mer in their bloodlines."

"A mermaid who isn't given her soul-stone at birth never fully develops," Gwen said. "The symbiote inside just shrivels up and dies because it hasn't got any energy to feed on. It could be part of the reason we've become so endangered. It seems like, over the years, most Mers wanted their daughters to be plain old humans."

"Nobody wants to be plain old human," Jake grumbled. "It's boring. You have such a gift, yet you choose not to use it."

Gwen's eyes narrowed with anger. "It's a not a gift if people treat you like a freak, Jake. Don't forget how good you humans are at destroying anything you find frightening or different."

Addison nodded her agreement. "Yeah. Don't forget, they were still burning witches until the nineteenth century. Just because we're in the twenty-first century doesn't mean people are more civilized. It just means they have more ways to exploit us."

"Kind of like you, Jake," Tessa pointed out. "Admit it. You'd love to bask in the glow of revealing a lost species to the world."

Kenneth inwardly winced. He didn't want to imagine where that sort of revelation would put Tessa and her sisters if their kind were exposed. One only had to turn on the nightly news or open a scandal sheet to see how the media ran any subject it deemed newsworthy straight into the ground. The press was relentless, ferocious in their pursuit of anything that would drive ratings and revenue higher. Like jackals scenting blood, they ran their prey to exhaustion before devouring all—blood, flesh, and bone.

The girls wouldn't have a chance.

"Maybe it would be better if this stuff stays at the bottom of the ocean," he suggested.

Jake immediately shook his head. "Whether the girls like it or not, this stuff is starting to come up. It won't stay hidden forever. There are a lot of treasure hunters on the high seas, and as the technology for deep-sea exploration improves, more will be found."

Pressing a hand to her forehead, Tessa closed her eyes. "He's right, damn it. If Ishaldi is there, it's going to be found."

Gwen shrugged. "So what? It's not like they can point at us and say there's a Mer just because they drag a few mermaid statues and coins out of the water."

Tessa let her hand drop. Face drawn, her green eyes snapped with raw will. "You're not getting it, Gwen. I'm tired of hiding and I'm tired of worrying if we're the last few Mer on the face of the earth. Maybe if we came out, others would, too. Who knows how many more Mer may be out there?"

Gwen threw up her hands in horror. "We are most certainly not going to do anything like that."

Frustration rolling through him, Kenneth stepped between the bickering sisters. "What about a compromise, then," he suggested. "Nobody has to know you as Mer. But they can know you as the discoverers of a lost world."

Jake rocked back on his heels. "That's something to consider," he allowed. "Both Tessa and Addison have worked with me on archaeological surveys of the state's underwater maritime resources. Bringing them back onto my team might be just what I need to reestablish my legitimacy with the state's sea grant program."

"Why would you need the state's involvement for something in the Mediterranean Sea?" Kenneth asked. "If I remember correctly, you work with a salvage and rescue outfit."

A slight look of embarrassment skittered across Jake's face. "Worked." He cleared his throat. "Unfortunately, all operations have recently ceased due to a little mismanagement."

Though he might know nothing about the Mer, Kenneth understood the hard realities of business. The one thing he'd learned as a business owner was that you didn't spend more than you earned and you didn't overextend your line of credit. "How much mismanagement?"

Silence filled the basement.

Shoving his hands in his pockets, Jake's golden brows furrowed. "We've run out of money to continue our excavation of the site," he admitted after a long pause. "Between getting the equipment, paying the crew, and fighting off the bill collectors, we've flat run out of funds."

Kenneth nodded. "I see. But aren't there are always investors in this sort of thing?"

One expensive leather boot scuffing the bare floor, Jake snorted. "Try getting investors when your reputation among your colleagues is shot to hell. No one takes me at my word because no one believes Ishaldi or the Mer ever existed. It's like Atlantis, Shangri-la, El Dorado, or even the Lost Dutchman's Gold Mine. There're lots of stories, but everyone thinks they're myths. And with today's economy hitting rock bottom, people want a solid investment for their money."

"So what were you planning to do?" Kenneth asked.

Jake fidgeted, rocking his weight from foot to foot. "I'm trying to arrange for a museum to purchase the artifacts. The immensity of the find is staggering, so I'm hoping such an organization would grant the necessary funds to return to the location before another outfit moves into the area."

Gwen looked at Jake sharply. "What other outfit?"

Jake shrugged. "We've got competition. EU Explorations, a Spanish outfit, is also working the area. Unfortunately we didn't get all the artifacts the fishermen brought in from the initial haul. Word's out there's gold, and a lot of it. Though they haven't got the actual location yet, they've got the money and equipment to stay out on the water until they do find it."

Tessa blew out a breath. "Shit. As always, you're a day late and a dollar short, Jake."

The archaeologist threw up his hands. "Tell me about it. The thing is, I'm in it for the find, for the preservation of a lost civilization. They're in it for the haul, the loot. If the EU Explorations divers get in there first, they'll strip it and market it the way looters used to plunder Egyptian tombs before it became illegal. None of it will hit the museums and the cultural revelations will most likely be lost."

"So it's an all-you-can-locate buffet," Addison said. "Finders keepers, right?"

Jake grimaced. "Twenty-one modern states have a coastline on the Mediterranean Sea, but Ishaldi's location lies outside the coastal regions of most. Whichever country gets there first is probably the one that's going to try to declare it theirs. As a research vessel, we'd be under the authority of the United States."

Tessa nibbled her lower lip. "We wouldn't want someone else to steal this out from under our noses." By the look on her face, the gears in her head were turning full speed ahead. Of the sisters, Tessa seemed to be the one who wanted to seek an actual connection with her lost heritage.

"If anything came out of it, we would want control," Addison added.

Kenneth nodded. What he'd heard so far made a lot of sense. "So what happens to a find of that magnitude? Where exactly would its artifacts end up?"

Jake beamed, enjoying his role as the resident expert. "Barring that you haven't already got a significant university or museum attached, you start your own. Though some archaeologists are of the mind not to disturb a significant find, others think it's fair to remove the artifacts to spare them further damage and deterioration."

Gwen perked up. "Say no one else is involved. Is it possible we could open our own museum to share the discovery with the public? Do something right here?"

Tessa's head swiveled toward her sister. "You mean here, in Port Rock?"

"Why not? If those artifacts have to come up, where else would they belong? The local lore about mermaids is already part of our tourist trade, something we need desperately to make a living. Adding a museum to go with the hotel would really add to our cachet as a tourist destination."

"Attaching a conservation and research laboratory would add to its legitimacy," Jake added. "I could head the department myself."

Kenneth eyed the archaeologist but said nothing. He'd already noticed Jake was good at maneuvering things to his advantage. An hour ago he'd been a rotten bastard. Now he was a conquering hero. It was amazing how men like Jake could walk through shit and still come out smelling like a rose. Somehow guys like Massey always found a way to land on their feet even when pushed off the gangplank.

Still, some people weren't completely fooled, or blind to the ulterior motives of others.

Addison rolled her eyes. "How is it you're against everything Mer until cold hard dollars enter the equation?" she asked Gwen. "You're starting to sound like Jake."

Jake frowned, washing his expression in innocence.

"Thanks, but I am not just in it for the enhancement of my checkbook."

Gwen shot everyone a look. "Well, I would be. And if we're going to do this, it's going to have to be with the full consent of everyone involved. While I am not wild about the idea of coming out as a Mer, I can see the advantages of being part of a significant archaeological find. If we happen to make money off it in the process, well, all the better. We still have to eat."

Tessa nodded. "I would agree with that."

But Gwen wasn't finished. "The one thing I don't agree with is bringing in a lot of outsiders. I want this kept in the family." She shot a look at Jake. "Don't get to thinking this gives you a free pass. You've still got a lot of ass kissing to do to make things right."

Jake grinned and waggled a lecherous brow. "I'll kiss any ass that presents itself."

Ignoring the crude remark, Gwen sent a look toward Kenneth. "And I still don't know how you fit in," she said through a sigh. "But you do."

Kenneth kept his own face neutral. Getting kicked out of the inner circle now would truly suck. "Thanks."

Tessa narrowed her eyes. "He fits because he knows we're Mer." After a brief hesitation, she added, "And because he's with me."

Shaking his head, Jake rubbed his eyes. "Okay, let's say we keep this to present company only. It takes a hell of a lot of money to run an operation like this, and someone's got to step forward and write the checks." Hand dropping, his gaze swept the room. "Somehow I don't think anyone here has the ability to fork out a few million dollars."

Faces fell all around. The fanciful speculation of the

last few minutes deflated like a balloon with a slow leak. Talking about an expedition of that magnitude was one thing. Actually accomplishing it was quite another.

Though he listened closely, Kenneth kept his face carefully neutral. On one single point, Jake Massey was dead wrong.

Though he said nothing that would reveal his interest in the expedition, he'd already calculated the necessary figures. With a single phone call he could easily lay his hands on the cash needed to finance the recovery.

Only a single question remained.

Should he make the offer?

Chapter 10

Kenneth set his duffel bag down on the bed. Tessa's bed. In Tessa's room. He'd been kicked out of his quarters since Jake had commandeered the lighthouse as his personal command post. Not that the archaeologist knew Kenneth was supposed to be living there. Since Tessa had earlier identified them as a couple, Jake had naturally assumed they were sharing a room.

Tomorrow Jake planned to hit the phones, touching base with his old contacts. Though his professional reputation was frayed, he still had a good shot at finding the necessary funding. He planned to show the newly discovered artifacts to a few select collectors who had the muscle of money.

No one was happy about the idea of bringing in outsiders. All three of the sisters were feeling a personal connection, and bringing in an outside investor would mean giving up a portion of any artifacts recovered.

Given the excitement of the day, both Gwen and Addison had decided to sleep over, and both currently occupied their old childhood rooms. As the fourth bedroom had been converted into storage after Tessa moved into the master suite her parents had occupied, that left the couch for Kenneth.

Not that he minded. All he needed was a place to stretch out. Didn't matter how comfortable, either. As long as he was on his back, he could sleep. All he needed to do was borrow Tessa's bathroom for a quick shower and he'd be set for the night.

Kenneth unzipped his bag, digging out some fresh clothes. Since he didn't own a pair of pajamas, he'd just put on a pair of fresh jeans and a T-shirt and call it good.

He glanced toward Tessa. She presently stood on the small balcony outside her room, which afforded a fantastic view of the lighthouse and the open water beyond. Leaning against the railing, she stared out into the distance. She'd let her long hair down and it streamed around her shoulders and down her back like liquid fire.

Looking at her, Kenneth felt his throat tighten. Heat boiled in his core, his body hardening with instant response.

He swallowed, fighting to keep his desire in check. Tessa's shoulders and back were stiff with tension. She wasn't happy.

Kenneth knew why. *She's thinking about selling.*

After Jake had departed to set himself up in the lighthouse—Addison had the good sense to retrieve Kenneth's belongings before the archaeologist had taken over the loft—the sisters had sat down at the kitchen table and begun to talk. Over a few glasses of wine and multiple cups of coffee, Addison and Gwen had broached the subject that seemed to upset Tessa most of all: selling the island.

Though Kenneth hadn't been privy to the conversation, he couldn't help overhearing bits and pieces as he helped Jake repack the artifacts. He'd expected Tessa to put her foot down and say no, to kibosh the idea with her usual fierce resistance.

Except she hadn't.

Kenneth cleared his throat, reminding her of his presence. "I'll just catch a quick shower, then be out of your way."

Tessa glanced over her shoulder. "What? Oh, don't worry about it. You can stay if you want. The couch downstairs sucks to sleep on."

The bed. Ah, he could almost imagine the feel of sinking down into that delicious oasis of pleasure with Tessa pressed beneath him.

Except he had a feeling she wasn't in the mood for any naughty business. Her mind was definitely on another subject. She'd probably made the offer to be nice, perhaps even to spare his back a few aches.

Kenneth shrugged. No reason to make a pest of himself. "The couch will do me fine."

A slight smiled turned up her cherry red lips. "I would have thought you would have jumped at the chance to get into bed with me again." She shook her head. "You're too nice for your own good."

He laughed. "Well, you did kick me out earlier and say you didn't want to get involved."

She grimaced. "Then I opened my mouth and inserted my foot by telling Jake we were a couple."

"I was wondering when you were going to mention that. There are certain liberties that go along with being a team."

A spark of interest glinted in Tessa's eyes. Pursing her mouth, she asked, "Such as having sex?"

Kenneth shook his head. "I've got something else in mind."

Her eyes widened. He clearly wasn't taking the bait she'd tossed his way.

Not yet, anyway.

"What?" she asked.

Retrieving a pack of cigarettes from his bag, Kenneth walked out onto the balcony. Carrying the bracing scent of seawater, the night's cool breeze caressed his skin. The sounds of the water sloshing against the rocks filled his ears. Above his head, the sky was clear and filled with stars. Stars that reminded him of the glittering crystals Tessa had revealed. Like her, the island was magical. Special. He had a feeling one couldn't exist without the other.

Tearing the cellophane wrapper off the top, he tapped one out of the pack. Rolling the rest up in the sleeve of his T-shirt, he dug out a plastic lighter.

Kenneth sucked on the tip, inhaling a deep, calming rush of nicotine-laced smoke. "A couple usually implies two people working toward a common goal. Two people who want the same thing at the same time."

Tessa gave him a wary look. The one-night stand she was into. The long-term thing spooked her. "Uh, yeah. I guess you could say that."

Kenneth released his breath. "And while it's true I would love to get into those silky little panties of yours again, there's something I want more than sex."

Sparks of cynicism glinted in the depth of her eyes. "That's a first."

He flicked away gray ashes. "I'm thinking about a partnership, something that might be mutually beneficial to both of us."

Tessa's brows lifted. "What kind of partnership?"

Kenneth had her stumped. He'd turned down sex, yet was proposing an affiliation. "I know you're considering selling the island to finance Jake's venture, but I don't want you to do that."

"I don't want to do that, either," she admitted after a moment. "But it seems to be the only way we can raise the funds without going to an outside investor."

Kenneth considered the trail of smoke wafting up from his cigarette, quickly whisked out of existence by the night wind. "I'm not an outsider," he said quietly.

Tessa narrowed her eyes. "Don't be an ass. I'm not in the mood for games."

Heart thumping hard against his rib cage, Kenneth shook his head. "I'm not playing games with you, Tessa. I've got money—a substantial amount."

She blinked at his statement. "Right. And you can just pull millions of dollars out of your back pocket."

Taking a final drag, Kenneth snuffed out the remnants of his cigarette. Flipping the butt over the edge, he reached for his wallet. Unfolding the worn leather, he picked out a folded piece of paper. "Read this." He handed over an article cut out of the newspaper.

Tessa glanced at the headline. "Marsham heiress murdered in carjacking." She shot him a puzzled look. "Your wife?"

Kenneth's stomach knotted. "Yes. If you'll read the article, you'll see I was married to Jennifer Marsham."

Tessa read the article. Her mouth moved a little as she scanned its contents. "The Marsham Investment firm," she murmured at one pertinent point. "Dr. Jennifer Marsham . . . worth millions." She glanced up in confusion. "You're barely mentioned."

"Jennifer used her maiden name for career purposes," he explained. "That and the fact her parents didn't like me."

Her lips pursed. "Oh?"

Kenneth showed her his hands, which were battered and scarred from years of work with the tools of his trade. "They hated that their darling little girl married a grubby mechanic. In their eyes I wasn't good enough for Jen."

It was reaching the point where she began to believe it, too, he thought ruefully. Although he hadn't wanted to admit it, their marriage had been on shaky ground when Jen died. Their planned trip to Maine was more than an anniversary vacation. It was going to be an attempt to keep things together.

Tessa growled. "That sucks. They should have been glad she found someone she loved who would treat her right."

Kenneth mulled Tessa's words. He'd done his best to please Jen. He worked hard, didn't carouse, came home after work. If anything, it was his wife who'd kept the late hours, failing to show up for social events or missing appointments. She blamed it on the pressures of her blossoming career.

He'd understood, tried to be patient.

Jennifer had even agreed she needed to slow down, take some time off. The monthlong vacation they'd planned was going to be a celebration, too. With a baby on the way it, seemed to be a sign that things were going to work out. All they needed was a chance to start over . . .

Feeling the twinge of a headache creeping in around his temples, Kenneth rubbed his eyes. Damn. To lose the woman he loved just when things were starting to look up was like taking a spike through the heart. The damage was irreparable. The ache would always be there.

No. Their marriage hadn't been perfect. But he believed they could have fixed what was going wrong—if only Jen's parents would have butted out. He'd learned the hard way that when you married one Marsham, you married them all.

A compassionate hand settled on his arm. "You okay?" a soft voice asked. "You're awfully quiet."

Brow furrowing with frustration, Kenneth quickly lowered his hand. "Sorry. I was just thinking about other things."

Tessa's hand fell away, leaving a cold spot in its wake. Her expression grew somber. "Didn't mean to stir up bad memories."

Kenneth shook his head. "You didn't do anything wrong."

Digging up bones, examining the past would do him no good.

Jennifer was gone and so was the life they'd attempted to build together. Whatever mistakes they'd made, whatever choices they'd settled on meant nothing, wiped away in an instant by the bullet fired from the carjacker's gun.

Tessa folded the delicate piece of newsprint, offering it back to him. "I'm going to assume they circled the wagons after her death."

Kenneth accepted the paper, closing it in his fist. He had no idea why he'd carried it for so long. He certainly didn't need the reminder. Just thinking about the way he'd been treated by Jennifer's family was enough to cool his thoughts.

"They cut me off cold. And the first thing they did after Jen's funeral was take me to court."

Tessa's eyes widened. "Why?"

Kenneth considered the crumpled piece of paper he held, as dry and coarse as he felt inside. "Along with her life insurance, Jennifer had quite a substantial amount in a trust fund her grandfather had set up for her. As her husband, I was entitled to inherit a portion. They fought tooth and nail to disinherit me, even accusing me of arranging her murder to get my hands on her money."

She sighed sympathetically. "Holy shit. That must have been awful for you."

Tossing the article away, Kenneth raked his hands over his numb face. "Awful doesn't begin to describe that nightmare. Even though I was proven innocent, it still left a bitter taste in my mouth."

"I would think so."

He leaned against the railing, closing his fingers around the edges until his knuckles showed white. Muscles knotting, he could feel the stress all the way to his bones. "To make a long story short, I inherited quite a bit of money from Jen's estate."

"Oh." She hesitated. "That must have helped."

Kenneth mentally recoiled at her comment. He knew she meant it in a good and kind sort of way. Jen's parents had treated him like a sleaze, a gold digger.

"Not really," he said, attempting to distance himself from the bad memories. "I've never touched it. I never wanted to. It felt like I'd somehow profited from her death."

Tessa's brows puckered. "I can't even begin to imagine what you must have gone through."

Drawing a breath, Kenneth forced himself to let go of the anger and guilt he'd carried through so many long months. There was no reason to go into details with her. She wasn't involved. The past, how he'd gotten the money, wasn't anything she had to concern herself with. It was the future he was contemplating. And though he wasn't exactly sure of what he wanted for his future, he knew he wanted Tessa in his life somehow. If she needed his financial support, he'd gladly help her out. He wasn't relieving a guilty conscience, but he would welcome relief from the burden.

"I finally know what I want to do with the money. I want to give it to you."

His words made her frown, transforming her expression from compassionate to alarmed. Her eyes widened with shock. "That's not right—" she started to say. "I couldn't accept it."

Kenneth let go of the rail. He reached out, catching her hand. His fingers closed around her smaller, more delicate ones. "I want to invest the money in the recovery of your homeland. I know you want to find out more about who your people were, where they came from."

Tessa nodded. "That's true. But I can't take money from a stranger."

Kenneth interrupted her protest by pressing a finger across her lips. "After what we did last night, I'm not a stranger anymore."

Heart skipping a beat, Tessa closed her eyes. Her pulse roared in her veins. His touch was electric, setting her to boiling. Last night she'd found a lot of pleasure in making love to him. His body inside hers had felt so good, so right. They fitted perfectly together.

Yet she'd been the one to push him away, demanding distance. She'd said she wasn't ready, didn't want a serious entanglement.

So what do you want? a small inner voice demanded insistently.

I don't know, came her silent reply. *I just don't know*.

Frustrated, Tessa forced her eyes open. She took a step back, putting some distance between herself and

Kenneth. She needed to cool off, get her head back on straight. One more touch from him and she'd melt into a gooey pool of need.

"What happened last night isn't connected with what you're offering right now." She pressed a hand against her abdomen. An uncomfortable feeling curled in the pit of her stomach. "Last night was just sex. This is something on a whole different level."

"Why?" He shrugged. "I have the money. I want to give it to you. I don't have a problem with that."

Tessa immediately waved her hands in front of her. "Oh, no, no. Last night you slept with me and today you're offering me money. That would make me no better than a whore, and we're not going there."

Kenneth's gaze darkened. "I suppose a lot of people would think of it that way. You slept with me, now I'm paying you."

Tessa nodded vigorously. Although she was touched by his offer, the truth was she barely knew the man. Yes, there was an attraction between them. That was true enough. They'd both felt the sparks flying, and had taken advantage of the moment. But one night wasn't a commitment, not of her heart or her mind.

Her head spun. Sex was the clash of two bodies, all hormones and heat. Something that should have been easy to leave behind. However, Kenneth wasn't making it easy for her to walk away.

Even worse, he seemed ready to jump in, both feet first. He'd already been hurt once. She didn't want to see him burned again. She definitely didn't want to be his rebound woman. Relationships like that never worked out. When she went in again, she wanted a solid foundation beneath her feet.

She drew a deep breath. The scent and spice emanating off his muscular frame wafted on the night breeze, arousing her voracious craving to be taken again, and again.

Quickly shaking off the carnal notions, she cleared her throat. She had to dig deep and be honest. "I think it's great of you to make the offer. But there's no way I could accept. It wouldn't feel right." A small shiver swept down her spine. "You know. Sleeping with you because I need the cash."

Kenneth's gaze found hers. His dark eyes, the color of coffee cut with cream, glittered with longing. "Are you refusing the money because you intend to sleep with me again, or because you aren't?"

His question caught her by surprise. "What?" She swallowed a laugh, not quite understanding the meaning—or the implications.

His gaze never left hers. Desire flamed in their depths. "If you won't give me a chance to be with you because I have money, I'll get rid of every last penny I have."

Tessa blinked. "That doesn't make sense."

"Makes perfect sense to me. If you like me better as a poor man, then I'll be as poor as you want me to be."

Tessa threw up her hands. "I don't want you to be poor," she said. "I just want you to be happy." The words popped out before she'd even had time to think about them, or examine their meaning.

Kenneth drew a deep breath. "I'll be happy if you give me a chance. But if you can't, I won't shrivel up and die. I'm a big enough boy to take my pink slip and move on down the road. However, I didn't offer you the money to entice you into being with me."

She eyed him, taking in his tall frame and plain but open features. A shiver took hold. Desire? Uncertainty? Probably both. Kenneth was a nice man, a good man.

The decent sort of man most women wished they'd meet and marry. There was no doubt he'd be reliable, dependable, a rock to cleave to when times got hard. "You didn't?"

He shook his head. "No. I offered because I really see the desire in you to know more about Ishaldi, and where your kind came from. It's a wonderful chance for you to rediscover your people and their culture. I have the money and I can think of no better way to spend it than by funding your expedition."

Tessa could hardly believe her ears. "That's awfully generous. But what if you spend it, just to find Jake's wrong?" she asked, trying to be sensible. People lost fortunes in the pursuit of treasure every day. She didn't want to be responsible for tossing good cash away in the pursuit of an empty dream.

Kenneth burst out laughing. "So what? It's only money." He held out his hands. "As long as I've got use of these and a strong back, I can make a good living, Tessa. A mechanic's wage might not put you in a mansion on the hill, but it'll keep a roof over your head and food in your mouth."

Tessa thought about the news clipping he'd shown her. Despite his words, Kenneth was a man who'd married into money. He wanted better, had known the finer things in life. Why would he want to saddle himself down with a woman whose only asset was an island with a crumbling house and a lighthouse that really wasn't even needed anymore?

She fought to swallow past the tightness in her throat. "That's easy for you to say, but it's different when you're dead broke. I'm broke, absolutely busted. The insurance money my parents left behind is all but gone. This month I can pay the bills, but next month I can't." Her

jaw tightened. "The island is going to have to be sold . . .
Just not to fund some dumbass thing Jake's pulled out
of the air."

Kenneth reached out, catching her hands in his. He
tugged her closer, bringing her within kissing distance.
"I'm not deaf. I overheard you and Gwen fighting about
money yesterday. I also heard your reasons for not wanting to sell the island—so you'd always have a home for
the daughters you hope to have someday."

Throat closing, Tessa tipped her head back. Her vision blurred. A single tear slipped down her cheek. "It's
all we have left," she whispered, fighting to breathe past
the lump rising in her throat. "We can't lose this place.
It's our home. More than Ishaldi, it's where we belong
now. I can let that dream go, but I can't lose this place."

Kenneth's grip on her hands tightened. "You don't
have to let it go. I can help."

Tessa blinked, refusing to let another tear fall. If there
was one thing she hated, it was being weak. Pathetic.
She'd always taken care of things for her younger sisters,
made things right so they could survive—and thrive—
in the human world. "It wouldn't be right. I've always
taken care of things. I'll just have to work harder." She
tried to pull her hands away.

Kenneth tightened his grip, refusing to let her go. "All
my life I've been told that people who come from the
wrong side of the tracks couldn't succeed. I've never believed that. I've worked hard to prove naysayers wrong.
I got myself through college, and even had the luck to
marry well."

She shrugged. "Luck just wasn't on my side. And I
wasn't born an heiress."

Kenneth shook his head. "I'm not trying to say I've
had all the breaks and you had none. What I am trying

to say is that I know what it's like to go through the trials alone. I don't like alone, Tess." He tugged her closer, guiding her hands around his narrow hips. "I want someone there, standing beside me. I want you."

Lowering his head, his mouth brushed hers, excruciatingly light and deliberately slow. He simply conveyed his desire without pushing for a response from her side.

The ball was in her court.

She could refuse to play the game and walk away. Or she could follow through with the return.

Untangling her fingers from his, Tessa curled her fingers into the loops of his jeans. Kenneth, she thought as she pushed herself up on the tips of her toes to deepen their kiss, was as relentless and tenacious as a bulldog. He knew what he wanted and went after it.

Lost in the moment, she let sensation take over. His lips were warm, his touch restrained. By the tremble rumbling through his body, she knew he was holding himself back, trying not to spook her with the intensity behind his desire. There was no doubt. He wanted her. Would do anything for her.

Too good to be true?

Maybe.

Did she care?

At the moment, no.

The need for breath pulled them apart. As the moment ended, Tessa drew away, tingling to her toes, stomach fluttering as a sweet ache spread through her.

Kenneth's lips brushed her forehead. "Feels like you've changed your mind." His hand slid up, cupping her left breast. He brushed a thumb over her rapidly hardening nipple with an arousing pressure. Pressed hip to hip, she felt his erection pressed between them.

A long breath shuddered out of her. "You've worn

me down. It's just easier to stand still." She waited in suspense for the surrender she knew she would willingly make to his hard male body. All he had to do was make the move and she'd melt.

Kenneth's brows arched, concern lighting his features. "You're shaking."

His nearness wasn't helping her think straight either. "I know." Unable to wait any longer, she began tugging his shirt out of his jeans.

The pressure of Kenneth's hands circling her wrists was strong and sure. "We don't have to do anything."

Tessa considered his words. "So you're leaving it up to me?"

He nodded. "Pretty much. I want things to happen between us, but I'm not going to force the issue."

"And if I say no, and keep saying no?"

He maddeningly refused to be baited. "I'll accept it."

She nibbled her lip. "And still give me the money?"

He grinned and let go of her wrists. "As much as you need."

Tessa nodded. If his intent was to intrigue, he'd certainly managed to do just that. She didn't figure him to be the sort of man who played games. Rather, he seemed to be one who shot straight from the hip. "I see."

A roll of his broad shoulders was indication of his shrug. "Just call me a decent guy."

She laughed. "Hasn't anyone told you nice guys finish last?"

He flashed a cocky smile. "Not this one."

Tessa cocked a brow. "So how much money are you talking about anyway?"

Kenneth folded his arms over his chest. "Honestly?"

Narrowing her eyes, she nodded. "Honestly."

He did some mental figuring. "Almost eight million."

Tessa sucked in a startled breath. If her jaw hadn't been attached to her face, it would have hit the floor at her feet. "Did you say million?" She gulped.

Eyes crinkling around the edges, he cleared his throat. "Yeah. As in six zeroes after the number eight."

Holy cow. Given the simple clothes he wore and his lack of material possessions, Tessa would have guessed he barely had two nickels to rub together. For a millionaire, he was pretty down to earth. Marrying into money obviously hadn't turned his head. One of the many things she liked about him was his simple, honest manner. He didn't consider himself too good to work.

Open your eyes, idiot, an insistent inner voice prodded. *Look at what's in front of you.*

Tessa looked. Though she couldn't read his mind, she had a feeling that he wasn't deceiving her, or trying to take advantage of what he'd discovered about the Mer. He wanted to help. Even if it meant no strings attached.

"I never would have guessed." She sounded too breathless for her own liking.

Kenneth grimaced, his expression momentarily hardening. "I don't like mentioning the money. People treat you differently when they know you've got it. Everyone turns into a phony sycophant."

"I can't even begin to imagine what that would be like."

"I'm giving you the chance to find out." He eyed her. "So are you going to take the money?"

Tessa considered. Everything was crashing down on her, too much, too fast. The last twenty-four hours had been a roller coaster. She'd barely had a moment to catch her breath, much less get her thoughts straight. "I don't know."

Unrolling his cigarettes from his sleeve, Kenneth tapped one round cylinder out of the pack and lit it. "No pressure."

Exhaustion suddenly barreled in, pressing down on her with an oppressive burden. She rubbed tired eyes. "Can we talk about this later? I need to think."

Exhaling a stream of white smoke, he nodded. "That's fair."

Feeling the weight of the world on her shoulders, Tessa stepped off the balcony and walked back into her room. Her muscles were tight with tension. "I always do my best thinking in the shower."

His throaty laugh sounded behind her. "Just don't use up all the hot water."

Something about the sound of his voice vibrated inside her mind, pinging off her senses like pebbles tossed against glass.

Tessa made an impulsive decision, one that would change the direction of her life. A new adventure was opening up and she'd be a fool not to seize it.

Casting a glance over her shoulder, she arched a suggestive brow. "Who said I'd be showering alone?" Reaching down, she snagged the bottom of her T-shirt. Pulling off her top, she let it slip through her fingers. "Care to join me?"

Chapter 11

Tessa, Gwen, and Addison sat on the living room floor. Several bottles of wine had been uncorked and drank, the alcohol absolutely necessary to achieve an ultimate purpose: to get Gwen to loosen up and embrace her inner Mer.

The crystals Tessa had brought out of hiding were scattered across the carpet in no particular order. She picked one up, rolled it in the palm of her hand. The green-tinged stone glinted in her hand. "This is one of the ones I've had a lot of luck with." She showed the piece to her sisters.

"What is it?" Addison asked, riffling the pages of a thick clothbound diary. Though it wasn't exactly a how-to book, their mother's descriptions of her dabbling did help give them a grasp of their own potential.

It also gave the girls a glimpse into Jolesa Lonike's mind. She too was afraid of hurting people with her power. Like her middle daughter, she squelched the instinct to embrace it. Their father, on the other hand, had encouraged his daughters to hold on to their inner Mer. He'd often gone behind his wife's back to remind his daughters all three of them were special and could do anything they set their minds to.

Special was one thing. Unique was, too. But to be nonhuman in a world in which 99.9 percent of the people happened to be human wasn't easy.

Not everybody would consider a scaly tail cool.

Tessa rolled the stone across her palm. She considered its smooth surface.

For the most part, the few humans who were aware mermaids truly inhabited the bay were loyal, proudly and fiercely guarding a privileged secret. And even though he'd attempted to bring their civilization to the attention of the archaeological world, even Jake hadn't specifically pointed fingers their way.

Still the word *freak* hovered in the back of her mind.

A lump rose in her throat. She forced it down. *If we knew more about our power, we could control people, let them see only what we want them to.* Turning the notion into reality enticed.

"It's fluorite," she finally said, dragging her mind away from the wicked thoughts. The first thing their mother had warned them about their magic was an ironclad rule: Do no harm.

Addison found a page. Strange symbols and odd lettering covered the paper. "I wish I had learned more of the Mer language," she said, frustrated. "But I think this part covers that stone." She offered the book to Gwen. "Here. Didn't you learn quite a bit?"

Swallowing down a gulp of her favorite Pinot Grigio, Gwen waved her hand. "No. I will not get involved in this. You know I am firmly against using our Mercraft."

Addison harrumphed. "Don't be stupid, Gwen. It's our nature to use magic, kind of the way humans have to have air to breathe."

"Uh, we need air, too, Addie." Tessa bounced the stone on her palm. "According to Mom's diary, this piece is a grounding stone. It balances and stabilizes intuitive powers. It's also excellent for mental coordination."

Gwen sucked down more wine. After half a bottle to herself, she was more than a little bit tipsy. "Then the damn stone should tell you I am not interested in being Mer. I just want to be plain old Gwen, owner of a successful hotel."

Addison whacked her recalcitrant sister with the diary. "That's boring. Imagine all you could do if you just used a little magic. Instead of wishing for dollars, you could just conjure them into existence."

Tessa nibbled her bottom lip. "I don't think it quite works that way, Addled Brain. We can't just wave our hands and make the dollars appear." If that were possible, she'd have already done it a long time ago.

The sound of plaster and wood collapsing interrupted their discussion.

"Just the bedroom wall coming down!" Kenneth called from upstairs. "Better steer clear."

"We're making a wide berth," she called back.

"We'll get this place in shape in no time," be bellowed.

The sound of men wielding power tools resumed.

Tessa shook her head. Over the last few weeks, the man had lived up to the term *handy*, tearing into house repairs like a demon possessed. Not only had he hired a small crew to help out; he'd already redesigned the house.

Gwen cocked her head. "Sounds like he's really into his work."

Taking a sip from her own glass, Tessa rolled her eyes. "I can't begin to tell you all he's got in mind. The plans get more elaborate every day. He's adding both a den and an office, and he's redoing the master suite and bathroom, as well. If he doesn't stop, this place is going to be triple the size it is now."

Gwen's jaw dropped. "Must be nice to have Prince Charming sweep in and take over with his checkbook." She swirled the last dregs of wine in her glass. "Don't know how bitchy old you deserved that."

The drunker Gwen got, the sharper her tongue. Not to mention the green-eyed monster was beginning to poke its head out. It didn't help that she'd just kicked her longtime boyfriend out of their apartment. If anyone needed a good man and some hot sex, Gwen was a definite candidate.

Addison refilled her own glass. "By the goddess, that man is a catch. He's not sack-ugly, he works hard, and he's willing to spend his dough on you. I'm with Gwen. You should have forked him over to one of us. We'd appreciate him."

Tessa snorted. "It's not that I don't appreciate him. I'm just taking things slow. If there's one thing we Mers have to be sure of, it's our men. Pick the wrong one and we're stuck."

Gwen snorted back. "Oh, don't give me that bullshit, Tess. You know this one's a keeper. Right now you're like the heroine of a romance novel." She lifted her hands, framing the picture. "Poor girl plucked from obscurity by the tragic brooding guy who needs help to heal his broken heart. That's almost precious enough to make me puke."

Addison laughed and joined in. "Oh, I can even see the title: *The Secret Millionaire's Mermaid Bride*."

Tessa stuck out her tongue. "Both of you are just jealous as hell."

"Damn right." Gwen swallowed more wine. "I don't see how a bitch like you even gets men. You're just a mean, cranky Mer."

Ignoring the envy, Tessa petted the stone in her hand. Gwen was having a rough time, and putting in all those long hours at the inn had frayed her nerves. "I've got the touch, baby." As if in response to her words, the stone rose slightly from her palm.

Addison eyed the floating crystal. "Oh, that is fucking awesome. I still haven't quite got the knack yet."

Tessa drew a careful breath, trying not to disturb the stone's gentle hover. She'd only just learned to make the mental connection with her symbiote, using its energy to direct matter on the outside of her body. "I've just got the hang of kinetics down."

Gwen eyed the floating crystal suspiciously. "So what are you and that rock supposed to do next? Have sex?"

Tessa grinned. Gwen's words were more accurate than she knew. "Believe it or not, this stone has a charge inside it, kind of like a battery is juiced. By concentrating on its unique vibrations, I can make a connection and draw that energy into myself. Reprocessing it through my symbiote means I can then add its power to my own and make it remanifest in the physical world."

"I am so going to learn this." Addison clapped her hands. "So make it do something!"

Nodding, Tessa concentrated. And pushed. The stone immediately whizzed away from her palm. Aim uncontrolled, the crystal blasted straight through the nearest window. The pane of glass shattered into a billion tiny shards.

Jake immediately came rushing up to the blasted window. Cell phone in hand, his face was dead pale. "What the hell was that!"

"We're just playing with the crystals Mom left us," Addison called.

Stomach lurching, Tessa winced. "Oops." Cold was beginning to seep through her veins. She'd pushed too hard and too fast and the sudden loss of energy chilled her. She'd have to take a little more care until she fully mastered control of her symbiote. The greedy little fucker inside always wanted more. Bigger, better, faster, and stronger.

A little smile turned up her lips. If her mind ever took a turn toward the dark side, all hell would break loose.

Jake thrust his arm through the broken window, showing the scorch mark across the back of his hand. "That thing damn near took my hand off. Just an inch closer and I'd be waving a stub."

Addison flipped him off. "And if she'd have aimed lower, you'd be singing like a choirboy before puberty."

Jake returned the socially unacceptable gesticulation. "I get no fucking respect around here," he grumbled, returning to his precious cell. Because of the problems with the signal, he could only use it outside, on a clear day. Reception from the mainland wasn't guaranteed, no matter how terrific the carrier's worldwide network claimed to be. His only other option would be the two-way radio in the lighthouse. And the only operator monitoring that signal was the fire department.

"Like you deserve it," Gwen called back.

Jake checked his precious BlackBerry. Just as Kenneth was tied up with his plans for the house, Jake was busy plotting his return to the Mediterranean. His every waking moment was spent on the phone, pulling the vital details together. He certainly wasn't shy about spending Kenneth's money, either. He'd burned through two hundred and fifty thousand dollars in the blink of an eye.

But Kenneth wasn't just blindly trusting Jake and blithely writing out the checks. Taking over the basement, he'd set up a command post, going over the details with Jake. As the man wielding the checkbook, he wanted to know everything before he gave the final okay. Since Recoveries, Inc., was bankrupt, Jake had no choice but to shut up and smile.

All that mattered to the archaeologist was getting back to the ruins he claimed belonged to the lost city.

Curling his lips, Jake repeated the rude gesture. "Someday you'll get my side of the story," he said before disappearing to continue his phone calls.

Tickled by the display, Addison picked up a crystal, rolling it between thumb and forefinger. "I love the way this works." Her breath caught. "My goodness, I can actually feel the vibrations in this thing. It's like it's talking to me."

Reading her entranced expression, Tessa nodded. "I told you."

Though Gwen had a strong vibe for craft, she refused to embrace it. Addison wanted it, but was still a bit clumsy with the concepts she was introducing. But once Addison mastered the basics, nothing would stop her. It was just a matter of time. Of the three of them, Tessa definitely felt Addison would be the strongest.

Gwen settled back, eyeing both her sisters warily. "You're both playing with fire. Don't you remember how Mom always warned us about the *darkness* inside?"

"Mom wasn't saying we couldn't use our abilities," Tessa reminded. "She just reminded us not to let the viciousness of our natures get out of control and hurt people."

Addison nodded her head. "Humans are part of our survival. Well, at least the men are. Don't know about the women, so much. Could do without them, I suppose, then just keep the males for breeding."

"That's how it was supposed to be in the old days," Gwen reminded them.

Tessa considered the crystals. "Do you think it's true that humans and Mers were at war?"

"Wouldn't be so far-fetched," Addison put in. "Mankind is a pretty warlike species. And we Mers do have our tempers. Could be they found a way to wipe us out deliberately, and only a few escaped to survive. Kind of like the settlers taking the land away from the natives. The strong survive; the weak succumb."

Tessa picked up another stone, a cluster of crystal quartz. The stone was said to enhance psychic ability. "It's a possibility. There may have been a time when the Mer were hunted and slaughtered because of the power they had . . . we have."

"But if we have the power, wouldn't we be the ones who won?" Addison questioned.

No one had time to answer. Hammer in hand, Kenneth wandered into the living room. "Why is Jake yelling?" he asked, shoving a handful of catalogs under Tessa's nose. "And which do you like better for the floors? Carpeting or tile?"

Closing her eyes, Tessa pressed her fingers to her temple. Good goddess almighty. Her quiet life had certainly been turned upside down since Kenneth arrived and Jake returned, going from peaceful to unbelievably surreal in the blink of an eye. Suddenly she had a thousand things to take care of, most of which she didn't care about. Paint colors, carpet textures, tile designs. It was all a little overwhelming. Sure, the house had been a little run-down, maybe even a little shabby, but it had been hers. A nice quiet sanctuary far away from the troubles of the outside world.

A sanctuary falling down around your head. Whether she wanted to admit it or not, she'd needed someone to give her a shove. She couldn't keep hiding out.

Tessa let her hands drop. "I think I'd prefer tile," she said, making the effort to add a smile to her answer. She really didn't care what he put on the floor. Redoing the house was all Kenneth's idea, something he'd made his own personal project.

It didn't take a lot of figuring to guess Kenneth Randall was a take-charge kind of man. He liked to be in control, make the decisions, and call the shots. Being married to a rich, willful woman with a career of her own must have felt like castration to him. Mechanics just couldn't compare to neurosurgeons.

It also didn't take much brainpower to figure out he was a man who needed to be needed. He clearly liked home and hearth, futzing with repairs and clucking over the little woman.

He was almost too damn good for his own good. He put a hundred and ten percent into whatever he did. She, on the other hand, was pretty laid-back. She definitely preferred crystals to ceramic tile.

"Good. I agree." Kenneth paused, redirecting his thoughts. Nothing got past him. Not a single thing. "But you didn't answer my question. What's Jake bitching about?"

Addison pointed to the broken window. "Tessa accidentally sent a crystal through the glass and almost blew Jake's hand off."

Kenneth's brow furrowed. "I thought you were aiming for his head."

Tessa smacked his leg with the catalogs. "Funny. Haha. I wasn't aiming for anything, actually."

He walked over and examined the broken window.

"Looks like you blew right through it. Guess this means I'll need to order a replacement."

"Any chance we can get shatterproof?" As long as they were redecorating, might as well upgrade.

Kenneth thought a moment. "I'll check." He ambled off, heading back to work.

The girls watched him go.

Gwen shook her head. "Unbelievable." She laid a hand on her sister's arm. "Don't treat him bad, okay? If you're just going to use him, cut him loose."

Bristling, Tessa pulled her arm away. Getting drunk and jabbering like a baboon on crack was one thing. Saying hurtful things quite another. "Why would I hurt him?"

Gwen looked at her through soft green eyes. Her momentary jealously had bled out, replaced with sincere concern. "You're arrogant, Tess. We all are when it comes to humans. Even though we don't like to admit it, we do treat them like lesser beings."

Tessa's mouth quirked down. She had to admit there were lots of times when people—humans—just annoyed her. After they'd answered her beck and call she wanted them gone. Period.

The realization made her feel a little sick. "I won't do that to Kenneth." She raked her fingers through her long hair. A moment ago she'd been near freezing. Now she was burning up, beads of perspiration dotting her forehead.

She really didn't want to talk about how she would or wouldn't treat Kenneth. It was none of her sister's business anyway. Gwen wasn't the woman in Kenneth's bed.

But she'd like to be.

Gwen studied her through an all-too-perceptive gaze.

"Just make sure the *darkness* doesn't get the best of you."

Despite the fact she was burning up, Tessa shivered. Things were getting too complicated, too fast.

Kenneth frowned at the line of rot running along the base of the wall he'd just knocked down. He'd hoped the damage hadn't seeped down into the floors of the house, but one look revealed the worst.

He cursed under his breath. Damn. Looked like it was going to take a lot more work than he'd initially estimated.

Hands on his hips, he cast a look around the room. The workmen he'd hired had called it quits for the day, promising to be back first thing tomorrow morning. He'd definitely have to adjust his original plans and re-figure his budget to cover the extra costs of replacing the floors.

Kenneth shook his head. *It needs to be done.* No getting around it. He'd just have to roll up his sleeves and plunge right in. The old house was in terrible shape. Battered by wind and water for generations uncounted, it had suffered badly through the years.

Regular maintenance might have helped allay a lot of the damage, but it was work a single woman on her own definitely couldn't manage. The sort of repairs the house needed definitely called for a man's hand. Several men and several pairs of hands, in fact. After a few days of working on his own, he'd quickly figured out the job was too much to tackle alone.

Some might think renovating the house was his way of repaying Tessa. In a way, that was true. She'd given him back his life. But being alive didn't necessarily mean the will to live. He'd had to rediscover that for himself. It felt good to have a purpose, goals to pursue.

Of course, he'd consulted Tessa before plunging in. There was no way he'd enter into a major renovation without her say-so. While it was true they shared a bed, his place in her life was still tenuous. They were still learning their way around each other's moods, the slow dance that came with getting to know a person and their preferences. He'd already learned the hard way that Tessa was moody. She was a woman who sought independence, but had no way to maintain it.

Since she couldn't very well refuse, she'd agreed to let him handle—and pay for—repairs on the house. He'd asked for control and she'd granted it.

He did so with an eye toward the future. He wanted to make things work between himself and Tessa.

Simply put, he wanted a future. With her.

But Tessa wasn't the kind of woman to go along for the ride just to see the scenery. She wanted a destination in mind before running off. In that respect she was careful, wary, almost afraid of being tied to a man a second time.

She needed her space.

Kenneth knelt, digging at the moldy rotting wood with the tips of his fingers. He was willing to give Tessa what she needed. Putting a solid roof over her head would go a long way toward soothing her insecurities. He had the means and he had the money, so why not? Whether he'd be living there in the future or not didn't matter. He had other plans simmering on the back burner. If the time came to move on, he'd be ready to pack his bags and hit the road.

A commotion behind him alerted him to the presence of another person.

Jake Massey stumbled in, picking his way through the wreckage. He clutched his ever-important BlackBerry in his hand. It was a wonder the handheld didn't blow up. The poor little machine was in constant use.

"Geez, Louise," Jake said, eyeing the damage. "It looks like the *Titanic* sank here."

Kenneth rose to his feet. "It gets worse. Looks like part of the floor is going to have to come up, too."

Jake shook his head. "I'd been waiting for word that this house blew into the sea, never to be seen again."

Kenneth tapped a foot. "Foundation's solid enough, but the storms have taken their toll."

"You going to fix it?"

He nodded. "Every last bit. By the time I get finished, there won't be a single problem with the house."

Jake leveled a cool gaze his way. "Awfully nice of you to do for a woman you just met."

Kenneth narrowed his eyes. "Just like it's terribly nice of me to fund an expedition back to the Mediterranean for some two-bit archaeologist I just met."

Jake's face turned two shades redder. "Touché."

Kenneth tossed his hammer aside and rubbed his hands down the front of his pants. "So what's the latest?" Like Jake, he had to admit he'd gotten caught up in the mystique of the Mer. The idea of recovering a lost civilization excited him beyond words.

Jake lifted a hand, ticking off key points. "The company's debts have been cleared and the liens have been withdrawn, so we've got the boat and equipment in place. The captain's calling the crew back in now."

"How long will that take?"

Jake shrugged. "Oh, at least a month, I'm sure. But the time lag is okay. We've got to get an attorney into court as soon as possible to stake our claim."

Kenneth's brows rose. "We do?"

Jake nodded. "We've got to ask the courts to determine a salvage award and establish legal guarantees on any artifacts recovered, ensuring that they remain intact as a collection. Some pieces recovered earlier have already attracted private buyers. Because Ishaldi's ruins lay in international waters, Recoveries, Inc., needs to gain exclusive rights to salvage the artifacts."

Kenneth digested that chunk of information. He'd had no idea one needed a team of lawyers to defend a claim on something lying untouched at the bottom of the sea for more than a thousand years. "No wonder you've been burning up the dollars."

Jake shrugged. "Tell me about it. But we've got to protect our claim, this one more than others. We're not just pulling up relics from a shipwreck. We're delving into a lost civilization, something that exists only in legends."

"Kind of like the Loch Ness monster?"

Jake laughed. "Well, I don't know if our fair Mer would want to be compared to it, but I wouldn't mind being in on that discovery, either."

"So how do we get the courts to see things our way?"

"In seeking a salvage award, Recoveries, Inc., has to document the labor devoted to previous expeditions, and the risks incurred bringing up artifacts from a depth stretching almost three miles under the sea. The archaeological value of the ruins and its artifacts speaks for itself. The rediscovery will literally knock the archaeological world on its ass."

Kenneth rubbed his jaw. "Not to mention everybody else."

Jake grinned. "Exactly."

"Well, it sounds like you've got everything on track."

Jake consulted his BlackBerry. "There is one other thing I need to talk to you about."

Kenneth shrugged. Most likely Jake was about to ask him to write another check. "How much?"

Jake flagged a hand. "I'll probably need more money later. But that's not what's on my mind right now."

"Okay. Spit it out."

"My partner in Recoveries, Inc., is getting out. Part of the money I've spent has gone toward buying his half of the business. It's now mine. Every bit."

That put a sour taste in Kenneth's mouth. Jake was subtly amassing full control. "Congratulations on your acquisition."

"Not so much," Jake countered. "While it's true the company is now running debt-free, it won't stay that way long unless we have an influx of ready cash."

Kenneth raised an inquiring brow. "And?"

Jake sighed and rolled his eyes. "I'm offering you half of the business. We'd be partners, fifty-fifty. There's a lot of wreckage in those oceans and I intend to find as much of it as I can before I die."

Though his face was schooled to hold an impassive expression, inside Kenneth was bursting to come right out and accept. He definitely had to admit the treasure hunting bug had bitten him. Hard. This was the most exciting adventure he'd ever set out on in his life. He liked the idea of rediscovering the lost, bringing it up from the water to share again with the world.

But fools rushed in where angels feared to tread.

He also had a few considerations. And a few reservations. The first and foremost was did he like Jake Massey enough to want to go into business with him?

Although he hadn't wanted to admit it when he'd met the man, he could honestly check the box yes now. Sure,

Jake was clearly a predator, and out for himself. But he was also an intelligent man who knew what he needed to get where he wanted to go. His biggest stumbling block was that people didn't like Jake. Most everyone saw through his razor-sharp ambition—and didn't like the idea he might just stab them in the back to get what he wanted.

The second biggest consideration was how would Tessa feel about her current boyfriend (could he even call himself that?) and her ex-fiancé going into business together? So far she'd treated Jake coolly but civilly, making a wide berth around him.

The third consideration was what did he, Kenneth, want to do? Since selling his own business, he'd put himself on an aimless path. He had no goals, no responsibilities. He also had nothing holding him back from doing what he wanted to do, when he wanted to do it. For the first time in his life he was footloose and fancy free.

If he and Tessa stayed together, great. If not, he'd have something to fall back on.

Either way it seemed workable.

It didn't take long to make a decision.

He held out his hand. "I'll buy in."

Jake returned the shake. "Terrific. Welcome aboard, partner. I'll get the attorneys to put the legalities in place. Pull out your pen and get ready to sign."

Kenneth let his hand drop. "Haven't I been doing that already?"

"True. And you're going to be doing more of it soon, sure enough." Lifting his BlackBerry, Jake gave it a good shake. "Damn, I've lost the signal again. I'll have to go outside to make the call."

"Call away."

Jake picked his way back through the mess. He

paused at the entrance. "Oh, there is one thing I've got to let you know."

There was enough bait in his statement to make it interesting.

Kenneth's inner antennae rose up and honed in. His muscles knotted reflexively. "What's that?"

"Tessa. You do know I'm going to try to steal her back. We have some, ah, some business I'd like to finish."

The statement was made with such blithe confidence that Kenneth couldn't be offended. It reminded him of two dogs sniffing around, sizing each other up. "If you think you're man enough to get her back, then be my guest."

Jake's eyes glittered. "Well, I'm man enough to try. Question is, are you man enough to hold on to a woman like that?" Cocky, self-centered, and self-assured, he obviously thought a lot about himself and his abilities. Didn't matter if he won or lost. He wanted to play the game. In short, it was a show of macho virility.

Who had the bigger set of balls?

Kenneth's first instinct was to laugh the challenge off. His second was to punch the sucker out right then and there. A third part of him had to wonder. Did he have what it took to hold on to a woman like Tessa Lonike?

Jake seemed to read his thoughts. "What's the matter? Can't you handle a little friendly competition?"

The gauntlet had been thrown down.

Kenneth had to pick it up. "Toying with the woman you walked out on doesn't make it sound like you have friendly intentions."

Jake looked at him a long moment. "Oh, man. You definitely don't have the whole story there. There's another side to everything."

Kenneth scowled at him suspiciously. Like he would believe anything Jake had to say on the matter. "Oh?"

"You won't hear it from me. Best to let you figure things out on your own. The thing you'll find out about Mers is they're slippery. Hard to hold on to." Jake snapped his fingers in the air. "Blink, and they're gone. Like that."

"Sounds to me like you didn't hold on hard enough." Kenneth cocked his head. "Or haven't got enough staying power to keep up with a woman like Tessa. *Staying* is the key word there, you know. Anytime you walk away, you give up the right to what you left behind."

Jake swore under his breath. "This time I'm not walking."

Refusing to be intimidated, Kenneth folded his arms across his chest. Jake had a lot of nerve fucking him around like that. But he'd already figured out Jake's number. His shtick was ten percent sincerity mixed with ninety percent bullshit. Jake liked to push buttons, see how far he could get before someone sent him packing.

No doubt a partnership with the archaeologist would make for some interesting times. Throwing Tessa into the mix only made it that much more interesting.

"I'm not walking, either."

Jake's gaze danced, merriment laced with a hint of malice. The race was on. "Looks like we're on our way, doesn't it?" He slapped the side of the doorframe with his hand before prancing out of the room. "Let's get this show on the road."

Indeed.

Staring in his wake, Kenneth had to wonder. *What the hell have I gotten myself into?*

Chapter 12

Mediterranean Sea
Six weeks later

Tessa stood on the port bow of the *DreamFever*, staring out toward the far horizon. The tranquil waters around the ship glimmered, lit by the vanishing light of the sun. Fiery red-orange and deep blue mingled to form a deeper, richer shade. The sea stretched on, open and endlessly wide. The view was glorious, absolutely breathtaking.

Pulling in a deep breath, Tessa tasted the tang of salt on the cool breeze. She could hardly believe she was standing on a ship in the center of the very sea that was the uniting element and center of world history. These waters were rich with history, having claimed lives, fortunes, and, in some instances, entire cities. It was through this very sea that diverse civilizations had met and mingled, seeking to move beyond the boundaries of their homelands.

Her gaze scanned the darkening waters. Though they wouldn't reach their destination for another twelve hours, Tessa was sure the strange quickening in her veins was the tug of her people calling her home. Having made several experimental dives, she believed she felt the vibrations from the Mer who'd once inhabited the fathomless depths. When she swam, the crystal around her neck seemed to hum with energy it picked up from an outside source.

A sense of peace, of contentment, washed through her. *It was once here. Home.*

For the first time in a long time she felt like she belonged. The water was where she needed to be. Not just any water, but that which had spawned her race. The Mer might branch out, traveling far and wide, but the need to return to their birthplace was a primal one that couldn't be ignored.

The sound of a voice from behind pulled her out of her contemplations. "You've been spending a lot of time up here."

Tessa turned her head in time to see Jake sauntering her way. "I'm just excited about the idea of seeing Ishaldi."

Jake smiled and looked out over the water. "Feels like old times, doesn't it? You and me on our way to another adventure."

Caught in a mellow mood, Tessa nodded. "Yeah, it does kind of seem that way." As the expedition had come together, she'd found Jake's company more than tolerable. The bad feelings she'd nursed had faded. When his mind was on the hunt, Jake was a keen and intelligent researcher. He gathered every iota of data, then distilled it into terms a layman could easily understand. The discovery of Ishaldi and its artifacts would probably catapult his career into the stratosphere.

And I'll be a part of that.

"My people will finally have a place in this world."

Jake glanced at her. A slow smile unspooled across his handsome face. "Definitely."

Though they'd been traveling aboard the ninety-five-foot R/V cruiser for weeks, he was nattily turned out in one of his blazers and impeccably pressed slacks. Sunglasses perched on his head, his shoulder-length hair streamed around his face. The wind pulled a few sexy strands across his high cheekbones, even as the fading light added a glow to the deep blond shade.

Heart skipping a beat, Tessa's breath caught in her throat. He looked good. Really good. Pure eye candy. He hadn't lost his haughty vibe, either. His *I'm hot, you're not* strut was still very much in evidence.

The moment reminded her of the time when they'd first become acquainted, more than five years ago. With more than seven hundred ships resting off Maine's rocky coast, Jake had been one of the archaeologists working in the state program to identify and catalog the wrecks for preservation and recovery. She'd been one of the divers assisting with the surveys.

It hadn't been love at first sight. Tessa had immediately disliked Jake, thinking him a rude, arrogant know-it-all. He'd treated the divers like flunkies, insisting they go into the water again and again to get the information he wanted—even if it meant taking some big risks.

She'd been the only one who could satisfy his insatiable quest for knowledge, easily penetrating wreckage other divers refused to venture into. Of course, she had an unfair advantage. A mermaid never had to worry about a tank running out of air or getting snagged in a small space.

Tessa suppressed her frown. *We were two people who never should have been attracted to each other, but were.*

As compatible as gasoline and a lit match, they'd despised each other. Until they bickered.

At such times, the sparks flew. Somehow the chemistry simmering between them boiled over. Before they knew it, angry words had turned into deep, fierce kisses. Eager hands had ripped away confining clothing. Sex between them was fierce, bordering on brutal.

Remembering the aftermath, Tessa shivered. *Oh man.* The climax was addicting, pure heaven on earth. Jake liked women. And more than anything else, he liked fucking them.

Feeling heat rise to her cheeks, Tessa pulled in a quick breath to cool herself off. Just thinking about the nasty, frenetic sex they'd had was enough to set her off. She couldn't erase the past, nor could she entirely forget it. She did the next best thing by simply tolerating it, something not as hard to achieve as she'd first believed. Through the six weeks it had taken to get the expedition into gear, she and Jake had become something she'd believed impossible: friends.

Her hand traveled to the crystal hanging around her neck. "I never thought Ishaldi would be found. Ever."

Jake laughed. "I will admit you were my inspiration to go looking for it. All I needed was a little time and luck."

Tessa suppressed a frown. "We all thought you were taking advantage."

He shook his head. "That is one point you badly misjudged me on. I'll cop to being a bastard, but I'm absolutely serious about my work. Learning about the Mer was something I couldn't toss aside and ignore just because we broke up."

Tessa nibbled her lower lip. "It's hard to keep a secret like that. Though a lot of Port Rock's local lore is built around mermaids living in the bay, people believe that's just to bring in the tourists."

"Where there's lore, there's usually a little bit of fact involved," Jake said. "Somehow I don't think people would have a problem with the Mer coming out of the closet, so to speak. Your family has lived on the island for quite a long time. Those who do know you are Mer have accepted it just fine." He looked out over the water. "And I think once we begin bringing up the relics from Ishaldi, the rest of the world will, too. Once word is out, more Mer may come out of hiding."

Thinking about her aunt Gail and the cousins she didn't even know anymore, Tessa sighed. "One would hope."

Jake cocked an eyebrow. "That's why it's important to let the world know about the Mer. The race is bordering on extinct, as far as we know. Why not do everything you can to save your people? If our positions were reversed, and Mer were the majority and humans the minority, I know I'd be shouting from the rooftops."

His words made sense. Did she really want to be one of the last of her kind? Belong to a species with no hope of future survival?

The thought sent a chill through her veins. Since revealing the cache of crystals to her sisters, she'd begun to work harder on her craft, attempting to master the various elements behind her innate abilities. The pieces she'd always felt were missing from her life were beginning to fall into place. It wasn't just that she was an outsider always doomed to look in, but in closing herself off from the mystical side of her nature, she also closed the door on her senses.

For years she'd walked around half blind and half deaf, only partially aware of her potential. In learning to work with the crystals and the symbiote that was a part of her very soul, she'd begun to blossom. She was alive and ready to embrace the potential of what a Mer could really be: a strong, powerful woman in control of her own destiny.

Tessa turned around, leaning back against the rail. "Though I never thought it would be possible, I think I agree with you. The Mer obviously had a place in this world at one time. Why shouldn't we have it again?"

Jake grinned. "That's exactly what I've been trying to tell you for years."

She shook her head. "I hate to say it, but I think you were right."

"Told you so." Acting like a know-it-all prick had always given Jake a perverse charm women found irresistible.

She laughed. "Ass."

Leaning a hip against the railing, he eyed her. "Adventure suits you, Tess. You look alive for the first time since you quit working search and recovery."

Smiling, Tessa pulled her fingers through her long hair, enjoying the feel of the cool breeze on her skin. The last bit of daylight faded away, changing the sea from bruised blue to deep purple. Stars were beginning to appear in the velvety fabric of the night sky, glinting like the crystals she coaxed secrets from.

Before she knew what was happening, Jake swung around in front of her. His hands gripped the railing on either side of her hips, penning her in. "I was a fool to walk away."

Tessa lifted her hands, intending to push him away. Her palms settled on his chest, strong and broad under her touch. She felt his heart beating hard beneath his rib cage, belying the calm of his manner. It took only a second for her to read his intent.

He wants me back, came her wild thought.

She pressed forward, trying to push him away. "Come on, Jake—quit kidding around."

Instead of letting her go, Jake maneuvered closer. "I'm not kidding around." His mouth came down on hers with a deliberate, calculated slowness, his searching lips mastering hers.

His hand lifted, curling around her neck even as he worked his knee between her legs to press his thigh between hers. The pressure against her sex was instant and electrifying. She gasped, but had no time to protest.

Tessa broke away, breathless, tingling to her toes. Goddess above. If there was one thing Jake knew, it was how to make all the right moves on a woman's body. Her insides quivered with arousal, an all-consuming ache suddenly pulsing through her veins.

"Don't." She swiped a hand across her mouth. "I'm with someone else."

Jake snorted a laugh. "Yeah, I know. Kenneth." His hand crept to the top of her blouse, fingers expertly undoing her buttons. "Here's what I think about that." He undid a second button, then a third. "I don't think you're really into him."

Tessa slapped his hand away. "You don't know what you're talking about. Kenneth and I are—"

Jake persisted, undoing a fourth button. "Not sleeping together—I know." He increased the pressure of his thigh against her most sensitive place, increasing the friction.

Tessa's breath locked in her throat. "How do you know?" The sensations of his thigh rubbing between her legs sent shivers up her spine.

Treating her to a slow grin, Jake tugged open her blouse and tweaked her left nipple through her sports bra. His touch burned through the thin material. "It's a small boat, honey, and the walls are thin. When someone's getting their brains fucked out, you know it."

"Maybe we're just considerate of the crew," she shot back. The lame excuse fell flat. The truth was, she and Kenneth shared the same quarters but were sleeping in separate bunks.

Tessa inwardly grimaced. She hadn't been treating Kenneth especially well lately. Her mind was on her magic. And while her skills were blossoming at a rapid pace, the relationship with the new man in her life was dying on the vine. The hours she put into practice disappeared, leaving little time for personal pursuits. Or pleasure.

Jake rolled his eyes. "Spare me your consideration, please. Besides, if you two were tight as thieves, you'd have already slapped me silly and stormed off." He clicked his tongue and undid the last button. "Methinks there is trouble in paradise."

Tessa squirmed. Big mistake. The pressure of his thigh coupled with the chafe of her jeans against her crotch doubled the thrilling sensations between her legs. "Thinking with your dick doesn't count."

He studied her through an enigmatic blue gaze. The luminous shimmer dancing on the water reflected in the depths of his eyes. "Oh, but I have been thinking. About you and how good we were together."

Trying to wrestle her mind away from all the good feelings he stimulated, Tessa gritted her teeth. "If we were so good, why did you leave?"

Tracing his fingers along the lines of her plain sports bra, Jake slid his fingers under the material. "As I recall, your feet got cold before mine. You wanted to wait."

"I didn't say no. Just that I needed more time."

Tugging up her bra, Jake bared her left breast. Her exposed nipple puckered, then rose under the caress of the cool sea air. "We were together long enough for you to be sure." He flicked the tip with his finger. "You weren't then, but I think you are now." Easing her back against the rail, he lowered his head. His eager mouth captured the hard little bead.

Tessa whimpered, automatically tangling her fingers in his long blond locks. The sensations swamping her body were exquisite. She gasped in dismay as he painted soft circles around the hard tip. "Jake, please . . . This is so wrong . . ."

A voice from behind broke the illicit spell. "So am I to take this to mean you two are back together?"

Tessa immediately froze. Alarm shot through her. *Oh shit.* Kenneth. Though his voice was calm, she sensed currents of disappointment and hurt in his tone.

She shoved Jake, something she should have done in the first place. "Get away from me, you big lug."

Jake laughed, taking his own sweet time. Giving himself a quick check to make sure everything was in place, he turned around. "Oh, goodness," he said, very much tongue in cheek. "Looks like you caught us red-handed."

Kenneth eyed the pair. "And very exposed."

Tessa glanced down. Heat immediately scorched her cheeks. Her shirt was unbuttoned and one breast totally hung out.

A slow groan seeped past her lips. "It's not what it looks like." She tugged her bra back into place. Numb fingers fumbled with her buttons. She couldn't seem to make them work.

Jake snorted and threw an arm around her. "Oh, drop

the pretense," he said, throwing her a wink. "It's exactly what it looks like."

Kenneth arched an eyebrow. "Which is?"

Jake tossed his head. "I'm keeping my word to you, Kenneth," he said.

Refusing to be baited, Kenneth shrugged. "Tessa is a free woman, fully capable of choosing what she wants. I'm not going to try to tell her what to do with her life."

Jake snorted. "Oh, man. What a pussy." He rolled his eyes and snickered. "You let her take your money and fuck another man. I don't know what to call you. It's not noble, so it must be plain stupid."

Awkwardly clutching the front of her shirt together, Tessa broke in. "Shut up, Jake!" Heart slamming against her ribs, she shoved past him. "Don't listen to him."

Kenneth cocked his head. "What he says doesn't bother me." His eyes narrowed. "What I saw does. You weren't exactly fighting him off."

"Of course she wasn't fighting me," Jake interrupted. "She still wants me. Bad."

Kenneth stabbed a finger at the archaeologist. "I'm not interested in what you have to say. Being an asshole seems to be a part of your nature. With you, I know what I'm dealing with."

Jake spread his hands. "Leopards don't change their spots, man."

Kenneth's gaze raked over the archaeologist, scathing but distant. His right hand curled into a fist. "More like hyenas never lose their stink."

"Don't you just hate being right?" Jake sneered back. "It's like I warned you. Mer are slippery women." Flashing a contemptuous smile, he flexed his fingers in an obscene manner. "But they're oh, so damn hot when you get your hands on one."

Kenneth took a step forward. "There's only so much shit I'm going to take from you, Jake."

Heart pumping ninety to nothing, Tessa threw herself between the antagonists. "Just stop it, both of you," she said, fearing the two men might come to blows. "This is getting out of control."

Kenneth's face took on a guarded expression. His preternatural calm disturbed her. "You're the one who's out of control." His tone was low and steady, non-committal.

Giving her no chance to respond, he simply turned on his heel and walked away.

He didn't glance back. Not once.

Staring in his wake, Tessa felt her stomach twist. Guilt flayed at her heart.

I'm such an idiot! How is it I screw up everything I touch?

Jake's warm fingers curled around her arm. "If he really wanted you, he'd fight." He grinned, pulling her back into his embrace. "Now that he's gone, I think we can finish what we started."

Disgusted and ashamed by her momentary lapse in judgment, Tessa yanked away from his grip. "Oh, go to hell."

Stalking to the quarters he shared with Tessa, Kenneth slammed the door behind him. The image of Tessa locked in Jake's embrace played over and over in his mind, taunting him.

Blinking hard to banish the hateful images, he rubbed his hands across his face. Jealousy slithered through him, coiling into a tight knot in his stomach. He had to hand it to her. She'd definitely gotten under his skin.

Pulling in a deep breath to cool his anger, he glanced around the room. The luxury quarters were crammed with the general clutter of two people living in limited space. Away from home, Tessa let her housekeeping skills lapse. Her idea of unpacking seemed to consist of dumping her suitcase on the bed and digging through the pile. What she didn't need, she tossed on the floor. Ironing something and hanging it up seemed to be a knack she'd never mastered. Even the crystals she used to enhance her craft were scattered around.

Walking to his desk, Kenneth picked up one of the stray gemstones. Since taking the stash out of hiding, Tessa had revealed the surprising power of telekinesis, or the ability to manipulate matter with her mind. Since he'd witnessed her ability to shift, it hadn't really surprised him that she possessed other unique powers. He simply accepted them as a part of her Mer identity.

The stone he held was familiar. Tessa had explained that red garnet helped to release anger. He definitely needed that right now. But there were other meanings, as well. It was a balance stone, bringing what the bearer needed, be it passion or serenity. Garnets were also said to bring success in business.

Fingers closing around the carmine-shaded stone, Kenneth closed his eyes. If he concentrated hard enough, he fancied he could feel vibrations emanating from the stone's cold heart.

His mouth drew down. *A heart Tessa seems to share.*

He always seemed to choose strong, difficult women—perhaps because these types were the only kind he understood. From an early age he'd watched his own mother grab the wheel and do the driving. Not that she'd really had the luxury of choice. She took control out of necessity. With two young boys to raise, she'd had to make sure they didn't swerve off the road.

Jennifer, too, was a strong woman with a mind of her own. Her career was first. Her husband second.

Kenneth didn't like being number two. Second place was shit. He'd hoped he'd found the perfect balance with Tessa. She needed a mate, but was willful enough not to fold up like a wet paper sack when challenged. He liked feisty. It made things interesting.

The trouble was that nothing between him and Tessa had been the slightest bit enticing lately. And even though he'd always been good at holding his temper when frustration set in, he was getting a little tired of being put on a shelf and ignored.

He sighed, shifting restlessly. They were not sharing a bed and that irritated him. Even though each maintained a separate bed, they'd always managed to begin a night together, when they would indulge in the delights of each other's body. Usually he was the one to slip away when she fell into the grip of sleep.

But as her mastery of Mercraft increased, Tessa grew more restless, avoiding his touch. Having turned her attention to magic, she'd stepped onto a different plane of existence.

She isn't human, he thought. She belonged to a race much more advanced than plain old Homo sapiens. Compared to the Mer, human males were still knuckle-dragging apes.

A sigh winnowed past his lips. *When one door closes, another one opens.* By now he believed that. It had happened too many times in his life not to be true. There had been a time when he'd wanted to shut that door, forever. But something had spared his life, giving him a second chance to make things work.

The only thing he wasn't sure of was whether or not Tessa would continue to be a part of his second chance. Unfortunately, the garnet didn't seem to be helping passion out one little bit.

The sound of footsteps outside alerted him to the approach of another person. The door unlatched, easing open slowly.

Half a woman's face peeked around the door, a single green eye under a shock of red hair. "Can I come in?"

Tossing the garnet on his desk, Kenneth shrugged. "The room's half yours."

Tessa stepped in, shutting the door behind her. Her clothes were back in place, shirt buttoned to the chin. She cleared her throat. "I guess you're pissed."

Muscles in Kenneth's neck and shoulders tensed. "Of course I'm pissed. If there's one thing I won't tolerate, it's a cheat."

Her gaze was filled with guilt. "I'm sorry. I don't know what happened. One minute we were talking and the next minute Jake was putting the moves on me." She pressed a hand to her forehead. "It just happened so fast, I got caught in the moment."

"Remembering when things were good?" Self-aware enough to recognize his jealousy, he tried not to let it bait his temper. Turning into an asshole wouldn't help his case one bit. He'd only manage to come off as pathetic, a needy loser.

Control, he reminded himself. Keep a cool head. Tessa was a wild card. She might jump into Jake's bed, but that was no reason to let her destroy the partnership he'd formed with the archaeologist.

A woman was one thing. Business was another. You didn't mix the two.

What he couldn't control, he'd accept.

Tessa's hand dropped. Mouth turned down, her expression was grim. "Yeah, I guess so."

Kenneth nodded. Walking across the narrow room, he bent and snagged a few pieces of Tessa's clothes off the floor. He tossed them on the unmade bed along with the rest of the general mess. "I'm sure Jake will be tickled to have you as his bunkmate."

Her eyes widened with shock. "What? You're kicking me out?"

Kenneth narrowed his gaze. "I'm not kicking you out. I'm stepping aside."

She blinked in disbelief. "Just like that?"

As angry as he was, there was no reason to turn into a ranting maniac. Cool, quiet, and calm disturbed more people than fierce, raving anger. "Just like that. Or don't you remember me telling you I wasn't interested in playing games?"

Hands lacing in front of her like a repentant child, Tessa swallowed hard. "I guess I do. The first night we were together."

Kenneth tightened his jaw. "I won't share you with another man. If you're going to be with Jake, then be with Jake, damn it. But you're not going to have your cake and eat it, too."

Tessa thought for a minute. An impish smile lit up her face. "Maybe you could make things easier by just tossing his ass overboard."

"I can't. Jake's not expendable." He pretended to think. "You, on the other hand, are."

Her brows rose. "Me?" Though she tried not to show it, she was clearly stung.

Kenneth nodded. "You're the one element not necessary on this salvage. We could manage it without
you. Jake is the brains." He pointed to himself. "I'm the
money. You're—"

"The mermaid," she reminded him.

"Yeah. That."

"Just that? Are you tossing me away?"

He eyed her. "Maybe before you toss me."

"But I'm *not* tossing you."

Kenneth held up a hand. "Come on, Tess. You're not
fooling anyone. Somehow I think Jake wasn't the one
who couldn't commit. I think you were the one who
kept pulling back. He simply got tired of waiting and
left. I've experienced it myself. Sometimes you're fire;
sometimes you're ice. One day you burn me; the next
day you freeze me out. The two definitely don't make
for a good relationship."

Tessa's expression crumbled. Her shoulders sagged.
"Maybe it was me. I'm the one who told Jake I thought
we needed to wait to get married. I didn't know he'd just
call the whole thing off and walk. I thought he'd wait."

"For what?"

She threw up her hands. "A Mer gives up so much
to be with a human. I was only twenty-seven. Taking
a mate and having children would have cut my life in
half. I guess I felt I needed more time. But humans don't
have that time."

If he'd thought he didn't understand the Mer before,
he definitely didn't understand them now. "What do you
mean it would have cut your life in half?"

Tessa's hands dropped. "A Mer doesn't age the way
a human does. But we can't have our children until we
synchronize our internal clocks to match that of the
mate we've chosen. So when a Mer decides to take her

mate, she has to begin aging normally in order to activate her fertility and bear his children." She shrugged. "I
guess I wasn't ready to give up my youth."

It took a moment for him to fully understand the
implications behind her words. "Are you telling me you
don't get old?"

Tessa shook her head. "I didn't say we don't get old. I
said we don't age the same way."

Kenneth threw her a questioning look. "So how long
does a Mer traditionally live?"

"We can survive a very long time if we keep ourselves
healthy," she answered simply.

The proverbial bulb hovering over his head was finally beginning to shed some light. Tessa wasn't being a
cheat so much as she was trying to find a suitable mate
to help her continue her species. The old saying was
probably true. A girl had to kiss a lot of frogs to find a
prince.

Kenneth wondered if he was going to be another one
with warts. "And single?"

Tessa nodded. "Yeah. Trouble is, we're infertile until
we take our mates." She grimaced. "But once we do
make our choice, it's for life. We can't just get a divorce
and move on to the next man because nature adjusts our
eggs to accept only one man's sperm."

Kenneth frowned. "Sounds a little complicated."

She spread her hands in helpless dismay. "Maybe it's
the reason we're almost extinct. We're too damn picky."

"Must be hard choosing a man worthy enough to sacrifice your youth."

Tessa lowered her head guiltily. "I'm sorry. I've been
a bitch, a total bitch, and there's no excuse. My mother
always cautioned us not to give in to the selfish Mer
side of our natures. Somehow it's just a part of our spirit

to relegate humans to a lesser status. I just shoved you aside, assuming you'd be there when I wanted you."

"It doesn't work that way."

Straightening her shoulders, she nodded. "It's give and take, I know. And I've been doing all the taking."

Kenneth thought about her words. *It was true—she'd been tough to deal with lately.* But he knew he wanted her, knew that he wanted her to choose him. He wasn't about to lose her to Jake.

Making a sudden decision, he walked over to Tessa. Fingers curling around her arms, he pulled her close. Tessa had the right to choose the man she wanted. But he had the right to try to change her mind.

Kenneth was tired of sucking it up, being the nice guy. It was true. Nice guys finished last. Real men took what they wanted. Period. "You're not putting me off anymore." A second later, his mouth claimed hers.

Tessa's lips parted willingly under the searching invasion of his tongue. She tasted sweet, musky, and sexy. Her arms rose, circling his neck. Her hips pressed against his, creating a most enticing friction.

Kenneth's mouth left hers. His fingers threaded impatiently in the masses of her hair, tipping her head back so he could look into her eyes. Her gaze glittered with craving. "If Jake was any kind of a man, he wouldn't have let you walk away. Not then, not now. I'm the one who wants you."

Tessa shivered and closed her eyes. Silky lashes feathered across her rosy cheeks. "I can't make any promises," she murmured. "I can't . . ."

Breathless with reckless exhilaration, Kenneth growled, "I don't care." He needed her. Now. "Just give me today." Tomorrow would have to take care of itself.

She made a helpless, tiny noise of acquiescence.

Spurred on by pure instinct, Kenneth tugged impatiently at her shirt. Somehow he got it open, pushing it off her shoulders. Her flimsy bra followed, baring her breasts to his eager hands. He teased her nipples, plucking at the rosy tips. Heat curled around his cock like a woman's warm, silky fingers.

Tessa's breath hitched. "Goddess . . ." She whimpered. "That feels so good."

Nibbling at her lips, Kenneth cupped the curve of one breast. Capturing the sensitive pink tip, he rolled it between thumb and forefinger. At the same time, the primal male inside him raised its head. Jake had already explored this territory. Traces of his tacky aftershave still lingered on her skin.

He'd soon erase it, branding her with his own unique scent.

Kenneth fumbled open the top button of her jeans, tugging the zipper down. Pushing the faded denim down her hips, his hand slid past the elastic of her panties. Crooking a finger, he stroked her with a slow, steady motion. She was wet and ready to be taken.

Oh, yes, he thought, sliding the tip of his finger into her depth. Tessa was definitely worth the fight.

And he wasn't giving her up, come hell or high water.

Chapter 13

A day later, Tessa looked up at the men gathered around to watch her make the first dive. Because she would be plunging to a depth of almost three and a half miles under the sea, it had been necessary to reveal her secret to the crew. Given that a human diver could manage only about four hundred feet max, those working the salvage had to know. Even with the three-man submersible the Swiftship carried, the crew wouldn't be able to penetrate the areas she could. She'd have to handle the majority of deep-sea scouting and mapping.

Since most of the crew had served with Jake on earlier expeditions to locate Ishaldi, they were familiar with the lore surrounding the mermaids and their lost civilization. At first Tessa was a little apprehensive about showing her skills to a cadre of strangers. But once she hit the water, she found she enjoyed the attention. The crew of five men and three women thought it was wonderful to have a mermaid on board. It certainly made the other divers a little less apprehensive about the depths they were facing. No one had ever heard of a mermaid losing consciousness and drowning.

Everyone was excited about being a part of something huge.

Swimming up to the ladder that allowed divers to climb back on board, Tessa laughed. "You guys sure you don't want to join me?"

Jake bent over the edge. "I would be glad to, babe. All you have to do is give me that magic kiss."

Scrunching up her face, Tessa stuck out her tongue. "I wouldn't toss a glass of water on you if you were on fire, Jake Massey."

Jake frowned, clearly unhappy about missing the chance to hit the deep sea and do a little exploring. "Come on, babe. You know how important this is."

Tessa shook her head. "I don't even want to talk to you after that little stunt you pulled last night." She'd already refused to take him down with her. There was no way she'd ever lock lips with the lying dog again.

Kenneth clapped the archaeologist on the back. "Sorry, man. I told her all about your little wager."

Tessa pinned both men under her gaze. "I'm still pissed you two have been haggling over me like I'm a piece of furniture."

Jake gestured helplessly. "I wasn't playing around. I was honestly trying to get you back."

Kenneth gave a show of hands. "And I'm just trying to keep you safe from this lech."

"I'll make up my own mind, thank you very much," she said to both men. "Right now we've got work to do."

"How deep will you be going down?" Kenneth asked.

Tessa considered a moment. "Well over three miles, so I won't be back before sundown. If you'd like to take the first dive, now's the time to hit the water."

Kenneth hastily shook his head. "I think I've had enough of the water to last me a lifetime. You are welcome to have the honor."

Tessa nodded and pushed away from the ship. "I'm off, then." A second later she slipped beneath the radiant blue waters of the Mediterranean Sea.

Plunging straight down, she abandoned her legs and shifted into her true form. Since learning to manipulate the energies contained in her soul-stone, she'd mastered the technique of shedding clothing. The wet suit she wore simply melted away. The downside was that her clothes were never to be seen again. She had no idea where they ultimately ended up. But at least she'd advanced to the point where she could call different clothing to her when she exited the water.

A thrill suddenly went through her body, from her fingertips to her toes. The freedom of her newfound abilities had expanded her horizons tenfold. There was no more shame in being different. For the first time in her life she felt special. She felt . . . *empowered*.

Brimming with a sense of infinite strength, Tessa became aware that being a Mer made her close to being truly divine.

Intoxicated by her thoughts, Tessa plunged deeper. Though the waters of the Mediterranean were normally warm and made for pleasant swimming around the beachfront area, the waters deep below the surface of the open sea were chilly. But she didn't feel the cold at all. To her the water was warm and tingling, an effervescent living thing that welcomed her into its bosom. The water seemed to glow and shimmer, flowing around her body with a silken caress.

Cutting through the water at a speed the human eye couldn't even keep up with, Tessa made her way toward the bottom of the sea. The other occupants of the water quickly darted out of her way. Her visibility was good a clear five to six miles on the bottom. Light from above was murky thanks to a layer of plankton hovering at a twenty-meter depth. A human this far down would have already lost consciousness.

The dangers still didn't stop divers from trying to find the mother lode. The Mediterranean, with its three thousand years of maritime history, temperate climate, and easy access, was one of the best diving sites in the world. There were literally hundreds of wrecks and remnants littering the waters—relics from Phoenician times and the Roman-era amphorae, WWII war casualties, modern barges, and trawling wrecks.

Tessa swam on. The craggy sea floor was hardly a hotbed of treasure. Now and again she stopped to examine an object that caught her attention. Eventually a few objects began to emerge from the murk: a few large Grecian-style pots, some brass circlets that might have been bracelets, a scattering of coins.

Promising, she thought, and kept going.

Putting more distance between herself and the surface, she followed the steep decline of a sudden drop in the sea floor. Volcanic activity and earthquakes had created a valley of deep crevasses. At this point even an automated rover would have to stop the search. There was no way a machine could navigate the unstable depths.

Swimming deeper, Tessa peered into the murky gloom. At this depth, vision was getting iffy, even for a mermaid. She couldn't be sure, but she thought she could make out some tall, tilted objects straight ahead.

She stopped suddenly, brought up short by the sight of a headless statue positioned amid a scattering of fallen pillars.

Tessa gasped, reaching for the crystal around her neck. A flurry of small bubbles floated past her face. *By the goddess. There's really something here to be found.*

She maneuvered closer. Though the statue had only a single arm, there was no mistaking the fishlike form of its lower body.

Her first instinct was to dart to the surface to tell everyone the good news.

Reining in her excitement, she forced herself to take a few steadying breaths. No reason to leave just this moment. All too soon, this first significant find would be revealed to the eyes of a prying, invasive world. This would literally be her only chance to have it to herself.

She skimmed as close to the seabed as she could, digging amid the debris surrounding the statue. A series of polygonal stones soon emerged.

As she poked among the crusted debris, the rise of tears blurred her vision. She couldn't help but think what a joy it would have been to be able to share the moment with her sisters. Though she'd wanted them to come, they had declined. They both had ties, commitments holding them back. Not to mention the fact that someone had to stay behind to finish supervising renovations on the house, as well as lay the groundwork for the maritime museum Jake planned to found in Port Rock.

Tessa blinked hard. She'd memorize every moment for them. When they were together again, she could share her impressions.

Twitching her tail, she kept swimming. There had to be more.

Swimming through the wreckage, Tessa stopped to examine a strange object. It looked oddly familiar, but took a moment to identify. Giving it a look from all angles, she finally concluded it was a chariot of some kind. Of course, it sat on no wheels and any decorations and trim it would have had were long gone. It occurred to her that softer materials, such as wood, fabric, and any sort of remains, would have been devoured by undersea organisms.

As she examined the bits and pieces she found, Tessa became acutely aware of the strange vibrations thrumming through the water.

Drifting with no real thought of destination, she imagined how the city might have looked all those centuries ago. In her mind's eye she saw great temples sitting above the water, bustling with life. Surely humans would have walked the cobbled streets as well, merchants and explorers seeking trade with the females inhabiting the island—perhaps even trying to woo a Mer woman into marriage.

As to the destruction of Ishaldi, Jake had theorized the island might have been taken down by some sort of seismic disturbance. Currently the most common geological effect plaguing the region was volcanic action, which could have certainly triggered some sort of massive disaster.

Tessa contemplated the idea. Though it might not be the correct conclusion, it certainly made sense. A volcanic earthquake would probably have struck without warning, sucking everything in a single gulp. The sea would have been a boiling, toxic brew, suffocating human and Mer alike.

There would have to be survivors, though, Mer who escaped the chaos. They probably scattered onto various shores throughout the Mediterranean, taking refuge among the native populations. Some of the Mer would naturally have drifted into the wider waters of the Atlantic Ocean, eventually making their way toward the Americas. She knew several of her ancestors had swum into the Penobscot, finding refuge with the local Indians. That was how the island of Little Mer gained the name it was known as to this very day.

Lost in her exploration, Tessa swam on. Another mile disappeared, then another. A cache of piled stones that appeared to be purposely fashioned by hands caught her attention. It took a few moments to realize she'd found a fully intact temple.

A closer examination revealed a series of dark sculpted blocks arranged in a circular pattern, vaguely resembling the shape of Stonehenge. Capped with thick stones, there was only a single narrow space through which to enter.

It didn't take someone with Jake's knowledge to realize the edifice hadn't been part of the surface world. This arrangement looked as though it had been constructed under the water to begin with. To enter it, one had to swim, and with the dexterity of an underwater creature.

Curious, Tessa peered into the crack between the stones. She couldn't be sure, but she thought she detected a faint glow coming from within. She reached out, touching the rock. The surface beneath her bare palm hummed, vibrating with a strange energy.

Now would be the time to turn back, she warned herself. Report the findings. Get Jake's advice.

But she didn't.

Wriggling through the space, she found herself in a tunnel-like passage. Once inside, the rock walls seemed to have a different sheen, acting as a dim but definite source of illumination.

Eager to see where the passage led, Tessa flicked her tail. Several minutes passed as she made a sharp descent.

If she hadn't known better she would have sworn she was heading toward the core of the earth itself.

Her journey ended as abruptly as it had begun. At the end of the corridor she was surprised to find a wide stone staircase leading . . . *upward*?

Her brow wrinkled. *That certainly doesn't make sense.* Curiosity tugged. She definitely had to explore.

Swimming as far as the water would allow, Tessa quickly shifted into human form and followed the steps to their top. Alone, she didn't bother with clothing. It would have been a waste of energy since she anticipated shifting back soon.

Tessa gasped. "Holy shit." Rubbing her eyes, she blinked hard. She appeared to have stumbled into some sort of antechamber.

She looked around, gazing upon a place no one had seen for centuries. A glorious vision to behold, the artistry of nature had been finely tempered by the hand of a nearly lost race.

Ishaldi's artists had fashioned their temple out of pure stone. The shade of the walls and floor was incredible— the deep burgundy of iron ore, the blues and purples of manganese oxide, blotches of pink and coral and, lastly, calcite as pure and polished white as any pearl.

Rectangular in shape, the chamber was lined with a series of columns stretching from floor to ceiling. Seemingly lit from inside, the columns glowed with pale luminescence.

Labradorite, her mind filled in. *A high-energy, powerful stone.*

More incredible was the fact it was not submerged.

She drew a breath to test the air. Her lungs rose and fell. There was oxygen, breathable oxygen. A little stale and definitely damp, but perfectly breathable.

Given the expert set of the stone, she guessed the chamber to be impermeable by water. The temple's ancient builders had somehow found a way to create an airtight sanctuary beneath the sea.

Progressing deeper into the chamber, Tessa shivered. The ethereal gleaming of the columns cast strange shadows on walls covered with all sorts of unusual images.

At the rear of the chamber, seemingly fixed into the wall, was a tall arched doorway. The edges were scored with strange symbols.

Walking toward it, Tessa held out her hand. Her fingertips brushed the surface of something that looked vaguely like crystal aragonite. Growing in an odd formation, the mineral branched into finely spun spiderwebs of stone, seemingly so delicate they would shatter into billions of shards if touched.

The stone webbing was beautiful. Exquisite. And eerily realistic.

The fine hairs on the nape of Tessa's neck rose. This part of the chamber gave her a different feeling, distinct and unappealing. It seemed strangely devoid of energy, and Tessa sensed stark, cold death. Overall, the entire place reminded her of a mausoleum.

Goose bumps prickling her skin, she let her hand drop. "I don't like this," she murmured. "Man, I wish the guys were here."

Suddenly a figure appeared beside her. Surprised and more than a little bit startled, both of them instantly jumped back.

Tessa gaped at the man beside her.

Staring into the water, Kenneth heaved a sigh. It seemed like hours since Tessa had disappeared into the murky depths. Checking his watch, he turned toward Jake. "How long can she stay under there?"

Gaze raking the calm sea, Jake shrugged. "Forever, if she wants. She's a mermaid, dude. Swimming is what they do."

Annoyed by the simplistic answer, Kenneth rubbed the back of his neck with a hand. He'd stared into the water so damn long the muscles in his neck were beginning to ache. "I know she's a fucking mermaid. But aren't you worried it might be dangerous down there? What if she meets something nasty, like a shark?"

Jake didn't blink an eye. "The shark population has declined ninety-seven percent over the past two hundred years. In fact, large predatory sharks are facing extinction unless current fishing pressures ease."

Kenneth shot the archaeologist a look. As usual, the smart-ass had an answer at the ready. He wondered if there was any subject Jake wasn't up to speed on. The man was a walking encyclopedia, and too damn smart for his own good.

"I'm not worried about the dead fuckers. It's the live ones that concern me." Kenneth's stomach twisted. He glanced back down into the water and swore. "Where the hell is Tessa anyway? She should have been back by now."

Jake flicked a hand through his long hair, casually flipping it off his shoulders. One could almost hear the whir and click of the cameras as he posed for shots for the press. "A mermaid can outswim about anything in the ocean. She'll come back when she's ready."

Kenneth was starting to lose patience. "The least you could do is show a little concern."

Jake shrugged. "Why? These are most likely the waters that gave birth to her kind. She's practically home."

Just as Kenneth began to consider wrapping his hands around Jake's throat and squeezing, the damnedest thing happened.

He winked out of existence.

For a moment there was nothing. Blank, black nothing. It was like a giant hand had smothered the world and everything in it except for him. His universe spun like a top.

Kenneth panicked. He bolted, taking a mighty step forward . . .

He instantly reemerged in a strange, luminous chamber. A figure loomed before him. Skidding on his heels, he reversed his momentum seconds before he slammed into the other person.

"How the hell did you get here?" a familiar voice demanded.

Barely registering the change in venue, Kenneth shook his head. His heart slammed against his rib cage, threatening to steal the breath from his lungs. His head spun, as if plucked off his shoulders and set to ride on a maniacal carousel. "I don't know." He blinked hard to clear his blurry vision. Recognition slowly drizzled back into his scrambled brain. "Do you?"

Tessa blinked back. "Uh, it's weird. I was just thinking you guys should be here, and all of a sudden you were."

Kenneth swallowed hard, glad to feel his nausea receding. Having the world yanked out from under his feet hadn't been fun at all. "You said *guys*." He looked around, taking in all the details of the unfamiliar chamber. The entire place looked alien, definitely unwelcoming. "I don't see Jake here."

Tessa nodded. "As much as I hate to say it, we sure could use him about now."

Jake immediately appeared, blipping in out of thin air. He stumbled, dropping to his knees. He'd obviously been in midstride when Tessa snatched him. Hitting the floor hard, he cursed. "What the fuck!" Rolling onto his back, he looked around. Dazed confusion colored his expression. He didn't seem to recognize anyone. "Where the hell am I?"

Kenneth stepped forward and held out a hand. "I don't know. Ask her."

Jake gratefully accepted the help. Hoisted to his feet, he clenched his jaw and swallowed. "Christ, I feel like my guts have been ripped out." Pressing a hand against his forehead, he blinked hard.

Tessa touched his arm. "Are you okay?"

Jake's hand dropped. "I think so." He grinned at her, his smile turning lewd. "Oh, man. I love seeing you after a swim."

Disgusted, Tessa quickly covered vital parts of her anatomy. Her right hand slammed across her breasts even as her left dropped to cover the soft thatch of curls at the crux of her thighs. She'd clearly forgotten she was stark naked. "Lech!"

Jake defended himself. "How could I not look? I'm a man. It's what we do."

Focusing, she conjured her clothes. "You and me and naked is never happening again, Jake." Kenneth recognized her favorite faded jeans, kick-ass Goth T-shirt, and combat boots. It was the fastest he'd ever seen a woman get her hands on clothes. "You're getting pretty good with that teleporting stuff."

Dropping her clothes into a pile on the floor, Tessa quickly sorted the pieces and dressed. A minute later she tugged on her boots. "It's the best thing I ever learned how to do."

Kenneth eyed her from head to foot. "I didn't know you could move people."

Tessa tossed up her hands. "Until today, I couldn't. It's like my power has suddenly become supercharged."

Taking note of the unfamiliar surroundings, Jake explored the chamber. A low whistle broke from his throat. "This place is absolutely fantastic." He shot her a look. "I'm going to assume you're the one who brought us here."

Hand rising to the crystal around her throat, Tessa nodded. "I think so. When I found this place, I thought about you two being here and—" She made a wide gesture with her arms. "All of a sudden you appeared."

Whipping his BlackBerry out of his pocket, Jake snapped off about a dozen quick pictures. "You do have the ability to teleport things," he reminded absently, absorbed with checking his handiwork.

"Yeah," Tessa agreed. "Small things, usually."

Giving her answer half an ear, Jake futzed with his handheld. The archaeologist's first instinct was to record and transmit data. "Why do I never have a freaking signal when I need one?" Annoyance laced his words. "I thought AT&T was a global network."

Kenneth snorted. "I'm sure they didn't count on you sending e-mails from the bottom of the sea." He'd definitely missed the technological revolution. The computer was a foreign beast and he had almost no working knowledge about his own cell. He could receive and make calls. That was it. Give him a wrench or a hammer and he was fine. Ditto heavy equipment.

Neanderthal definitely lingered in his DNA.

Tessa was caught in her own dilemma. "But I've never moved a whole man before."

Giving her closer attention, Kenneth held up a couple

of fingers. "Two. Right about now the rest of the crew should be freaking out." He was definitely unsettled. While he'd known Tessa and her sisters had some interesting abilities, he'd had no inkling they could pull some major rabbits out of their hats. Seeing a rock shifted from place to place was one thing.

Being the rock was quite another.

Kenneth looked around. "So let's have some details."

"We're in a temple I found," Tessa began to explain. "On the outside it's almost perfectly intact. I'm not sure, but I think it was built specifically under the water. The place it's located can't be reached unless you're a Mer."

Realizing a lost cause when he saw it, Jake pocketed his precious device. "It would make sense the Mer would have done some construction beneath the water," he broke in, uninvited. "While humans of the time would obviously have been present on land, the Mer would probably want private areas to themselves."

Kenneth's brow wrinkled. "Kind of like a 'no humans allowed' policy?"

The archaeologist nodded. "I'm thinking so."

"So how is it we're under the water, but this place isn't submerged?" The air was heavy and damp, but not hard to breathe.

"My best guess is an air pocket," Jake said. "Based on the architecture of the room, I don't believe it was intended to be submerged."

"I'd guess that, too. But how long is the air going to last?" Kenneth didn't want to imagine what it would feel like when the limited supply ran out. It probably wouldn't be pleasant to experience.

He hoped Tessa would be able to get them the hell out when the time came. Otherwise, they'd be screwed with a capital S. As much as he wanted to be in on the discovery of the lost city, he hadn't counted on being transported several miles under the sea. Staying topside had suited him just fine.

Jake shrugged. "I don't imagine it would be a problem for a Mer, as they breathe oxygen and have lungs that filter oxygen from water when they are submerged. It's the humans who would have a problem—not that I think humans are supposed to be here in the first place." He walked around the chamber, inspecting it from all angles. The strange obelisks drew his attention. "Tessa, what is this stone?"

Tessa said, "Labradorite."

Jake reached out, placing a hand against one. "This is a power stone for Mers, isn't it?"

"Very much so."

"These could be the things that supersized your ability to teleport larger objects. You probably drew off them unconsciously," he speculated.

She nodded. "That's what I thought. It's definitely a high-energy area. I can feel the vibrations running through me." She visibly shivered, running her hands up and down her bare arms. "What do you think this place is?"

Jake slowly took in the entire circumference of the chamber. "Judging by the look, it's definitely some sort of ceremonial chamber." He licked his lips. "Can't be sure just yet, but I think we're in some sort of burial vault."

His words sent a chill skittering up Kenneth's spine. "Are you saying there are bodies here?"

"The way that rear entrance has been marked and sealed off, yes." Jake pointed. "It's an absolutely incredible find."

Kenneth's stomach squeezed. By the gleam in the archaeologist's eyes, they wouldn't be leaving anytime soon.

He drew a long breath. "So now what do we do?"

Tessa dropped her hands, letting them dangle at her sides. "We stand around like morons," she said, the barest trace of a smile parting her lips. "Until Jake tells us to get our shit together."

Kenneth barely suppressed his chuckle. "I guess he would know." He had to admit he had no idea what to do next.

His partner was definitely the man of the hour.

Busy with his examination of the chamber, Jake pointed to some of the hieroglyphs etched into the walls. "Can you read any of this?" he asked Tessa.

Tessa shook her head. "My mother spoke Mer to us when we were kids, but I've never seen the language written like this. It looks like nonsense to me."

"I doubt you would be able to read an ancient version of the text even if you were completely familiar with the Mer language," Jake commented.

Tessa swallowed. "How ancient are you talking about?"

Jake considered the chamber. "Judging by the construction of this place, the Mer were a highly advanced civilization for their time. Two influences I'm definitely seeing are Greek and Egyptian—which makes sense since the location of the ruins lie between these two major powers. The script style certainly fits the timeline, too, as this way of recording their history was widely used by many ancient cultures."

Kenneth looked, too. None of it made any sense to him either. "So what you're saying is that we're looking at their version of a book?"

Jake nodded. "Absolutely. This will be the most exciting find of the twenty-first century, I'm sure."

Tess walked to the nearest wall. She reached out, tracing a few of the etchings with the tip of her finger. "So what's all this supposed to mean?"

Jake examined the etchings. "These usually depict a deity or other important person. As you can see, many of these drawings show a woman with a great aura of energy around her." He pointed. "Look at the halo. I would venture to guess she is very a significant figure."

"Atargatis?" Tessa ventured. "As creator of all the Mer, she would be a figure of power."

"It's possible," Jake mused. "The same woman appears several times in these hieroglyphs." He shrugged. "No telling for sure until we learn a little more about the language and find a way to produce a credible translation."

Kenneth strolled over to the wall. Most everything Jake said went over his head. Trying to look intelligent, he studied the symbols and drawings etched into the stones. "I'm not an expert, but doesn't it seem like these pictures show some of the things Tessa has?"

Jake barged in for a closer look. "Where do you see that?" he demanded.

Kenneth jabbed a finger. "Here, look at this. What does she appear to be wearing?"

Tessa moved closer for a better look. She hadn't really examined the drawings closely. It might have been her imagination, but it looked like a soft glow lit the drawings from behind. She blinked hard, clearing her blurry vision. "It looks like a sort of collar," she ventured.

Jake nodded. "Close, but think again."

Kenneth answered. "The choker."

Jake's hand moved to another portion. "Right. And

this hovering ball must be the orb." He looked from Tessa to the wall, and back again. "You certainly seem to have several of the items that represent a powerful female in this society."

The archaeologist moved on to a third depiction of the queenly figure. "But here she seems to be holding a scepter of some kind. Look how the rays beam out of it. What appears to be a sky and mountains are cracking open."

"Didn't see anything like that in your treasure box," Kenneth said.

Tessa's mouth turned down into a small frown. She shook her head. "If Mom ever had anything vaguely resembling a scepter, I never saw it."

Jake sighed heavily. "Too bad. It seems to be a very powerful piece."

Tessa held out her hands. "Sorry. You're shit out of luck. If I had something like that, I'd know it."

"What about your aunt?" Jake shot back. "Is it possible she might have it?"

Tessa's brow wrinkled. "Now that you mention it, I do vaguely recall her and Mom arguing over what they called the 'family jewels.' My grandmother settled it by saying to divide everything."

"So it's feasible the scepter might have gone with your aunt?"

"I don't know for sure." Tessa made a knee-high gesture with her hand. "You have to remember, I was this big when all this was going on."

Jake set to postulating out loud. "If your family as a collective truly held all the items shown around this deity female in the hieroglyphs, do you know what that could mean?"

Tessa threw up her hands. "That some thieving ancestor of mine knocked her in the head and stole her stuff?"

Pressing his palm against the wall, Jake shook his head. "I believe it would mean you could be a direct descendant of this person. And judging from the details, I'd say she was a queen."

Hearing his words, Tessa suddenly went very pale. "No shit."

Noticing her lag, Kenneth slipped a worried hand around her waist. "What is it?"

Accepting his support, Tessa gratefully leaned into him. Such a revelation was incredible. Who could believe it?

If he's even right. Jake's speculation had been known to be liberally laced with a lot of bullshit.

Tessa pulled in a weary breath. "When I was a kid, no older than five or six, my grandmother would tell me and Gwen stories about a great queen named Nyala."

Jake stared at her through narrow eyes, as though he suspected she'd deliberately withheld vital pieces of information. "What kind of stories?"

She laughed shortly. "About how we were descended from Nyala, how she was the last to wield a vast and terrible power. I always thought they were just fairy tales."

"That matches up with what we have here," Jake observed after a brief pause. "Hypatia's account calls the females of Ishaldi a warlike race. And most accounts in legend brand the Mer as unfriendly toward humans."

Tessa rolled her eyes. "That's not true."

"In a way, it is," Jake countered. "Every country in the world has some story about mermaids and most of them are the same."

"Yeah, I know. We lure ships onto rocks and drown the crew." Tessa gave a quick thumbs-up sign with one hand. "Yeah, that's exactly what we want to do. Drown you humans and take over the world."

Jake returned her glance with one of his own. "Don't kill the messenger, please. I'm just referencing what I've learned from my research. It's nothing personal."

Crossing her arms over her chest, Tessa shot him a scornful look. "I'm not so sure about that."

The two set to bickering, slinging a series of personal insults back and forth.

Kenneth winced, stepping between them. "Let's get back on track," he suggested. "What if Tessa is somehow descended from this queen?"

Tessa gave him a quick jab with her elbow. "Stop it. Those were just stories. I'm not royal."

Tucking ruffled feathers back into place, Jake shifted back into know-it-all mode. "Think about it, please. The powerful objects depicted in these hieroglyphs would only be entrusted to a person of very high rank, most likely someone the people considered royal."

Kenneth looked down at Tessa. Even though she wasn't doing anything, he could feel the energy emanating from her. A lot of power boiled beneath the surface of her skin.

A chill skittered through him. *All she has to do is think it, and it'll happen . . .* It vaguely occurred to him there might have been a time on this earth when humans had a reason to fear the Mer. He'd learned enough from Jake to know most legend had some basis in fact.

He quickly squelched the negative thoughts and focused on what the moment meant for Tessa.

"What if it's no fantasy, Tess? Who else would have held such important symbols of power but a sovereign? As incredible as it sounds, you might be a descendant of royalty."

Chapter 14

It took every bit of willpower Tessa possessed not to snort a laugh back in Kenneth's face. "Come on. Don't be stupid." She made a gesture, circling her finger near her temple. "Both of you have lost your minds. The air must definitely be thinning if you think that's true."

Both men stared back at her, two sets of eyes holding absolute conviction.

"I think it's true," Kenneth said, a note of wonder in his voice.

"I'd second that," Jake added. "The pieces we've put together certainly make the scenario seem plausible."

As much as she wanted to deny it, Tessa had a nagging feeling the guys hadn't lost their minds. Based on the stories she'd heard in her childhood about a powerful queen, the idea wasn't so far-fetched. It was entirely possible her grandmother wasn't weaving fanciful tales for her granddaughters; rather she was passing on some kind of an oral history.

Still . . . Believing she was one of the highborn felt utterly ridiculous. "It just can't be."

Losing the look of superiority, Jake's eyes assumed

the cast of wonder. "Except for the scepter, you have most of those items in your keep, Tess," he said, interrupting her sinister contemplations. "Your mother and her mother before her and even your great-grandmother all worked to carefully preserve those pieces."

Deep inside, Tessa felt her stomach loop into tight knots. Tension tightened her shoulders even as a feeling of nausea crept up from her stomach. "What for?" she demanded. "These things aren't of any real value. The stones aren't even precious."

"But they are a part of your Mercraft, correct?"

Tessa nodded. "That's true. But what am I supposed to do with them?"

"Command your people," Jake said. "Holding such objects would make you the figure of power."

Tessa lifted her hands, pressing her fingers into her temples. All of a sudden pressure was ranging behind her eyes, beating against the confines of her skull. "All this is starting to give me a headache," she said with a sigh.

Jake ignored her exhaustion. Leaving the hieroglyphs behind, he walked toward the arch. Lifting his arms, he pressed his palms against the solid layers of opaque crystal, sealing it shut. "This is a quite interesting way to seal a tomb," he remarked. "It's like the stone has been woven into webbing. I wonder how we'd get through it."

Tessa's hands dropped. "You mean, like, open it? Now?"

Jake glanced over his shoulder. "No time like the present." Stepping back, the archaeologist eagerly rubbed his hands together. "The logistics are going to be difficult given the depth we're dealing with, but we're going to have to figure out a way to get equipment down to begin recovery."

Kenneth shot him an incredulous look. "You can't be serious."

Jake immediately cut him off with a huff. "I'm very serious. It's what we do. Remember?"

"You don't even know if that's what it is," Kenneth shot back. "Right now all you're doing is guessing."

Jake just stared, affording Kenneth all the interest he'd give an insect he was about to crush. "Hands-on research is part of the recovery," he snapped nastily, pointing toward the sealed area. "If we find a chamber of any kind, we open it. If there are bodies inside, we pull them out."

Kenneth immediately rejected the idea. "The dead should rest undisturbed. What you've found so far is enough."

Jake turned to Tessa. "Explain to this moron the meaning of *search and recovery.* If we find it, we bring it up."

Tessa put her hands on her hips.

Though she understood the side Kenneth was taking, she'd also worked enough recovery missions with Jake to understand the intention behind archaeological expeditions. The mission was simple: Uncover and record the findings.

An unbidden chill swept down her spine. Sometimes the findings included remains. The coast of Maine was littered with wreckage from ships and airplanes that had gone under when misfortune struck. The last wreck she'd worked on with Jake wasn't a ship, but a WWII fighter. Surviving family members had been elated when the wreckage was located and identified. And though the bodies of the crewmen trapped inside had been reduced to bones, she'd worked to bring them to the surface with the few personal effects she could locate.

Closing her eyes, Tessa inhaled a deep, calming breath.

Should it be any different with the Mer? Her throat worked as she swallowed back the bile rising from her stomach.

Licking dry lips, she turned to face the two men. "I think it should be opened."

Jake's icy blue eyes lit up with the fervor of a fanatic finding true religion. "Excellent decision. We're on the edge of a historic discovery."

Kenneth didn't look as convinced. "It feels like sacrilege to me."

Tessa rubbed her hands across her face. "Why don't we argue one step at a time?" She eyed the crystal seal. "Right now we have no guarantee we can even get the thing open."

Kenneth snorted. "Oh, give Jake a hammer and he'll get through."

Jake scoffed back. "I am not a philistine. Our mission is to preserve and protect, not bash and carry. The less damage we do, the better."

Kenneth threw up his hands in frustration. "I don't like it, but I suppose the two of you will outvote me on this one."

Tessa cleared her throat. "I'm not siding with Jake when I say I want to keep going with this," she said, choosing her words carefully. "But this is a significant find and we can't ignore its value. The Mer deserve to have their place in history, too."

Kenneth's expression was wary. "I understand that," he said. "I just don't understand the hurry."

Jake shot him an angry glare. "This stupid argument is costing valuable time. Now let's figure out how to get this show on the road."

Kenneth shook off his partner's nasty look. "If you're going to try it, better do it fast." He drew a deep breath.

"I don't know about you two, but it seems to me the air's starting to thin."

Jake processed the information. "We are working with a limited resource." His gaze swung to Tessa. "I don't suppose you would know anything about opening a Mer tomb?"

Tessa eyed the crystal webbing. "I'm not sure, but I think it's been energy spun."

"Which is?" Jake asked.

"If you take a crystal and apply enough heat, you can turn it molten, literally weave it into other shapes and forms," she said, attempting to explain. "I've tried it a few times, but I'm not really good at getting it to take shape yet. It takes an incredible amount of psi-energy to do it."

Jake glanced back at the hieroglyphs. "Those drawings depict the choker and the orb as emanating a great energy. I don't suppose you happened to tuck those in your back pocket?"

Tessa laughed. "Of course not." Those things were back in Maine, safely hidden away. She'd had no reason to pack them for a trip out to sea.

"We could have them flown in," Jake started to suggest, then stopped himself. His gaze sparked. "Or Tessa could whip them up here."

She raised a brow. "Whip them up?"

Jake snapped his fingers. "Why not? You whammied us straight to the bottom of the sea. What's so hard about bringing down a few trinkets?"

Tessa rolled her eyes. "You were on a ship just a few miles away. Those things are half a world away. I doubt I could fetch them from that far. It might have been a fluke that I could bring you guys down here in the first place."

Kenneth paled. "God, I hope not."

Sensing his growing discomfort, Tessa looked at him and frowned. "Don't worry. I'll get you out of here. If we run out of air, I'll swim you out." She pointed to her lips. "I've got the magic kiss, babe."

"I'd take one of those," Jake said. "Teleportation makes me sick."

Tessa shot him a middle finger. "You'll take this and hope you can hold your breath long enough to reach the surface."

Jake pouted. "You sure have gotten touchy since you've learned to do all that shit."

She narrowed her eyes. "Better watch it, or I'll send you to the far side of the moon."

Kenneth brightened. "Can you do that?"

Jake threw up his hands. "God, sometimes it feels as if I'm dealing with Tweedledum and Tweedledee. Can you get the items or not?"

His request instantly sobered her.

Tessa licked dry lips as uncertainty seeped through her veins, sharp and painful as shards of glass. For a wild moment she doubted her ability. Everything she'd learned in the last few months seemed to drizzle away, leaving her brain a useless pile of mush. "I don't know. I can try."

Jake nodded. "Then do."

Tessa waved her arms, moving the men back. "Give me some space."

Both moved toward a far wall.

Satisfied she had enough room, Tessa pressed her hands together in front of her. She'd easily mastered kinetics and had successfully learned to move small stones and other objects from one place to another with the flick of a thought. It shouldn't make any difference whether the item was a foot away or several thousand miles away.

In her mind's eye, she plucked the choker from her jumble of memories. Remembering how it had looked to her eyes and felt under her curious fingers, she envisioned holding it in her hands.

Taking a deep breath, she reached into her mind and connected with the memory. This, she hoped, would allow her to grasp the physical item.

The crystal pendant hanging around her neck warmed. Gathering its energy, she pushed it outward, willing it toward the desired object. When she was sure she had a firm grasp, she reeled the energy back in.

A little spark of light exploded in front of her eyes. Her hands shot out, cupping together to form a cradle. Seconds later the desired object rested against her palms, still warm from its travel through kinetic space.

A low whistle broke through her concentration.

"Jesus, that's amazing," Jake complimented.

Kenneth managed a nod. "I knew you could do it."

Tessa's heart gave a convulsive thump. No, he wasn't exactly thrilled by her unworldly ability. The unspoken rift between them widened a minute fraction. He was very aware he was all too human and she was not.

Shaking off his silent disapproval, Tessa gave a little bow. "Thank you very much," she said, holding the prize out toward him. "Would you hold this for me?"

Kenneth stepped forward and claimed the trinket. He cradled it carefully, as if she'd handed him the most fragile and rarest of objects.

She waved him back. "Now for the orb."

Tessa repeated the process, a little easier the second time around. More confident in her ability, she easily managed the incredible task. A minute later she held it balanced in her hands.

Jake clapped. "Excellent."

"You handled that like an old pro," Kenneth observed.

"Let's get to work," Jake said.

Tessa looked to Kenneth. "Would you help me put it on?"

"Sure." He claimed the piece. A clasp at the back allowed it to be opened, widened, and fitted around the neck.

Tessa lifted a hand, fingering the regal ornament. The fit was tight, uncomfortable. But she had to admit the choker was an impressive piece. Like fine diamonds, the stones had been sized, cut, and polished into a marquis shape before being embedded in a band of solid gold. Altogether there were five thin rows, giving it an overall height of about three inches.

She thought of the queen being chained and choked by the incredible responsibility that went along with wearing the piece.

She frowned. "Damn, I'd hate to wear this every day."

Kenneth noticed her discomfort. "Feel okay?"

Tessa swallowed, feeling the muscles in her throat contract in rebellion against the metal. "I'll be glad to take it off."

It's wrong, a voice whispered in the back of Kenneth's mind. *We shouldn't be doing this.*

But he said nothing. Despite his reservations, he had to support Tessa's decision to open the tomb. As she'd said earlier, she had the right to learn everything she could about her people.

Kenneth personally felt some things were best left undisturbed. Sometimes things were hidden for a reason. And once concealed, were meant to remain that way.

He glanced at Tessa. She looked pale, a little unsteady on her feet. "Are you sure you can breathe?"

Forcing a finger between her skin and the tight collar, Tessa tugged the choker. "This freaking thing feels like a choke chain," she gasped through a series of shallow pants. "I'll be glad to get it off."

"Don't forget the orb," Jake put in.

Tessa frowned at him. "I can handle this, thank you very much."

Jake sniffed and looked down his nose. "I'm just offering a few suggestions."

Kenneth couldn't suppress a wary look. Jake loved flaunting his knowledge. And he took his occupation as a know-it-all very seriously. "Maybe you should shut up and just let Tessa handle things."

Jake scoffed, but Kenneth had to say his piece. There was a fine line between the spirit of discovery and rushing in like fools. "I just don't like all this guessing, especially since you two are messing with something unknown. What if something goes wrong and the whole damn place collapses around our heads?"

Jake stared right though him. "When you take on a job like this, you take on the risks that go with it. If you're going to keep whining like a baby, maybe Tessa can send you back to the ship."

In other words, Jake was calling him a pussy.

Ouch.

He made a snap decision. "I'm in."

Jake raised a brow. "All the way?" he asked, lacing his question with dry sarcasm.

Straightening his shoulders, he looked at Tessa. "To hell and back."

She smiled. "That's the best thing I've heard all day."

Although he couldn't be sure, Kenneth thought she looked more than a little relieved by his reply. But then again, the idea of having Jake Massey watching your back wasn't a very inspiring notion. Beneath the surface of his personal allure, the archaeologist had a devious streak a mile wide. It was best to keep loose change and sharp objects out of his reach.

"So what exactly are you going to do?" Kenneth asked.

Tessa eyed the arched doorway. "The seal looks like crystal aragonite. I think if I apply enough heat I can weaken its cellular structure, crack it open, so to speak."

Alarmed, Jake waved his hands. "Be careful," he warned. "We want as little damage as possible."

Positioning herself in the center of the chamber, Tessa looked at the imposing seal. "I'll do my best," she promised. Setting her feet apart, she extended her arms. The orb rested in the center of her upturned palms. "An instruction booklet would definitely help," she mumbled before closing her eyes.

Kenneth watched as the stones circling her neck began to flicker. Tessa wasn't only drawing their energy in, she was going to have to redirect it out, toward the globe.

Face twisted with intense concentration, Tessa opened her eyes.

The choker around her neck lit up, giving off a thousand-watt glow. At the same time, it emitted a beam of pure energy, striking the crystal orb in her hands. Lightning flickered within the sphere, flaming out from its heart and striking the hard crystalline shield. The red-hot beam sparked and flared against the stone before completely spluttering out.

Trembling from head to toe, a low groan passed Tessa's lips. "Damn it," she slurred. Her knees buckled, threatening to take her down.

Kenneth rushed in, catching her before she hit the floor. Holding her around the waist, he wrapped his arms around her and pulled her close. "Steady there."

Barely managing to keep her fingers wrapped around the fragile orb, Tessa pulled in long, desperate gulps of air. "By the goddess." She fought to catch her breath. "I wasn't expecting that."

His gaze shadowed with worry, Jake hovered. "What happened?"

Fighting to regain her equilibrium, Tessa slowly shook her head. "It's hard to explain, but when the beam hit the stone, the fucking thing turned on me. It started to suck the energy out of me." Jaw tightening, she shook her head. "I had to let it go or it would have sucked me dry."

Kenneth frowned. "That's enough, then. There's no reason to put yourself in any more danger."

Tessa twisted out of his grip like an unruly toddler, determined to have her way. "That fucker didn't like me trying to open it."

Kenneth looked at her. He didn't need to be able to read her mind to know what she was thinking. "No. You don't need to try again."

Tessa looked up, meeting his gaze with a stubborn one of her own. "I'm going to try again."

"If it's going to drain you, I'm inclined to agree," Jake

seconded. "Neither one of us can swim out of here if something happens to you."

Tessa brushed off their protests. "Nothing's going to happen. I think I know what I did wrong."

Kenneth folded his arms across his chest. "What?"

She made a vague gesture toward the crystal seal. "This thing was made to put up some heavy resistance," she started to explain. "It's not only locked, but double-bolted. Throw a little energy at it, and it's going to toss it right back in your face."

Jake nodded. "That would make sense."

Tessa looked around the chamber. "I need more energy, and I need it to come from a bigger source than the Herkimer diamonds I'm wearing." She eyed the softly luminous pillars. "There's the boost I need."

Kenneth compared the size of the pillars to the size of the woman standing in front of him. Those things were massive, huge, and, by the looks of them, full of power.

He eyed Tessa, measuring her slender body. Though she was taller than the average female, her five-ten height didn't even begin to measure half the height of those pillars. Pulling energy from a larger source into a smaller one didn't make sense. Logic said she'd quickly overload her system and burn herself out.

He shook his head. "You're crazy." The words popped out before he'd even considered saying them.

Tessa took a deep breath, then pushed it out. "Maybe, but I've got to try." Cautiously, she resumed her original position in the center of the chamber. "Step back, nonbelievers."

Jake hurried out of the line of danger, scuttling to the farthest side of the chamber. He wasn't dumb. He wanted to be as far away as possible if anything went wrong, such as a massive, rock-shattering explosion.

Kenneth shot his partner a disgusted look. You could always count on Jake to cover his ass first.

He wasn't willing to take that caution. He'd told Tessa he'd support her through hell and back, and by God, he was going to do just that. *She won't do it alone.*

Stepping up behind her, he wrapped his arms around her curvy frame. "I'll keep you on your feet."

Tessa relaxed against him. "You're assuming I can concentrate with you pressing against me like that."

Kenneth tightened his grip. "You'll have to make the best of it because I'm not going anywhere."

Tessa extended the orb again. "Here goes nothing."

It took only seconds for the magical tension to deepen throughout the chamber.

Holding Tessa tight, Kenneth felt the fine hairs on his body stand to attention as she began to filter the energy out of the labradorite pillars. Her control was stronger this second time around, her aim clear and precise.

Like something you would see in a mad scientist's lab, thin spikes of lightning snaked out from the pillars, striking the choker around Tessa's neck. A tingle of exaltation passed through him as the vibrant force throbbed between their bodies, leaving him miraculously unharmed.

Drawing the massive charge inside her own body, Tessa redirected it toward the orb. Filmy strings of red-hot light flickered within the orb's heart, gathering strength with each passing second.

A beam of pure white radiance leaped from the orb, striking the crystal webbing squarely in the center. Soaking in the radiance, the shield glowed with the brilliance of a sun going nova. Unleashing its potent energy, white whips of flame simultaneously spread out across the shell of stone, dissolving it like acid.

Kenneth felt the luminous energy through his eyes, vibrating the bones in his skull as if it would rip him to shreds.

Blood pounding at his temples, self-preservation kicked in.

This is going to pull us apart.

He had to get Tessa out of the line of danger.

Clenching his teeth, Kenneth bodily wrenched Tessa around, turning her away from the glowing beam of energy she'd unleashed. She sank to her knees as if forced by an intense pressure coming down on her shoulders. Her face twisted as the crystal orb slipped from her fingers. The sphere instantly struck the stone beneath their feet, shattering into a million tiny pieces. The shards crackled and snapped, then darkened into burned-out ashes.

The strange lightning filling the chamber flickered, then died. The pillars around them went dark, burnt out to the core.

The atmosphere around them was void, cold and empty.

Letting himself relax, Kenneth drew a tentative breath. The intense odor of burnt stone scorched his nostrils. Silence prevailed. Tessa lay like a deadweight in his arms. For a heart-stopping instant he was sure she was dead as he lowered her to the cold stone floor.

Kenneth shook her, limp and insensible in his arms. "Tessa?"

A low moan finally broke from her throat. She whimpered softly, making a clawing gesture toward her throat.

Jake hurried in from the shadows. "That was incredible."

Anger rising like a cobra, Kenneth shoved him away. "She better not be hurt. Or you'll be the one to pay."

Jake gestured helplessly. "I'm just trying to offer a hand."

"Stay the hell away, Jake!"

Panicked, Kenneth looked at Tessa's pale face. Wrenching the choker off her neck, he tossed the hateful thing aside. Like the orb, the Herkimers were burned out, charred to a crisp. "Tessa, sweetie. Are you okay?"

Dazed and disoriented, Tessa struggled to sit up. "What happened?"

He cradled her cheek against his palm. "It all blew up," he said. "Damn near fried us all."

Groaning in disappointment, Tessa closed her eyes. She lifted a hand, pawing ineffectively at her left temple. "God, it's throbbing. Feels like I've turned my insides out."

"Just be still," Kenneth urged. "You have to rest."

But Jake had wandered away from Tessa, staring straight at the doorway. He pointed. "You did it."

All eyes turned toward the circular arch.

Kenneth gasped, struck by the vision, dazzled by the sheer force Tessa had unleashed. The crystalline shell had vanished, replaced by a rippling blue veil of a mist-like substance.

A chill of dread and foreboding raced down his spine.

"I'll be damned," he murmured.

Hearing his words, Tessa forced herself to stand. Unsteady on her feet, she staggered toward the swirling mass. "It's open." Panting through her mouth, she spread her arms wide as if to embrace the glowing morass of light writhing in its center. At the same moment her legs gave out under her weight, causing her to sink to her knees.

Kenneth rushed forward to catch her. But before he

could wrap his arms around her and pull her back to safety, something incredible happened.

As though commanded by her gesture, the force swirling in the heart of the blue veil reached out. White-hot light flared, filling the chamber with a blinding glow.

Throwing up his arms, Kenneth shielded his face from the glare. He felt raw energy spreading through him, heating and intensifying until he was sure his flesh would be scorched to the bone.

The glare slowly faded.

Kenneth lowered his arms. He blinked, searching the empty space. Tessa had vanished.

Just. Like. That.

Kenneth froze. "What the fuck?" He threw a panicked look toward Jake. "What the hell did that thing do?"

Face pale, Jake said tremblingly, "I don't know what just happened. It took her. It just took her."

Gritting his teeth, Kenneth focused his full attention on the strange vortex. The sole source of light in the chamber, it continued to cast an ominous glow.

That thing had Tessa.

He wanted her back.

Rage and frustration boiled. "There's only one way to find out where she went," he growled.

There was no time to hesitate. No time to think.

Just do it.

Raw determination spurred him forward. He forced his body into motion, heading straight into the center of the glowing light.

Chapter 15

Gripped by the powerful force, Tessa felt warm. Content. Safe.

But it was only a matter of moments before she found herself rudely thrust outward. The radiant illumination abruptly winked out, taking with it its pure warm rays.

She barely had time to register the abrupt change before she caught a glimpse of a hard white surface below.

Tessa fought to break the eerie paralysis that held her. As one accustomed to performing tricky maneuvers in water, she instinctively twisted her body midair to more easily absorb the impact of the fall. Thrusting out her arms, she fell to the floor with a thud and rolled.

She ended up on her back, legs splayed wide.

For a moment she lay still, panting. Relieved she could breathe, she did a quick mental check. She had a bruise on her backside, but she'd manage to escape breaking a bone.

What the hell happened?

Making a grab for her bearings, she stared out into unfamiliar surroundings. A few minutes ago she'd been in the undersea temple, staring at some sort of energy mass. And then it had grabbed her, hauling her . . . *where?*

Still a little shaky, Tessa climbed to her feet. At the moment she couldn't begin to guess what had happened. In the blink of an eye she'd been forcibly sucked into a whole different world. It didn't take a rocket scientist to figure out the thing they'd opened wasn't a tomb, but something else. Something totally bizarre. And out of this world.

At the moment she had no idea where she was, but she had a gut-level feeling that she was about to find out . . .

Looking around, Tessa realized that she appeared to be standing on a high platform at the rear of a huge stone sanctuary that looked like it had been lifted straight out of a photograph of ancient Greece. Instead of ruins, though, the Parthenon-like structure was perfectly intact.

And occupied.

She wasn't alone.

Her gaze skimmed across a crowd of figures. She couldn't count the number, but she figured out by the startled look on the faces around her that she'd caught them by surprise. It took her a moment to realize why she could see everything so well.

She was standing high above the crowd. From such an advantageous point she saw the occupants of the temple were women. Women who shared strange, eerily unsettling similarities. Tall and pale skinned, they were all blond and blue-eyed. There wasn't an ugly or imperfect face among them.

The women were even dressed alike, most of them

clad in a style that might have been lifted straight out of some futuristic science-fiction flick: formfitting leather jumpsuits. Not the usual cowhide, either. They wore the exotic stuff, like eel and stingray. Decked out in a variety of colors and patterns, their outfits were studded with jewels and other precious metals like gold and silver.

Tessa's stomach twisted into tight knots of fear and disbelief. Holy shit. While she couldn't exactly be sure, the women looked strangely familiar.

Mers, she suddenly thought. *Great galloping goddess.* Living, breathing, weapon-toting Mers. She could barely believe her eyes.

And then the next thought occurred to her. Had they stumbled on Ishaldi?

The more she thought about it, the more she realized it was the likeliest explanation. She wasn't sure how, but she had a feeling she'd find out soon.

The women were armed. Heavily. In addition to the familiar Ri'kah worn by those standing on the periphery of the main group, she recognized a variety of weapons that would have been the latest technology had you lived a couple of thousand years ago. Daggers were sheathed in hilts, and spears were at the ready. She even thought she glimpsed a sword or two.

They were ready to rock. Seriously.

A cold chill rolled over Tessa's skin. If things turned nasty, she didn't have a single thing to defend herself with. She'd expended serious energy, leaving almost nothing for herself. Right now she doubted she had enough brainpower to flick at a fly. If things turned ugly, there was no doubt these Mer could stomp her into the ground before she even had a chance to lift a hand.

Oh, man. This can't be good.

Though they had obviously taken note of her presence, no one said a single word. The temple was absolutely silent. All eyes were fixed on her.

Several minutes passed, uninterrupted by any movement whatsoever. Just as she was sizing them up, the Mer were also sizing her up. They didn't show any fear. Merely curiosity.

One of the Mer at the foot of the altar finally broke away from the rest of the crowd. Hand positioned on the hilt of her dagger, she cautiously stalked up the wide stone steps. Reaching the top, she stopped a few feet away from Tessa. Her vivid blue gaze burned with curiosity.

Tessa cast a quick glance over her shoulder, checking out all avenues of escape. The eerie vortex swirled behind her like a giant, gaping maw. That thing had brought her here. Easing back a careful step, she hoped it would be just as good for getting the hell out.

No time to find out.

Kenneth burst through the gate's center, tumbling and skidding across the cold marble floor. Jake followed next, rolling head over heels in a most undignified manner. He landed smack on his face, a soft "oomph" sliding from his lips.

He pushed himself up on his knees. "What the hell happened?"

Jake rolled over on his back, then slowly forced himself into a sitting position. He panted. "I feel as if I'm going to vomit."

Tessa quickly hushed them both. "Be quiet, you idiots. I think we just stumbled onto a bunch of Mers."

Both men looked past her, mouths agape. One look at the tall, leather-clad, badass-looking chick with a knife in one hand and a sword strapped across her back shut them both up.

"Just let me do the talking," she warned, hoping she could find a way to communicate with them.

The tall Mer planted her hands on her hips. She cocked her head as though expecting an answer.

Tessa quickly extended her arms to show she held no weapons. "I come in peace." She winced as the words came out of her mouth. How lame. But she couldn't think of anything else to say.

"I don't think they speak English," Jake hissed from behind. "Don't you know any Mer?"

That made sense.

She gave it a try, speaking a little bit of the language she'd learned from her mother. The words felt strange rolling off her tongue. "Where am I?" A simple enough question.

They seemed to make some sense to the Mer who'd confronted them. A flicker of faint recognition flitted through her cornflower blue gaze. "Do you not know?" she asked.

Relief flooded through Tessa. The Mer's accent was strange, but perfectly understandable. Though not completely fluent in the lingua franca of the Mer, she was sure she'd learned enough to hold simple conversations.

As to the question of where she might be . . .

To show their shared connection, Tessa touched the stone hanging around her neck. "I am a Mer," she said, attempting to put confidence behind her words, "and I have come in search of my people."

Gaze immediately lighting with recognition, the strange Mer stepped closer. The soul-stone at the base of her neck started to glow, sending out a soft pulse of light. "The prayers of so many voices have at last been answered," she said. "I offer my most humble gratitude that you have freed your people from their cruel bondage, goddess."

Goddess? Good grief, did this woman honestly believe she was some sort of all-powerful deity?

"You honor me with such a welcome," she said. "I am pleased."

The woman pressed her hands together and offered a brief nod. "I am Doma Chiara. You have my welcome to the Temple of Thiraisa."

Tessa searched her mind for the meaning. The closest she could come up with was that *Doma* was an indication of rank. The woman was a priestess. A dagger-wielding, sword-swinging priestess. There had to be an oxymoron in there somewhere. To keep the goodwill flowing, Tessa copied the gesture. "My name is Tessa Lonike, but I am no goddess. I'm only a Mer who seeks the truth of her people's origins."

The woman's eyes widened. "Then the world outside the sea-gate still exists?"

Sea-gate? That was a new one.

Not exactly sure of the logistics between Earth and Ishaldi, Tessa ventured a guess. "If you speak of the world above the water, yes, it's still there."

A peevish voice interrupted their conversation. "What the fuck is going on?" Jake demanded from behind. "This damn hard floor is ruining my knees."

Tessa shot him a quick frown. "Forget your pants for a minute!" she snapped. "We aren't in Kansas anymore, Toto."

Jake snorted. "You think I haven't figured that out?" He hated being pushed aside and ignored.

"Shut up, man!" Kenneth broke in, eyeing the forbidding horde of Mer and the weapons they carried. "If you don't mind, I'd like to get the hell out of here in one piece."

Tessa cut her hand through the air with a kill-it motion. "Both of you be quiet," she snapped, ordering them to silence.

She scrambled to make sense of the entire scene. Right now she had a lot of pieces, but none of them fit together. It was going to take some work to assemble the entire picture. She wished it was as simple as sitting down over a pitcher of strawberry margaritas and dishing.

Unfortunately, she doubted her greeter, rigidly adhering to proper etiquette, would welcome such informality.

The priestess pointed to Kenneth and Jake, seemingly impressed. "I see your pets are well trained. You had them silent immediately. They seem to obey your commands well."

Tessa's brows rose with surprise. "My pets?" She looked toward Kenneth and Jake. "You mean these humans?"

"Humans, yes. That is what they were once called, though we have not used that term since the ancient age." Lips curling with disgust, Doma Chiara spat toward Kenneth. "They are useless creatures."

Tessa felt a slow sinking in the pit of her stomach. Oh, shit. Had the sea-gate been sealed because of a conflict between humans and Mer?

A war would definitely explain the lack of Mer in the ocean's waters at this time. After Ishaldi was taken down, any Mer remaining in the human world would probably have scattered, attempting to find a safe refuge wherever they could. Hunted, perhaps relentlessly, their numbers would have quickly thinned.

The gruesome picture of men slaughtering Mer the way they still massacred other defenseless sea life flashed through her mind.

Tessa attempted to will away the terrible images. "You speak as if you despise them."

Chiara frowned, nodding solemnly. "The inferiors have always caused problems." Her hand again moved to the weapon sheathed at her hip. "But we have done our best to control them."

Tessa's brows rose in surprise. "Inferiors?"

Chiara indicated the rear of the temple. "The *huslas*, our human slaves." She pointed out people hovering on the periphery of the Mer crowd. She sighed as though exhausted. "It has taken much time, but we have tamed their savage natures."

Tessa looked. Her brows rose in surprise. She hadn't even noticed them before. They were kept separate from the rest of the group by guards, who kept them in place with snapping whips.

Unlike the Mer, who were clad in elaborate leather outfits, the people wore almost nothing at all. Men were clad in little more than loincloths. Women wore loincloths and cloths binding their breasts. All wore shackles around their necks, wrists, and ankles. They were chained and kept like dogs.

These people, she guessed, were descendants of the people left behind in Ishaldi when the threshold between the two worlds closed.

Tessa felt her grip on self-control slipping through her fingers. Here she was in an unfamiliar land, among an unknown people who lived in a way she couldn't begin to understand. Any kinship she might have felt with Mer instantly evaporated. They were nothing like she'd expected.

Acutely aware a response was expected, Tessa affected an attitude of interest. Dismay gnawed deep in her belly. "I see you have succeeded well in that endeavor."

Since the Mer considered human beings to be a sub-par species, it might be safer for Jake and Kenneth if she went along with Chiara's impression that she owned the humans. They were under her care, so to speak.

Tessa swallowed the thick lump building in the back of her throat. "I assure you my pets will behave. I will see they are kept in their proper place."

Chiara nodded gracefully. "Of course. You must be tired from your long journey, Mira Tessa," she said, automatically granting Tessa the rank and status of an honored and esteemed guest. "I am sure you will want to rest before meeting with Queen Magaera."

That one took her by surprise. "I will?" She'd stupidly assumed she'd soon be on her way back through the thing Chiara had identified as a sea-gate. Of course, that was an insane notion. She'd just unlocked some sort of doorway sealed for almost two millennia. It only made sense the people locked inside would want information about a world they hadn't laid eyes on in, well, ever.

The priestess nodded. "Now that you have given us back our freedom, we Mer shall have a chance to reclaim the waters that are rightfully ours."

Fighting back a faint surge of nausea, Tessa inwardly gulped. The weapons the Mer carried weren't for show-and-tell. The women were armed and ready for a fight. Comparing the well-armed Mer to the pathetically kept humans, an uneasy suspicion crept up from the shadows in Tessa's mind. Cold awareness prickled the fine hairs on the back of her neck. She shivered faintly.

I think I've made a huge mistake.

*   *   *

Kenneth didn't like the looks of the shackles the Mer were fitting around his neck and wrists. Though the women were doing nothing to cause him undue harm, their attitude was one of distance and disinterest. He was just another human, and a worthless one at that.

A gut-level sense of dismay and embarrassment filled him. "Why do we have to wear these?"

Her expression tense but controlled, Tessa leaned in. Pretending to check the grip of the collar circling his neck, she whispered, "Humans are like slaves here." She spoke so quietly he had to strain to catch her words. "They regard you as little more than animals of low intelligence."

"Can't you tell them in your world you don't treat people like animals?"

Tessa frowned at him impatiently and shook her head. "I've tried to tell them you are my companions and quite intelligent, but they aren't buying it. In their minds, humans are untrustworthy and need to be fully controlled."

Attempting to dig a finger in between his wrist and the tight cuff to loosen the pressure, Kenneth jerked his head toward Jake. "So why the fuck are they so gaga over that asshole?" Instead of treating him like a mongrel dog, the Mer seemed to take more interest in the archaeologist. They petted and pawed him like a prize stallion.

Tessa shot a look toward her ex-lover. "It's his hair and eyes. For them, he's a perfect specimen for breeding."

Kenneth snorted. It never failed. He should have guessed Jake would find a way to take advantage of his looks and charm the ladies.

"So what am I? Chopped liver?"

"It's not you," Tessa explained. "It's your hair color. You're considered an inferior, not suitable for fathering their daughters. Your purpose is more like a slave."

Understanding dawned. "Ah, someone who does the heavy lifting."

She nodded. "Right."

He blew out a breath. "Figures."

The woman who had initially acted as greeter ambled over. She looked at Tessa. They exchanged a few words.

Kenneth shivered. The Mer tongue sounded like gibberish to his ears. He couldn't understand a single word and it made him feel like a second-class citizen.

His mouth drew down. *In their world, I am.*

He glanced around. From what he could see, all humans were shackled, both males and females. Some, he noticed, seemed to be treated better than others. Those who were poorly kept were pathetic creatures. In the human world they would be considered plain or merely average. In the Mer world, they had no hope. Hair shorn away, their skin was covered with bruises. Many were badly scarred, the damage inflicted by the whiplike lashes all Mers carried. Looped at their belts, the objects of punishment were within ready reach.

Those treated better included men—and some women—lucky enough to be born blond. Not only were they dressed a bit more nicely, but they were paraded on leashes the way some people would show off a pedigreed animal.

One of the Mer who had helped shackle them handed their leads to Tessa. Giving Jake a final warm pet, she sauntered back to her duties.

Tessa looked at the leashes. "I'm sorry. They require you to be leashed in public."

Jake perked up. Instead of fighting his shackles, he seemed to be enjoying all the attention he attracted. "Excellent."

Kenneth shot him a look. "Excellent? They've got us collared."

Jake shrugged. "When in Rome you do as the Romans do, my friend. It only makes sense that the Mer would be the dominant race. After all, this is their world."

"Yeah, but instead of being equals, they've made us into slaves."

"Which is exactly how our own human civilization evolved," Jake said. "When the strong roll in, the weak roll over. To survive means to adapt to the ways of the ruling race."

Kenneth grumbled. "I don't call slavery survival."

The Mer who had greeted Tessa hurried over. A look of disapproval pursed her lips. Handing over a whip, she made a slicing motion with her hand. The words that accompanied her gesture sounded sharp, scolding.

Tessa nodded her response, snapping the whip savagely in the air to indicate her understanding. "She thinks you are speaking out of your place and she wants me to punish you."

Jake eyed the forbidding whip. "Oh, kinky. A whip and chains." He waggled his brows. "Tell me, darling, don't you feel all butch now?"

Tessa cracked the whip, giving him a neat smack across the arm. "You'd better have a care with your tongue."

Jake rubbed the red patch rising on his skin. "Hey, watch where you're swinging that thing, damn it!"

Tessa smacked him again. "If they think I can't control my humans, they might take you away. I can't say what would happen to you if they did, but I don't think it'd be pretty."

The archaeologist flagged a distracted hand. "What are they going to do? Pet me to death? I don't have to speak the language to figure out more than one of those ladies would like to put me in her bed. How long do you think it's been since they've had new blood added to the gene pool?" He pointed toward his beltline. "What I've got down here is pure gold."

Kenneth shook his head. "I think I'm going to puke." Leave it to Jake to figure out how to feed his libido, and all in the name of new world discovery.

Tessa delivered a third smack. "You're pissing them off, and you're starting to piss me off. Put a lid on it before I really have to lay some hurt on you."

Putting on the face of an angel, Jake smiled and said nothing.

Kenneth breathed a sigh of relief. The last thing he wanted was to feel that leather come down across his skin. He had a feeling he wouldn't enjoy it half as much as Jake was. That asshole was just a glutton for punishment. If it were kinky, illegal, or immoral—preferably all three—Jake would be there in a second.

A tug on his leash reminded him he needed to start walking.

Trotting along beside Jake, he followed Tessa. Tessa in turn followed their guide, who led them outside the elaborate temple.

Catching his first glimpse of the city, Kenneth caught his breath. All the trouble it had taken to reach it was suddenly worth the risk.

A magnificent vision to behold, Ishaldi was vast, a metropolis stretching as far as the eye could see. Streets of pure limestone wound between temples and other buildings that served as public and private dwellings. Beautifully sculpted lawns and lush enclosed gardens were liberally sprinkled with pools of clear sparkling water and intricately carved stone fountains. It was like walking through a crack in time and somehow arriving in an ancient Greek city.

The atmosphere above the trees wasn't a wide-open stretch of endless space. Nor did any sun shine in the sky above. Ishaldi's heavens shined with a pure and incandescent white light. To stare directly into its depth was almost blinding.

It took Kenneth a moment to realize he wasn't looking at an overcast sky, but one formed entirely of crystal. The Mer world, the whole of it, existed entirely underground.

Interrupting his sense of wonder, Jake leaned close. "Amazing. I'm going to say the Mer live much as their ancestors did. My guess is their civilization has hardly changed since their world was sealed off from ours. They've had no outside influences to integrate into their civilization for almost two thousand years."

"It feels like the whole place is part of a giant terrarium," Kenneth whispered back. "How can their world exist under the freaking ocean anyway?"

Jake pondered a moment. "I'll agree they have a very unusual ecosystem going on here. So much so that I'm beginning to suspect that their world and ours inhabit the same space, but in different dimensions."

That brought his eyebrows up. "I don't get it."

"Wormhole," Jake mouthed.

"What's got worms?"

"Not *got worms*, idiot," Jake corrected. "A wormhole is a shortcut through space and time."

Kenneth glanced around. "Are you saying we're on another planet?"

Jake quickly shook his head. "Based on the architectural similarities to our own ancient cultures, I'd wager we're still earthbound. It's a long shot, but I'd say some glitch in dimensional shifting aligned their world beneath ours."

Kenneth grimaced. "Is that even possible?"

Jake shrugged. "It's physics. The thing we stepped through seems to be some sort of wormhole. But instead of taking the traveler through outer space and time, it transports intradimensionally through two different points in the planet's evolution."

Kenneth resisted rolling his eyes. "I guess that makes some kind of cockeyed sense."

They followed Tessa, who in turn followed the woman called Doma Chiara. Their guide led them toward a fine chariot, elaborately designed and gilded in gold. Instead of horses doing the grunt work, several men waited to pull the chariot to its destination.

Kenneth looked at the men. They waited patiently for a command, as docile as any well-trained animal. He doubted it could have been easy for any human, male or female, to assume the role of slave. But then again, did the humans of Ishaldi even remember freedom? They'd apparently been kept in captivity and bred like animals.

Doma Chiara climbed up to take the reins. Saying a few quick words, she made a motion for Tessa to join her.

Tessa resisted. A quick exchange passed between them. Neither woman appeared happy.

Tessa finally shrugged and threw up her hands. "I'm sorry," she said to Kenneth, joining their hostess. "While

it's a custom for their petted ones to ride, the true inferiors are expected to walk."

Kenneth frowned. "What the fuck is that supposed
to mean?"

Jake grinned and stepped up into the back of the
chariot. He looped his hands around Tessa's waist, cradling her close, making a show of protecting his mistress.
One hand slipped up, cupping her breast. "It means I
ride with my lady and you walk with the dogs."

Kenneth's jaw dropped in disbelief. "What kind of
twisted shit is that?"

Wriggling uncomfortably in Jake's grasp, Tessa gave
her ex-fiancé a sharp elbow to the gut. "Get your hands
off!"

"Hey!" Jake moved back, rubbing his aching solar
plexus. "Have a care there. I'm a prime specimen."

Kenneth's hands balled into tight fists. *Prime specimen, my ass.*

Catching his anger, Tessa gave him a surreptitious
look. She quickly shook her head, sending a silent signal.
Cool down, it said.

He looked up at her and frowned. "I don't like this
place."

"Bear with it," Tessa mouthed. "We haven't got a
choice."

Doma Chiara snapped her whip. The men pulling the
load took off at a steady trot.

Kenneth felt a tug on his collar. He reluctantly pushed
his body into motion, jogging beside the chariot. Damn
good thing he'd gotten himself back in shape. He had no
choice but to keep up. His leash was looped around a
peg designed specifically for the purpose.

Tessa had better figure out a way to make nice with
the Mer and then get them the hell out of here. The

shackles were beginning to make him itchy and nervous. He didn't like losing control of his hands.

For now he'd have to play along. The last thing he wanted to do was endanger Tessa. The Mer seemed to be accepting her as some sort of conquering heroine. Acting up would only damage her credibility.

He was going to have to be a good boy and play by the rules. Even if those rules sucked.

Slipping on a mask of blank acceptance, Kenneth trotted on beside the chariot. Right now all he could do was hope that his final destination didn't involve a dog-house and table scraps.

Chapter 16

The sanctuary of Queen Magaera was a multistoried building spanning five and a half acres of land, which housed not only the regent, but numerous chambers for private dwelling, a throne room, multiple pools for bathing, and a courtyard sculpted entirely in stone.

In addition, the fortress held inside its walls a central antechamber branching off into various corridors, leading to the administrative chambers of the queen's advisors. But that wasn't all. There were enormous storerooms stuffed with trade goods, as well as workrooms for creating the intricate leather fashions and jewelry the Mers seemed to favor for personal adornment. Weapons, too, were created from the precious metals.

An intricate plumbing system tied everything together. Life at the palace hummed with a machine's precision. Everyone had their place, and kept to it.

As an honored guest, Tessa and her human companions had received a grand tour. Though Kenneth had the sense to keep quiet, Jake had jabbered on, comparing everything he saw in Ishaldi to similar instances in the human world. Fortunately their guides took his excitement with good grace, pampering him with extra attention.

It was enough to make a person sick.

"I can't believe the way those women are fawning all over you," Tessa commented once they were ensconced in a suite overflowing with every luxury the Mer had to offer. At last they had a moment alone to catch their breaths, compare their impressions.

Jake sniffed at the carafe of wine a servant had recently delivered. Finding the vintage to his liking, he filled an earthenware cup. "They know a good thing when they see it."

Kenneth looked up from the couch he had collapsed on; a simple wooden frame with rope webbing and mats lay on top. Having kicked off his shoes, he was giving one foot a liberal rub. "Damn. These boots definitely weren't made for that much walking. It felt like we went ten miles, maybe more."

Since Jake wasn't offering anyone else a drink, Tessa poured another cup of wine. Carrying it over to Kenneth, she sat down beside him. "I'm really sorry. I'm going to try to get us out of here as soon as I can."

Kenneth accepted her offering. "Thanks." He took a deep swallow. Lowering the cup, he grimaced and wiped his lips. "Man, that's some strong stuff."

Jake swirled the remnants in his own cup. "Wines in the ancient world weren't the best vintage. The heavy taste of spices is usually added to disguise spoilage."

Kenneth hastily set his cup down. "I think I'll pass on having any more." He eyed the archaeologist. "Why are you drinking that stuff if it's spoiled?"

Jake sipped. "Our hosts have offered it, and it is our duty to accept it."

Letting his head fall back, Kenneth pushed out a long sigh. "More of that 'when in Rome' shit, I suppose."

Jake's eyes narrowed. "It's called playing the game. We are literally at the mercy of the Mer."

Shoulders slumping with exhaustion, Tessa pressed her head into her hands. "Just stop bickering, you two. Please. I'm no happier than you are that we're in this mess." She blew out a long sigh of regret. "I shouldn't have insisted on opening that thing."

"Wormhole," Jake informed her. "It's some sort of passage between Ishaldi and our world."

Tessa thought a moment. "Chiara called it a sea-gate."

"So they're perfectly aware of what it is?" Kenneth asked.

Tessa nodded. "Seems that way."

Jake finished the last of his wine. "Did she happen to mention why it had been sealed? By the looks of it, that happened from our side, not theirs. It must have been something they had no control over. I mean, what society would willingly seal itself off?"

Tessa shrugged. "Nope, and I don't know. And if I had known what it was, I would have thought twice about opening it. The Mer don't seem very friendly toward humans at all."

Kenneth laid gentle hands across her shoulders. "You couldn't know, babe. No one could." Strong fingers expertly worked the pressure points around her neck and shoulders.

Tessa forced herself to relax. Being tense and on edge wouldn't help matters one bit.

She lifted her head, smoothing her tangled hair away from her burning face. "Though I don't like this situation at all, we've just got to play along. Once I meet with their queen, I will express the desire to return to the sea-gate. She has no reason to hold us here, right?"

Stubbornly, Jake shook his head. "Wrong."

The single word hit like a slap in the face.

Tessa looked at him with blank dismay. "Why wrong?"

Jake curled a lip. "Sometimes I think you fell off the turnip truck yesterday."

Kenneth gave Jake a glare. "I think we can both do without the insults. We're not exactly unintelligent."

"No, but you aren't putting much brainpower into thinking this out," their resident expert countered. "Remember, we've just walked into a world that's been cut off from human civilization for centuries. Yes, we see the Mer have gone on and survived quite nicely. But now that the sea-gate is open, what do you think they're going to want next?"

"Chiara mentioned they were anxious to return to the seas," Tessa confessed.

Jake's eyes narrowed thoughtfully. "Of course they would be eager to regain what they lost when the sea-gate closed. I imagine they once had a ruling command over much of the Mediterranean waters. But they wouldn't just rush out into a world that is essentially unknown to them. Times have changed. They can tell that just by looking at our clothing and listening to us speak."

"Tessa seems to be getting along with the language barrier all right," Kenneth said.

"I'm still a little iffy on some of the terms she's using," Tessa admitted. "The conversations I had with Mom were pretty simple."

"Still, you are managing to communicate and that is what counts," Jake said.

"And you think they're going to want me as some sort of guide?" she asked.

Jake shrugged. "I'm just guessing at what I would do if our positions were reversed." He sauntered away, heading toward an open balcony. "It's beautiful here. Ishaldi is absolutely pristine, untouched by any of the degradations of an industrial age."

Giving the archaeologist the stink eye behind his back, Kenneth slipped his boots back on. "I think I prefer our good old nasty world."

Tessa barely managed to suppress a shiver. "It's creepy the way they keep humans as slaves and treat them like animals."

"Slavery was an accepted way of life in ancient times," Jake tossed over his shoulder.

Kenneth perked up. "Come to think of it, don't you think it's odd we haven't seen any animals? I mean, have you seen a dog or a cat, or even a rabbit? Since this world evolved similarly to our own, wouldn't they have the some kind of wildlife?"

Jake turned around, propping a hip against the elaborate stone railing of the balcony. "Now that you mention it, I don't recall even seeing birds in the trees."

Tessa pushed herself off the couch. She walked over to take a look for herself. Outside, the light emanating from the crystal sky had begun to fade. Shadows from the coming darkness began to creep across the land.

She looked out over the wide, thick growth of the forest. "During our ride Chiara told me the crystals mimic sunrise and sunset. At night the crystals rest, recharging themselves. They don't have seasons either; and no wind, rain, or violent storms. The whole of their world is sustained by underground reservoirs. If there is one thing Ishaldi has, it's plenty of water."

"Something mermaids would need, I suppose," Jake mused.

"It's all too freaky for me," Kenneth said from behind. "All I see in my head when I think of this place is some prehistoric insect trapped in amber."

His last remark brought something to mind that had nagged Tessa throughout their journey. She couldn't easily shake off the feelings of misgiving nagging her. "Don't you think it's eerie the way everything is so perfect?"

Jake eyed her impatiently. "What do you mean?"

Sighing, Tessa made a helpless gesture. "I can't exactly explain it, but it feels as if this place isn't an actual living city, but a model of what the Mer think one should be. Nothing out of place, but still it seems "—she searched for the words she wanted—"artificial."

"It just feels that way because we're out of our element," Jake scolded. "Imagine how they would feel seeing our world after all this time."

Tessa pursed her lips. Her hand lifted to her soul-stone. "It's more than that," she insisted. "Even though I've tried to make a psychic connection with Chiara and the others, I can't. It's like some sort of dampening field is all around me. The energy's there, but I can't key in."

"I'm sure their security is set on high alert," Jake commented. "I doubt they'll let down their guard until they know what our intentions really are."

His answer rankled. Jake didn't understand the innate unspoken impression an empath could pick up. The cues of thought and emotion might be subtle, but they were usually detectable in both human and Mer. But these Mer . . . It was like walking among the living dead. Both emotion and energy were rigidly controlled.

Tessa wanted to argue the point, but she had no time

to follow through. The doors to their chamber opened and an unfamiliar woman swept in, followed by a retinue of Mer and their human servants.

Well armed and alert, the Mer stationed themselves at various points around the chamber. Spears in hand, sharp daggers were sheathed at their hips. A few of the women wore the deadly Ri'kah.

Seeing the laserlike weapon, Tessa felt her mouth go bone dry. No doubt about it. These women were probably experts with the technology.

The human servants bore silver platters. They carried them to a large wooden table, arranging the selections in a manner pleasing to the eye.

Her smile quick and cheery, the woman introduced herself. "I am Arta Raisa, and I will be seeing to your comfort."

Tessa stood up, taking the dominant position in front of her men. She understood the woman's prefix to roughly imply the position of chief administrator. "Thank you for your service."

Raisa indicated a couple of wooden benches sitting nearby. "We have brought food for your humans," she said, directly addressing Tessa. "Please tell them they may eat."

Catching sight of the food, Tessa's stomach rumbled. The time lapse between this morning and the present couldn't have been more than three or four hours, yet it seemed as if days had passed. Her last meal had consisted of some saltines and cheese. Since she'd be diving into deep waters, she hadn't wanted to load herself down with a heavy meal.

She relayed the message to the men. "She says you can eat."

Jake lifted his hands in a gesture of thanks. "Thank

heavens. I was about to faint from hunger." He hurried over to the table, picking through the food.

Rising silently, Kenneth ambled over a little slower. "I have to admit I could eat."

Tessa joined them, gaze skimming the elaborate presentation. A variety of fruits, some familiar, some strange, greeted her eyes. Fish and other seafood were also laid out, and she recognized a few of the more common varieties: oysters, shrimp, crab, eel, and some kind of fish that looked vaguely like haddock.

"The sea life seems to be thriving," she commented.

"They obviously maintain some sort of fishery," Jake guessed. "I would think this would be a diet more suited to a sea-based creature."

Tessa scrunched up her face. Seafood had never been her favorite. "This Mer likes her steak, thank you very much."

Kenneth eyed the fish, a dubious look crossing his face. "Is all this raw?"

She looked closer. "I think so."

He shook his head. "I'm not eating it."

Jake kept his selection to the fruits. "Maybe it's how the Mer eat their food."

Tessa's stomach lurched. "There is no way I am putting that in my mouth." Despite her words, her stomach clenched. Hunger was beginning to gnaw a hole through her middle. She reached for something that looked like an apple. "I'll do the vegan thing, too."

Shooting her a look of disapproval, Raisa slapped her hand. "This food is fit only for slaves. They are still dependent on the physical."

Tessa looked at the Mer through narrow eyes. Had the woman lost her mind? "I'm still dependent on the physical, too. Just like them, I need food to eat."

Eyes taking on a glassy stare, Raisa's mouth turned down into a frown of intense disapproval. "You still eat with the mouth?"

Picking up the vibe that she'd done something very wrong, Tessa slowly nodded. "Of course. Don't you?"

Suppressing a fine shiver, Raisa immediately shook her head. "As food began to grow scarcer we learned how to use the energy of crystals to nourish and energize our bodies." Again she pressed her hands together in the particular manner resembling the act of prayer. "It is our sole nourishment."

Tessa inwardly flinched. Just when she thought she was beginning to understand things, they took a turn from curious into downright bizarre. Like Alice going down the rabbit hole, she'd entered an upside-down world. Very little was familiar, and similarities were few and far between. Even the Mer, her own kind, were strangely unfamiliar.

Tessa licked papery dry lips. "Of course . . ." If she didn't get something to eat soon, she'd faint dead away.

But it wasn't Raisa who answered. Another newcomer broke in, interrupting.

"I have received word of a visitor from the outside," an imperious voice spat. "Let me see with my own eyes this otherworld traveler."

Tessa whirled on her heel. A tall woman, proudly erect, stood behind her. With hair the color of spun white silk and eyes so pale blue as to almost be colorless, her face was so finely molded as to be chiseled. Adding to the impression of her stone-cold beauty was the fact that her skin was pale, almost lifeless in appearance.

Slender and fine-boned, she wasn't clad in the traditional leather Tessa had become accustomed to seeing the Mers in, but a filmy sort of gown spun of a material as light and flowing as a spider's webbing. The strange fabric shimmered like frost.

She looked almost too ethereal to be real.

Arta Raisa immediately dropped to one knee. "Behold Queen Magaera."

The queen flicked an impatient hand toward Arta Raisa. "Leave us," she commanded. "I wish to speak to our visitors alone."

Raisa immediately bowed. "Shall I take the guard?"

Queen Magaera shook her head. "Take your huslas and be gone."

Raisa bowed. "Yes, Majesty."

Tessa watched Raisa hustle the servants out of the chamber. The door closed behind them. Only the guards—still very much armed and at the ready—remained.

Tessa clasped her hands together as she'd seen Arta Raisa do, and offered a brief bow. Hesitantly, she dared to speak. "Thank you for your welcome. I am most honored, Majesty."

Queen Magaera immediately frowned and shot her the evil eye. "Cease your groveling," she snapped. "Your sniveling words mean nothing to me."

Struck dumb by the blatant rudeness of the insult, Tessa shut up. The woman clearly wasn't happy.

Magaera drifted closer, gliding effortlessly. The soft folds of her gown whispered around her as she moved. The vague odor of something cold and loamy clung to her skin.

Tessa immediately wrinkled her nose. The smell reminded her of wet stones after a hard snow had begun to melt. It occurred to her most of the Mer carried the scent, though none so strong as Queen Magaera. It was, she realized, the smell of pure crystal energy—the sole sustenance of the Mer.

Queen Magaera studied Tessa intently. "I never thought I would lay eyes on the seventh dynasty again."

Tessa stood, openmouthed and confused. "Seventh dynasty?"

A look of disdain tightened Magaera's face. "I speak of your symbiote's markings. They show you to belong to the Tesch Dynasty."

A nagging suspicion came to Tessa's mind. "Would it have anything to do with Queen Nyala?"

Queen Magaera deigned to nod. "She was the last Tesch queen to rule before the obliteration."

Obliteration. That didn't sound promising at all.

Tessa stood motionless, her feet rooted to the floor. "I'm sorry, I don't understand." She felt so stupid. So utterly stupid.

"The Tesch Dynasty was erased from Ishaldi's historical record because of Nyala's betrayal of her people." A small smile tweaked up one corner of the queen's cruel mouth. " 'Twas my own grand dame who ordered the Tesch Dynasty into oblivion. She could not bear to let her people remember a Mer queen betrayed them."

Her words delivered a hard jolt. Gulping back shock, Tessa's stomach turned cold. "I don't know anything about it," she admitted slowly.

Gazing at her in silence, Queen Magaera gave a fleeting smile that might have passed for amusement. The fine lines around her eyes tightened. "Because of her love for a land-walker, Nyala chose his people over her own."

Tessa felt the dull thud of her heart against her rib cage. Hearing the queen's words left her dumbfounded with shock. "I—I don't understand," she stammered. "Land-walker?"

Magaera's lips momentarily thinned with disgust. "Humans."

"Nyala loved a human?"

"Yes. But it is forbidden in our society. They are the lessers, good for nothing except breeding and servitude. Nyala saw them as equals, those who should walk beside the Mer instead of behind them. During the war she wished to make peace with them, but her council advised her to hold steady."

A sense of foreboding crawled down Tessa's spine, chilling her. "So it's true we were at war?"

Queen Magaera laughed bitterly. "Of course. There was a time when Mer owned the waters of the land-walkers. The price was heavy to cross our waters, but they needed the bounty of the seas to sustain themselves. Soon they turned against us, began to hunt and slaughter our kind. To make peace would have been unacceptable. As our goddess Atargatis intended, the Mer have always been the dominant race."

Deeply unsettled by the unfolding narrative, Tessa tried to keep her voice steady when she dared to speak again. "But wouldn't peace have benefited both worlds?"

The ruling monarch stared for a moment, and then snapped, "Why should our people bend when Atargatis gave us the power to rule both land and sea?" She slammed her hand down. "If only the council had acted sooner to assassinate her, the Mer would still be a force to be reckoned with outside Ishaldi."

Shock coursed through Tessa. Nyala's own council planned their queen's death. "That's barbaric, the act of traitors!" she protested.

Magaera smirked, a strange stretch of her lips. "A Mer queen rules until her last breath. If she is strong, if she rules with an iron hand, she has a long life. If she is weak . . ." She didn't have to say any more. What she left unsaid was perfectly clear.

Tessa's mind whizzed back to the hieroglyphs she'd seen in the chamber outside the sea-gate. They seemed to make sense now. The figure depicted must have been Atargatis granting her people her power. The choker, the orb, and the scepter. All of them would grant a Mer queen the power of a living goddess.

Nyala had all in her keep. But instead of using them against humans, she'd turned on her own people.

"Nyala sealed the threshold between the two worlds," she finished in a half-numbed voice. "And she never intended for this place to be found."

At last the pieces had all been put into their rightful places. Tessa finally understood the great secret her mother's people had concealed for so long. Instead of trying to preserve their heritage, they'd been trying to hide it.

Eyes narrowing, Queen Magaera raised her chin. "I can sense by your inner vibrations that you knew nothing of this." She gave a short laugh. "So the Mer are not the only ones Nyala deceived. Fitting, is it not?"

Tessa shivered as a chill rushed down her spine. *I shouldn't have meddled.*

Queen Nyala had loved a human. And had done something about it. It must have taken a lot of courage to leave her homeland, knowing she would never again be able to return. The act would brand her as a traitor.

Forever.

Tessa's shoulders drooped. She felt sick to her stomach. "I don't think I need to hear any more."

Magaera's smile dropped from icy to subzero arctic. "Given the service you have performed, it is a shame I can't allow any survivors of the Tesch bloodline to continue. But your blood is muddied by inferior breeding." She sniffed. "Your mother clearly had a taste for the common, just like Nyala."

Tessa's hackles rose. "I'm not inferior." The bitch was starting to piss her off, and in a mighty big way.

Queen Magaera cut her short. "Of course you are." She laughed. "And the circle of betrayal is now complete. As Nyala turned against her own people, it is only fitting I punish those daughters who survived her."

Kenneth didn't like the look on Tessa's face. Grim didn't suit her at all. Though he couldn't understand what was being said, the gist of the conversation definitely wasn't pleasant.

This is bullshit. I'd like to know what the hell is going on. Clearly the visitor—who, judging from the look of her, could only be Queen Magaera—had Tessa rattled. And that, in his opinion, was a problem.

Breaking away from Jake, who seemed happy enough stuffing his face with fresh fruit, Kenneth tried to join Tessa. He'd taken no more than two steps before a couple of the Mer guards stepped in front of him, blocking his way with the spears they carried.

"I'd get the hell back, man," Jake warned. "You definitely don't want one of those sticking out of your gut."

Kenneth shot his partner a nasty look. "I'm tired of being told to keep my goddamn place."

Speaking in a sharp tone, one of the Mer gave him a hard jab in the chest. The tip went right through his shirt, breaking the skin beneath. Blood oozed from the cut.

Kenneth winced, pressing a hand against his breast-bone. He could imagine the serrated edge of that obsidian point sliding between his ribs and puncturing his heart. "Ouch, be careful with that thing, damn it." Though the weapons appeared primitive to the modern eye, they were still perfectly good when used for killing.

No reason to test that theory.

He raised his hands. "I just want to join my mistress," he said, speaking clearly and slowly.

Tessa glanced his way. "Now isn't a good time. You're probably going to want to stay as far away from me as possible."

Finished with his meal, Jake perked up. "What's going on?"

Tessa pressed her lips together. "They say my great-something-grandmother betrayed her people when she stole the crown jewels of Atargatis and sealed the sea-gate. And that I have to be punished for her crimes against the Mer."

Kenneth fought to collect his thoughts. "That can't be right."

Tessa's shoulders drooped. "I'm afraid it is. The sea-gate looked like it was sealed from the outside. That's true enough. We all saw that with our own eyes."

The strange woman in the diaphanous gown made a motion with her hand. "At least you can accept your Nyala's betrayal," she said in perfectly understandable English. "A small credit in your favor."

Tessa, Jake, and Kenneth looked boggled.

Jake was the first to break the silence. "You understand us?"

Touching the crystal at the base of her neck, the woman nodded. "Your simple language is very easy to understand."

"Then why haven't you been speaking it all along?" Kenneth demanded.

An icy stare pinned him down. "It is beneath a queen to speak to inferiors."

Kenneth returned her stare with one of his own. "I'm not an inferior. And in the twenty-first century we don't keep slaves, human or otherwise."

The queen tilted her head, studying Jake and Kenneth closely. "It is my understanding the world outside the threshold has changed in ways we Mer do not yet comprehend." She spread her hands in a magnanimous gesture. The guards holding him at bay lowered their weapons. "Therefore, it is my intention to personally welcome you to Ishaldi as ambassadors of your people."

Jake perked up. "Ambassadors? Now that's a whole different ball game." He held out his wrists. "Do you think the shackles and collars can come off? They clash with my outfit."

Kenneth rolled his eyes. Oh, brother.

The queen snapped her fingers. The guards stepped up, quickly removing the accoutrements of bondage. "I hope you find that more to your liking."

Kenneth rubbed his wrists and grunted. "It'll do for now."

The woman steepled her hands in that particular manner of the Mer. "I am Queen Magaera, and my attention is yours. I regret if you have suffered any indignities, and will do all I can to remedy the matter to your satisfaction."

Jake looked around their luxurious quarters. "I think we can forgive the misunderstanding."

Kenneth ignored his partner, pointedly walking over to join Tessa. Surrounded by the queen's guards, she stood stark and alone. He didn't care if it earned him a prod. He wasn't going to let Tessa stand alone like a leper.

Tessa gave him a weak smile. "I'm sorry for dragging you into this."

Recognizing her need for comfort, Kenneth slipped his arms around her slender body. "It's okay." He kissed the top of her head. "We'll figure this out." It helped that he and Jake had been granted some recognition and status. If he could use it to help Tessa, he would.

She pressed against him, snuggling into his arms. "Hope so. I just want to go home."

Kenneth tightened his hold on her. No matter what, he'd make sure they stayed together. "Why would you punish Tessa for something she didn't do?" he asked, addressing the queen. "Shouldn't she be hailed for opening the sea-gate and freeing her people?"

A small line formed between Queen Magaera's brows. "Hailed?" She laughed. "What a ridiculous notion. When Nyala sealed the threshold, she handed the Mer a death sentence."

Jake's brows lifted in surprise. "I think you'd better let me do the talking here." To Queen Magaera, he asked, "How did Nyala doom your world?"

Magaera curled her lips. "She cursed us with the sickening."

Kenneth glanced at Tessa. "What's the sickening?"

Tessa shrugged and shook her head. "I don't know," she said. "But it doesn't sound good."

Jake clearly didn't think so either. Face paling a little, he took a deep breath, then let it out slowly. "Explain the sickening."

Magaera sighed as if impatient with the questioning. "To see is to know."

Beckoning them to follow, she led the visitors to the

wide stone balcony overlooking acres of lush, pristine, heavily forested land. The last of the day's light glinted off the greenery. "How does it look?" she asked, lifting a hand to indicate the vast beauty of her kingdom.

Tessa frowned in confusion. "It's beautiful, but I still don't get any feeling from it."

The queen glanced at her, disdain etched into her features. "Once, it was breathtaking. Now it is ruins."

Tessa looked at her. So did everyone else.

"I see nothing out of place," Kenneth remarked, taking a second long glance over the thick expanse of trees.

A hint of sadness replaced the anger in Queen Magaera's face. "Most of it is an illusion."

Kenneth didn't understand. "I don't get it."

Magaera laid a cool hand on his arm. "What you see, human, is all facade. All you see now is energy particles strung together to create a more pleasing picture than reality."

"Molecular energy," Jake filled in. "She's saying their world is strung together by an energy net."

Magaera nodded. "At night the sky-crystals must rest to recharge themselves. As the darkness comes, the nets begin to unravel, revealing the true face of Ishaldi." She pointed. "Behold, our degradation."

Everyone looked again.

As though fire burned away the image of a magnificent painting, so did the fading rays bring a change to the landscape around the elaborate palace. It was like the hand of death reaching out, withering all that fell under its devastating touch.

Kenneth gasped. The land was sterile. Where life had once thrived, only stark remnants stood. The trees shrank back, leaves falling away, branches growing skeletal and thin. Other greenery was sparse, fighting to grow in the haggard conditions. What wildlife remained was in danger of extinction, as it had become constant prey for a desperate and starving human population.

The devastation stretched as far as the eye could see. The outlying lands offered no respite from the terrible drought gripping the land. An endless expanse of steppes stretched below a gathering of colossal mountains. Majestic in height and breadth, the limestone peaks ruled absolute over the wreckage of a dying world.

Kenneth swallowed tightly. It was eerie and unsettling to look at.

Jake stirred beside him. "My God. It's almost dead."

Tessa's mouth dropped with shock. "This happened because the sea-gate was closed?"

Magaera nodded. "Although I was not yet born at the time, the scrolls kept by my grandmother, Queen Anthusa, confirm our world as prosperous in the beginning. Although Ishaldi had lost contact with the other side of the threshold, it was believed we had enough renewable resources to sustain ourselves indefinitely."

"Sounds familiar," Jake muttered.

"But resources had to be controlled. Because humans bred so much sooner in life than Mers, the first thing we had to do was contain their reckless breeding. We couldn't let the population outgrow what we could reasonably support."

Jake cocked a knowing brow. "So you began to cull them, choosing the superior and disregarding the inferior."

Magaera nodded. "Yes, selective breeding. To keep Mer bloodlines strong, we wanted only the strongest. The rest became inferiors, of no real value except to work."

"So you turned them into dray animals," Tessa accused.

The queen narrowed her eyes. "Their breeding has to be controlled."

"You still haven't explained what the sickening is," Kenneth broke in. He wasn't quite ready to buy into all Magaera said. Though no psychic, he sensed that a current of deception ran under her cold calculation.

He had no real proof. Just a gut feeling.

Magaera fiddled with one of her elaborate crystal bracelets, twisting it around her slender wrist. "No one knows why it came," she admitted after a moment's silence. "It's like a virus, a corrosive rot poisoning everything it touches. It spares nothing, not animal, insect, or plant. It has even begun to poison our water. With each passing day, more of our land grows uninhabitable. Even magic will not hold the disease at bay."

Clearly horrified by the narrative, Tessa pressed a hand to her mouth. "By the goddess. How have you survived?"

"Through careful isolation, we have managed to preserve some of the needed species," Magaera said. "But still our efforts mean little. We have only enough food to sustain the lessers, and that will not last. Given another century of such relentless onslaught, the remainder will surely perish, and then we Mer shall have nothing but ourselves and the stones that sustain us."

"That's why the Mer no longer eat," Tessa informed them. "They've discovered their symbiotes can convert the energy they pull from crystals into a food source to sustain the physical." She shook her head in amazement. "I'd never have imagined it was possible, though it makes sense."

Queen Magaera smiled ironically. "Strangely, as our

world dies around us the Mer found a way to triple the span of our lives. You may have noticed we have no lack of stones."

Jake gave the queen a once-over. "How old are you anyway?"

Magaera paused in thought. "I have seen the worst of the sickening, watching my world shrivel up through seven hundred long years."

Tessa couldn't conceal her gasp of surprise. "I knew we could live a couple of hundred years, but I've never heard of Mers living that long."

Queen Magaera gave the younger Mer a sardonic look. "It is an age you will never achieve, Tessa of the Tesch Dynasty. Come the morrow, you will pay for the crime of extinction Queen Nyala perpetrated against her people."

Face going pale with shock, Tessa's hands dropped, dangling uselessly at her sides. "I'd hoped you'd forgotten about that."

"Not at all," Queen Magaera said as the Mer guards moved in from all sides. "It was my intention the moment Doma Chiara informed me of your arrival. No one but a descendant of Nyala's would have tried to return to Ishaldi."

Kenneth stepped in front of Tessa, braving the points of at least a half dozen spears. He eyed the vicious Mers. Eyes glinting, they glared back. The looks on their faces hinted at their delight in carrying out their monarch's orders.

"You're not taking her anywhere." What the hell could he possibly do? They were outnumbered and he didn't have a single weapon at hand. Somehow he doubted the few karate moves he knew would handle the job. Chuck Norris, he wasn't.

Queen Magaera flicked a careless hand. "Stand aside or both of you shall share her fate."

Jake stepped up a little more reluctantly. "Now, hold on one minute," he said, trying to ease the tension. "When we first arrived, Tessa was hailed as a goddess."

Queen Magaera's gaze held an edge of intent. "We are grateful for our freedom and the chance to begin restoring what we have lost. But even if the girl were not a Tesch, she would never be accepted anyway. Among the Mer she is an impure. Again, that makes her an outcast." She flicked a careless hand. "By our law, she has no right to live."

Tessa rolled her eyes. "My red hair and green eyes mark me as genetically inferior."

Kenneth winced. It wasn't the first time in history the pursuit of racial superiority had destroyed innocent lives. "You just granted us the status of ambassadors," he said, trying to pull the proverbial rabbit out of a nonexistent hat. "Surely you could extend the courtesy to Tessa, as well. She is the reason we are here."

"As a Mer born and raised on the human side, technically she belongs to us," Jake added.

Magaera's eyes went as hard as stone. "Technically you are all alive because of my good graces," she countered icily.

"And we do wish to stay on your good side, merciful queen," Jake backpedaled, ever the expert ass kisser.

Kenneth gaped at the archaeologist. He should have figured when push came to shove, Jake would be the first to jump overboard to save his own worthless hide. The rat.

Magaera looked at them all, her expression grave. "As I said earlier, I require guidance as I plan the Mers' return to the human world."

Kenneth's inner antennae went on high alert. There was no way in hell he'd help the Mer return to the human world.

Snapping his resolve into line, he cleared his throat. "I'm not helping you."

The queen's expression was utterly unconcerned. She didn't look one bit impressed that he dared to speak up against her.

Magaera laughed. "You mistake your value in my eyes." Her eyes flared, pale and almost colorless. "I require only one of you, and I have made my choice." Her lips stretched into a mirthless smile. "Like the ill-bred Mer you unwisely defend, you are expendable."

Just like that, the hammer delivering her judgment came down.

Hard.

Chapter 17

Hands on her hips, Tessa surveyed the cell. As far as she could tell the walls surrounding them were fashioned from sheets of snowflake-colored obsidian. Though no more than a few inches thick, the smooth, shiny surface was impenetrable. And appeared to be absolutely unbreakable.

"There has to be a way out of this."

"You tell me," Kenneth said from behind her.

Tessa pivoted on her heel. Kenneth sat on the cold stone floor. Back against the wall, he sat with one leg bent at the knee, his arm casually propped on top. His hand dangled. The obsidian glowed faintly, just enough to provide a filtered, gloomy light.

"For a man that's just been condemned to death, you're taking things pretty calmly."

He shrugged. "Not much I can do about it. We've been over every inch of this cell, and there isn't a crack in the walls. And unless you can somehow conjure a sledgehammer, I doubt we're going to be busting out of this place anytime soon."

Tessa inwardly winced. He was absolutely right, damn it.

Walking over to the nearest wall, she pressed both her palms against the glassy surface. The stone was negatively charged, amplified until it had the strength of steel.

Shit. I can't draw a charge off these. It was like having a flashlight and a handful of dead batteries. Neither would do her any good.

She shook her head. Claustrophobia was beginning to set in. It was like being locked in a giant glass cube. "I doubt a sledgehammer would do the job. The stone's been drained so no Mer can draw energy out."

"I suppose after that go-round with the sea-gate you haven't got any charge left to throw at it anyway."

Tessa's hands dropped. She'd almost burned herself down to a crisp trying to channel enough energy to open the sea-gate. Right now she'd need a mountain-sized crystal just to generate enough energy to flick a pea. "I wish I did, but I haven't got a drop left."

He shrugged. "Guess we sit and wait it out, then."

Nerves upsetting her empty stomach, Tessa felt sick. "I wish you'd at least look a little bit worried."

"You just have to accept what you can't change."

She tried for a smile but found none. "How about you changing what you can't accept?"

He drew in a deep breath, then blew it out. "Feel free."

Tessa sighed. "I wish I was."

She trekked over to sit beside him, plopping down. Unlike the luxurious chambers aboveground, the dungeons below the queen's sanctuary were cold, stark, and forbidding. They were given no furniture to sit on and no food to eat. Their sole luxury was a thin stream of water issuing from a slit in the wall. The water filled a circular stone basin; a drain carved around its edge prevented overflow. The water was clean, clear, and ice-cold.

At least we won't thirst to death, she thought. Of course, the flip side, starvation, wouldn't be pleasant with or without water. She hoped that wasn't going to be their fate. The idea of slowly wasting away into skin and bones wasn't on her list of ways to die. At the very least, she hoped they'd go fast.

Preferably without a lot of pain.

"I'm sorry I got you into this mess."

A pent-up breath rushed from his lungs. "It's okay."

Tessa shook her head. "No, it's not. Because I insisted on opening the sea-gate, you're about to be executed." She slammed her palms against her forehead over and over. "I'm so damn brainless."

"Hey, stop that!" Kenneth's fingers circled her wrists, bringing her hands down. "You couldn't have known what was behind that thing when you opened it. Hell, I think we all wanted to know."

She shook her head stubbornly. "You didn't. You warned us it could be trouble messing with the unknown. If you'd have been smart, you wouldn't have followed me through."

Kenneth gave her an incredulous look. "Do you honestly think I could have stayed behind, not knowing what happened to you? There was no way in hell anyone could have kept me from going through that gate after you vanished."

Her vision blurred. "I signed our death warrants when I opened the sea-gate."

A wry smile parted his lips. "Except for Jake's. He seems to be getting along quite well."

Tessa blinked back her tears, refusing to let them

fall. "That rat bastard. Somehow he always manages to slither away untouched."

"Maybe it's our one advantage. Given some time, he may be able to convince the queen it's in her best interest to release us."

She sniffed. "You really think he'd do that?"

He nodded. "Jake's crafty, and so is Magaera. She clearly plans for the Mer to make a return to our world now that the sea-gate is open. But they just can't exactly come swimming out. She'll need help."

Tessa considered. "Maybe Jake can convince her she needs our cooperation. The moment the Mer come out, the whole damn world's going to freak."

"We can hope." Kenneth's fingertips trailed slowly down her cheek, raising an exquisite sensitivity. "Meanwhile, stop beating yourself up. Let's just wait and see what happens."

She smiled. "How did I get lucky enough to find a man like you?"

He arched a brow. "You found me, remember? You're the one who fished me out of the water."

Tessa laughed. "Looks like I caught myself a keeper." The filtered light cast gentle shadows across his face, lessening the severity of his angular features.

His gaze fastened onto hers. "When I said I'd follow you to hell and back, I meant it. I love you, Tessa. I think I've loved you from the day your lips first touched mine."

Tessa tilted her head to look up at him. "Really? You're not just saying that because we're about to die?"

One corner of his mouth tugged up. "I'm not just saying that. I mean it. I want to be with you, whether we've got five more minutes or fifty more years."

Drawing a deep breath, she shook her head. Wow. She couldn't say for sure how she would've felt had their positions been reversed. Betrayed. Maybe even angry. She'd run roughshod over him and he'd taken it. If that wasn't the mark of a patient man, she didn't know what was.

She inwardly cringed. *And I've been such a bitch, insisting on getting my way every time.* "That's . . ." Emotion clogged her throat, cutting off her words.

Kenneth leaned closer, closing the narrow distance between them. "Called commitment. And if you haven't already figured it out, I'm very committed to you." His mouth slowly covered hers.

Lips parting under his, Tessa eased into the kiss. Sensing his need for control, she allowed him to take command. He eased his tongue in, delivering a velvety stroke. The taste of him was rich and smooth, like taking a bite of rich dark chocolate.

Her internal temperature hitched up a notch. So did strategic body parts. *Goddess, I want him.*

Now.

Tingling with anticipation, Tessa's hand began to trace the inside of his thigh.

Kenneth pulled back, letting out a reluctant groan. "Better be careful." He darted a glance toward his hips. "I don't think I could hold back."

Body temperature inching higher, Tessa breathed a soft sound laced with need. "I want to." Heat curled through her, traveling lower. Moistness dampened her panties. "This might be our only chance to be together again."

Tipping back his head, he blew out a breath. "God, I wish it wasn't here, like this."

She cupped her hands around his face, forcing him

to look at her. "So it's not moonlight and roses." She pressed another quick kiss to his mouth. "It's you and me being together."

Kenneth lifted a strong hand, brushing a few stray locks of hair away from her face. His gaze searched hers. "You really want this?"

Tessa swallowed over the lump in her throat and nodded. "Yes." All she knew was need, the desire to touch and be touched. Licking dry lips, she glanced down, exploring the bulge beneath his jeans. "And I doubt you're in much of a position to say no right now."

He smiled crookedly. "I damn sure wouldn't want to."

Tessa stretched out over his lap. "You don't have to." Unbuttoning his jeans, she tugged his zipper down.

Kenneth gasped as her fingers circled his shaft. "Oh, God, I can't believe you're actually going to . . ." His gasp of surprise filled her ears as her lips closed around the plum-ripe crown.

Tessa pleasured him with her mouth, tonguing his length with slow circles and wicked little nips. She continued the sweet torment, making him moan more than once.

Fighting through the pleasure to catch his breath, Kenneth tangled his fingers in her long hair. "If you don't stop now, I'll lose it."

She smiled. "Just let it happen."

But Kenneth wasn't content to just let it happen. He needed control.

Absolute control.

With a groan of effort, he assumed the superior position, pulling her up onto her knees and turning her around. "You're not running away from me anymore, Tessa." His strong hands circled her waist, ripping the front of her jeans open. He fiercely tugged them over her hips.

Hands pressed firmly against the floor, Tessa glanced back over one shoulder. When they'd made love before, he'd always been a gentle, considerate lover.

Now he'd turned into a tiger, and his carnal appetite made her the prey. There was no way she could resist his hard, sleekly muscled body. There was no way she wanted to. Her body pulsed in anticipation.

She caught a glimpse of his erection. "Come on," she challenged with throaty gasp. "Make me yours. Only yours."

Answering her cry, Kenneth gave a single, unsparing thrust.

Shuddering in surrender, Tessa felt every inch. Her nails scraped against the cold stone floor as he moved in and out. Each jolt of his hips against hers only stoked the flames higher.

Wildly aroused, she moved her hips to meet him. It wasn't long before waves of pleasure took over her, giving her no chance to catch her breath. Tessa came with a strangled cry. The sensations went on and on, spreading through her like a searing wildfire consuming dry prairie grass. Kenneth's body shuddered as final release claimed him, and they collapsed together, a heap of tangled limbs.

Gathering her into his arms, Kenneth pulled her close. His arm pillowed her head. Limp and stunned, Tessa couldn't move. Not one single inch. The exertions of the entire day had suddenly caught up with her and she was too damn exhausted. They lay in the semidarkness for a long time, her back pressed to his front.

Just as she was about to slip into a dreamy sleep

of contentment, a portion of the obsidian wall began to glimmer. A slice of the stone vanished, leaving a doorway-sized opening.

Tessa hurriedly sat up as Jake Massey stepped inside. A Mer guard followed closely at his heels.

Blue eyes glittering, he eyed her half-naked body. "Well, well, looks as if we've caught you two doing the nasty. Unfortunately, in Ishaldi it's a crime against nature for a Mer to mate with a motley inferior."

Despite the languor seeping through his bones, Kenneth snapped instantly awake. Pushing to his knees, he struggled to pull his clothing back into place. Beside him, Tessa was cursing as she fought with her own zipper. He'd given it quite a yank earlier and she couldn't seem to get it up again. Her cheeks were flushed, blazing with embarrassment.

"Who the hell you calling motley?"

Ignoring her question, Jake kept his sultry gaze pinned on Tessa. "She's a great lay, isn't she?"

"Jake," Tessa cried angrily. "Now isn't the time for your games."

Clothes back in place, Kenneth stood up. "What the hell are you up to, man?"

Jake waved a hand casually. "Queen Magaera has given me the chance to come and say good-bye."

Kenneth felt a cold spike go straight through his heart. Any confidence he'd had that Jake could help them escape certain death fizzled away. "What do you mean, say good-bye?"

"Although I tried to change Her Majesty's mind, I'm afraid the queen is still set on executing you both."

Tessa let out a gasp. "Doesn't sound as if you tried very damn hard."

Jake shrugged. "I had no choice in the matter. I have to stay on her good side."

Kenneth felt the rise of anger. "Why? Because it benefits you?"

Jake smiled with smug self-satisfaction. "Don't you see what's happening here?"

Kenneth shook his head. "Aside from you continuing to kiss ass to get your way? No, I don't."

Raising his hands in front of him, Jake clenched his fists. "I've found Ishaldi," he said. "Don't you see what that means? My entire career is about to rise from the ashes."

Kenneth could only stare at him, utterly speechless.

Tessa sprang to her feet. "That's it?" she yelled. "You're going to sacrifice my life and Ken's life for a fucking career move?" Lunging into motion, she shot across the cell, intent on taking the archaeologist down.

The Mer guard accompanying Jake immediately raised her arm. The Ri'kah curled around her hand pulsed. Kenneth caught a bright flash of energy just before Tessa reached her target.

The flash shot out, striking Tessa squarely in the chest. The force slammed her violently back against the wall. She slumped to the floor.

Heart pounding in long jarring beats, Kenneth immediately dropped to her side. "Tess. You okay?" He checked the back of her head. A nasty lump was beginning to form.

Eyes out of focus, Tessa's gaze wavered. "I-I'm okay."

"What the hell are you doing?" he spat furiously toward Jake. "Why are you helping these people? Can't you see what they are?"

Jake grinned. "I'm saving my ass." His eyes glinted deviously. "In this case, the needs of the many outweigh the loss of a few. The Mer must return to our waters to survive. Once there, they can begin rebuilding their sovereignty as a sea-going people."

"With you as the man easing their way, I suppose?"

"Of course," Jake said cheerfully. "Not only will my long years of research be vindicated, but my credibility will be totally restored. History will be rewritten and I will be immortalized."

Kenneth barely resisted rolling his eyes. "You've got to be kidding."

Jake sneered. "No, I'm not. But don't worry. When I tell the story of how the sea-gate was unsealed, I'll be sure to include a bit about the heroic effort you both made." He clucked his tongue. "Too bad you had to die in the end."

Pressing a shaking hand to her head, Tessa shot her ex-lover a nasty glare. "You bastard. You used me. Now you're using my people."

Jake's contemptuous smile widened. "They ceased to be your people when Queen Nyala chose to seal the sea-gate."

Kenneth swore silently to himself. He'd seen right through Jake from the beginning, but had tolerated him because of Tessa. Her dream, her life's dream, had been to discover the truth about her people. Everything she'd hoped for had turned to ashes in her hands.

Kenneth eyed the dangerous guard, wondering if he could move fast enough to evade a bolt from her weapon. By the look of disdain on her face, she'd love the chance to take a few more potshots at the humans.

Talk about feeling impotent, totally useless.

Hands clenching into fists, he got to his feet. Maybe he'd just try it. What did he have to lose anyway?

The Mer caught his move. Her weapon came up. "Do not try me," she warned in perfect English. She bared her teeth viciously. "You will not survive."

Jake smirked. "All it takes is a flicker of a thought for her to set that thing from stun to kill." He raised a brow. "Though their technology dates back a few hundred centuries, it is amazingly effective. Their weapons rival some of the best we have today. I think when the Mer emerge, they will be taken very seriously, if you get what I'm saying."

Kenneth smiled coldly. "It must thrill your tiny ego to be the leader of an army of women."

Jake ignored the insult. "My ego's doing just fine, thanks very much." He smiled, pointing to himself.

Kenneth's heart lurched. "You're really going to do this, aren't you?"

Flicking his long blond locks off his shoulders, the archaeologist smiled. "I have no choice. It's destiny." He laughed, giving a flash of straight white teeth. "Vindication has the most delicious feeling about it. It almost sends a shiver down my spine. Not quite as good as being rich or Mer, but it's damn close."

Shaking off the blow she'd taken, Tessa climbed unsteadily to her feet. "Fuck you, asshole."

Jake sauntered out of the cell. His Mer guard paused long enough to restore the wall to its former solidity.

Once again they were locked in. The stone walls seemed to bear down from all four sides, crushing them in a relentless grip.

Without warning, Tessa launched herself against the wall. "Fuck you, you son of a bitch! You lying bastard!" She pounded at the stone wall with her fists.

Fearing she would hurt herself, Kenneth rushed to grab her. Arms closing around her waist, he dragged her away from the wall. "That won't help anything," he said, attempting to get her under control.

Slipping free, she started kicking at the unbreakable obsidian. Tears poured down her cheeks. "First chance I get, I'm going to kick Jake's ass to hell and back."

Kenneth tried again. Coming in from behind, he wrapped his big body around hers like a straitjacket. Pressing her against his chest, he simply held her. "It's okay, babe. Just calm down."

"I don't want to calm down," Tessa said between angry sobs. "I want to kill that asshole."

He kept his hold firm. "I know, I know. I'm pissed, too. But beating down the walls isn't going to work. If I thought I could kick them down, I would."

She relaxed in his hold, the whole of her weight suddenly sagging against him. "I know you would."

He kissed the top of her head. "Okay to let you go?"

A long minute passed. She finally nodded. "I think so."

Kenneth released her. She managed to stand on her own. Brushing matted hair away from her sweaty skin, she offered a weak smile. Her face was swollen, skin blotchy and red. "Sorry about that. I just lost it for a minute. I'll be fine."

"You sure?"

She planted her hands on her hips and glared at the wall. "Yeah."

Kenneth dragged a hand through his hair, staring at the unblemished surface. *Man, what I couldn't give for a keg of dynamite.* "No use in throwing a fit. It isn't going to budge."

Sighing heavily, Tessa dragged herself over to the

shallow basin and sat down on its edge. Dipping a hand into the water, she splashed her face. "At least it's cold." Filling her hand a second time, she took a long drink. "Too bad this isn't poison," she muttered.

Her remark caught him squarely in the gut. A chill slid down his spine. He remembered the day he'd tried to take his own life, the sense of hopelessness filling him like a black and bitter acid. "Don't talk like that, Tess."

Tessa looked up, her gaze drained of all hope. "Our backs are against the wall. They're going to kill us no matter what."

Kenneth tried to distract her. "Right now I'm thinking about wringing Jake's neck."

She allowed a reluctant smile. "I should have sucked the life right out of Jake when I had the chance." Her hand lifted to the crystal she wore around her neck. "Did you know a Mer can siphon the energy right out of you?"

Kenneth shook his head. "I don't see how that's possible."

"The human body is full of minerals, which are unformed crystals. All a Mer has to do is latch on and she can drain you." She snapped her fingers. "And like that, you're dead, all your energy sapped away."

An idea glimmered in the back of Kenneth's mind. "What do you do with the energy?"

She shrugged. "Anything I want. It's the most powerful magic a Mer can use."

"Could you use it to teleport us out of here?"

Tessa blew out a deep breath. "These walls are too much of a psychic damper to try to get through. The best I could do would be try to blast a hole."

"Then do it."

Startled, Tessa looked up. "Do what?"

"Take the energy from me." Kenneth pointed to himself. "I'm a pretty big guy. There ought to be a lot of charge in me."

She shook her head. "I can't."

"Why not?"

"It's forbidden to use *D'ema*, death magic."

"But if you use it, there's a chance you could get us out of here, right?"

"Yes," she admitted slowly. "But you might die in the process."

He thought a moment, then shrugged. "So? I'm dead if we don't try. And if I have to, I'd rather die by your hand than have some Mer zap me with her little laser gun."

Tessa looked at him long and hard. The idea clearly distressed her. A silent minute passed, and then another. "No. I'm not going to do it." Her voice trembled with pent-up emotion.

He persisted. "Why not?"

"I thought we weren't doing the suicide talk anymore." Her forehead furrowed a little. "You talked me out of it, remember?"

Suicide was one thing. Sacrifice was another.

I have what she needs.

Determined to persuade her, Kenneth moved toward her. Grabbing her by the shoulders, he gave her a little shake. "Think straight for a moment. If there's a chance you could get one or both of us out of here, you should take it."

Tessa adamantly shook her head. "I won't be bullied into using my magic against you."

Kenneth gave her a harder shake. "I'm not bullying you, Tess. I'm trying to give you a way out of here. If one of us can survive, then we have to try."

She twisted out of his grasp, putting as much distance between them as the cell would allow. "How can you ask me to kill you when I've just figured out I love you?" Her glare was hot, filled with confusion and anger. "It's not fair. It's not fucking fair!"

Kenneth froze, stunned by her words. *She loves me?* came his dazed thought. In the back of his mind he'd suspected she cared for him. But loved him, truly loved him? He never would have believed it was possible.

Her confession strengthened his resolve. "Nothing about life is fair. But you've got to take the chance if it means getting out alive."

Clenching her fists, she shook her head. "Don't make me do it."

Kenneth walked over to her. Reaching out, he slipped his fingers beneath the crystal hanging around her neck. Heat pulsed from the tiny stone. He almost believed he could feel the beating of a tiny heart resonating from within its depth. "If you won't do it for yourself, do it for me."

Her throat worked. "I—I can't. It's bound to be painful." She shook her head adamantly. "I don't want to hurt you."

Letting go of the stone, he reached for her hand. "I can take the pain." Kissing the cold tips of her fingers, he pressed her palm against his chest. "Do it now, and do it fast."

Shivering, Tessa tried to jerk back. "No."

Kenneth held on, keeping her hand flat against his chest. "Do it. Then do your damnedest to get the hell out of here."

Worn down by his badgering, Tessa wavered. "I'll try to just take a little," she finally agreed. "Just enough to break through the stone."

He nodded tightly. "Take what you need."

She hesitated. Tears began to roll slowly down her cheeks. "I'm going to hate you for this. I'll never forgive you."

He licked papery dry lips. "So hate me for the rest of your life. You need a charge and I'm it."

Tessa reluctantly lifted her hands, pressing the tips of her fingers against his face and temples. "I've never done this to a living person before. Just inanimate rocks."

He smiled. "There's a first time for everything, babe."

Blinking hard, she offered a wavering smile. "I wish you were Jake. I'd gladly suck the life out of him."

His jaw tightened. "Can't say I wouldn't mind that myself."

Tessa's muscles tensed. She pressed a little harder. "If I can get to him, I will," she promised.

Kenneth nodded and closed his eyes. *Good enough.*

Tessa closed her eyes and murmured, "Don't be afraid. You'll free a pressure in your head, but that's only me."

The force invading his body came slowly, creeping in through his skull. Latching on with steel-tipped claws, Tessa's symbiote burrowed deep. Pain spiked through his brain, hot, crimson, and definitely hungry.

Biting back a moan, he fought to remain conscious as fiery hot tendrils ran down his neck, shoulders, back, and abdomen. Blazing with pain, he felt as if his insides were boiling.

Tessa cried out softly. "I'm not going to take everything." Her voice sounded panicked, afraid.

But her symbiote kept going.

Kenneth's vision wavered, suddenly going dark. He was vaguely aware of his skin growing cold.

He clenched his teeth. *Tessa has to get out of here.* That's all that mattered.

Her symbiote dug deeper.

He suddenly realized she had no control. It would take until glutted.

The pain exploded.

Kenneth couldn't react, not even to scream. Darkness stretched endlessly, and he felt as if he were about to fall into it.

He struggled to cling to consciousness, acutely aware his body was beginning to shut down.

So this is what it feels like to die.

Self-preservation was curiously absent. He didn't care.

He was completely anesthetized. It wasn't true an entire life flashed before one's eyes. In fact, he was aware of nothing except his inability to respond to what was happening to him.

Legs crumpling beneath him, Kenneth tumbled. He hit the cold stone floor with bruising force.

Chapter 18

The air in the cell felt cold and empty. Save for Kenneth's soft moan of agony, silence prevailed.

Horrified by what she'd done, Tessa dropped to her knees beside his trembling body. His face had gone bone white under the strain of losing so much so fast.

Cradling his head on her lap, she quickly checked for a pulse. It was faint, but there. She breathed a sigh of relief. *I didn't kill him.*

"Kenneth, can you hear me?"

His lids fluttered open. His gaze was blank, unfocused. "Get out, Tessa." His words were barely discernable.

Looking at him, Tessa felt a vise grip her heart. Just a few minutes ago, he'd been so strong and vital. Now his face was plastered with pain, his body contorted with suffering. Dark circles ringed his eyes.

Smoothing his hair off his sweat-soaked brow, Tessa bent close. "Hang on." She reached out to claim one of his hands and squeeze it tight. "I'm going to get us out of here." Her own body trembled alarmingly, not from weakness or exhaustion but from the searing surge of energy she'd taken in.

Right now she felt as if she had enough power to light up half the globe.

Kenneth struggled to draw in a breath. "Don't waste time." He struggled to lick dry, cracked lips. "Just go." Drawing in a final breath, his eyes slipped shut. He sighed and went limp.

For a shattering moment, Tessa thought he had died. She pressed a hand to his chest. His heart continued to beat, but weakly.

She gently lowered his head to the floor. By the goddess, he'd given everything and had nothing left. Not one whit of strength. She could tell just by touching him that she'd almost drained him dry. One more minute and he would have died for sure.

And she wasn't sure he'd survive now. She'd never heard of a human surviving D'ema. When a Mer used it, it was usually with the intent to kill.

Tessa sprung to her feet. Somehow she had to get him out of this wretched place. No way she'd let him die here. Not now. Not when they had a fighting chance.

"Hang on," she said fiercely. "We're not going to be here much longer."

Focusing her concentration, Tessa hurried toward the nearest wall. Pressing her hands against the smooth obsidian, she began to examine it, not with her eyes but with her senses. Going past the physical, she delved into the molecular level of the stone.

Its solid face faded away, allowing her to see the mass of particles and energy that gave it form. As she'd guessed, the Mer had reversed the stone's charge from positive to negative.

Tessa continued her exploration. It took a few moments to find a weak spot in the stone, but it was there.

If she focused her energy strongly enough, she might be able to blast through it.

Pressing her fingers against the weak spot, Tessa reached for the crystal around her neck. Gathering the energy she'd harvested from Kenneth, she gritted her teeth and concentrated on channeling it outward.

The tips of her fingers began to glow, taking on a strange luminescence. The air around her quivered, crawling over her skin like a thousand tiny insects. Behind her eyes she felt a sense of pressure, her body's reaction as the energy she'd taken in began to drain away. The sensation wasn't painful.

I can take it.

Tessa pushed a little harder. Tiny cracks formed beneath her luminous fingers. But it wasn't enough. She needed to give a little more.

Narrowing her eyes, she recentered her energies and prepared for another attack. Body stiffening, she pressed her other hand against the obsidian wall. The tiny cracks grew larger. The floor wavered under her feet.

The pressure behind her eyes suddenly increased. A twinge shot through her temple. She ignored it. Now was not the time to draw back.

She pressed on, full speed ahead, leveling more mental energy into the heart of the stone. The cracks suddenly spread across the wall with unnerving speed.

Feeling the pressure behind her eyes turn to pain, Tessa refused to stop. Her brain began to burn. The sensation took off like wildfire, zipping down her neck and shoulders, intensifying as it spread through her chest and down her legs.

Tessa collapsed, her body slamming into the floor.

A long minute passed, and then another.

Lying as if a deadweight, she didn't move. Darkness flowed around her. She gasped painfully. Teeth chattering, her head and heart pounding, double time. *I can't give up*, came her vague, indistinct thought. *Too close . . .*

Dazed, she lifted an unsteady hand to her temple. Locking her jaw against a rush of nausea, she pressed her fingers against her skin, attempting to ease the pain.

Struggling to sit up, she blinked hard. Her vision was badly blurred, the four walls around her doubling to eight.

Still shaken, she tried hard to focus on the wall.

All she'd managed to do was crack it a little.

She felt defeated. All that energy wasted for nothing. "Shit." She'd done almost nothing to damage it.

A single tear fell down her cheek. Kenneth had given her a chance and she'd wasted it.

They were still trapped. Still doomed to die.

Unbidden, another tear fell. She wanted to cry more, but there was no more to give.

She glanced toward Kenneth. He lay so still and pale. She'd drained him, leaving him as dry and barren as a desert plain.

She crawled toward him. She kissed his cheek, his cold, cold lips. "I'm sorry, so sorry."

Kenneth stirred a little in returning awareness. "Did it work?" His words were slurred, almost indistinct. His head shifted toward the wall she'd tried to break through. Weak as he was, he had to check for himself.

Tessa lowered her head, kissing him on the mouth again. "No," she murmured softly, cupping his face in both hands. "But it doesn't matter. We're together, and we're going to stay that way."

He didn't reply. Exhaustion crept in, dragging him back into unconsciousness.

Attempting to add her body's heat to his, Tessa pressed herself closer to him. Neither of them could last very long at this rate. She was acutely conscious of the lack of energy in his body. He might possibly survive if they had food, warmth, and time to rest.

Rationally Tessa knew they weren't going to survive. As it was, they had nothing. The Mer granted the condemned no comfort, not even a single scrap of material to use as a blanket to cover their shivering bodies.

A pang of homesickness filled her. She hated to think she was going to leave this world without seeing her sisters one last time. She missed Gwen and Addison. She missed her island. And her life hadn't been as boring and worthless as she'd believed.

If she could turn back time, she would've refused to see Jake that fateful day he'd arrived with the artifacts. Instead, she'd fallen to that siren's call, forever beckoning souls to their doom.

It pained her to realize she'd doomed not only herself, but Kenneth, as well. He was a good man. He deserved better.

She closed her eyes, wishing she could take it all back.

Just as she was about to drift off, there was a commotion, sounds outside her cell.

Tessa raised her head. "What the . . . ?"

She had no time to finish the sentence.

A sliver of the obsidian wall slid away. The Mer guard who'd earlier accompanied Jake stepped into the cell.

Tessa climbed painfully to her knees, attempting to shield Kenneth's inert body. She had an ounce, maybe two, of his energy in reserve. It wasn't a lot, but it might be enough to blast the bitch to hell.

Fear clutched at her throat. She'd never used her

magic to take down another Mer, but desperate times called for desperate measures.

Tessa concentrated, gathering the last remnants she possessed. Her vision wavered, jagged flickers of color dancing in front of her eyes. This was it. She was going to give it everything, every last drop she had. If she tried and failed, she probably wouldn't care what happened next.

She'd be dead.

Trembling with effort, Tessa threw up her hands.

Sensing her intent, the Mer guard reacted instantly. Making a quick gesture, she dropped to her knees. "Do not," she cried, raising her arms as if to shield her body. "I am here to offer my aid."

Tessa slowly lowered her hands. "Did you say you were here to help?"

The Mer climbed to her feet. "We all are." Returning to the threshold, she made a quick gesture. Two more women appeared.

Tessa's eyes widened. Unlike the guard, who was a beautiful blonde with crystal blue eyes, the newcomers had darkly shaded hair.

The Mer guard stepped up. "I am Cyntheris, and we have come to help."

Tessa looked at the women in confusion. "I don't understand. I thought you served Queen Magaera."

Cyntheris frowned. Her nostrils flared with disdain. "In name I serve her." She spat. "In spirit I fight for what is right." Her contempt, though unspoken, resonated.

A Mer with chopped chin-length black hair and deep black eyes stepped up. "My name is Kleio." She offered a smile. "Like you, I am one of the outcasts, with no right to live."

"Not all Mer believe that way," Cyntheris added.

"And we are fighting to regain what has been taken from us."

The third Mer spoke up, the eerily identical twin of Kleio. "We must go, and fast. Too soon our treachery will be discovered."

Her mouth a grim, set line, Cyntheris agreed. "Kallixeina is right."

Tessa reluctantly moved aside, revealing the unconscious man. "I can't leave him."

Kleio knelt beside him, touching his pale skin. "He has been almost completely drained."

Tessa felt like a criminal under her gaze. What she'd done was wrong and she knew it. She had no excuse. She should have known better. "I channeled his energy to try to break us out of here," she finally admitted, pointing to the damage she'd inflicted on the obsidian wall.

Shivering faintly, Cyntheris shook her head. "The stone is strengthened so no one can take it down. You could have drained a thousand humans without success."

Her words went through Tessa's heart like a spike. "Then I sacrificed him for nothing."

Kleio glanced up. "He is weak, but your symbiote didn't drain everything. As long as he has a pulse he can be restored." She looked at the other two Mer. "But I can't do it here. We have to get him out of here."

Kallixeina stepped up. "I will help carry him."

Tessa moved to help. "I can, too," she said.

Cyntheris caught her arm. "You are weak yourself. You will need all your strength to make the journey across the dead lands."

Tessa gulped. "That doesn't sound promising."

Kleio looked at her levelly. "It is the only place where

Queen Magaera's people refuse to go. Their fear is the only thing keeping us alive."

Tessa made a quick decision. She had no other choice. She'd do whatever it took to save's Kenneth's life.

"We'll go."

Kenneth lay helpless, his senses muffled by the grip of an intense headache. His pain prompted a groan. He opened his eyes. Confusion buffeted his senses. This place didn't look familiar at all.

"Where the hell am I?" he mumbled numbly. The words falling from his mouth hardly sounded as if they came from a human being. Lost in the pain, he remembered only pieces. Right now, he only knew he was alone and that he was hurting. Death would have been preferable to the terrible agony crashing through his skull.

He tried to concentrate through his suffering. He heard his heart beating in his head, felt the reverberating thud in his chest.

Drawing in a deep breath, a strange scent caught his attention. Just the faintest hint. He filled his lungs again. The aroma was unmistakable.

Meat. Roasting meat.

His stomach rumbled, reminding him of how hungry he was.

He tried to sit up. Couldn't. His limbs just wouldn't obey the commands of his brain. He fell back, weak and spent.

Seeing only shadows and haze, he squinted. Hovering at a doorway, a flickering figure set into motion. It floated a moment, then began to advance, gliding closer until it had settled beside him.

Though everything else around him was blurred, he could see her perfectly. She looked vaguely familiar, but he could not place her. Her long hair was a rich honey shade. A straight nose, fine mouth, and strong jaw completed her face. She didn't move for several long minutes, fixing her eyes upon him with a wonderfully delighted expression. Her presence lent the chamber an otherworldly spellbinding charm.

Gulping, Kenneth tried to swallow past the lump forming in his throat. His spine stiffened. A hand of fear touched him, held him immobile. A ghost? Nonsense! Clearly he'd gone quite mad. Pain must have driven him over the edge and now he was hallucinating. He closed his eyes tight. But when he opened them, the specter still hovered.

The woman smiled warmly. Up close he could see that her skin was pale, almost translucent.

"Who are you?" he asked, the words fumbling past slack lips.

"I am Doma Atheia." She reached out, stroking the tips of her fingers lightly across his forehead. His heart skipped a beat. Her touch, though cool, was not unpleasant. Between her parted lips he could hear wisps of breath.

Kenneth trembled as his fuzzy memory produced a few vital pieces. "Tessa," he started to ask. "Where—" Again, he struggled to get up.

Atheia's hand moved to his shoulder and she gently urged him back. "She is fine."

Kenneth sank down, too tired to resist.

"I can help you," Atheia added. "If you will let me."

Fist clenched tightly, she lifted her right hand over his chest. Hand hovering, she unwrapped her fingers to reveal what she held—an oval amethyst about the size of a fifty-cent piece. The glow of an unearthly radiance seemed to emanate from its heart, as though it generated its own inner light source.

She smiled again, looking from the stone in her hand to his face. As she did, the crystal rose from her palm, powered by an unseen force.

A flash of intuition reassured him she would do him no harm. "Please . . ."

Placing the hand holding the stone palm down on his chest, she began to chant the words of a melodic spell.

Doma Atheia began to speak softly. "Elements of day, powers of the night, I call upon thee, goddess of light, heal his pain with all thy might."

As if generating some sort of lightning storm, fiery bolts emanated from the stone.

Closing his eyes to shield them from its glow, Kenneth felt tiny fingers of luminous warmth caress his skin. He could feel tense muscles relax as the warmth slowly advanced through his body.

For a long moment there was silence. He felt as if he were floating on air, his body buoyant, mind untrammeled. He was close to drifting off to sleep when a featherlight stroke across his cheek brought his eyes open. Immediately he could see that the stone with its mysterious healing light had vanished.

"Has your pain gone?" the Mer priestess asked.

Swallowing, his mouth suddenly dry, Kenneth nodded.

"It has," he affirmed. "How did you . . . ?"

A familiar figure knelt down beside him. "Kenneth? By the goddess, how do you feel?"

Kenneth gingerly propped himself up on one elbow. Rubbing a hand across his face, he did a quick mental check. "I feel pretty damn good, actually. Better than good."

Tessa smiled, relief etched into her face. "I shouldn't have taken it out of you to begin with."

Vaguely aware that he lay on some kind of low pallet, Kenneth looked around. The huge stone-walled chamber was simply furnished, lit by a simple lamp made of a clay pot filled with oil and a wick. Around the room, clay pots of oil with floating wicks brightened and warmed.

He looked at the two women. "Where the hell are we?" The last he remembered was lying on a cold stone floor in the obsidian-walled cell, praying he'd hurry up and die.

"We're in Thonissi," Tessa said. "One of the dead cities."

Sitting up, Kenneth swung his legs over the edge of the low couch. "Dead city? I don't understand."

The Mer who'd introduced herself as Atheia answered. "Thonissi was one of the first cities affected by the sickening," she explained. "It was abandoned a long time ago."

That answer definitely confused him. That and the fact she was speaking a language he could understand. "How is it I know what you're saying?"

Atheia laughed and touched her soul-stone. "Our soul-stones allow the Mer to communicate on a psychic level. That way we can speak with each other when we are unable to use our mouths."

"Like under water," Tessa put in. "And once we synchronize our soul-stones to the same wavelength, we can share information easily." She touched the small stone hanging around her neck.

"But you didn't do anything like that with Magaera, did you?" Kenneth asked, more than a little confused.

Tessa shook her head. "No. I didn't."

"Tessa was kind enough to share her knowledge

of your language with us, so that we could speak with you without an interpreter," Atheia explained. "As for Magaera . . ." she said with a shiver. "Our queen knows ways of invading the mind without your consent." A fine tremor shook her. "To the rest of us, it is forbidden knowledge. But to a sorceress . . ."

Kenneth wasn't sure whether it made sense. The more he learned about the Mer, the less he understood.

He decided to ask a question that might get an answer he could make some sense out of. "So why are we in a dead place?"

Atheia laughed. "Because slowly but surely life has begun to return. We are learning to overcome the sickening, return life to our lands."

Tessa's smile backed up her words. "Come on. You must be hungry. We'll explain while you eat."

As if to second her words, Kenneth's stomach rumbled. He remembered what had first pulled him out of his comatose stupor. The smell of cooking meat. "I'm game. Take me to your food. Please."

After taking a few minutes to wash up and relieve his bladder, Kenneth followed the women through a series of broad corridors. In the lead, Atheia conducted them into a suite of rooms with wide fireplaces and shuttered windows. In a kitchen-type room, several women worked around a stone hearth, preparing the day's meal. Unlike the priestess, they weren't all perfectly blond and blue eyed.

More surprising than the domesticity of the Mer females was the sight of the men who worked beside them. Instead of cringing and cowing, shackled and whipped, these men stood confident. And free. And they weren't all blonds, either. They looked more like him—big, brawny. Just average men.

Atheia led them to a bench in front of a table. "Please sit. We will bring food."

Kenneth sat down. Tessa took the space beside him. He leaned toward her. "Are we still in Ishaldi or am I really dead and don't know it yet?"

She nodded. "This is the way it was before the Mer began culling humans for slavery and breeding."

"Then these men—?"

"Are their husbands."

"I thought the Mer took mates only when they were ready to have their daughters."

Tessa's cheeks reddened. "It's still true. In their minds, a happy life is worth more than a long one."

He looked at her, wondering if she remembered the words she'd told him earlier, in the cell. He did. He'd never forget the moment she admitted she loved him.

But was it true, or something she'd said in the heat of emotion? People under stress often said things they didn't mean.

His gaze found hers. He hoped she remembered. And he hoped she meant the words. "That doesn't seem so far-fetched."

Breaking their gaze, Tessa rubbed her cheek. "I know." She looked around, drinking in every detail. "This is how I imagined Ishaldi would be."

Kenneth studied her thoughtfully. Without really thinking about it, he put a hand on hers. He squeezed. Just a little. "You're not locked down yet, Tess."

Her expression suddenly softened. To his surprise, she squeezed back. "I am," she admitted in a low voice meant only for his ears. "You just don't know it yet."

What? Kenneth looked at her closely.

But there was no time to think about it.

Several Mers delivered platters heaped with food.

While he recognized some of the fruits, the first thing he noticed was that they didn't limit their diet to raw seafood. An animal that looked vaguely like a snake had been skinned and roasted.

Atheia held a dish toward him, indicating he should serve himself. "Please, have your fill."

Kenneth gingerly selected a piece. He took a polite bite. The meat was chewy, but flavorfully seasoned. "I thought the wildlife had died out here," he said after he'd swallowed.

A Mer with black hair nodded. "Most wild game has died out, and we try to preserve the little that remains. Most of our food comes from the water. What you are eating is eel from the reservoirs."

Kenneth blanched, trying not to pull a face. Food was food and he should be grateful he was getting a meal. He'd feel a lot better on a full stomach. "Tastes okay." Finishing off the first piece of meat, he reached for a second. He was hungrier than he thought and the eel didn't taste that bad.

"Our world would have a chance to survive if the queen and those who worship her would stop draining our natural resources," the woman added with a frown.

Atheia nodded. "Kallixeina speaks the truth."

Concentrating on his meal, Kenneth shook his head. "Queen Magaera told us the virus was unstoppable."

Another Mer with black hair stepped up. "It is unstoppable because they choose to make it that way."

"Kleio's right." Tessa munched her own selection, something that looked like a cross between an apple and a pear. "The sickening is the result of psychic burning," she began to explain. "In an effort to make themselves immortals, some Mer have begun to eschew the physical. They take in energy, but return nothing. Minerals form the basic framework of all life. Drain them away and everything dies. Stone begins to disintegrate, soil becomes sterile, plants and animals die. The viruslike disease killing Ishaldi are the Mer themselves."

"It is D'ema, the death magic," Kallixeina added. "And it is forbidden to use."

Kenneth thoughtfully chewed his meat. "Then why don't they simply stop?"

Everyone looked at him like he'd lost his mind.

"Such power is a disease itself," Atheia said slowly. "And now that the sea-gate is open again, the human world is vulnerable to Magaera's hungers. Soon, she and her army will go forth to continue the old war. Once they regain freedom in the seas, they will glut themselves."

Kenneth glanced at Tessa. The more he found out about the Mer, the worse the news got. He found it hard to believe such beautiful women could belong to such a vicious and destructive race.

As if able to read his thoughts, Tessa nodded slowly. "During the war between humans and Mers, Queen Nyala had to choose the human world, or her own. She chose yours."

Kenneth swallowed down the lump building in his throat. The food he'd consumed sat like lead in his gut. The remainder of his appetite vanished. "Why would a queen turn against her own people?"

Tessa indicated the women and their mates. "Because Nyala, too, saw value in peace between our races. Her council would not let her end the hostilities. Her own life was in danger and she saw only one way out."

Kenneth nodded. "I can see how that would be lucky for us," he said, pushing away the leftovers.

Guilt flashed across Tessa's face. "And then I came along and ruined everything." Her hand settled on his arm, fingers digging tight. "With Jake's help, Magaera's legions will swarm the oceans. What they can't conquer, they'll kill."

Kenneth's shoulders slumped. Oh, shit. He'd completely forgotten about Jake Massey. "It would be just like that bastard to want to set himself up as a god."

Until that moment the men hovering in the background had been unusually silent, letting the women do the talking. Now one broke free from the group, stepping forward to speak.

Unable to understand the language he spoke, Kenneth shook his head. "I didn't catch what he said."

Kallixeina translated. "My breed-mate says we must stop Queen Magaera from vanquishing the land of his ancestors."

Kenneth didn't have to think about it. "Any reasonable man would say that."

Kallixeina gave her man a fond smile. "His reasons are stronger than most. For most of his life, Cydros has been a slave, a lesser in our society. Under Queen Magaera he has no rank and no rights. He may breed only a lesser woman because he is considered an inferior to mate with a Mer female. His son or daughter will also be a slave, and their lives will not be their own."

Kenneth understood. "I couldn't imagine living the life of an inferior. I've been treated like one and I didn't like it."

"Then you understand why we battle Magaera," Atheia said.

He nodded. "Of course."

Tessa put a hand on his shoulder. "Queen Magaera now has control of the sea-gate."

"That makes sense. With Jake advising her, she's probably got that thing on lockdown."

Tessa pulled a deep breath. "There's more. They're going to try to get us home. But we only have two very slim options."

He didn't like the sound of that one. "Which are?"

She gave him a long, searching look. "One, we win and get to live."

Kenneth clearly saw the conflict in her face. "And two?"

She grimaced. "We lose, we die."

Atheia looked at them both, her face taking on a drawn, grim expression. "Out here in the dead lands our numbers are still small, yet undetected by Magaera and her council. To fight we will need every person able to command a weapon. But once we step out, we will all be revealed. Every last one of us. There will be no place to run, no place to hide."

Listening to her speak, cold awareness rushed over him. Though her even, neutral voice had betrayed nothing, he had a sneaking suspicion that all hell was about to break loose.

And we're right in the middle of it.

Kenneth looked at the small band of people around him, human and Mer. Somehow, amid the violence and devastation rolling through their world, they'd managed to carve out a reasonable semblance of life. Their world was torn by the strife of civil war, as many realms were, but they'd clearly managed to survive the conflict. Perhaps they would have flourished, given time.

But time had been taken from them when Tessa opened the sea-gate. Magaera and her ilk now had access to an unlimited source of energy—energy that would surely increase her power a thousand times over. She would also be goaded on by a man who would show her the ways of the human world—and how best to rape its almost limitless resources.

Magaera had the potential to become a god. First she would reclaim the seas. Then she would strike out for land.

And the world would crumble under her fist.

"If you're asking me to fight," he said evenly, "I'm in."

Chapter 19

The Mer rebels kept their weapons hidden below-ground, deep inside a series of limestone caves that had once been part of a reef laid down by an inland sea millions of years ago. A rabbit warren of tunnels twisted off in various directions.

Men and women, human and Mer, worked together, preparing for the conflict ahead. Everyone was serious, concentrated in their efforts.

Kenneth examined the dagger he'd been given. "Is this all you've got?"

Cyntheris nodded. "Yes."

He grunted and turned the weapon in his hand, trying to get a feel for it. The short, etched-silver blade glittered in his grip, sharp and deadly. A series of strange runes were incised in the steel. "I guess it will have to do."

Cyntheris looked at him, a quizzical expression crossing her features. "Do you no longer have blades in the human world?"

Kenneth frowned. "Oh, we've got them. Definitely. It's just that our weapons have advanced to the point where a man can take down hundreds with a single weapon."

No reason to mention the bombs and the hundreds of thousands those could demolish. The Mer didn't need any encouragement.

He braced himself, wondering if he could actually use the blade. Though he'd owned a gun before Jennifer's murder, he'd fired it only on a practice range. He'd gotten rid of it soon after her death. It would have been nice to have the 9 mm now. Self-defense was a concept he definitely grasped and approved of. He'd already made up his mind to fight. And he had to be prepared to follow through.

It was kill or be killed and Kenneth didn't intend to be the one doing the dying.

Cyntheris lifted her arm, showing the Ri'kah she wore. "We can do a bit of damage with these." Leveling her crystal-powered weapon, she aimed toward a nearby rock. A few quick laserlike blasts sped through the air. The rock disintegrated into dust.

Kenneth raised a brow, impressed. "Nice." He pointed at the Ri'kah. "Now if only we had a few dozen more of those."

Watching from behind them, Kallixeina smiled. "Unfortunately, those are reserved for the queen's guard. The rest of us must make do with the primitive weapons." She cut the sword she held through the air. "But it will still send a head rolling."

"If you can get close enough to wound them," Kleio snorted.

He cocked his head. "I've seen a bit of Mercraft. Why do you even need weapons when you can move things with a simple thought?"

The Mer women around him laughed.

Kleio stepped up to him and lifted her hand. "I will show you," she volunteered. "Raise your hand."

Kenneth did. "Like this?"

Kleio pressed her palm against his. "See if you can move my arm."

Tongue going into his cheek, Kenneth nodded. Of course he could move her hand. He was bigger and naturally stronger than a woman. "Okay." He pushed.

Kleio's hand didn't move. "Harder."

He pushed harder, but the Mer didn't budge. "I can't." His hand dropped. "What did you do?"

Kleio laughed. "That is what I am trying to show you about Mer-magic. When a Mer goes against a Mer, if both are equally strong, neither really affects the other. I could throw out a bit of energy, but my enemy could easily shield herself or try to turn it back on me with a spell."

"I think I understand the concept now."

She arched a brow. "Do you really?" She suddenly karate chopped Kenneth's hand at the wrist, taking the dagger out of his hand. In a flash she retrieved it, coming up under his chin with the sharp edge. "Make an enemy of a Mer and she will give you no mercy."

Kenneth's heart hammered against his sternum. Tension raced through him. He'd not only been checked; he'd been mated. Kleio could have slit his throat before he had a chance to draw a breath.

It was a lesson he clearly needed to learn.

Fast.

Kenneth pulled in a breath to slow his pounding heart. Damn. She was fast. "I think you win."

Those four words eased the tension. Everyone laughed and relaxed again.

Kleio drew down the blade. "I am sorry to have to do that to you." She flipped the dagger in the air, caught it by the blade, and offered the hilt to him.

More than a little embarrassed, Kenneth retrieved his weapon. "That's okay. It's something I needed to know." Better to nurse his wounded male pride in the company of friends. He had a feeling Queen Magaera's defense force wouldn't be so forgiving.

Cyntheris's gaze swung to his face. "You have to be a little faster and trickier than your enemy. Those serving Queen Magaera are trained to be utterly ruthless with their power. They know all the ways to bring death and will not hesitate to use them against us."

Kenneth looked at the tall, blond Cyntheris. She definitely stood out among the rest of the darker-haired, and in some cases, darker-skinned Mer. "Tessa told me you helped get us out of the cell. But aren't you one of the ones they consider part of the elite?"

Cyntheris paused a moment in thought, then replied, "I am, but that does not mean I do not see the folly of their ways." She indicated a dark man working to sharpen several spear points. "Brison is my husband, though few know that truth. We must conceal our union because he is not acceptable as a Breema for a Mer of my status and rank."

Kenneth sneaked a glance at the strong, barrel-chested man. He had curly black hair and skin the color of dark toffee. Brison was handsome, a real stunner. He was the kind of man that made women pant. "And he's not acceptable because of his looks? That's all that makes him inferior?"

"That is all." Cyntheris frowned. "In order for me to take a mate, I must apply to the queen's council and wait for a suitable male to be chosen from the breeding pool."

"One they consider genetically perfect?"

"Yes."

Sperm donor? That raised his brows. "And the Mer want one uniform look, which they consider to be perfect?"

The blond Mer regretfully nodded her head. "Somehow the old ways have become so terribly twisted."

"Yet you've defied them."

"Many do, but our numbers are still so small." Cyntheris sighed. "If my treachery were discovered, I and my husband would both be executed." She sent a fond glance his way. "But I think he is worth the trouble."

They didn't have any more time to talk further. Tessa ducked into the underground cavern, followed by several other rebels.

"Everything almost ready here?" she asked.

Cyntheris answered, "Yes, we are almost ready to go."

Kenneth's gaze strayed to her slender figure. Her long red hair shined like a beacon in the low illumination emanating from the stone walls. But it was her eyes that really got him, a deep jade green. Sometimes her gaze was hot, filled with heat and passion. Other times her gaze went cold, distant and detached. He'd felt both the heat and the ice. No doubt about it, a raw energy radiated from her.

But the one thing he'd never gotten out of those eyes was love. He'd never seen Tessa look at him the way Cyntheris looked at her husband.

Emotion tightened his throat. *She said she loved me*, he reminded himself. He had to believe it, hold on to it. Right now it was the only thing getting him through this nightmare. He had to hold himself together. For both of them.

As if drawn by his thoughts, Tessa walked his way.

"Wow, you look all medieval." She eyed the blade in his hand.

He rubbed a hand over his jaw. "Not exactly a Smith & Wesson, but I guess it's going to have to do." He gave Kleio a look. "It even came with a little lesson on how to use it, so I think I'm all set."

Tessa hugged her arms around herself. "You think you could actually use that on someone?" Her voice was strained, a little thin.

Looking at the deadly blade in his hand, Kenneth felt goose bumps form. Aside from a few bar fights in his younger years, he'd never seriously scuffled with anyone, male or female. Without even stopping to think, he already knew what his answer had to be. "I don't want to, but I will if I have to." He lifted his gaze toward hers. "I'll do anything I can to defend you."

A weak smile tugged at one corner of her mouth. "You're braver than I am," she admitted in a rush. "I don't know if I can do this."

Kenneth watched her wrestle with her emotions. She was clearly having a hard time with the idea. She looked so alone, so afraid.

He took a step closer, wrapping his arms around her. That's all he'd really wanted to do through these last confusing hours. Hold her. Just hold her. "It's going to be all right," he murmured into her silky hair. "Somehow, we'll get home."

Releasing a tremulous breath, Tessa tipped her head back to look at him. "Do you really think we can?"

Kenneth's heart lurched. "We'll make it," he said to reassure her. "I swear to God I'm going to do everything I can to keep you safe." He meant what he said, one hundred percent.

•

Tessa snuggled deeper into his hold. "Promise me you'll always be there."

Lowering his head, Kenneth brushed a kiss across her lips. "I'll never leave you, Tessa."

And then he kissed her, long and deep.

The Mer rebels had decided to strike as quickly as possible. In an hour, the dungeon's guards would change. Cyntheris's treachery would soon be discovered.

Since they could not enter the city of Quanous, where the queen's palace was located aboveground, it was decided to make the attempt from belowground. Thanks to an elaborate system of plumbing, a grid of tunnels stretched beneath the metropolis. Reaching the Temple of Thiraisa would be a simple matter.

Taking care of what they might find there wouldn't be.

"Getting inside is going to be easy," Cyntheris said. As one of the few armed with a Ri'kah, she had taken the designated role of leader. "There is a grill for drainage and overflow in one of the purification chambers. Once inside, we can make our way toward the threshold. Hopefully we can get you through before Magaera's guards stop us."

Tessa nodded. "You think the sea-gate is guarded?"

Cyntheris nodded. "Most definitely. But at this hour, the number will be few because Magaera believes you are still imprisoned. We must act with haste before you are discovered missing."

Tessa shivered, remembering that cold, awful place. "You took a terrible risk helping to free us."

Cyntheris didn't glance back as she continued up the narrow passage. It was cold and damp, and everyone was miserable from the dirty sludge water seeping into their shoes. "I would like to cross into your world myself. I want my husband to see the land of his ancestors, perhaps even raise our children there."

Tessa's throat tightened. "I hope you can."

The small band of rebels continued on.

Just as it seemed they would be doomed to wander the twisted passages for all eternity, Cyntheris at last halted. "We are in the main bathing chambers." She peered through a narrow iron grate.

Kallixeina stepped up. "Do you see anyone?"

Cyntheris did a quick count. "Two guards."

Brison stepped up behind his wife. "They must die quietly. Quickly." He made a slicing motion across his neck.

"I agree," Cyntheris said. "We don't want to alert others who will be in the main temple. One scream will carry through the entire place."

Brison lifted his weapon, a small, elegant athame, or short-bladed dagger. "I will take care of them."

Kenneth moved in. "What's going on?"

Tessa hastily relayed the plan in a low whisper.

Kenneth nodded and eyed the grate. "Going to need some help lifting that," he said, and went to work. Trying to keep noise to a minimum, the two men carefully moved the grate. Kenneth supported its weight and Brison slid through the constricted opening.

Everyone watched, breathless, as he darted around a wide oval pool of shimmering, ethereally blue water. The pungent aroma of incense, a cloying mix of musk and cinnamon, scented the air.

In a split second, Brison and his deadly blade moved into action. Creeping up behind the unsuspecting guards, he killed both Mer guards before Tessa could think to blink. He moved with grace and speed, intent on carrying through his mission. The first woman had not yet begun to fall before the second drew her last breath.

Quickly securing the area, Brison did a little bit of scouting. He disappeared, a move that forced everyone to hold their breath.

The ongoing silence pumped up the tension another notch.

Tessa gritted her teeth and swallowed hard.

Seeing her waver, Kenneth reached for her hand. "You okay?"

Tears welled in her eyes and it was all she could do to hold them back. "I've never seen anyone die before," she admitted, blinking hard. "It's horrible."

"I know. Trust me, I know." His grip on her hand tightened. His skin felt warm. Solid. Real. "If you need to stay here, we can handle things."

Knowing he was trying to spare her further horror, Tessa looked into his face.

Kenneth truly was one of the good guys. She'd known that all along. Without considering his own safety, he would sacrifice himself for others. He'd done that since they'd arrived in this hellish place, without complaint. He'd even offered his life to give her the chance to go free. Men like him didn't come along every day. He was a rare prize.

Good grief! she thought, swallowing hard. She'd almost pushed him away with her own petty selfishness.

That wasn't going to happen again. Somehow she'd figure a way out of this mess. And when they were home, and safe, she'd treat him like a king instead of a convenience.

"I'm going, too." She steeled her nerves. "There's no

way you're leaving me behind. Wherever we go from now on, it's together."

Though she suspected their chances of getting back through the sea-gate were slim to none, there was no way she was going to let him walk into the battle alone.

Kenneth lifted his hand. His warm palm curved around her left cheek. "I'll try not to let them get close to you, Tess. Somehow I'll get you through."

Lifting her hand to cover his, Tessa smiled at him. "I know you will."

There was no time to talk about anything else.

Brison appeared a few minutes later. He made a motion with his hand. "Magaera has posted only half a dozen of her guards. If we move quickly, we can take them."

Cyntheris considered his report. "That is reasonable," she allowed. "Magaera believes she still has you imprisoned, so she has no reason to expend her soldiers' efforts. Soon enough, though, that ruse will end with the changing of the guard."

Tessa's heart accelerated. "Then I guess this is it. We're going in."

Wiggling through the narrow gap, she vowed not to let fear distract her.

Staying focused was absolutely essential.

Chapter 20

Crouched behind a pillar in one of the purification chambers, Tessa felt defeated. So many of them had died already.

Though they had initially overcome the guards posted at the sea-gate, one of them was able to escape and alert Queen Magaera's defense forces. In moments, they easily outnumbered the rebels. Kallixeina and Kleio had already sacrificed their lives in the initial push to take the sea-gate. Their bodies lay near the bodies of their husbands.

Tightening her grip on the dagger she held, Tessa swallowed painfully. She'd managed to kill one Mer, but she wasn't sure she could do it again.

Death. It was a smell she would remember all her life.

Which might be shorter than she thought. Magaera's soldiers had them boxed in like rats in a trap. Attempting to retake the sea-gate had been the errand of fools.

Not that they'd had a choice.

A desperate whisper came her way. "Holding steady, Tessa?"

Tessa shot a glance toward Kenneth. Sword clutched in his hand, he looked pale but determined. They'd managed to hold off the first attack, but Magaera's soldiers had regrouped.

They were coming back, stronger than ever.

"Not so steady," she called. "But I'll do my best." Anticipation sent her heart into a faster rhythm.

He ducked as a stray energy bolt from a Ri'kah smashed into the stone above his head. Sharp pieces of debris rained down on her. "Now would be a good time to try that teleport thing."

Swallowing hard, Tessa quickly shook her head. "I wish, but the stones of the temple have been negatively charged. No Mer can draw off them—to them it's a sacred space."

"But not one I want to die in."

A sudden movement behind Kenneth caught her attention. A blast coming out of nowhere took down a portion of the wall shielding them. Stone turned to rubble as a half dozen heavily armed Mer poured through the newly made opening. Catching sight of the enemy, several of the women lifted their weapons.

"Tessa, look out!" Kenneth warned.

Paralyzed by the sight, Tessa barely felt her dagger slip from her numb fingers. For ten, maybe twenty seconds, she couldn't move.

One of the Mer tackled her. The two hit the ground, rolling.

Gaining the superior position, the Mer slammed a knee between Tessa's shoulder blades, stealing her breath. She fought the woman viciously, thrashing like a wild horse attempting to buck out from under its rider.

The vicious Mer refused to be shaken. She dug her fingernails deeply into Tessa's brow, wrenching up her head. The cold blade of a dagger slipped beneath her neck.

Tessa clenched her eyes shut. Shit. She was about to die.

"Do not kill her," she heard a voice say. "This is the one Magaera wants alive."

The weight on her back lifted.

Two more Mer soldiers stepped up. Grabbing her arms, they hauled her to her feet. She struggled, but her captors held her in an iron grip. Three more Mer moved in, cutting her off from the rest of her comrades.

Kenneth swung into immediate action. By the look on his face, he was ready to take it all the way. Catching the closest Mer with a tackle, he slammed his opponent into a nearby wall.

Kicking and twisting against his weight, the Mer screamed with rage. "Die, inferior!" she snarled. The blade she carried flashed in an upward arc, slashing a long slice in his arm.

Weapon skittering from his grip, Kenneth hissed in pain. "Shit!" Catching the woman's wrist, he twisted hard. The bone beneath his grip snapped like a stick. "Sure do hate doing that to a lady." He panted. "But you ain't no lady."

Dropping her dagger, the wounded Mer howled in agony.

Catching sight of another attacker, Kenneth caught the strap of the first woman's belt. Digging his fingers in deep, he slung the Mer around in front of him. At the same moment, her comrade thrust the spear intended for Kenneth. The serrated point impaled the Mer all the way through, back to front.

With a sharp sound of surprise, the first Mer sank to her knees.

Kenneth immediately spun toward the third female soldier, swinging his bare fist in a roundhouse blow. His hand made contact. Hit with a full-force blast, she dropped like a stone.

He whirled on the women who'd captured Tessa. He narrowed his eyes, and a half smile came to his lips. For him the fight was just beginning and he intended to keep on kicking ass.

One of the women surrounding Tessa stepped forward. She drew her finger across her throat in a crude gesture of execution. "Stay back," she warned. "Or I will kill her myself."

Kenneth came to a dead halt. He immediately raised his hands to show he wasn't armed. "I'm staying," he said. "No fast moves."

More Mer soldiers came through the destroyed wall. Half the great temple was in a rubble, but it didn't matter. In less than an hour, the rebels had fallen.

Swarmed from all directions, Kenneth cursed as a couple of Mer came to avenge their slain sisters. They retaliated without mercy, driving him to his knees. Scant minutes later his body bore the deep cuts and bruises— wounds not deadly enough to kill but sufficiently vicious nevertheless.

"Deliver the death blow," one soldier urged.

Another shook her head. "We are commanded to take the outsiders alive."

Struggling to escape her assailants, Tessa kicked and screamed like a madwoman. "Stop it, you bitches! Leave him alone."

One of the Mer gave her a hard slap. "Hold your tongue, animal! He gets no less than he deserves."

Tessa blinked, recognition flooding her mind. *Chiara*, her mind filled in. But the woman who had greeted her and hailed her as a goddess was not the same. Outfitted in a tight leather jumpsuit and boots, she'd shaved her long blond hair. Only a Mohawklike strip remained. On one side of her scalp was a small tattoo, a symbol Tessa recognized to mean death.

Magaera's warriors were prepared to follow the bidding of their queen. To fight and to conquer was their sole purpose. They wouldn't stop, not even when faced with death.

Such was the true nature of the Mer.

"Are you so blind that you can't see what your queen is doing to Ishaldi?" Tessa demanded.

The priestess laughed. "The chance to be immortal, to be a true goddess, is worth the price. Your world has the resources we need to make it so."

Tessa's heart sank. Nothing stood between the Mer and the human world. Nothing at all. "I wish I had never opened it."

Chiara frowned. "Unfortunately, you didn't. The sea-gate still blocks us."

Shoved by rough hands, Tessa and Kenneth were hustled to the undamaged portion of the massive temple. The wide stone stairs leading up to the sea-gate were perfectly intact, as was the altar. Several of the rebel Mer and their human mates huddled at the base of the stairs. Faces pale, their eyes were rimmed with fatigue and defeat.

Tessa recognized Atheia, Cyntheris, and several others among the group. At least a few had survived. Though probably not for much longer. No doubt they'd all face the executioner.

And that was definitely something she didn't want to contemplate.

Hands on her hips, Queen Magaera stood at the top

of the altar. Arta Raisa stood on one side. Jake stood on the other.

Seeing him, Tessa frowned. *Bastard.* It wasn't fair that he'd walk out of this disaster unscathed.

Chiara prodded her in the back. "Walk."

Barely giving them a chance to lift a foot, the Mer soldiers practically dragged them both up the stairs. They couldn't seem to deliver the prisoners fast enough.

Queen Magaera's gaze raked her captives. "There you are, you silly little bitch." She arched a brow. "Did you honestly think you were going to get away?"

Reckless bravado surged through Tessa's veins. "Gave it my best shot."

Ignoring her, Magaera turned to Jake. "I wonder if she knows how painful her flippancy is about to become."

"Go ahead and get it over with," Tessa said defiantly.

The queen chuckled. "Oh, you shall not be the one to be sacrificed. Not yet, anyway." She snapped her fingers and pointed toward the huddled prisoners at the foot of the altar. "Bring Cyntheris. It is fitting a traitor should be first."

Doma Chiara and another Mer guard wrestled Cyntheris to the top. Swaying a little, Cyntheris moved with concentrated effort, as if sheer force of will could help her overcome her body's weakness. Bleeding from several wounds, she was unsteady on her feet.

Magaera pointed at the sea-gate. Its entire center blazed, roiling like a star gone nova. "Send her through."

"My death is not the end," Cyntheris cried out before she vanished into the swirl of energy. Her screams of terror echoed on even after she'd vanished.

No one moved. Or dared to breathe.

A heap vaguely resembling a person came spilling

back. The skin on the corpse was leathery, sucked down to the bone. Cyntheris's body had been completely drained of every last mineral.

Too shocked to think clearly, Tessa gasped, horrified. Her mouth dropped open and it was all she could do not to scream. She pressed a hand to her mouth. "By the goddess," she breathed.

Kenneth's eyes were equally wide with shock. "What the hell just happened?"

Jake ambled over, prodding the corpse with an expensive leather loafer. "That's just the problem," he said. "We don't know yet. Every time we send someone through the gate, it spits them out. Right now we're just testing a few theories."

Tessa smiled sweetly. "Why don't you give it a try?"

Jake bared his teeth right back. "Actually, sweetheart, I was saving that honor for your boyfriend. He came through the gate unscathed, so I'm thinking it might be safe to send him back." His smiled widened. "Or not."

Icy fingers wrapped around Tessa's heart. Her breath caught in her lungs. She shook her head. "No."

Jake ignored her. "How about it, partner? Are you feeling lucky today?" He pointed to the gate as if a sideshow barker. "There's a fifty percent chance you'll get through."

Kenneth shrugged. "Why not? I seem to be into investing in losing ventures. I took a chance on a fucker like you, and look what it got me."

Jake tsked. "Oh, come on. It'll be the biggest adventure of your insignificant life." He arched a cruel brow.

Face livid with pain and rage, Kenneth stared through simmering, narrow eyes. "You're welcome to have the honor."

The archaeologist laughed. "No dice. That's why they

put the monkeys in space first. The theory had to be tested with big dumb animals."

The eyes of the two men locked, each assessing the other, both refusing to back down from the path each had to pursue.

The Mer guards pushed Kenneth toward the sea-gate.

Maddened by the thought of losing him, Tessa struggled to break free from her captors. "I'll go."

Queen Magaera smirked. "That is the idea, my dear. Although I can't be sure, I believe I know exactly why we cannot get through the sea-gate."

"But it's all speculation at this point," Jake added. "You were first through the sea-gate. We're thinking you might be the answer to getting back to our side. It's a long shot, but it's all we've got at this point."

"And if it kills me?" Tessa shot back.

Jake shrugged. "Tough shit, babe. Better to be alive on this side, than fried to a crisp trying to go home."

Tessa bared her teeth in a fierce scowl. "Your sentiment truly touches my heart, asshole."

Thrust toward the sea-gate, Tessa stumbled. She landed on her knees, barely a foot away from the roiling mass separating Ishaldi from the human world.

Shivering from head to toe, she looked into the center of the mass. *That thing's going to eat me alive.*

Struggling to master her fear, Tessa slowly climbed to her feet. She stepped toward the gate, held out her hand.

"Tessa, don't!" she heard Kenneth call.

She refused to look back. *I love you*, she thought, and passed through the threshold with a single determined step.

A rush of energy came at her from all sides, snatching her off her feet. The electric tension grew, a mass of flame and heat detonating all around her.

Shaking, burning, Tessa felt as if she were about to shrivel up into ashes and blow away. She tried to scream, but the sound was locked in her frozen throat . . .

The moment Tessa stepped through the gate, Kenneth caught and held his breath. His first instinct was to turn his head away. He didn't want to see her remains spat back like so much refuse. Despite his fear, he forced himself to watch. And wait.

One endless minute dragged by. And then another.

Magaera smiled, pleased. "She's made it through."

Jake smiled back, simpering. "I thought that might be part of the problem."

The Mer queen nodded. "It would have taken only seconds to reject her. If our theory holds, we should all be able to pass through now."

Jake paced in front of the sea-gate. "Only one way to find out." He jerked a thumb toward Kenneth. "If he makes it through, our theory is sound. After that, I'll go through."

Magaera considered his proposition. "But how do I know I can trust you once you are on the other side?"

Jake's mouth twisted briefly, cynically. A tormented look flitted across his face. Then it vanished. "I have sworn to serve you in every way. My life's work has been devoted to the rediscovery of Ishaldi and bringing the Mer back to their rightful place in Earth's waters. I would never betray your trust."

Queen Magaera's face tightened. "Yet are these not people you once called friends?" she questioned, watching the archaeologist closely.

Kenneth watched, too. He sincerely hoped Jake was one hell of an actor. It would be nice if he was helping to secure their release instead of twisting the knives he'd planted between their shoulder blades. Tessa had gotten through the sea-gate and that was a point in Jake's favor. Whether it was by accident or design, he had yet to discover.

Jake waved a dismissive hand. "I can make new friends."

Kenneth cursed under his breath. The SOB seemed to be driving the blades deeper.

Arta Raisa stepped up. "May I suggest chaining the prisoner? He will be more easily controlled on the other side."

Eyeing her prisoner, Magaera nodded. "Put the heaviest shackles on him, and see that chains span his hands."

The Mer guards quickly moved into action.

Kenneth balked, resisting the impulse to fight back against the degradation of being chained like a dog. Jake batted nary an eye. His face was schooled to impassivity, a cautious blank. If he had any thoughts on the matter, he concealed them well.

One of the Mer guards offered the archaeologist a blade. "To control him." She handed it over.

Jake considered the dangerous weapon. For a moment he wavered, swallowing hard. "I'll handle him."

The Mer guard led Kenneth to the sea-gate. The energy emanating from its center was electric, raising the fine hairs on his forearms. He didn't want to think about what would happen if something went wrong.

Refusing to be cowed, he jutted out his chin. "Let's get this over with."

Jake stepped up beside him, just as he had the first

time they'd gone through the gate. "I fucking hope this works," he muttered under his breath.

Kenneth arched a brow. He'd like it just fine if the sea-gate chewed Jake up and spat out his bones. "Guess we'll find out."

They launched through the portal in a single bound.

The light shimmered around their bodies, attacking from all sides with a heady, suffocating weight. The power came fast, like fire rushing down a tunnel. It felt as though his skin were slowly turning itself inside out. Heat shot down his spine as arcs of light burrowed through his eyes to enter his skull.

Suddenly the light winked out.

It was all over.

Kenneth emerged on the other side. Dizzy and nauseous, but safe.

He stumbled forward, clumsily trying to break his fall with chained hands. He skidded across cold stone littered with sharp pieces of glass—the remnants of the crystal orb. Though the labradorite pillars were completely drained, the sea-gate provided a dim but workable illumination.

The sound of a body hitting the floor beside his told him Jake had passed through, as well. "Shit! That hurts!"

Tessa hurried over from the far side of the chamber. "Guys?" The tone of her voice was relief mingled with delight.

Happy to see she was safe, Kenneth pushed himself up. "Are you all right?"

Eyes wide and anxious, Tessa helped him stand. "I'm fine."

His gaze locked with hers. "You should have left."

She shook her head. "Couldn't do it. I had to wait for you."

"Aw. Isn't love grand?" Dagger in hand, Jake rolled to his feet. "I can't believe it worked. We're back."

Tessa eyed the weapon in her ex-lover's hand. "Do you think you can put that thing away?"

Jake considered the sharp-edged blade in his hand. "I—I . . . can't."

Head still spinning, Kenneth climbed to his feet. "Snap out of it, man. It's over. We're out." His stomach squeezed, boiling with anxiety. "This is our chance to get going before those bitches get through."

"You're not seriously on their side," Tessa added. "You can't be. They're evil."

Jake's mouth thinned. "As much as I want to, I can't let you go."

Wrong answer, Kenneth thought.

Seeing his chance, he had to take it. His hands might be shackled, but his legs weren't.

Acting with split-second timing, he launched a hard kick toward Jake's legs. Caught by surprise, the archaeologist crumbled. He blindly slashed out with the blade.

Tessa's foot came down hard across his wrist. "Let go!" She smashed down hard.

Jake howled and tried to roll away. "You're hurting me!"

"Tough shit." Kenneth slipped his cuffs over Jake's head, making a garrote. "Don't make me kill you, man." He applied enough pressure to let Jake know he was serious. "I will if I have to."

"We just want to get out of here," Tessa added. "You can stay."

Jake's fingers scrabbled at his throat, digging at the thick chain pressing into his windpipe. "Okay, Okay!" He half coughed, spittle running down his chin. "Go. Just go."

Kenneth eased up. "Once we're gone, you can do whatever the hell you want."

Tessa's sudden yelp tore through the chamber. "Oh, God, look out!"

Half a dozen Mer soldiers swarmed around them, tackling Kenneth from all sides. Something hard and heavy knocked him soundly on the left temple.

"Back off!" one of the women ordered sharply.

Head reeling from the blow, Kenneth staggered back. Had he been on his own, there would have been no hesitation. He would have continued to fight. But Tessa . . . No, he couldn't risk her life.

Full of bitter conflict, he ceased all movement. "I'm backing off," he mumbled. One minute they'd been ahead. The next minute they were outnumbered.

Jesus, he thought bitterly. *We almost made it.*

Queen Magaera's commanding voice cut through the melee. "Cease!" Her forehead ridged in anger. "There's no use resisting further."

"Stay still," one of the Mer commanded, pushing him toward the rear of the chamber.

Two more Mer soldiers seized Tessa, shoving her roughly. "Don't touch me," she shouted back, twisting out of their grip.

Gasping for breath and holding his injured throat, Jake climbed to his feet. "It's about time you got here," he snapped. "They damn near killed me."

Queen Magaera ignored his outburst. Her attention lay elsewhere.

Walking with purpose behind her steps, she surveyed the labradorite columns scattered throughout the chamber. "The dim-witted girl," she sniffed, touching one of the burnt-out stones "Just as I suspected, she pulled too much energy too fast and reset the resonance of the gate."

Jake flexed his wrist, testing for damage. "Is that a problem?" He pointed toward the twisted remnants of the choker Tessa had worn. "That's all that's left."

Magaera's eyes narrowed in displeasure. "She has destroyed the jewels of Atargatis. They are irreplaceable, granted to the Mer by the goddess herself."

Jake frowned. "How important were they?"

"Very important. They were the tools that granted the reigning monarch absolute sovereignty over land and sea." Magaera's mouth thinned. "It pains me they are destroyed."

"Some pieces still remain," Jake hurried to assure her. "The scepter is . . ."

"Something I intend to recover," Magaera snapped. "Just as soon as I regain control of the sea-gate."

Jake eyed the shattered orb. "Can it be done without those pieces?"

"Of course. The threshold is a magnetic force, one we can manipulate by amplifying our own telepathic energies," Magaera answered precisely in a tone that sounded layered with displeasure. "Presently it is under the command to accept the psychic imprint of the last person to open it. She must go through first before others may safely follow."

Jake mentally processed the information. "So that means Tessa has become the key."

"Right now we may leave Ishaldi, but we can't go back without her in the lead," Magaera confirmed.

Jake frowned with frustration. "I'd hoped we could get rid of her," he mumbled. "Both of them, actually."

One corner of Magaera's mouth turned up. "It will be

inconvenient. But once I confiscate her soul-stone, she will simply answer as my slave." A wry chuckle escaped her.

Catching bits and pieces of their conversation, Tessa shook her head. "I'm not doing jack for you, bitch."

Doma Chiara hit her soundly across the legs with the shaft of her spear. "You will do exactly as my queen commands, or I will gut you myself."

Tessa stubbornly shook her head. "Rot in hell."

"Be careful, Tess," Kenneth whispered.

Tessa looked at him through teary eyes. "I won't give up my soul-stone." A small muscle in her jaw jumped. "And I'm not going to let them use me to control the sea-gate."

Kenneth's heart stalled in his chest. "What are you talking about?"

Her gaze went distant, brooding. "Just wait," she murmured. "I'll redeem myself yet." A chilling smile of satisfaction played on her lips.

Kenneth didn't like the sound of those words. "Don't, Tess," he warned under his breath. "Whatever you think you've got in mind, don't do it."

Magaera's stare landed on Tessa. "Bring her to me." She cocked her head. An evil little smile danced on her thin lips. "The sooner we get started, the sooner I can control the sea-gate."

Chiara shoved her spear in Tessa's back. "Move." Tessa reluctantly walked forward, swearing bitterly to herself. Kenneth watched her fearfully, worried about what stunt she might pull.

Queen Magaera touched the pendant around her neck. Unlike the lighter crystal stone most Mer wore, hers was heavier, more prominent. And as black as her soul.

Kenneth watched closely as the queen stepped up to Tessa. He tried hard to quell his agitation.

"I hope you will make this easy," Magaera instructed. "Will you match psychic vibrations with me willingly, or are you going to make me take your soul-stone by force?"

Kenneth saw a look of fear sweep over Tessa's face. Then he saw horror. "No. You can't have it."

Magaera smiled. "I'm afraid you don't have much of a choice."

Tessa's fingers clutched at the crystal hanging around her neck. "I'm not giving it to you."

Kenneth watched Tessa and remembered something she had once told him. For a Mer to lose her soul-stone was worse than death.

Queen Magaera laughed. "If you won't willingly give it to me, I'll take it by force. It's the only way I can ensure complete control of the sea-gate."

Cursing the chains holding him immobile, Kenneth could only watch. And wait.

As Queen Magaera reached for Tessa's soul-stone, he felt another presence in his mind, strange yet somehow familiar. It took him a moment to realize it must be Tessa. Though they'd never been psychically linked before, he wondered if their joining in the cell had caused a new connection between them.

He looked at her. Eyes narrowing, her mouth tightened. *I can't go through this alone,* she seemed to be saying. *We need to take her* down.

As Magaera took hold of her soul-stone, Tessa's body shook violently.

All of a sudden, he felt Tessa inside of him, and before he knew it, the energy was being ripped out of him.

Her voice cut through the scorching heat and pain,

calm, focused, and oddly comforting. *I've got to take from you one more time.*

Kenneth's legs quivered beneath his weight. He didn't have much, but what he did have was hers. *Take it all*, he silently urged.

She did, draining him until he could barely stand. Then, suddenly, their tenuous connection abruptly snapped.

Vision gone dead black, Kenneth hit his knees. He had nothing left to hold him upright. The pressure in his head and chest had passed the point from painful to downright unbearable.

But the energy emanating from Tessa grew brighter. Stronger. Ripping herself away from the queen's hold, Tessa stumbled back. Her soul-stone blazed around her neck. A pulsing illumination seemed to flow through her veins, lighting her up from inside with an otherworldly incandescence.

Throwing her arms straight out in front of her body, she hurled a bolt of pure unfettered energy straight into the floor. For a second the limestone seemed to turn to liquid. Then dozens of huge cracks formed beneath their feet.

Jake jumped back, trying to dodge the danger. "Stop it! You're going to kill us all!"

Tessa grinned like a goddess gone atomic. "That's exactly what I'm going to do."

Shading his face from her radiant gleam, Jake swept his eyes along the cracks in the limestone. Long and deep, they threatened to shatter the entire chamber if they opened any wider. "You don't have to do this. We can figure this out," he tried to say.

"I've already made up my mind, Jake. Remember my face when you're in hell."

"She cannot do this!" Magaera screamed savagely.

"Take her down," she ordered her soldiers. "But do not kill her. We need her alive."

The armed guards rushed into the fray, weapons at the ready.

Outnumbered and unarmed, Tessa pulled out her final card. Drawing deep on her last reserve, she hurled a sudden blast of energy straight into the ceiling.

The chamber rocked, the ceiling over their heads shattering violently as thousands of gallons of seawater rushed into the previously airtight cavity.

Kenneth felt the roof crashing down around him. He instinctively caught his breath as he attempted to scramble out of the water's relentless path. But there was no way to escape the giant waves rapidly spreading around him.

Icy water closed over his head, instantly plunging him into the heart of an inky, all-consuming abyss. Suddenly he couldn't breathe. The idea he was going to die, really die, this time, skittered through his frenzied mind.

Hands bound, he had no chance to swim. He was sinking, going down fast. Losing oxygen, his lungs burned as if someone had opened his mouth and poured acid straight down his throat. He clamped his mouth shut, but that didn't stop the brackish seawater from seeping in and taking over.

So this is what it really felt like to drown . . . to die when you wanted to live.

But he would never find out for sure.

Just when he thought his body would give up its life to the sea, something warm and pliant pressed against him. Familiar arms encircled his neck.

And a woman's lips touched his . . .

Epilogue

Twenty-four hours later

Standing aboard the *DreamFever*, Tessa stared across the bright blue surface of the Mediterranean. The sea stretched on for miles, tranquil. Undisturbed. A light gust of wind whipped her hair around her face. The ship rocked gently, swaying beneath her feet. The salty odor of the water permeated through her senses, soaking down to the bone.

It felt strange to be back in the real world. Everything had changed.

The crystal around her neck vibrated softly. Its resonance was weak, but steady. Queen Magaera's attack had weakened her, but not conquered her. She recalled surging with pain, feeling her life's very force drain away.

Anger spiked through her, sharp enough to take her breath away. *I know you're down there*, she thought darkly. *But where?*

The sound of footsteps on the deck behind her alerted her to the presence of another.

"You okay?" a familiar voice asked.

Giving herself a mental shake, Tessa lifted her head. Showered and dressed for the day, Kenneth Randall rubbed a hand over his freshly shaven face. Right now the man looked like he'd been through the ringer. A series of cuts and bruises mottled his face. He looked pale and tired, with dark circles rimming his eyes. It would take a while before he looked normal again.

A spike of pain tore through her. He'd taken the abuse. For her. "Yeah," she said, memorizing every wound. She'd never forget what he'd done for her. Never. "You?"

Pulling a breath, he leaned against the railing. A twinge of pain visibly moved across his face. "I'll live," he answered with a wry grimace. His shadowed gaze turned to the silent depths of the still water. "Do you think anyone else made it?"

Closing her eyes for a moment, Tessa sighed. Though she hated to admit it out loud, a feeling of failure nagged her. She wasn't sure why. She'd done her damnedest to destroy the sea-gate. But that didn't mean she'd succeeded. Though those who had followed her into the human world could not go home, the sea-gate was still keyed to allow other Mer to pass through unscathed. The sea-gate wouldn't close again unless she went back.

And she would never go back to Ishaldi.

Never.

"Yeah," she admitted. "I think they're there."

Surprised, Kenneth inclined his head. "Why?"

Tessa slowly shook her head. "Call it a Mer's intuition."

"You think Jake—?" he started to ask.

She gave him a sharp glance. The idea of laying eyes on him made her skin crawl. "Let's not talk about that bastard," she answered tightly. "As far as the crew is concerned, he was killed in the quake." Nobody on the face of the earth had to know she'd caused the disturbance.

Kenneth nodded. "I guess for now it's best he stays dead. But we are going to have to tell the authorities everything, you know. Jake ... the sea-gate, the Mer ..."

Her jaw tightened. "I have no idea who we can tell without looking crazy." Her grip tightened on the railing, knuckles going white from the force. "Or worse—endangering myself and my sisters."

"Well, it's only a problem if they survived," Kenneth added quietly. "That whole place came down so fast, it's a wonder any of us got out alive."

Brooding, Tessa returned to her study of the unfathomable depths. The idea of picking through the rubble disturbed her, though she doubted there would be any bodies. Queen Magaera and her ilk were, after all, Mers, too.

"Oh, make no mistake about it. They're down there. Soon they'll come up. When they do, I have a bad feeling all hell will break loose."

Kenneth's strong arms circled around her, a solid shield of protection. He pulled her close and kissed the top of her head. "When they do, we'll be ready." He spoke as if he believed they could go through it all over again. And win.

Tessa's heart surged. Tipping back her head, she gazed into his dark eyes. *By the heavens, I'm a lucky woman.*

Kenneth gave her everything she'd ever dreamed of having in a mate. Sympathy, support, and the freedom to be herself. She didn't have to hide anything. He accepted everything about her with no hesitations.

She loved this man, this wonderful brave soul, with all her heart. And, incredibly, he loved her. She had a second chance for a real future with a man she loved.

She definitely wasn't going to blow it this time.

Winding her arms around his neck, she pulled him closer. "There is one thing we haven't discussed," she murmured against the protective wall of his chest.

Kenneth treated her to his most endearing gaze, his dark eyes filled with honesty, sincerity, and love. "What's that?"

A combination of warmth and need raced through her. It was always that way with Kenneth. It always had been, from the first day they met. "I've been thinking we should make things a little more, you know, permanent."

He raised an eyebrow. "What are you saying?"

Tessa smiled. "I'm saying I want you to be my breedmate. I'm saying I want to marry you." She took a quick, steadying breath. "I love you and I can't think of a better man to father my children."

He drew back. "But that would mean—"

Tessa held him tighter, never wanting to let him go. "It would mean we'd be growing old. Together." She tightened her grip around his neck. "Think you could handle me as a cranky old Mer?"

Kenneth's grip tightened around her waist. "Probably not." He laughed, a low warm sound. "But I'll do my damnedest to try."

Please read on for an excerpt
from the next book in the Dark Tides series,
available from Signet Eclipse
in February 2011.

Turning into the hotel parking lot, Blake Whittaker guided his black sedan into the nearest available space and killed the engine. Instead of making an immediate grab for the bag in the passenger seat, he simply sat, staring into the distance.

It was amazing how things had changed since he'd last been in Port Rock. Almost seventeen years had passed since he'd last set foot in the small Maine fishing village. And while the familiar old landmarks were still in place, a lot of things looked different. The hotel, for instance, was new. Back when he was a kid, the oceanfront acreage overlooking the bay was undeveloped and offered an unobstructed view of the open water and the small island that lay about a mile offshore.

Little Mer Island, he thought. That's where he'd be heading first thing tomorrow. To get there he'd have to rent a skiff, cross the wide-open waters of the bay.

A flush prickled Blake's skin as his heart sped up. Despite the humidity permeating the warm summer night, he shivered. He hated deep water of any kind. Aside from a shower, he did his best to stay far away from the stuff. It didn't matter if it filled only a swimming pool, or the vast ocean. The less he saw of it, the better.

Mouth going bone-dry, his grip on the steering wheel tightened as a series of images flashed through his mind. For a brief second he wasn't a thirty-three-year-old man, but a four-year-old boy facing an insanely furious woman filling a deep, old-fashioned claw-foot tub with ice-cold water . . .

Forcing himself back toward calm, Blake blew out a few quick, hard puffs, filling his lungs and then quickly expelling the air. The strain of clenching his jaw made his teeth hurt. The last thing he needed was a full-blown panic attack while sitting in the parking lot. Thank God the parking lot was abandoned. There was no one around at such a late hour to see him melt down.

Catching hold of his fear and forcing himself to stuff it away, he slowly uncurled his fingers. A low curse slipped between his numb lips. "Damn." Just thinking about his mother made him twitch, set his nerves on edge.

He hadn't expected that memory to come crawling out of nowhere and ambush him. He did his best not to remember those petrifying moments when his mom was tanked up on vodka and raging with homicidal malice.

Men. She hated them. Every last blasted one and . . .

And some things are best left alone, Blake reminded himself. Remembering his mother was like sticking his hand into a den of poisonous snakes. He was bound to get bitten, but in this case he just couldn't stop prodding the deadly reptiles.

He'd better stop it or he was going to get bitten. Badly.

Coming back to Port Rock certainly wasn't helping matters. When he'd finally gotten old enough to leave it, he hadn't intended to come back. Not ever. At the age of seventeen he'd gotten the hell out, going as far away as he could. A one-way bus ticket and a suitcase had been all he'd had to his name. If he hadn't joined the army, he would've had nowhere to go at the end of the trip.

Blake rubbed his burning eyes. To be sane himself, to continue being sane, he had to quit tearing at the scars that marked the old wounds. There were a lot of ghosts lingering in his past, a lot of skeletons shoved into his family's closets.

Shut them, bolt them, and go on. That's the way he'd always gotten things done. As a kid he'd kept a stiff upper lip, taken the beatings, and gone about the business of living as best he could.

He'd survived.

Sighing again, he shifted in the uncomfortable seat, feeling the cramps in his legs and ass. The three-and-a-half-hour trip through a massive thunderstorm had taken its toll on his nerves.

Palm rasping against a day's growth of whiskers, he reached for the cup balanced between his legs. He took a gulp of its contents: unsweetened black coffee. It was cold and tasted like shit. The churning acid rose to the back of his throat as the bitter brew mixed in his stomach to burn away another millimeter of tissue. Pain immediately sliced through his gut, feeling as though a razor were wending its way through his bowels.

As much as he didn't like coming back to Port Rock, he had a job to do. Not a difficult one. Just ask a few questions, poke around a little. It wasn't rocket science.

But it was top secret.

As a special agent, Blake presently worked in the A51-ASD division of the FBI. Had it not been a highly covert organization, the A51 would have been familiar enough to tip off most Americans as to its purpose. After all, Area 51 was the nickname for a military base presently located in the southern portion of Nevada in the western United States. Supposedly the base's primary purpose was the development and testing of experimental aircraft and weapons systems.

That was partly true. And anyone not presently situated under a rock knew about the intense secrecy surrounding the base, one that had made it a popular subject among conspiracy theorists who held a belief in the existence of alien life on planet Earth.

The crackpots weren't wrong, either. Blake Whittaker knew for a fact the federal government took the existence of aliens very seriously. The genesis of the current operations stemmed from an incident that happened in 1947 in Roswell, New Mexico. At that time the military had supposedly recovered an alien craft and corpses, purportedly held under lock and key, and never to be revealed to the public.

It was absolutely true in every respect.

The ASD had been created to cover not only future occurrences of possible alien activity, but also to investigate other incidents deemed alien, paranormal, or inexplicable.

Curious. Strange. Bizarre. You name it, the ASD had an agent on it.

And that was why he was presently in Port Rock. Because something curious had taken a bizarre turn.

It had all begun in the 1950s, when an intense concentration of electromagnetic energy was located in the Mediterranean Sea. There was no rhyme or reason as to why the energy should be at that precise spot, or what caused it. Using the latest technology in deep-sea exploration, scientists had yet to discover the source. Given the location of the disturbance, most theories ranged from a geothermal field due to volcanic activity, to some sort of alien homing signal or beacon.

For the most part, the energy seemed to be harmless, a phenomenon never to be explained. Naval ships in the area monitored it, and no changes had been reported in the past sixty years. Whatever it was simply *was*.

And then something happened.

From the data he presently had, Whittaker knew that an undersea salvage group called Recoveries, Inc., had moved into the area. The outfit had recently filed in federal court for salvage rights for what they claimed to be the lost civilization of Ishaldi. Nothing unusual there. Treasure hunters regularly hit the Mediterranean in search of everything from ancient Egyptian barges, to Spanish warships, to World War II aircraft. After all, for three-quarters of the globe, the Mediterranean Sea was the uniting element and the center of world history.

What exactly had occurred was still to be explained. During the first dive, tragedy had struck—some kind of seismic activity had taken place deep beneath the water. The resulting quake was strong enough to be detected by hydrophones, and was unlike anything scientists had ever heard through decades of listening.

The undersea quake had also claimed a victim. Jake Massey, the archaeologist leading the recovery efforts, had been reported as missing at sea. A month had passed since that fateful day and his body had yet to be recovered.

More interesting than the quake and the regrettable loss of life was the fact that the former low-level energy field had gone haywire. The electromagnetic field had suddenly tripled in strength. Its signal—if it could be called that—had begun to interfere with radar and radio transmissions, seemingly swallowing up everything electronic in a single gulp. It was as if a big black hole had suddenly opened at the bottom of the sea. No ship could get within ten miles of the location without interference. As the area was one of the most heavily sailed shipping lanes in the world, it was a pain in the ass for seacraft to detour around.

In the grand scheme of things, Blake's job was fairly simple. He'd been sent to question Massey's partner about the incident. The feds wanted to know whether Massey's crew had seen, heard, or encountered something outside the norm during their time underwater. Given that the seismic activity had taken place at a depth of more than three miles below the water's surface, Whittaker sincerely doubted they would have any useful information to offer.

Blake grimaced and tossed the empty cup onto the floor on the passenger side. Flicking on an overhead light, he consulted his notes, random chicken-scratched information on a pocket-sized pad.

According to intelligence, Kenneth Randall presently lived on Little Mer with his wife, Tessa. Since the loss of Jake Massey, the group had suspended all salvage efforts and the company had gone inactive. An investigation by the U.S. Coast Guard, which monitored recovery efforts in the Mediterranean, had ruled Massey the victim of an unfortunate accident.

Still, the A51-ASD had a job to do. And that meant sending an agent to ask a few questions and poke around a little. His conclusions on the matter would be the deciding factor on whether a follow-up was warranted or whether the matter was marked closed.

The barest trace of a smile crossed Blake's lips. Most of the incidents he looked into turned out to be bogus, of no real scientific value. He'd worked for the agency for almost five years and had yet to see anything unusual or out of the ordinary. Logic and science could usually explain away most of the reported phenomena.

Tucking his pad away, Blake ran his fingers through his hair. He caught a brief glimpse of half his face in the rearview mirror, a thatch of messy black hair and bloodshot blue-gray eyes. Lines of disgruntlement puckered his forehead. Shadows lingered behind his gaze, the ghosts of disappointment and disillusionment. One of his irises had a thin streak of amber through the lower half, as though someone had taken an eraser and begun to rub out one color before replacing it with another. People, especially the crazy ones, were frequently unsettled by that odd eye. It was something he used to good effect when employing his best "don't lie to me" agent stare.

Blake glanced at the single bag he'd packed for the trip. Aside from a change of clothes and his Netbook, he carried only a wallet, his cell, and his service weapon. Spending a lot of time on the road had taught him to travel light. He didn't plan to be in Port Rock for more than a day.

The sooner I can leave, the better. He didn't want to hang around his old hometown, rehashing memories that were better left alone. Some things needed to be stay buried.

The deeper, the better.

Opening the car door, Blake got out. The cool breeze winnowing off the bay was like a balm on his flushed skin. A day's worth of sweat clung to his flesh. He felt wet patches under his arms, trickles of perspiration making their way down his spine to his underwear. Sweat fogged his vision as he pushed a sticky hair off his forehead.

He pulled in a deep breath, letting the crisp sea air

clear his clouded mind. Stretching his arms wide, he rolled his shoulders, trying to relieve the ache at the base of his neck. He'd wasted enough time. Right now what he needed most was a hot shower and cool, clean sheets.

Grabbing his bag off the passenger seat, he locked the car and headed toward the brightly lit lobby. *Wrap things up tomorrow and I'll be on my way to Boston by six.*

ABOUT THE AUTHOR

Devyn Quinn resides in New Mexico with her cats, seven ferrets, and shih tzu, Tess. She is the author of twelve novels. This is her first novel with Signet Eclipse. Visit www.devynquinn.com.

Coming February 2011
from

Devyn Quinn

SIREN'S SURRENDER
A Dark Tides Novel

Gwen Lonike has never embraced her mermaid heritage,
preferring to live as a human. So when her sister, Tessa, returns
from the Mediterranean with news that she inadvertently
opened the gateway to a lost mermaid kingdom—and
accidentally let the ill-intentioned and dangerous queen escape
into the human world—Gwen is concerned about the
potential threat to her idyllic life.

Meanwhile, a covert ops group has caught wind of paranormal
activity in the Mediterranean and traced the action back to Port
Rock. Agent Blake Whitaker is far from happy when he's
assigned to his hometown to stake out the situation. But when
he discovers his target is the sister of Gwen, his high school
crush, memories and feelings come flooding back to him. Can
Blake hide his true mission from Gwen—and can Gwen keep
her mermaid identity a secret, even as the queen hunts
desperately for the Lonike sisters? It's only a matter of time
before the truth comes out on both sides, but as the danger
rises, both must choose to surrender their trust to each other.

Available wherever books are sold or at
penguin.com

Penguin Group (USA) Online

What will you be reading tomorrow?

Tom Clancy, Patricia Cornwell, W.E.B. Griffin,
Nora Roberts, William Gibson, Robin Cook,
Brian Jacques, Catherine Coulter, Stephen King,
Dean Koontz, Ken Follett, Clive Cussler,
Eric Jerome Dickey, John Sandford,
Terry McMillan, Sue Monk Kidd, Amy Tan,
J. R. Ward, Laurell K. Hamilton,
Charlaine Harris, Christine Feehan...

You'll find them all at
penguin.com

*Read excerpts and newsletters,
find tour schedules and reading group guides,
and enter contests.*

Subscribe to Penguin Group (USA) newsletters
and get an exclusive inside look
at exciting new titles and the authors you love
long before everyone else does.

PENGUIN GROUP (USA)
us.penguingroup.com